# Appointment
# on
# Lake Michigan

By
Dennis Kenyon

*For Helen*

*Hope you enjoy my yarn!*

*Best Wishes*

*Dennis Kenyon  April 2008*

This book is for my son,

Dennis, Jr
1981-2000

"For the wonderful boy he was and the amazing man he would
have become"

Published by Electrocution (www.electrocution.com)

Printed and bound by Antony Rowe Ltd, Eastbourne

## Author's Note

I'm occasionally asked why I wrote this story. The answer is I once found myself in a Menominee hotel a couple of days too early for a meeting. The outside temperature was minus forty and the nearby Lake Michigan was frozen over

Alistair Craig is not me, although I have relied quite heavily on my own travels and flying experience, and once made the flight I describe. Some of the characters are based on aviation friends for originality, and if you recognize yourself…. I ask forgiveness.

The places used are real and 'Top Risk' was a real racer—a fine horse I have ridden and loved. The *Champagne Princess* was a real yacht, but I do not know who owns her now.

And finally the politics of my story will of course change, as will the value of money. I just pray that future years will see our world problems resolved.

*Dennis Kenyon*

Ashington
West Sussex
England

August 2005

# Glossary Of Abbreviations

| | | | |
|---|---|---|---|
| ADF | Automatic Direction Finder (Navaid) | ILS | Instrument Landing System Landing Aid |
| AOP | Air Observation Post | IFR | Instrument Flight Rules |
| APB | All Points Bulletin (American Term) | KHZ | Kilo Hertz (Radio Frequency Range) |
| ATA | Actual Time of Arrival (Navigation) | MHZ | Meg Hertz (Radio Frequency Range) |
| ATC | Air Traffic Control | KTS | Nautical Speed Measurement |
| ATIS | Automated Traffic Information Service | LED | Light Emitting Diode (VHF) |
| AWAC | Airborne Warning | NASA | National Aeromautics Space Administration |
| COM | Communication (VHF) | NI-CAD | Nickel Cadmium (Battery) |
| CCTV | Closed Circuit TV | NM | Nautical Mile. |
| CIA | Central Intelligence Agency | NSA | National Security Agency |
| ENT | Ear, Nose and Throat | PSI | Pressure Per Sq Inch |
| ETA | Estimated Time Of Arrival (Navigation) | PBX | Private Branch Exchange Phone System. |
| EST | Eastern Standard Time | RAF | (British) Royal Air Force |
| FBI | Federal Bureau of Investigation | RPM | Revolutions Per Minute. |
| GPS | Global Positioning System (Nav Aid) | RT | Radio Telephony Radio Communication |
| GCHQ | Government Listening HQ | UHF | Ultra High Frequency Range |
| H | Helicopter Landing Pad | UTC | Universal Time Clock. International time |
| HI | High Intensity Strobe Light | VFR | Visual Flight Rules |
| Hi VIZ | High Visibility | VHF | Very High Frequency |
| HOTOL | High Speed Take Off Landing | VOR | VHF Omni Range |
| HSCT | High Speed Commercial Transport | WILCO | Will Comply (Radio Call) |

# 1

A voice on the radio crackled.

*"Descend to fifteen-hundred feet and report entering the zone.... Follow Heli-Route 'Haitch Seven' to Barnes.... Squawk.... Seven-Fower-Tree-Zero."*

Alistair Craig squeezed the collective lever down in response to Air Traffic Control's curt instruction and set the transponder digits that would uniquely identify him to London Radar. The altimeter swung lazily around the dial to indicate the new height.

Five minutes to go for the Battersea Heliport landing, and as Craig entered the busy airspace of Heathrow's control zone, he could never have dreamed in a hundred years how today's flight would change his life so dramatically.

A light early-morning haze obscured London's skyline as Craig navigated the H7 Helicopter route, to the quaintly named Nonsuch Palace at Banstead.

The Caesar's Camp reporting point on Wimbledon Common passed a thousand feet below as Craig called the Radar service to confirm his position. The helpful London controller cleared him to the next radio frequency. *"Roger, helicopter Zulu-Zulu."* (Craig's call sign for the day) *"No further traffic information for you.... Maintain standard altitudes on 'Haitch-Fower' and call the Heliport on frequency 'Wun-Two-Tree-daycimal-Niner.'"*

The Heliport Controller was an old friend and recognised Craig's professional radio patter. They had shared one or two monumental booze-ups in their Royal Air Force days. He responded to Craig's initial call informally. *"OK Alistair, your passengers are waiting.... We're using approach 'Zero-Tree' and you're cleared to land and park on stand Eight."*

Craig acknowledged the instruction with a formal *"Wilco"* and set the helicopter into a steady descent that would take him past the four chimneys of the derelict Battersea Power Station to the landing platform that juts out into the muddy river. Some turbulence from the tall chimneys kicked at the controls, causing a light vibration in the yaw pedals. Craig applied firm pressure with his right foot to offset the reduction in power and maintain heading for the assigned landing pad. As the helicopter dropped the last few feet, he flared with the cyclic, raised the collective lever and settled into a stable hover.

A swirl of light dust followed Craig as he smoothly air taxied to the allocated stand, where a ground marshaller wearing a yellow Hi-Viz jacket beckoned. With a flash of the landing lamp, he acknowledged the marshaller's signal, and manoeuvring inches from the tarmac, he touched the Agusta Executive 109 down exactly in the centre of the white H landing spot.

Alistair Craig called the Control. *"Helicopter Zulu Zulu is on the ground at stand Eight. Closing down."*

Craig carefully cooled the two Rolls-Royce jet engines at ground idle for the mandatory two minutes, closed down the fuel pumps and ignition, and braked the rotors. With the auxiliary services switched off, he entered the flight times in the Technical Log, and prepared to offer his passengers the courtesies dictated by the Company Rule Book.

Two men appeared at the door of the passenger terminal. The first was tall and elegantly dressed. The other, shorter, man had a nut-brown complexion and dark sideburns. He seemed an unlikely companion. Probably, a Middle East National, maybe a Saudi or perhaps Moroccan. He wore a loose-fitting overcoat gathered at the waist with an old fashioned wide belt, and unusually for an Arab, he was clean-shaven. The hair was cropped short, and dark glasses shaded his eyes. Craig guessed them as Ray-Bans. Someone had money, he thought uncharitably.

The tall man would be the racehorse owner, Craig judged. He'd be fifty, about six feet and would weigh 180 lbs. The wavy hair was dark, contrasting with a pale complexion. Unusually pale for the time of the year.... prison pale perhaps? Wisps of grey hair showed at the temples and should have softened the man's image, but it was a hard, expressionless face with blunt, chiselled jaws and pointed nostrils. The deep set, probing eyes were very brown. They looked out at the world with suspicion, and might not smile easily.

Then, as he moved closer, Craig noticed a curious feature. The man had no eyebrows or eyelashes, and the broad expanse of forehead lent the face the classic appearance of a scholar.... similar to the high-domed features drawn in sci-fi strip cartoons to illustrate aliens from space. The racehorse owner appeared to dislike the feature, and, like Adolf Hitler, disguised the high forehead by pulling his hair forward at an angle to the left eye. The jaws were clean-shaven, with a moon shaped cleft below the thin, rather cruel lips. The moon cleft extended to the cheeks. Yet it was not an ugly face, and to many women it might even be handsome, with its rugged hint of masculine authority.

The man was dressed formally with a single-breasted lounge suit in dark brown. The suit was casually cut, but probably tailored in Savile Row. A fashionably colourful tie was held in place by a gold clip where a solitaire diamond twinkled in the morning sun. The silk shirt was pink, with a long 1980's style collar and concealed buttons. The sleeves discreetly displayed the English gentleman's one inch of cuff, nicely matching the pink handkerchief that just showed at the top pocket. Immaculately pressed trouser seams broke correctly above soft calf leather shoes. The shoes looked expensive, and were fastened by bronze side buckles that hinted Gucci.

This man has led a hard life, Craig thought, as he climbed down from the helicopter. Probably made plenty of money from the horses, and was now spending it on good living, Bond Street clothes, helicopter travel and so on. Craig wished him well. At least he wasn't like some of his baseball-capped passengers, who wallowed in unwarranted wealth, didn't bother to dress or speak properly, and couldn't even spend their newfound money with taste.

Craig greeted the two men with a big smile and offered his hand to the racehorse owner. The man shook it briefly. Possibly a Mason's touch! Craig brushed the thought aside.

"Good morning, gentlemen. Nice day for the races. Can I take your bags?" Craig kept the regulation smile going.

Two suede leather cases with Saudi Airline labels were handed over. Craig stowed them in the luggage compartment as the men waited. He turned the key in the lock and opened the rear passenger door.

"Make yourselves comfortable, gents." Craig continued with good humour as he guided them to their seats. "Flying time to Goodwood is thirty-five minutes…. This morning we'll follow the river through the centre of London. You'll get a terrific view of the City. Today's racing papers are in the seat pockets with headsets if you need them to chat." Craig remembered the required safety brief. "Oh, and can I ask you to spend a moment reading the safety leaflet. You'll find it in the seat pockets, too."

The racehorse owner looked intensely at Craig. The voice was indifferent. "Thank you, pilot." It said flatly.

The absence of response to Craig's cheerful bonhomie was unsettling, and the close scrutiny of the man's laser-like eyes seemed to bore through to the back of his skull. He didn't like it. Best to ignore the man, he thought, as he strapped himself into his seat.

He slipped on the David Clark headset, set the Master switch to 'On' and ran through the pre-start drill. Instrument readings, jet pipe temperatures and fuel pressure were OK for the start sequence, and with the Air Traffic start clearance received, he acknowledged the 'thumbs up' signal from the waiting marshaller, idly wondering if the man knew the origins of the ancient virility symbol. He returned the phallic gesture with a smile and pressed the engine starter. A high-pitched 'Zing' rang out from the igniter as the number one compressor whined, and with an exciting surge of power from the turbine, accelerated to 65% idling speed. The whine changed to a howl as Craig started the second engine…. then opened both throttles to full power, carefully monitoring the engine temperatures as they soared to almost one thousand degrees.

The readings quickly stabilised and, with the rotor tips whirling at maximum speed, Craig obtained departure clearance from the Control Tower. Pulling on the collective lever, he lifted off the Battersea Heli-pad, raised the landing gear and headed east, following the course of the winding river as it flowed through the greatest city in the world.

A blunt-nosed tug, pulling a heavily laden barge chugged by, low in the water, with its chimneystack belching smoke as the craft struggled against the tide. Below, a motley mix of office blocks, London's big railway stations, and Kennington's famous cricketing Oval, passed beneath Craig as he climbed to the assigned fifteen-hundred feet.

At times like these, with an interesting new day ahead, and the warmth of the sun in the cabin promising a fine day, Craig knew why he loved flying. London's famous buildings lined the banks of Old Father Thames, where they jostled for every inch of precious space. Ten thousand pounds for every square yard, a property man once told him. The intricate Gothic stonework of the Houses of Parliament beamed brightly in the morning sun, contrasting with the simple, post-war geometry of The Royal Festival Hall. Beyond Hyde Park, the classical Portico of Buckingham Palace smiled down the Mall to Lord Nelson's column and the Admiralty Arches, but scowled up at her unwelcome neighbour.... the twenty storey Hilton Hotel, which peeps disrespectfully into the gardens and private quarters of England's Queen.

Craig's thoughts turned to the empty plinth in Trafalgar Square. Now whose statue would 'Red Ken' have placed there alongside Landseer's four famous lions? Probably his own!

Further down river, the stark reflection of the New London Bridge rippled in a slack morning tide. Craig wondered how the Americans were treating the graceful arches of the old bridge, unceremoniously carted off stone by stone in the 1950s and rebuilt on the Arizona desert, where they now spanned a river of Pepsi Cola cans and tourist trash.... A sorry ending for so much history. He glanced back at his two passengers who were studying the spectacular panorama of London's skyline, as it unfolded around them.

"We'll be entering London City shortly." Craig enthused. "You'll see Saint Paul's Cathedral and the Tower of London.... further down river is the Millennium Dome built on the Isle of Dogs.... it cost the British taxpayer almost a billion pounds, and its been empty for years," Craig snorted. "Typical of Government waste!" He continued enthusiastically: "But then you'll see the more successful commercial areas." Craig pointed ahead. "The wonderful Cutty Sark, permanently docked alongside Sir Francis Chichester's Gypsy Moth and the Docklands development of the old Canary Wharf." Craig paused for a routine check of the instruments as he resumed the standard tourist cockpit commentary.

"That's the new HSBC building.... one of the tallest in Europe, you know. Plenty of bank money, I'll bet." Craig grinned. "A new building every time I fly over the area.... they're springing up like mushrooms."

The two men seemed unimpressed.... Nothing was said.

'What's with these two guys thought Craig.... Struck dumb! Just forget the tourist chat and get on with the job,' he said to himself.

The world famous picture postcard view of Tower Bridge appeared as Craig made the mandatory position report. *"Helicopter Zulu-Zulu is passing Tower Bridge at fifteen-hundred feet."*

*"Roger Zulu Zulu."* The Battersea Heliport controller responded. *"Call Thames Radar leaving the London Control Zone at Greenwich, and caution, there's a police helicopter patrolling the Lea Valley between five and fifteen-hundred feet. Have a good day at the races."*

*"Copied the traffic."* Craig acknowledged with humour. *'We're visual with the Copper Chopper."* He smiled at his own joke. *"I'll be calling on the way back Jeremy."* Craig set the throttles to 75 per cent max continuous power and allowed the speed to settle at a respectable 140-knot cruise, as he continued along the river.

The Greenwich Observatory appeared on the south bank of the great Thames loop that encloses London's Dockland, and Craig reflected that, while dear old England was rapidly losing her international status to Europe, at least the whole world still followed Harrison's latitude and longitude system of navigation which originated at the Greenwich Zero Meridian, and which was passing beneath Craig at this very moment.

The remainder of the flight was uneventful as Craig competently liaised with the Air Traffic controllers en route. First the wartime Spitfire aerodrome at Biggin Hill, the original home of Winston Churchill's famous 'few' who, in the summer of 1940, had won the Battle of Britain almost single-handed. Next came the long black scar of Gatwick Airport's two-mile runway, and its mighty four-engined Jumbo Jet traffic. A brief period of radio silence followed as Craig crossed the Pilgrim's Way westward. He pointed out the British

Aerospace Airfield by the pretty Surrey village of Dunsfold, now disused, but still routinely blasted by the effervescent Jeremy Clarkson as he compered his BBC car show, 'Top Gear.'

Craig's tall passenger was silent, but not uninterested. As a younger man, he'd flown with the Irish Air Force and was aware of Alistair Craig's professional handling of the executive helicopter. He could see Craig was a good pilot, and had already decided that he was the one they needed. Later today he would put the proposition to him.

Craig left the Gatwick Control Area and, scanning the horizon, set course for the chalk landmarks on the Sussex Downs thrown up during the Alpine Geological storm sixty million years ago. Goodwood racecourse came into view. Craig disliked the spiky plastic roof of the new Grandstand, which desecrated an area of outstanding natural beauty. Modern architecture gone mad.

"Approaching the racecourse now," he called to his passengers. "Where would you like to be dropped? I can't fly too near the stables.... Might spook the horses."

"Alongside that car park will be fine." The racehorse owner pointed animatedly. "Can you land on the grass by the white rails?"

"No problem. There's a marked H for our helicopters." Craig replied, and with little fuss, manoeuvered the Agusta 109 neatly against the railings and landed precisely on the designated parking area. Craig closed down both engines and, with the drooping rotors ambling to a halt, jumped out to help his two passengers with their bags. The landing site was a short walk from the main Grandstand. Craig looked up at the large black dots perched high in the tall Poplar trees surrounding the Heli-Pad.... Rooks? .... Crows perhaps? Bloody noisy whatever. No wonder the big buggers weren't scared off by his helicopter!

Craig turned to his tall passenger.... time for some social chat.... and information perhaps!

"I hope you enjoyed the flight, sir," he opened cheerfully. "Isn't London a great sight from the air?" He switched on the company smile again. "Oh, I'm Alistair Craig. I follow horse racing, too. I don't suppose you've any racing tips, Gentlemen?" he ventured, immediately regretting his cheek.

The racehorse owner scrutinised Craig. The eyes narrowed and the hairless eyebrows dropped a fraction. He pursed his lips and spoke to

Craig with an Irish accent, probably Dublin, or perhaps, Craig thought, the so-called mid-Atlantic accent. The voice was soft but with the firm authority of a Sotheby's auctioneer accepting a final bid.

"The name is O'Rourke, Ryan O'Rourke," it said. "I'm from the Irish Republic." He gestured to his companion. "My colleague is Sheikh Makhtoum, a business associate who controls our Casablanca Office.... we're in the oil industry.... Anglo Arab Oil." For the first time, O'Rourke smiled and spread his shoulders proudly. "So you enjoy a gamble, my dear boy?"

Craig did not like the patronising, 'dear boy' which the man pronounced with a rolled rr.... He looked at both men, from one to the other. Was this O'Rourke man a queer? Craig disliked the type.... If he was? He looked a bloody tough one!

Craig looked back squarely at the bland forehead. The eyes were steel and challenging. Craig wanted to turn away.

"I'm not a regular gambler," he replied defensively after a pause, "but I guess being a racehorse owner, you must be in the know," he added, forcing a grin.

The racehorse owner continued to fix Craig with the laser eyes and a glazed expression. His Arab companion was showing more interest.

"*Top Risk* in the three-fifteen race, Captain Craig," he said eventually. "If you want to win some real money, put everything you've got on the nose. I mean to win. But don't complain to me if you lose your money.... dear boy."

Again the irritating expression. Craig looked sardonic, shrugged his shoulders and cocked his head with polite indifference.

"Well that's kinda nice of you, Mr. O'Rourke. Thanks for the tip. I'll take my chance and just hope I'm in luck. Oh, and what time would you gentlemen like to leave?" Craig thought by way of thanks he should show the required Company politeness.

The racehorse owner glanced briefly at a gold Rolex Oyster with a black dial. He wore it on the inside of his left wrist. "Ten minutes after the last race, dear boy," came the reply, "but I'd like to talk with you before then. Why not take a drink with me in the owner's bar about three-thirty? If you don't see me, ask any of the stewards for Ryan O'Rourke, the owner of *Top Risk*."

"I'll be there, Mr. O'Rourke." Craig said and, before he could enquire further, O'Rourke and his poker-faced Arab partner left, chatting enthusiastically as they headed for the member's stand. Craig's eyes followed the two men until they were out of sight.

He was deep in thought.

Now why would a racehorse owner want to talk to him? Surely not to buy him a drink. What an odd pair, though. An Irishman and an Arab.... partners in the oil business. Sounded like the old Englishman, Irishman and Scotsman joke!

Nice of them to give him the tip, though.

He shrugged away his thoughts and spent ten minutes securing the Agusta's four rotor blades with the tie-downs, fitting the engine intake muffs and locking the cabin doors. With a final check around the helicopter, he sauntered leisurely to the Grandstand, leaving the noisy birds squawking in the trees behind.

The sun was gaining strength as it climbed in the clear September sky and with its warmth on his cheeks, Craig's spirits lifted in anticipation of a day at the races, and a wanton gamble on O'Rourke's horse.

He walked through the dirty concrete tunnel under the main Grandstand entrance, to be greeted by a hum of expectancy from the excited race-goers. What a terrific atmosphere of occasion and a superb view of the racecourse.

Looking around, he chose a seat close to the rails and sat on the rough wooden bench, thinking of Mr. Ryan O'Rourke and his Arab friend....

*The unexpected invitation was ringing in his ears!*

9

# 2

Two months earlier, on a wonderfully warm summer day, Alistair Craig was taking his regular Sunday walk along the Sussex Downs, south of the medieval town of Steyning. He made the short steep climb from Wiston Village, following an ancient track through the woods, to the popular Chanctonbury ring.... a prominent clump of majestic Beech trees that cling to the summit of the South Downs, and a landmark, which can be seen from London, fifty miles away.

The circle of trees was planted in the eighteenth century and covers an ancient earthwork that hides an interesting history. In prehistoric times, Iron-Age hill farmers inhabited the site, cultivated the soil, and mined the chalk for flints. Several hundred years later, a tribe of woad-painted Britons led by King Cogidumnus settled on Chanctonbury, but were eventually forced to flee before the all-conquering Roman army. The invading Centurions re-fortified the camp and built a temple for their new Christian faith, where they flourished for more than three hundred years as they steadily integrated with the local population. When the Roman Empire collapsed, the soldiers left, the wooden ramparts rotted and fell into decay, and seventeen centuries of wind and rain reduced the structure to rubble. Today, with the thinning Beech trees nearing the end of their natural life, only the circular ditch and the earthworks remain to reveal Chanctonbury's long history.

Craig liked exploring historic sites, but today, because of the sunny weather, he just wanted to sit down under the gnarled old trees and think out his future. He spread his walking jacket on the grass by the newly planted Beech saplings.

Alistair Craig was not overly handsome in the conventional sense. He possessed an 'Erudite' appeal, with fairish wavy hair, blue eyes, and the honest, ready smile of the sportsman. At college, he'd been an athlete, specialising in the mile.... once approaching the magic 'four minutes' of his day. He was almost the classic 'six footer' with a medium and fit build. He had an arrestingly English accent and laughed often. When not on flying duty, he dressed casually, sometimes in blue jeans and a polo neck sweater or jacket. He never wore body jewellery, tattoos or a baseball cap!

He was nearly forty, and his qualification as a helicopter pilot ensured a steady £35,000 each year. He got by on his salary OK, but earlier in the year, things had changed dramatically and he'd become obliged to live in a rented flat in Brighton. He had a few worthwhile assets, which included his car, some antiques and paintings, and a few thousand pounds saved in the local Barclays Bank, but little else.

So if he added it all up, his total worth was barely thirty-thousand pounds. Not very good, he told himself, and allowed his thoughts to return to the better days.

Before the accident, his finances had been very different. He'd lived comfortably on two incomes with his pretty wife. Tracey had been the very centre of his life, and as a close husband and wife team, they worked hard over the years, and between them earned enough to buy a period flint cottage. The cottage had just two bedrooms, but was classically thatched, and nestled comfortably in a fold of the South Downs, close to the quaint village of Wiston.

Apart from the beautiful cottage, their prized possession was the white E-Type Jaguar that had cost £10,000. The Jaguar was thirty years old, and something of a classic, but it could still outpace the foreign rubbish that disgraced the English roads. The thought intrigued him. He smiled wryly. So he possessed a streak of patriotism!

They were a happy couple, and spent their hard-earned money improving the cottage, building an extension and carefully developing the garden. They added a conservatory and some new period windows turning the cottage into a spacious and very desirable family home.

Craig loved the house, and as the marriage matured, he could not have been happier. A wonderful wife, a good job and a lovely home. Their happiness was complete when Tracey presented him with a fine baby son.

But then came the terrible day when his world collapsed.

They were driving to his parent's home in Brighton, for a family Christmas, when a Mercedes, whose driver was later convicted of being drunk, crossed the centre of the road and collided with their Jaguar. The car rolled twice before ramming a solid roadside wall. The massive impact severed the seat belt anchorage points, throwing Tracey and his young son out of the car on to the open road. When he regained consciousness, Craig found himself trapped by the legs with the Jaguar burning. He winced as he recalled the agonising wait for the rescue services and the terrible pain as the firemen cut him free. In his nightmares, he re-lived the scene....Tracey's limp body being lifted into the ambulance.... her cries for help, and the horrible sight of congealed blood staining her white party dress as her life ebbed away. God... How he wanted to die with her.

Then the devastating moment a grim-faced police officer had to tell him his son had also been lost in the crash.

There were the sirens, the police cars with their flashing lights, the ambulance, and the curious, staring faces of the crowd. A happy family had been destroyed in a heartbeat. Craig pushed the ugly memories away.

The hospital repaired his burned legs with surgery, and he spent many painful weeks hobbling about on crutches, but being unable to work, the next blow came when he lost his job and found his capital draining away. He couldn't meet the bills. The bank helped for a short while, but then came the news he was dreading, that in view of the extensive mortgage arrears, the company had to repossess the cottage. Craig was lost in despair as his world slowly fell apart about him.

In vain, he pursued the insurers, only to find the foreign Mercedes driver was not insured, and his claim for damages and financial support became locked in a legal wrangle.

The weeks dragged into months, until the sad day he had to hand over the keys and leave the cottage. He lost interest in work, and tried to come to terms with the change in his life, as he continued to battle with the insurers.

Then came the day he remembered so well, when the morning post brought him two pieces of news…. The good and the bad. He was to have his flying licence renewed by the CAA, and could work again…. But a second letter told him the mortgage company were putting the cottage up for sale by auction. To be sold to the highest bidder…. although he was eligible to bid! To bid for his own home, he thought bitterly. The auction was to be held in London in six months time, along with a dozen bankrupt shops, a few local apartments and various derelict country properties and barns for the DIY worker.

Craig knew he had to find the money to get his cottage back. Somehow. Any way! So he could return to the home that had been so much a part of his life, and had such happy memories for him. But he had less than six months to get the money!

He took an air taxi pilot position with his old firm's rival, where he could keep his troubles to himself. Now he was working again, he tried for a new mortgage, but with his name black listed and relying on a single income, he was deftly refused by the lenders he approached. He did the figures. He would need something in the region of £100,000 to add to the money the cottage was expected to realise, once the mortgage and the debts were repaid. His new boss said they might help him with a small shortfall, repaid from his salary, but while that would help, it barely affected the big numbers he needed.

Craig turned his options over, and very soon realised they came to nothing. He needed to get his hands on the big money soon, and with the date of the auction getting closer by the day…. it had to be very soon.

But as the days became weeks, he became more desperate and to take his mind off the problem, he buried himself in his hobbies. He stayed most evenings in his rented flat, working on his paintings and antiques, especially his clocks, where he could delve into their movements…. just as their makers had hundreds of years before him. But each morning, he marked the date on his kitchen calendar, counting down the days before the auction. A day, when, unless he could get the money, his cottage would be lost forever.

His new female colleagues, who knew nothing of the accident or his financial problem, often ribbed him that his collection of museum pieces was nothing more than an attempt to fill an empty home, a home they would say, which could be vastly improved by their presence! He always laughed off the idea, reminding them that the three loves in his life were his job, his antiques and being single. And being single allowed him the freedom to travel, sleep late or enjoy quiet nights at home with his clocks and his music.

Craig looked out from the summit of Chanctonbury, taking in the spectacular view of the Sussex Weald.

He dragged his thoughts back to the present.

With the first cooling breeze of the day on his cheeks, and the constant drone of the bees in the hedgerows for company, Craig sat himself down on the lush downland grass which, in the height of summer, is tinged yellow by the ubiquitous armies of Buttercups and Dandelions. Fairy circles of yellow and white daisies, added to the seasonal colours beside the brambles and the Rhododendrons, and above him the warm sun filtered through the trees surrounding the 'ring.' A quintessential English summer at its very best, Craig decided.

But yes, he considered again.... He would change things, and alter the direction of his life. Take up the ladies' sexy offers, and socialise more. This time, he would be more selfish to make up for what the sodding world had done to him. Get more from life. The sort of money his posh Air Taxi customers splashed around. First the most important thing.... Enough money to buy the cottage. Then a new car. A Jaguar, of course.

He looked down to the cluster of houses that would be Wiston, and could just make out the white figures on the village cricket green, as they enjoyed their 'willow on leather' game. The 'Steyning Rebels,' they called themselves. How do you become a rebel at cricket? Craig smiled to himself.

Wiston was a tiny gem at the foot of the Downs.... a village post office shop, with beamed ceilings—a thatched pub, with hanging flower baskets, and the historic 'All Saints' Saxon church clock, striking the hours. The classic country scene.

He allowed his thoughts to wander again as he mused. First, he'd need to be the highest bidder at the auction. Appoint a solicitor for the conveyance, and get the contracts exchanged. Then along to the 'lanes' in Brighton for some interesting antiques for the cottage, and to update his Hi-Fi with the latest surround-sound system. Everyone had DVDs these days. And, of course, the car. Craig loved Jaguars, and the latest Walkinshaw TWR XK8 was a driver's dream. He would choose the white convertible model with red trim. Imagine the thrill of visiting the Jaguar showrooms in London to place his order.

A seagull screeched overhead. He looked up and studied the effortless ease with which the graceful bird soared in the rising air currents above the trees, and came to a decision. If he were to get his cottage back, he would have to do something special. A big job.... maybe even illegal! He'd have to take risks. Legal or not, he would have to do something.

He reviewed himself. What skills did he have? Not much to offer.... just his flying. He had had a good education at St Catherine's College and, after graduating, joined the Royal Air Force. He obtained his wings, the flying badge of the RAF, at Cranwell in Lincolnshire, and progressed to fast jets and eventually helicopters. After his commission, he left the service and swapped an RAF uniform for the black company tie and white gloves of his old firm, Executive Helicopters, the elite of the helicopter business. A steady air taxi job, which he'd done well and where he'd been well regarded.

And so to his new job, which brought him to today's thoughts, sitting under the Beech trees taking in the spectacular view. Somehow he had to get his hands on the money. A new life, his home and the luxuries he promised himself. He looked up to the seagulls once more, shrugged his shoulders and brought his thoughts back to earth and reality. What a bloody day-dreaming fool he was! What a Prat. A total Walter Mitty. Even if he was prepared to risk some dubious flying, it was unrealistic to think the opportunity was likely to come his way. His cottage and the new Jaguar were nothing more than a pipe dream, a pleasant dream perhaps, but a dream that couldn't become reality.

Alistair Craig clambered to his feet and brushed himself down. He'd do better to work hard for what he wanted, he told himself, and there wouldn't be any short cuts. Just be grateful for his health and the things the Good Lord had given him.

He picked up his jacket, threw it over his shoulder and started the gentle walk down to the National Trust's dedicated car park, at the foot of the Downs. He turned his thoughts to his favourite village pub, the 'Red Lion' where he would later enjoy a juicy steak alongside the local beer. Craig smiled.

Now who has ever really seen a lion coloured red!

# 3

Goodwood Week is the pearl in the English racing calendar. The "Top Peoples' racecourse" poses unashamedly on the aristocratic lands of the Duke of Richmond & Gordon, where each summer, the elite socialites and cocktail party set meet on the well trimmed lawns of the imposing Goodwood House to parade the latest in hat and dress fashion, but take scant interest in the racehorses, as they pound the course for the bookmakers and punters.

The special 'Ladies Day' is when the champagne flows fastest against a mix of posh society gossip and classic racing, and a day which also attracts the 'working ladies,' who arrive from London in chartered coaches with exposed bosoms, powerful perfume, hell bent on a good day out and whatever might follow.

The Downland setting for this annual parade of High Society is also a Mecca for the true horseracing fan. The contrast of brilliant white railings against the lush green of the turf, the electric atmosphere of expectancy from the Grandstand, the noisy punters and the colourful flower displays, more than justifies the description.... Glorious Goodwood.

Craig was happy. He had the best part of the day to himself, one of the perks of the job, and, although he was not an avid fan of the Sport of Kings, he liked to watch the horses race, and enjoyed the sense of social occasion, the boisterous crowd mixing happily alongside the jockeys and the mounting excitement that precedes a chancy gamble.

He would enjoy the racing, and from his seat in the Grandstand, he watched the ranks of loudly dressed bookmakers, waving their arms and chalking up the betting odds on tatty Tic-Tac boards. Craig toyed with the idea of how much he would bet on Ryan O'Rourke's horse and decided to join a group of race-goers queuing at a wooden chalet. The clapboard building smelled of fresh paint. The hinged front was propped horizontally to form a canopy and the rough wooden building was stocked with race programmes, and various sporting and horse publications. A dozen pairs of binoculars were suspended from different points of the stall and the temporary shop was doing good business.

Craig needed a programme, and as he waited, an attractive girl wearing a coarse tweed jacket and thick unflattering spectacles, collected a pair of binoculars and a copy of the Horse and Hound. Craig realised the binoculars were for hire and, having deposited a ten pound note, chose a pair of powerful Zeiss 10 x 30's and paid for the Sporting Life newspaper.

He walked over to the crowded saddling enclosure where the runners for the first race were on parade. Each horse was beautifully groomed, with shining coat and spotless racing tack, and Craig was intrigued to see the intricate geometric patterns often combed into the horses' flanks. Diamonds seemed to be the favourite. He couldn't help wondering how much each animal had cost its owner. Too many thousands, no doubt!

He found a ringside seat, where a vivid display of red and white geraniums and late chrysanthemums smiled up at the race-goers. It was a colourful, exciting, occasion and Craig felt privileged to be part of it.

A rattle of hooves drew his attention as a scruffy young groom struggled with the reins of her powerful charge. A magnificent bay wearing a dark blue rug embroidered in gold, clattered into the ring. The frisky mare suddenly stopped, and refused to pass a spectator holding a newspaper that flapped disconcertingly in the breeze. With a shrill whinny, the mare shied, but with a sharp tug on the reins, was quickly brought under control. Then, with a half-hearted buck of hind legs, the temperamental animal resumed a steady walk. The following horse, a tall grey with proud head and long white tail, passed without fuss, apparently quite unmoved by the offending newspaper and the earlier commotion.

Craig consulted his programme. The jumpy mare was listed as *'Chesapeake Bay',* owned and trained by Guy Harwood. Today's jockey was Ray Cochrane, and the horse was entered in the first race, a selling plate.

Craig checked further down the programme. The 3.15 was described as the Whitbread Cup for five year olds and up, to be run over one and a half miles. £10,000 was shown added to the stakes. *'Top Risk'* was entered at number seven, and its form given as 0.0.0. The horse hadn't won or been placed in any of its previous three races, and was described as aged six, carrying ten stone three pounds. Mr Ryan O'Rourke was listed as the owner. The colours would be Royal Blue, Gold diamonds and quartered cap.

The jockey was the highly successful Frankie Dettori. Craig had once flown him with Lester Piggott from Goodwood to an evening meeting at Windsor Park. They had obliged Craig by winning both their races!

Hmm.... O'Rourke's horse, an outsider at Ten to One. Never been placed before, but expected to win today. Could horse racing be that fixed, Craig asked himself?

He passed through a wicker gate to the public enclosure and chose a seat at the top of the Grandstand, where he would have a good view of the course. The start, about ten furlongs away on the far side, was followed by a sweeping left hand curve, leading to the long uphill run and the finishing post on his left.

Craig soaked up the traditional scene and found his thoughts cast back to the old newsreels, and the famous English Derby at Epsom. Whatever happened to the mysterious tipster and self styled 'Prince Monolulu' and his routine cry to the punters? *"I've gotta horse".*

Craig swept his binoculars over the magnificent backdrop of beautiful trees and lush green turf down to the distant starting gate. How much money would be won or lost today as each horse pounded by the finishing post? How many bottles of champagne were waiting to be popped? How many wives might be beaten when the losing gamblers arrived home, their money gone and the worse

19

for drink? It was all a part of life's winners and losers, Craig considered.... probably one that would never change.

A dusty Tannoy speaker in the Grandstand roof interrupted Craig's thoughts.

"Good afternoon, ladies and gentlemen. This is Robin Sullivan, your commentator for today. May I welcome you to the first day of our Goodwood week and I see we are starting with the fine weather arranged by our super efficient Clerk of the Course."

Craig cringed at the corny joke and wondered what might be coming next. The commentator continued breezily, going through the declared runners and giving the horses' form.

The first race was duly won by *Chesapeake Bay,* the jumpy mare Craig had seen in the saddling ring, and a tingle of excitement ran up his spine as the horse hurtled by the finishing post, eyes bulging, teeth bared and pounding hooves that churned up melon sized clumps of turf.

A roar greeted the winner as it thundered over the line and the following runners cantered home in line astern. Craig looked around the Grandstand where a flutter of betting slips littered the floor, discarded by the grim-faced losing punters.... perhaps having just blown a week's wages, but who were no doubt already planning how they would recoup their losses!

The race results appeared on the finisher's board, and the loudspeaker confirmed the race order. There was an hour before Craig's race, so he decided to look over the line of bookmakers who were already frantically signalling betting odds to their colleagues in the exclusive member's enclosure. Craig was not sure how much to bet on O'Rourke's horse, or the odds he might get. Not much good risking all he had on him just to get his money back!

As he reached the lower Grandstand level, the bookmakers were busy chalking up betting odds for the second race. He noticed that one or two boards offered a better price, so he would need to do some mental arithmetic and shop around, he decided, but first it was time for a drink. He stepped under a striped awning to the cafeteria.

Sipping an ice cold Pepsi-Cola, Craig listened to the commentary for the second race, which the favourite led from start to finish. He emptied his glass and followed the other punters back to the saddling ring.

As before, a dozen horses were being led around the ring, but now the central grass area was occupied by several small groups, presumably the owners, their trainers and the usual hangers-on. Craig was happy as he took in the scene. He liked the high fashion colours of the ladies' dresses, the bright jockey silks, the thick ranks of red Geraniums and the animated hubbub of conversation which hung in the air. He was amused to see how some of the posh ladies coped in the soft grass. A particularly fashionable lady with classic long blonde hair, looked stunning in a red, Carmen style dress, but was struggling for composure as her tall heels sank in the earth, while in the same group an equally fashionable, but older, companion, still looked great in a plain black dress and sensible flat shoes.

Craig soaked up the English garden party atmosphere and checked around the crowded ring to find a seat with a good view of the action. No doubt last-minute riding instructions were being passed to the jockeys, and Craig recognised one or two well-known faces. Dick Francis, the ex-champion jockey and now a popular author, looked incredibly small, but Craig envied his wealth. In contrast, the Irish five times champion, Keiron Fallon, seemed too tall to be a jockey as he chatted casually to a well-dressed owner. Probably discussing fees and profit sharing for his next win!

Craig spotted a female jockey looking very much out of place in this traditionally all male arena. Horseracing, the Stock Exchange, even the flight deck of today's airliners. The age of sexual equality had surely arrived. Craig admired the progress made by the fairer sex after years of waiting in the wings. But would women ever play the men on level terms at Wimbledon or St Andrews?

He looked anxiously for *Top Risk,* whose number was missing from the assembled runners, but, in a moment, a tall Chestnut trotted into the ring and for a second cantered nervously on the spot as a powerfully built stable lad held him in check. Craig was impressed with the outsider, which was tipped to win. The horse stood visibly taller than the others, perhaps seventeen hands high. Craig felt encouraged, although he guessed size probably had little to do with breeding, racing speed and stamina.

So how much to bet? Craig asked himself again. He felt a sudden flush of the daredevil.... Why not risk all? Take the cash from the conveniently placed ATM. Yes, he'd draw out to his maximum daily

21

limit and punt all the cash he had with him. Go for broke! About £250 would go 'on the nose' as his tipster had advised, but even as he came to the decision, *Top Risk* began his cantering trick again as the stable boy held on. For a moment horse and boy pulled hard against each other, and then almost as quickly, the big Chestnut relaxed his head and settled into a steady walk.

Craig overheard one or two comments from the other punters. It seemed that putting money on a nervous starter wasn't a good idea. Craig was reassured, surely that would improve the odds, and he had inside information!

The jockeys were called upon to mount. Once again, *Top Risk* repeated his cantering performance, and as Craig left to get his money and head for the bookmakers, he was not feeling too sure of his decision. It was only the deadly certainty with which his wealthy passenger had tipped *Top Risk* that prompted Craig to chance his hard-earned money.

Walking from one tout to another, Craig established the best odds at Ten-to-One and, even as he proffered his handful of notes, the bookmaker's clerk chalked the odds down to nine. Craig pocketed the betting slip, and once again climbed the Grandstand steps, in time to see the runners emerge on to the soft turf and take up a steady gallop down to the far away start.

At the rear, *Top Risk's* jockey was having a difficult ride as his mount cantered in circles. A sudden cry from the crowd made Craig raise his glasses. The fiery Chestnut had jerked his head back sharply and blood was streaming from Frankie Dettori's nose.

'Hell and Damnation!' Craig cursed to himself, but although the jockey's silks were heavily spotted with his own blood, he angrily kicked at the horse's flanks, and with a whack from the whip, *Top Risk* galloped off to the distant starting gate.

Craig felt defeated. Just his bloody luck. On his salary, £250 took some saving. His tipster had warned him. *Top Risk,* eh?.... Even the name was an omen.... What a mug's game*!*

Thinking he might as well get his money's worth, he trained his glasses on the start where the runners were being coaxed into the stalls. The commentator was burbling on about *Top Risk's* bad luck, which depressed Craig even more. Still, the horse had stormed off well in the direction of the start. If only he would repeat it in the opposite direction on his way back to the finishing post!

Craig scanned his glasses over the course and stopped on the big Tote Board. Not much difference in the prices, except, my God, *Top Risk* was being shown at 'eight to one.' As Craig watched, the odds changed again and settled at seven. Some big money must be backing O'Rourke's horse. Craig was pleased with his own stake. The runners were safely in the stalls and under starter's orders. The Tote betting was closed.

Craig wondered how many thousands of pounds in bookies bags and betting shops around the country were about to change hands. Just so long as some of it was destined for him!

The crowd went quiet and then roared, "They're off." Craig focussed on the starting line as the brown, black and grey mass charged off. Immediately a dark horse moved into the lead and rode across the pursuing pack to ride hard against the inside rail.

*Persian Alice,* a 'fifty-to-one' rank outsider, was leading by several lengths. Craig hoped some unknown horse wasn't going to upset the form, but then, the following two runners closed on the leader, and were joined by the 'two-to-one' favourite. *Top Risk* was closely tracking the leading four. Great, he was in with a chance.

The leading horse soon fell back. Now there were only four horses in front, a good three lengths clear, and as the field raced up the long uphill straight, the favourite moved smoothly into the lead, with two horses chasing hard. At the three-furlongs-from-home marker, *Top Risk* was still going well and galloping hard on the heels.... and now drawing level with the second and third horses, as he closed on the leader. By God, he was going to win!

Just a short length separated the leading horse from *Top Risk* with the Grandstand crowd howling for the favourite, and, as if this was a signal, *Top Risk* began inching closer, and with a furlong to go…. put his head down, flicked back his ears and galloped home as though he had just left the starting stall.

Craig's blood sang as *Top Risk* thundered past the winning post amid a flurry of hooves, colour and flying turf. Fantastic, bloody fantastic! Craig could hardly stop himself from running down the Grandstand steps to get to the bookmakers. Would there be a fuss?

Especially with the last-minute change of odds. After all, his winnings would amount to two and a half thousand pounds!

He joined a small queue of winning punters and anxiously proffered the winning betting slip with his heart in his mouth. But, without ceremony, the bookmaker's clerk took Craig's ticket and, one at a time, counted out five bundles of £50 notes on Craig's outstretched palm. His only concession to the event was a good-humoured, "Your lucky day."

Craig pocketed his winnings and stepped back to watch, as the other smiling gamblers were paid off.

Fingering the crisp notes in his bulging pocket, Craig pondered. What an incredible piece of good fortune! He actually had a big bunch of 'fifties' in his back pocket! Fifty of the lovely blighters!

But what of the tipster? The hard faced Irishman knew a thing or two about horses all right, and *Top Risk's* victory was obviously a foregone conclusion. Perhaps he expected a share of the winnings. Then again, he would have no idea whether Craig could afford to stake £50 or £550 when he obligingly told him how to bet. He hadn't asked.

Alistair Craig was a happy man and he looked forward to the meeting with Ryan O'Rourke. He would need to thank him in some way.

# 4

The race commentator commenced his standard run-up for the 3.45 pm race as Craig headed for the Owner's Enclosure. With a few minutes to spare, he waited at the entrance where a uniformed gate attendant was checking passes. The Grandstand clock showed exactly 3.30 pm as Craig approached.

"I've an appointment with Mr. Ryan O'Rourke," Craig said nervously.

"Sorry, he won't be here, sir," the man replied politely. "You'll find him at the Winner's Circle. It was his horse that won the last race."

"Thanks a lot," Craig tried to sound offhand, "I'll try him there."

Well, well.... Craig thought. So O'Rourke could not have been absolutely sure of the result of the Whitbread Cup. He'd definitely told Craig to meet him at the Owners Bar.

A large crowd was pressed around the railings of the Winner's Circle. They wanted to get a good look at *Top Risk,* the frisky Ten-to-One shot that had soundly trounced the favourite. Ryan O'Rourke was holding his horse by the neck rein as Dettori dismounted, unstrapped the light racing saddle and threw it over his shoulder. O'Rourke was laughing at a shared joke with the jockey as he left for the winner's weighing room.

Craig couldn't see O'Rourke's Arab friend.

*Top Risk* was steaming heavily from his triumph, and as a light rug was thrown over his rear quarters, he shied again. Frisky or not, *Top Risk* was a fine racehorse, Craig thought as the temperamental winner was led out, followed by the whizzing and whirring of a dozen camera motors.

O'Rourke spotted Alistair Craig and beckoned him into the ring. Rather self-consciously, Craig squeezed between a group of spectators and ducked under the rail.

"We'll follow *Top Risk*." O'Rourke said, jerking his head, and without waiting, set off in the wake of his horse. Craig caught up and walked alongside.

O'Rourke looked sideways at Craig and said in a matter of fact tone. "Did you put a bet on my horse, dear boy?"

"Yes. I got on at Ten-to-One," Craig replied, in what he hoped was betting parlance. "And thank you for the tip, Mr O'Rourke. You obviously know the form."

They arrived at the stables and stopped by the first loose box. Several horses were being exercised around the cobbled yard. O'Rourke took *Top Risk's* reins, while a stable lad opened the door. The boy checked the straw bedding and, taking the reins from O'Rourke, led the horse into the cool, cobwebbed interior. "Get some fresh water," O'Rourke directed and closed the lower stable door. The stable lad secured the outside bolt and ambled off across the yard, bucket in hand.

*Top Risk* pushed his head out as O'Rourke leaned against the door. He turned to Craig.

"How much did you bet?" he asked sharply.

Craig decided to tell the truth. "Two hundred and fifty pounds."

"Could you afford to lose that much?" O'Rourke's tone was accusing.

"No.... far from it." Craig shot back.

"You've risked a lot of money Captain Craig, so you're something of a chancer."

"I suppose I must be," Craig admitted. "But you seemed so certain of the win."

O'Rourke's eyes narrowed. He smiled, paused for several seconds and looked steadily at Craig. He put a friendly hand on Craig's shoulder. The voice held a hint of greed. "Would you like to earn some real money, Captain Craig?" O'Rourke said softly. "Say a quarter of a million dollars."

Craig froze. Had he heard the man right? What an odd coincidence! His thoughts did a double-take, not knowing whether to take the man seriously. It was as though O'Rourke knew all about him and his desperate need to get that sort of money. A quarter of a million dollars was around one hundred and fifty thousand pounds.... fifty thousand more than he needed! He thought back to the plans he'd made to buy the cottage, that sunny afternoon months ago at Chanctonbury, and how O'Rourke's money could change his life.

"What on earth do I have to do?" Craig asked with a trace of sarcasm. "Raid Fort Knox? " Craig's confidence had returned, and for some reason he felt he should show O'Rourke he wasn't the type to be pushed around.

"Well, you don't expect that much money for a cosy ride around the countryside in your little helicopter, dear boy, " O'Rourke said with a rigid smile. "It will be a difficult flying job and extremely important. If you get caught.... " The innuendo hung in the air like a Damocles sword.

Craig was confused and didn't know what to say. The numbers were enormous. Ryan O'Rourke was obviously used to manipulating people using money like a sledgehammer, but Craig couldn't stop thinking about the quarter of a million dollars and the cottage it would buy.

*Top Risk* nudged his head against Craig's shoulder.... He needed time to think. To hide his indecision, he reached up and rubbed the horse's pricked ears. *Top Risk* nibbled Craig's palm, hoping for a tasty treat.

"Well yes, I could be interested," Craig said eventually, "but I'll need to know what I'm expected to do."

O'Rourke's light-hearted expression changed. He rested an elbow on the stable door, looked carefully around the yard and moved closer. The voice was velvet.

"Now listen carefully, dear boy.... My company needs the services of a good pilot in America. You'll be asked to fly a helicopter from Lake Michigan, across the Canadian border to Lake Ontario. It will be at night and you can forget all about passports." Craig widened his eyes as O'Rourke continued.

"After a refuelling stop, there'll be another five hundred miles to the Atlantic, where you'll land on my yacht. The flying will need careful planning and accurate navigation. The lakes will be frozen at that time of the year, and you'll be in the air for four or five hours at a time, maybe twelve in all."

Craig wasn't having difficulty following O'Rourke's brief outline of the task, but why on earth would anyone need to make such a long flight in a helicopter, especially at night?

O'Rourke's voice fell to a whisper.

"You will join a specially assembled team, each experts in their field. The task is immensely important to my international financial backers, Captain Craig. Millions of dollars rest on its success. Your share and personal fee will be exactly two hundred and fifty thousand US dollars." O'Rourke looked hard at Craig to emphasise the point. "The money could be paid in sterling if you prefer.... at the usual exchange rate, dear boy. Give or take a few thousand!" He finished with a laugh. Craig looked back incredulously. What was this man going to come out with next?

"If you accept, you'll get a preliminary ten thousand when you start and another ten in America. The rest will be paid when you land on the ship." O'Rourke paused and shifted his feet, gauging Craig's reaction. "The flight will be in three months' time."

O'Rourke eyed Craig intently, the penetrating gaze boring into the back of Craig's skull. He looked away, still confused, trying to think what he should do.

"Well then, what do you say, dear boy?"

Craig found himself staring at the space where O'Rourke's eyebrows should be. The laser eyes bored deeper. He was still trying to take all this in!

He looked nervously about the exercise yard as he considered O'Rourke's incredible proposition. He was thinking rapidly. The job sounded like some sort of smuggling run, a few million pounds to be moved out of the country, gems perhaps, or a wealthy man on the run. But he wouldn't do drugs. A few years back, a pilot mate had flown the infamous Polly Peck fraudster, Asil Nadir, out of the UK to Cyprus for a fat fee. It had worked for him. Get caught and he might get let off with a caution, but complete the run and the money he desperately needed would be his, neatly tucked away in his bank.

He'd have enough money to go to the auction and buy back his cottage.

Now here it was…. a once-in-a-lifetime opportunity.

As he turned the possibilities over in his mind, something caught his eye. He looked past O'Rourke to the car park where a British Racing Green Jaguar XK8 was waiting at the exit with its engine idling, the autumn sunshine glinting on the stylish, highly polished coachwork. The powerful V8 Sports car paused for a moment before joining the main road and then, with a goodbye wave to someone Craig couldn't see, the driver accelerated fiercely up the road and out of sight, amid a welter of crackling exhaust and a kaleidoscope of flying colour.

The good life. He looked up at O'Rourke and said firmly. "I'll do it. When do I start?"

O'Rourke's expression registered no more than satisfaction.

"Good. Now here's the plan. You start working for my company next month." He opened his wallet. "Here's my card. Come to this address at twelve 'o clock tomorrow. Bring your passport. And telephone my secretary first. You've already got a few thousand pounds to show we mean business. I expect you to be there on time."

"Okay, Mr O'Rourke."

Craig wasn't sure whether he should offer to shake hands.

"Good, We'll be meeting again soon." O'Rourke concluded briskly. "And please have the helicopter ready to leave at five o'clock. I need to be in my office well before six."

"That's understood," Craig said to his new employer. "I'll have the engines running and ready for lift off at five exactly. We have a tailwind, so the return flight to London is only thirty minutes, so you'll have a little time in hand."

It wasn't too soon to show the Irishman that his choice of pilot had been right.

But Ryan O'Rourke had never had any reservations about Craig's ability and motive. He'd already been watched and investigated for many weeks before this day, and Craig would have been surprised if he'd known just how much of his personal history was already on the racehorse owner's file.

*Today's events had been the completion of the final planning stage in a daring operation that would shake the foundations of the world's security and economy. Two of the most feared terrorist groups in the world had joined forces, and were setting a trap that would cause international alarm and change forever the supposed superiority of the West.*

Craig arrived home with his thoughts still racing. That was one hell of a day! But he intended to do it. Hadn't he wished and wished for just such a chance to make the money for the cottage? And here it was.... presented on a plate. Only a fool would let such a chance go, he told himself. And one hundred and fifty thousand pounds was five years' salary. Money talked!

He slept fitfully through the night and was up at first light. He'd have a good breakfast, and then call his office claiming a 'rest day', which the company always accepted. Then he would take the morning train up to Victoria and a taxi to the address on O'Rourke's card. The Anglo-Arab Oil Corporation PLC. What else? He said to himself. Oil money, of course.

Craig's black cab efficiently threaded its way through London's morning traffic and down to the City area where he was dropped off amid the steel and glass architecture of London's newest buildings. O'Rourke's office was on the top floor of The Gherkin.... the controversial all-glass Norman Foster building that towers over the north bank, in an area he had innocently flown over so many times on the London Heli-Route. Craig waited in the reception area as various office staff dashed to and fro, carrying files. He studied the many aerial pictures of North Sea oilrigs he recognised. Brent, Alpha.... they were all there.

Ryan O'Rourke appeared on the dot of twelve o'clock, and invited Craig into his modern office with outstretched arms, and a welcome more appropriate for an oil baron. The office was everything Craig expected. Spacious, light, with soft carpets, and all-glass windows to take in the panoramic view of London. Lush architectural plants were set against rare woods and designer glass furniture. A well-stocked bar occupied one corner. Craig looked out to the view where the London 'Eye' and the Houses of Parliament stood solidly on opposite sides of the river. The gardens of Lambeth Palace were spread out below, where a sightseeing hot air balloon was tethered. A small crowd was queuing for tickets.

30

O'Rourke was a changed man. Now full of smiles. He took Craig's hand.

"Good to see you again, Alistair," he opened. "Welcome to Anglo-Arab Oil. Let's take care of the formalities first." He handed Craig a director's black leather brief case. "These are the plans for the project which you'll need to study. Just an outline at this stage. You'll get the full and final briefing in America, then collect the helicopter from the factory and fly it to my yacht from there." The voice became businesslike. "Remember it's a night flight over a thousand miles across Canada." He said sternly.

Craig knew what the job entailed. It had been ingrained on his brain since he first accepted O'Rourke's offer. A week's work perhaps and he'd be back to England with the money.

Moving to the bar, O'Rourke poured himself a small measure of Scotch Whiskey.

"Anything for you, dear boy? .... We need to get to know each other!"

Craig looked at O'Rourke with renewed interest. He certainly seemed to have a good business about him. This office would have cost a bomb! Big wins on race horses. Fat Cat-sized pay cheques for a few days' work! He recalled his old boss's oft-repeated dictum. 'If you don't have big money.... stand close to those that do!' But there was still something about the man Craig couldn't put his finger on— an inner tension as though a spring was coiled inside the man's body, waiting to be released.

"Can I say no, Mr O'Rourke? I'm not a daytime drinker, but I will take a soft drink."

O'Rourke settled behind a large Rosewood desk, as Craig sipped politely at a Coca Cola. "When you've read the notes on our project, please call me. At six tonight. Just confirm that you know what we need, and you don't see any problems with the flying. And check the BA tickets are in order. Here's my private number."

He gestured to the briefcase.

"You'll be pleased to know your first fee is there in sterling." He smiled at Craig. "Don't put it in your bank, dear boy. Banks don't like unusual amounts arriving against a normal pattern. They have to call Government security.... money laundering, you know. You'll find the address details of a safety deposit bank where you are to lodge the money. They will want to see a passport, but the safe box is totally secure and discreet, of course. You specifically ask for a Mr. Torreville. He'll arrange things... !"

Craig clicked open the briefcase.

The classic 'brown envelope.' He smiled inwardly. Included were several papers and a British Airways ticket folder. He checked the envelope.

Ten thousand pounds and more to come!

The first step to the cottage.

Craig closed the case and slipped the lock.

O'Rourke chatted inconsequentially for the next ten minutes until his desk phone rang. He stood up and stretched out his hand.

"I'll need to get on with my day, dear boy. We will be speaking later. My secretary will see you to the elevator," he concluded turning to his phone.

Leaving by the main entrance, Craig walked across the wide pavement and down to the river embankment. He turned back to the towering building, glistening in the sun, then looked back and leaned over the deep parapet to watch the swirling river.... thinking. He was becoming a 'City' man, brief case projects. Glass office buildings. Brown envelopes!

A long barge lay low in the water as it ambled down to the docks. From time to time short blasts echoed across the river as the vessel's Captain signalled his intentions. The tide was going out as the muddy water flowed swiftly against the stone walls, twenty feet below. He allowed his thoughts to wander. It was happening, and the first positive indication was the money he now had. He'd get a taxi to the Bayswater safety deposit box firm, and then return to Victoria Station and the train home.

It was a month later when he handed in his notice. His boss found it difficult to believe he would let go of such a good job. Craig had been a solid company man and one of his best pilots. The Chief Pilot's position wasn't far away. He was sorry to lose him. He wished Craig well, but was puzzled about why he wouldn't say what he was planning to do.

As Craig closed the door to his office for the last time, he said a sad farewell to the staff individually, putting up with the saucy 'have a good time' comments from the girls. The boss had paid him a

32

worthwhile departing bonus, with the words: 'Would like to see you back one day Alistair... Good luck with whatever you are doing.'

Two months later, on the first day of December, having made arrangements for a good friend to occasionally look in to his small flat, he found himself climbing aboard an early morning British Airways flight for New York and a connection to Menominee Airport in Michigan. His instructions told him to book in to the Holiday Inn at Marinette, where, precisely at nine am on the following day, he would be contacted.

Alistair Craig felt apprehensive as he stepped aboard the roomy interior of Boeing's comfortable Triple-Seven airliner, but excited at this dramatic change in his fortune. A change that would bring the material things he wanted. The flint cottage in Wiston, and a new convertible Jaguar in the garage.

As the flight stewards closed the passenger door firmly behind him, Craig looked around the cabin. The other passengers began fussing with the overhead lockers as they stowed their belongings, while Craig settled into his allocated seat and told himself that even if he was about to become a criminal, he'd be a wealthy one and, in any case, it was now too late to change his mind.

# 5

Alistair Craig padded across the shaggy pile carpet of his hotel room to examine the brass table lamp that is standard furniture in the Holiday Inn chain around the world. He fumbled for the On switch and squeezed.... nothing happened. He tried pulling the knob without success.... he cursed silently. Why the hell couldn't they simplify their lights! Then, recalling that switches in America rotated, he turned the knob and flooded the room with a bright light that made him squint.

Craig returned to the untidy bed thinking how restlessly he'd slept. He pulled the bedside telephone towards him and called for a time check. A dull monotone voice told him it was 7.35 am. Checking his watch, he adjusted the minute hand. Time to get going. He moved to the bathroom and switched on the television as he passed.

The bathroom was typical American $100-a-night stuff. Period, brassy, efficient. Alongside the bath, a half-round marble column supported an overhead trellis, from which trailed the leaves of a 'Swiss Cheese' plant. *Monstera Deliciosa,,* or a good plastic imitation, Craig thought as he fingered the broad leaves. He filled the bath, threw in some salts and slipped back in the warm soapy water. The clockwork infrared heat lamp set in the ceiling ticked noisily. Craig relaxed for ten minutes, reflecting that here, at least, was a slice of the good life he wanted, and if he could only make a success of this job, he could soon have his old home back, and might shortly be enjoying the same comforts for the rest of his days.

Climbing out of the bath, he reached for the green striped Holiday Inn towel, and dried himself under the overhead lamp. He then shaved with his electric Ronson and pulling the trousers of his dark blue suit from the hanger rail of the open wardrobe, he returned to the window.

In the half-light, he looked out over an empty car park to the frozen river beyond. It looked damned cold out there. Snow was heaped everywhere, on the roadside, the riverbank and on all sides of the hotel car park. Craig's attention was drawn to an urgent 'bleep-bleep' and flashing amber light from a reversing snow plough accompanied by the mechanical voice.... 'This vehicle is reversing'.... 'This vehicle is reversing.' A heavily muffled pedestrian scurried clear.

Further down the road, a flickering neon sign above a clapboard roof, spelled out the letters, 'First National Bank'. On the snow covered lawn in front of the building, the dull orange glow of a sodium floodlight illuminated the portico, which was designed, Craig observed, with the amusing anomaly of Corinthian Capitals set above four fluted columns of the Doric Order. A strange architectural combination, but presumably one intended to lend an appearance of respectability to the entrance of an otherwise plain building.

On the roof, a square clock face flashed its message in white computer-style figures. Minus ten degrees Fahrenheit, it said. Forty-two degrees below freezing point in old money, Craig quickly calculated, and as he considered the significance of such extreme temperatures, the figures flashed off and re-appeared a few seconds later in Centigrade. Minus thirty, they said this time. Craig whistled softly through pursed lips. Centigrade or Fahrenheit.... Either way it was going to be bloody cold for the job he had to do.

Craig blessed the efficiency of the intrusive, but warming hum of the air conditioning, and set the room thermostat a few degrees higher, so that the dial now stood at seventy-five. At least he might not have to face the Arctic weather for a few days.

He picked up the hotel brochure from the writing desk. The Holiday Inn in Marinette, it said, is pleasantly positioned on the Wisconsin side of the Menominee River. The white man was first attracted to the area by the vast tracts of pine forest, and it was in

35

1831 that the first water-powered sawmill gave the initial impetus to the lumber boom that was to last a hundred years. The introduction of man-made materials in the 1950's brought about the demise of the timber industry, and from the forecourt of the Holiday Inn, hotel guests can look across the Menominee river to the museum, where a Log trailer marks the great days of timber trading.

Menominee was once the site of one of the largest Indian Nations. It is twinned with Marinette and the two towns sit astride the broad dividing river, which serves as the Michigan-Wisconsin state line. In summer, the river flows down to Green Bay on the western shore of the mighty Lake Michigan. In winter, the lake is frozen to a depth of several feet and it is possible to drive across the ice to the Door Peninsula, then a further seventy miles to Cadillac on the far side of the Lake.

Craig put the brochure down and recalled what the barman had told him last night. Few of the locals ventured out too far, he'd said, just the dedicated fishermen or some of the more adventurous kids. But such activity was confined to the shore. The icy sheet was continually moving. Deep fissures could open and close in seconds, and at forty degrees below, a broken limb and saturated clothing could cause death from hypothermia in thirty minutes.

Opening his suitcase, Craig pulled out a light blue shirt and matching Paisley tie. Checking himself in the long mirror, he pulled the shirt over his head and adjusted the tie with a Windsor knot. He then sat back on the bed to wait for the TV weather report. He chuckled as Tom and Jerry appeared in a mad screen chase accompanied by the Donald Duck voice of the wonderful Mel Blanc. He switched channels only to find Bugs Bunny, more Mel Blanc and his crazy colourful cartoons.

He finished dressing, cleaned his shoes with the polish-impregnated cloth that never worked properly, and freshened up with his favourite Old Spice after-shave lotion. The cartoons were replaced by a well-groomed lady newsreader announcing the local TV station, W-F-R-V, serving the Green Bay area. The World news would be next, to be followed by the national weather, but first an important announcement from the sponsors!

Craig paid extra attention to the small screen. A squeaky clean, all-American housewife with the inevitable blonde hair, thrust a bottle of pills at the camera, assuring her early morning viewers that those nasty headaches could only really be cured by using Anacid pain reliever. Apparently Aspro tablets were no good! Hmm, mused Craig. Shouldn't someone tell the makers...?

The commercials were followed by a few minutes of world news and the weather, when the forecaster cheerfully predicted that temperatures in Michigan were scheduled to stay below freezing, with a 'Lo' of minus 30 degrees. Craig wondered how the helicopter would perform at such temperatures. Would the engine run normally? What were its low temperature limits? Could the fuel freeze? What other problems might the cold bring? The local helicopter people would surely have the answers, and while he was an experienced pilot, he'd never flown in such extreme temperatures, and certainly not at night. He thought about the consequences, and knew that this flying job was going to be risky, but that was what he was being paid for. And, as the big day got closer, he also knew he was in too deep to turn back. In any case, he reminded himself, he badly wanted the money.

With a last look at himself, he checked around his room, switched off the lights and stepped into the corridor. Now what would breakfast bring? He said a polite, 'good morning' to a black housekeeper pushing her large trolley heaped with small soaps, plastic drinking glasses, assorted striped towels and the various cleaning tools of her profession.

The lift doors opened obligingly before he could press the red arrowed 'down' button, and a plump woman with short brown hair hurried out, giving him a drawled, 'thank yew' as she brushed by. Craig stepped into the roomy lift, pressed the ground floor selector button, and idly glanced at the small advertisements as he rode down to the reception level.

The Holiday Inn boasted a Saturday night cabaret, and a coloured singer was pictured in a clinging gold dress that reminded him of the Golden Girl in the old James Bond film.

He decided he would see the show after today's meeting. The flying would start soon, but probably not for a couple of days. He also wanted another chance to talk to Christine, the English girl he'd chatted with in the restaurant last night. He thought for a moment.

She seemed reserved and a little apprehensive. Wasn't it unusual to find such a girl alone so far from home?

She was starting a new job and was very excited about the prospects. Craig hoped she wasn't being caught up in one of those dubious job propositions that lure girls to foreign parts and end in trouble. She was attractive, with the long blonde hair he preferred, and the classic looks you saw on the covers of women's fashion magazines. So why on earth come to this part of America? Menominee wasn't exactly Paris! Perhaps she was the type who liked to travel by working her way around the world meeting people. What a coincidence, finding two English people thrown together three thousand miles from home.

Craig realised he was looking forward to seeing her again. He might even persuade her to visit his room and the king-sized bed the hotel directors had so thoughtfully provided. He found himself thinking about her curvy figure. Why do men find the female breast so attractive? But it was always so, the physical emphasis of the essential difference of the sexes perhaps? The subconscious comfort of the child pressed to the mother's breast. Craig had toyed with the idea many times, and had once even discussed it with a psychiatrist friend, although not from his consulting couch.

He'd been in the bar of his favourite roadside village pub, the 18th century Sussex Pad in Sussex, and had been told that what was really interesting, was not that Craig was attracted to the female figure, but that he needed to discuss what he thought was a problem with a psychiatrist! And with this piece of mumbo-jumbo, Craig decided to forget the idea and resign himself to his physical preferences.

Wasn't there something in nature, about the Bumble Bee being unable to fly due to its high body weight and the insufficient lifting area of its small wings? But the humble bee didn't understand the basic aerodynamic theories of lift, drag and weight and just went ahead and flew anyway!

If Christine were at breakfast, he would suggest they meet up in the bar before dinner. Reaching the ground floor, Craig stepped through the opening lift doors and returning the smile of the hotel receptionist, he crossed the lobby to the 'Voyageur' restaurant.

A few of the early morning guests looked up to note his arrival, and as Craig hurriedly glanced over the tables he realised with disappointment that Christine was not in the restaurant. Blast.... and worst still, a bossy blue-rinsed manageress, waving a menu card and allocating seats for the guests, was beckoning him. She gave Craig a toothy smile and directed him to a table by the window where he would have a good view of the hotel entrance. A brown linen napkin was unfolded and placed intimately on his lap, and, drawing Craig's attention to the breakfast menu printed on the tablemat, 'blue rinse' gestured to a prim waitress who was already advancing to his table.

"I'd like a moment to decide, please," Craig said stiffly.

With a courteous "Certainly, Sir," the waitress retreated to a nearby table, where a colourful assortment of breakfast cereals was on offer. Craig rehearsed what he would say if Christine appeared. He would invite her to share his table. It wouldn't do any harm to enjoy a little company before the big day—hopefully, the most profitable day of his life. But wait a minute, Craig. You are about to start working for a mega-fat pay cheque. You've been chosen for your flying skill, so with money flying around at a hundred and fifty thousand pounds a time, perhaps you should devote all your energy to the job in hand. Put Christine out of your mind until the job was done and the money safely in your pocket.

He thought about the money. A hundred and fifty grand for one flight! What would his mates say? What was he doing here? He'd never done anything illegal in his life, and beyond his flying skill, he had no training for the sort of covert work he felt convinced this job must entail. Craig was beginning to regret the decision that had brought him thousands of miles from the comfort of his cosy flat. He was an ordinary chap, too far over thirty. Wasn't it a bit late to make his fortune now? But then again, it was the opportunity he wanted and he had made his decision to get the cottage. He must stick with it.

With conflicting thoughts, Craig resolved one thing. He would do this one job. Once the money was safely in the bank, he would have the life he wanted. Best now to apply himself to the flying with no mistakes. No romance with Christine. Just get the job done, get the money, and get out.

He looked at his watch. Eight-fifteen. His first contact was at nine. O'Rourke had promised Craig the second ten thousand 'on account'. He wondered how it was to be done. How do they do these things?

Who'd be his contact? How would he recognize him? Stop fretting, he told himself. He would know soon. His imagination was running away with him.

Craig shrugged his confusion aside and began checking the menu. A variety of eggs was on offer, cooked in different ways. What was it the Americans said? Sunny-side up or easy over? How do you get your eggs cooked the regular way? The second item on the menu was a sixteen-ounce Delmonico steak. One pound of meat for breakfast, Craig marvelled! So that was the secret might of the American nation, he mused. He'd never heard of an eggplant with chopped grits, so he decided to order an English breakfast. Better face the cold outside on a full stomach.

He looked up. A cute waitress was by his side.

"Two eggs, cooked on one side only, some tomatoes and a good portion of bacon and sausages," he ordered. "Oh, and if you have any mushrooms, I'd like them too."

"That's order number four," the waitress tinkled, ticking her pad without a flicker of interest. Large breakfasts must be the norm, Craig thought. Something to do with the long history of hungry lumberjacks working in the area perhaps.

The waitress eyed Craig pertly.

"Coffee?"

"Please, with milk and sugar."

"Coffee, with milk. No cream. You'll find Sweet 'n' Low sugar packs in the bowl."

Craig opened a crumpled edition of the Marinette Eagle Star left by a previous guest. The front page was devoted to the lifting of a moratorium on influenza vaccine. Health officials at the Advisory Committee on Immunisation Practices feared a connection between the vaccine and the Guillaine-Barre syndrome, a temporary paralysis that is often fatal. The Federal Centre of Disease Control in Atlanta had established a link between the vaccine and the syndrome.

Immunise yourself against influenza, and risk total body paralysis seemed to be the choice. Ah, the freedom of America.

Craig put the paper to one side and looked out to the frozen river where the thermometer was still showing forty below.

He was contemplating the efficiency of the double-glazing that separated him from a temperature drop of a hundred degrees, when a

Pontiac station wagon pulled up at the hotel, and braked to a halt on the packed snow. Perhaps this was his visitor? But the driver and her young child jumped out holding their hands to their ears and hurried into the warmth of the lobby.

The waitress arrived with his order and began fussing over the table. Breakfast on the tablemat, coffee pot to one side, iced water in a brown glass, and a tray containing packets of VLT milk, butter and a variety of jams.

Craig looked up into two blue eyes and gave a polite, "Thank you," which triggered off the universal, "You're welcome," in reply.

Craig was sipping his third cup of coffee when a second car drew his attention. A steel grey Cadillac Seville had parked with its engine running, billowing clouds of steam from the exhausts. A coloured man sat behind the wheel, killing time. This was his contact. Probably waiting for the exact meeting time. Very efficient and if this was a big organisation …. Just as things should be.

Craig finished his toast and gulped down the remains of the coffee. He checked the time and left the restaurant for the reception area where he waited for the scheduled nine o'clock meeting.

Another step, he hoped, towards his English cottage.

# 6

The great American clockmaker, Seth Thomas, produced some fine Grandfather clocks, one of which was standing solidly behind the reception desk.

As its bell struck nine, the hotel doors swished open with a hiss, and for a moment, an icy blast invaded the warmth of the lobby as the Cadillac driver hurried purposefully through the already closing doors.

The man was brown skinned with a physique and shoulders that suggested he was a bouncer or earned his living in the boxing ring. He'd be in his mid thirties, and would have grown up in the rough and tough back streets of city life. The broken nose and cheek scar said so. The crinkly black hair was clipped short at his chunky ears and shaved close at the nape of the neck

The complexion was dark and oily, and a shadow of stubble glistened on the man's chin, although he had probably shaved in the last few hours. The fleshy jowls were puffed like an adder, and the broad neck squatted on the man's massive shoulders like Mike Tyson's. The face was pitted with old smallpox scars and had a squint in the right eye where, as a baby, he'd been left unattended in an open cot. The flickering eyelid attracted the attention of a curious Jaybird, which pecked at the sparkle.

The surgeons saved the sight, but the damaged muscle no longer controlled the eye, which wandered independently of its companion, and was now twitching as he advanced towards Craig. He wore a loose jacket, which fell open to reveal a faded T-shirt and khaki twill trousers. The trainers were tatty.

Craig decided his contact was from the Caribbean, a Cayman Islander, probably a family fisherman. He visualised the man in a striped seaman's jersey, and a jaunty sailor's cap, with perhaps a peg leg and a shoulder parrot! One of the old pirates from the Captain Morgan's days.

The man acknowledged Craig with a slight nod, and raised his arm across his eyes in the old West Indian salute. He jerked his head towards the lift and spoke to Craig with an accent from the heart of George Town.

"Ah'm Leroy Brandt, Cap'n Craig. Ah need yo to come wit me man," the voice was neat syrup and grated amiably.

Craig rose from his chair, and dutifully followed Brandt across the lobby to the second of two lifts. He remained silent until the indicator registered the third floor. The doors slid open.

"Number two to you, to leave." Craig extended his hand to the door with exaggerated English politeness.

Brandt's eye flickered at Craig. He produced a curt laugh.

"No need for dem fancy words, Cap'n Craig. Yo're not flyin' now man, jest goddam follow me."

An interesting character, Craig thought, as they walked along the carpeted corridor in silence. Brandt stopped at room 303 and tapped once. The door opened an inch against the security chain.

"Brandt."

Craig instantly recognised the Arab who had flown with Ryan O'Rourke to the Goodwood races. So he was a part of the set-up. How intriguing!

The man pulled on the door and stepped back into the room.

Craig thought back to the helicopter flight. Yes.... definitely the same man, although he'd seemed quiet enough then, but now there was something menacing about the man's demeanour, and the Middle Eastern features seemed more pronounced, with a new air of charisma and authority. He stood still for a few moments looking at Craig.

He was dressed casually in a black sweatshirt, black trousers, and black polished shoes. A fetish all black outfit, Craig thought, popularised by the golfer, Gary Player.

Thick eyebrows hooded the deep-set eyes above a typical Arab nose. A swirl of dark brown hair stopped short at the neck, where flecks of grey made him look older. The cheeks were olive, and the man's smile revealed a gold tooth Craig hadn't noticed before, and he'd grown.... perhaps re-grown a beard. Craig was thinking of someone. An international figure. Yes, an Omar Sharif look-a-like. But ten years younger.

So the Arab was in O'Rourke's team. His number two perhaps? It wouldn't do to underestimate this pair, Craig decided. But why would O'Rourke have an Arab and a Caribbean working with him in America? An unlikely mix surely.

The water was getting decidedly murky!

The man stood within a step of Craig, spreading his arms in welcome. The gold tooth flashed.

"We meet again, Captain Craig. Please come in."

Craig wondered what his role in the organisation would be. He walked into the room. Brandt closed the door behind them and stood with his back to it, sentry like, arms folded.

The furnishing was the same as Craig's room. Two double beds, a long dresser, and a circular table in the centre of the room, above which was suspended a large lamp. Two armchairs faced each other by the balcony window. The decoration seemed to be the standard yellow and brown of the hotel chain. A well-stocked drinks tray was laid out on the dresser. The television was on with a CNN newscast showing.

Leroy Brandt threw a hostile stare in Craig's direction.

Craig's heart thumped.

"So Cap'n Craig, h'allow me ta hintra-duce yo."

Craig smiled at the way Brandt spoke and like many Cayman Islanders, sometimes added an H when one wasn't needed, but didn't use one when it was.

He might even get to like the man, he decided.

Brandt stuck out a rigid hand like a signpost. The deep voice was basically warm, even friendly. Craig toyed with the idea Brand had to put on an act to maintain his tough image. Tough or not, it was Brandt who was calling the shots for the time being.

Brandt gestured to the Arab.

"Dis is Sheikh Mohammed Makhtoum, Cap'n. Him's de financier from an' Arab bank an' helps wit de money. Yo'll git along man. Him used to fly fer de Saudi Air Force han' is one of der Royals."

Craig nodded politely to the Sheikh and put his hand forward to shake hands. He wasn't sure how he should address him. Couldn't do any harm to smile.

"Hallo Mr Makhtoum. It's good to meet again."

Craig decided he would be especially respectful to his new boss.

"I'm happy to be working with you. But as yet, I've little idea of the flying you need. I'm being paid good money and appreciate it must be very important."

Craig immediately regretted his stupidity. If Sheikh Makhtoum were in charge he'd obviously know all about Craig and the fees.

"Captain Craig," Makhtoum began easily, and with extra politeness. No doubt as taught in the English Public Schools, Craig noted. "I am pleased you are happy to be with us, and you understand the importance of our work." The voice was mellow with only the hint of a Middle Eastern accent. Probably from a good Saudi family and a well-educated Arab, which confirmed Craig's thoughts of an English public school education.

"Have you a radiophone with you?" Craig was surprised at the question.

"Yes, a Triband Nokia."

"Please allow me to look after it, I'm sure you know these things leave a paper trail a child could follow. So no calls at all while we are working together."

He arranged a cough. "I'm sure you understand."

Craig handed over the phone.

Makhtoum looked at the phone and said something to himself in Arabic.

He looked back to Craig.

"Thank you Captain Craig. None of us will be using these."

He slipped the Nokia into a drawer. Craig frowned. Careful bunch, it seemed.

"I'm sure you will be happy to know that our operation has been planned as a joint project by Mr O'Rourke and an organisation from my country."

A thin smile crossed Makhtoum's lips. "We are partners."

Craig liked the euphemism.

"I don't need to give you too much detail now. It's in your flying brief. The helicopter you will be flying has been purchased, and you will be collecting it on our behalf in two days time…. That will be the 4th of December. It's an Enstrom 480 Hawk, and is ready now."

Makhtoum produced another smile, and brought a white handkerchief to his lips to smother a light cough, and continued.

Craig cocked his head politely as he listened.

"I understand you learned to fly on the type, and will be familiar with its systems." His tone changed as he continued, now almost a chat.

"I have much respect for your English skills, Captain Craig. I also understand you are an ex-Royal Air Force pilot. I myself learned at your CSE Oxford Air Training School twenty years ago, before returning to fly for my country."

Craig nodded. CSE's Oxford business had been built on the training contracts for foreign nationals, so cleverly arranged by the two Lordships, Iveagh and Waterpark. 'Guinness and Aristocracy.'

What strange bedfellows!

But, leaving aside the Royal Air Force flying schools, their training at the well-run Kidlington Airfield in the Oxfordshire countryside, was the best in the world. Craig had visited the airfield while a student at his college.

Sheikh Makhtoum was obviously proud to tell Craig of his flying experience. He continued professionally like a Commanding Officer.

"The helicopter will need to be flight tested," he explained. "And I understand you are well qualified to do that. Just a check on the aircraft's systems, navigation equipment, extra fuel, and so on, as you will know. Then you are to prepare for the flight, which is to be at night. Our Mr Brandt will be with you to help with the fuelling stops."

He looked at Craig expectantly. Craig remained silent.

"I can tell you that you have been chosen especially for this task because of your excellent background, and RAF experience. The success of our project depends very much on you, which is the reason we are paying you so much money."

The Sheikh turned to Brandt. "Is there anything you desire to add, Mr Brandt?"

Brandt shook his head.

"Captain Craig, we will eventually meet again on Mr Ryan O'Rourke's yacht. Leroy Brandt has your briefing instructions. Please study them, and keep him informed of every stage of your progress, particularly if you see any problems with the flying you are being asked to do. I can only repeat that your flight is one of the most important aspects of our operation."

He gestured towards Brandt. "Now I am placing you under Mr Brandt's command until you arrive on the ship."

Craig liked what he heard. He'd always had a reservation about the Arabs, but here was a flying man who had an understanding of people. He'd be able to work with him. But he wasn't so sure of the rough and ready Leroy Brandt. Still, if he had been especially chosen too, he must know his job.

"Brandt has the second part of your fee," Makhtoum continued. "He is a good solid man, who is well experienced for this work. He is paid to look after us all, which he does well. I want you to work closely with him."

He looked back to Craig.

"Captain Craig, these are nervous times for Americans. You and I are foreigners in a highly security-conscious country, and we must not do things that might attract unwanted attention. You should maintain a low profile and not discuss this job with anyone."

He studied Craig closely in emphasis. "Now I do hope that is clear, Captain Craig."

"Yes, I understand the position exactly, Mr Makhtoum. You can count on my full co-operation."

The Sheikh shook Craig's hand and left the room with a parting, "We will meet again gentlemen."

Leroy Brandt plonked his burly frame on the bed and propped himself against the headboard with a pillow. He grabbed a glass. Craig knew most West Indians fancied a drop of the hard stuff.

"Drink?"

"Too early for me," Craig said casually. "But don't let me stop you."

"Yo won't." Brandt growled hiding a smile, He picked up a bottle of Bourbon and poured himself a generous three-finger measure. He swirled the glass slowly and emptied the contents with a single swallow.

"Now listen, Cap'n, let's git one goddam thin' straight," he growled. "Yo're de hired hand han' we want no patsy chit-chat or stupid slip-ups on dis caper or yo'll have us all in de goddam slammer."

The change in conversation amused Craig. It confirmed his impression Brandt was trying to act tough. With those enormous biceps, he was probably just retained for protection, but would he know what he was doing on this job?

In spite of Makhtoum's courtesy, he wasn't happy to be in the hands of this muscle man for the flying he had to do. He disliked the arrangement, but it was too late to back out now, and in any case, his brief encounter today convinced him he wouldn't be allowed to, but he certainly didn't intend to submit to Brandt's gruff behaviour.

Craig replied quietly, "Okay Mr Brandt, I'm sure we understand each other." He thought he might turn the conversation round. Take some initiative.

Pulling a chair towards him, he sat down, with a hand grasping his ankle, in what he hoped was a relaxed pose.

"Enlighten me Mr Brandt, how did you get into this job?"

"Like de Sheikh tells hit, Cap'n, ah'm de boss's minder when him's over here. Ah does de rough stuff, when needed, an' ah'm lookin' after yo Craig, an' de flyin' an makin' sho de goddam plan goes off right."

Brandt handed over a brown file. Attached was a smaller envelope.

"Der's ten Grand in dollars fer yo Craig," Brandt grated. "Don't blow hit all on dem girls." He added sarcastically. "Once yo gits de job done, ders a whole load more ta come fer us all, man. But first we have ta git our fancy boy to da ship."

Craig noticed the slip instantly. So it was a man who was to be flown out of America. Had to be a wanted man, no doubt a business fraudster wanted by the Government. That had to be watched. Another piece of the jigsaw in place.

48

Craig took out the dollar bills. He decided he wouldn't count them and returned the notes to the envelope.

"What ...." Craig began to ask.

"No need fer no goddam questions now." Brandt snapped. "Yo jest let me know when yo've finished fixin' de flight. Meet me here tonight. Make hit five o'clock. We need ta talk about gettin' de helicopter. Hokay?"

"Yes Brandt, Ahm okay," Craig replied, mocking Brandt's gruff tone.

He felt vaguely encouraged. He'd got something positive to do and was firmly on the hook. He would see this job through, and to avoid seeing the inside of a prison, he would use his RAF training to the full. Craig was confident, that once he was in the air, in his own environment, he'd know what to do.

With the first part of the money in his pocket, he was already on his way to getting his old cottage back, and the new life!

Brandt got up and handed Craig some keys.

"Here's yo car, Cap'n. A VW Passat, from Europe yo know, parked outside. Him's fitted with snow spikes. Yo drive careful, han' definitely no speedin', Cap'n."

Craig pocketed the keys. "I think I can manage that," he began....

"Thinkin' hain't nearly good enough, man," Brandt cut in impatiently, "Jest yo make damn sho, if yo wanna see de rest of dat dough."

Brandt opened the door and ushered Craig from the room.

Craig sat on the unmade bed of his own room. 'Phew,' he sighed to relieve his tension.

He opened the envelope, pulled out several sheets of instructions and, settling down at the table by the window, he started to read

\* \* \* \* \* \*

PILOT INSTRUCTIONS

FOLLOWING THE MEETING, TELEPHONE THE ENSTROM HELICOPTER FACTORY AT MENOMINEE AIRPORT (NUMBER 863 9411.) ASK FOR MIKE CARRINGTON, CHIEF PILOT. INTRODUCE YOURSELF AS

49

SHEIKH MAKHTOUM'S PILOT. YOU ARE TAKING DELIVERY OF HIS NEW HELICOPTER AND WILL CARRY OUT A PRE-DELIVERY ACCEPTANCE FLIGHT. THE SHEIKH WANTS YOU TO CHECK THE OPERATION OF ALL THE SYSTEMS AND EQUIPMENT

1. 720 CHANNEL VHF PLUS A STANDBY SET
2. A GARMIN MK 111 GPS AND VOR NAV
3. MEDIUM FREQUENCY ADF COVERING 200-1500 KHZ
4. TWO LANDING LIGHTS WITH EMERGENCY BACK UP
5. HEAVY DUTY NI-CAD BATTERY

THE HELICOPTER MUST BE READY FOR YOU TO FLY BY 12.00 HRS ON THE 4TH DECEMBER. THIS TIMING IS ESSENTIAL AND CANNOT BE CHANGED SO MAKE ABSOLUTELY CERTAIN OF THAT.

* * * * *

Craig frowned as he studied the notes and looked out of the window.

Well, nothing too special so far, but there was three more pages of instructions. What was coming up now?

He picked up the second sheet, which contained line after line of checkpoints, timings and radio frequencies. He continued reading.

* * * * *

MAKE ARRANGEMENTS TO TAKE DELIVERY AT 12.00 HRS ON THE 4th DECEMBER. CARRY OUT A TEST FLIGHT TO CHECK THE RADIO AND AIRFRAME SYSTEMS. REFUEL THE FUEL TANKS TO MAXIMUM THEN SECURE THE HELICOPTER IN READINESS FOR THE FLIGHT.

5th DECEMBER 14.00 HRS. CARRY OUT FINAL FLIGHT PLANNING.

FLIGHT SECTOR ONE.

5th DECEMBER. NOTE TAKE OFF TIME FROM MENOMINEE AIRPORT MUST BE 16.15 HRS. THIS TAKE OFF TIME MUST BE EXACT PLUS OR MINUS ONE MINUTE ONLY

16.15 HRS LIFT OFF FROM MENOMINEE AIRPORT TO FLY SOUTH. FLIGHT PLAN TO BE AT POSITION 12 NM NORTH OF ROCKWOOD CIVIL AIRPORT AT 16.55 HRS

16.56 HRS CHANGE COURSE TO MAINTAIN TRACK 095 DEGREES BY GPS. CLIMB TO 3000' AND ROUTE FOR THE FIRST LANDING SITE AT POINT 'ROMEO' ON LAKE MICHIGAN. POSITION IS 50 NM ON THE 145 RADIAL FROM VOR GRB.

17.10 HRS TUNE ADF TO FREQUENCY 1301 KHZ AND HOME TO POINT 'ROMEO'. IDENT CODE IS DOT-DASH-DOT. CALCULATE AIRSPEED TO ARRIVE AT 'ROMEO' AT 17.30 HRS. THE LANDING PAD WILL BE INDICATED BY SIX WHITE LIGHTS SPACED THIRTY FEET APART INDICATING THE LETTER 'H'.

17.30 HRS LAND AT THE MARKERS, CLOSE THE ENGINE AND STOP ROTORS. A GREY CADILLAC WILL BE WAITING WITH BRANDT AND YOUR PASSENGER. BOARD AND PREPARE FOR LIFT OFF FOR THE SECOND SECTOR AT 17.40 HRS. THERE WILL BE A FULL MOON

FLIGHT SECTOR TWO. 5th DECEMBER

17.40 HRS. FROM POINT 'ROMEO' TO POINT 'SIERRA' ON LAKE ONTARIO, NORTH OF CANADIAN BORDER. DISTANCE 480 NM, ETA AT 'SIERRA' IS 23.15 HRS. A HOMING ADF TRANSMITTER ON FREQUENCY 797KHZ, IDENT CODE DOT-DOT-DOT, WILL BE LOCATED AT 'SIERRA' THE LANDING AREA WILL BE MARKED AS BEFORE. THE HELICOPTER IS TO BE RE FUELLED FROM THE WAITING PICK-UP TRUCK. PREPARE FOR THE SECOND LIFT-OFF SCHEDULED FOR 23.30 HRS.

FLIGHT SECTOR THREE. 6th DECEMBER.

23.30 HRS FINAL SECTOR IS FROM POINT 'SIERRA' TO POINT 'TANGO' FOLLOW THE EASTWARD COURSE OF THE SAINT LAWRENCE RIVER. FLIGHT PLAN TO REMAIN CLEAR OF THE POPULATED REGIONS.

02.55 HRS 12 NM WEST OF OTTAWA CHANGE COURSE TO POSITION 'TANGO' APPROX 100 NM OFF THE COAST, DUE EAST OF CONCORDE, NEW HAMPSHIRE. LEAVE THE COAST ABEAM PORTLAND. A HOMING ADF TRANSMITTER, IDENT CODE 'TANGO', ONE SINGLE DASH WILL BE LOCATED ON THE SHIP. FREQUENCY 200 KHZ. ETA AT POINT 'TANGO' IS TO BE 05.10 HRS.

05.10 HRS LAND ON THE SHIP'S AFT DECK . ONCE ON BOARD YOU WILL COME UNDER MY ORDERS WHERE YOU WILL DISEMBARK. THE BALANCE OF YOUR FEE WILL BE AVAILABLE IN US DOLLARS

SPECIAL NOTES

ALL TIMES ARE 'ALPHA' LOCAL TIME (NOTE NOT UTC)
HEADING ARE DEGREES MAGNETIC
DISTANCES ARE NAUTICAL MILES
NO NAVIGATIONAL LIGHTS TO BE SHOWN
POSITIVE RADIO SILENCE TO BE MAINTAINED

FLIGHT BRIEF CONCLUDED

Craig turned his attention to the flight planning maps showing the aircraft's track and the three RV's: ROMEO, SIERRA and TANGO. The primary navigation aids had been coloured red, together with the en-route radio beacons.

But Hell! It looked an awful long way for a flight at night, but the wonderful moving map GPS would take the workload off the navigation.

He lowered the instructions to his lap. Well…. well, he thought, and mentally compared the detailed instructions with the examination paper he had sat to get his professional flying licence. But he knew he could do it! By God he could, and a comforting feeling of relief settled over him now that he knew what was wanted, and the uncertain skies of the previous days had cleared.

He read the instructions a second time, already committing to memory the radio frequencies, ETAs and identification codes. It was now that O'Rourke's careful selection of Craig was justified as his trained, methodical brain filed away the tracks, distances and timings.

He pulled out his navigation computer to make the fuel calculations and was horrified to find that the longest leg would leave him with only 30 minutes' fuel. But what if there was a headwind? He imagined it could blow very hard indeed in these regions. Better have 130 gallons of fuel onboard, but at a specific gravity of 0.72, the fuel alone would weigh nearly half a ton! Was that asking too much of the Enstrom Hawk? He made a note to check the payload and fuel consumption when he called on the helicopter factory.

The timing seemed critical. He would need a cruising speed of 120 knots. Would the Hawk be capable of that?

The final leg would be the easiest.... no fuel or time problem. He would plan to stay clear of the populated areas, and when in range of the homer, just go hell-for-leather for the ship.

Craig considered the long sea crossing and winced. Just so long as the engine kept going. He closed his mind to the consequences of an engine failure and a ditching in the Atlantic in winter. The specialist survival instructors he'd spoken to-assured him the human body lasted just thirty minutes in freezing water!

He packed the instructions, and pulling out the keys, decided he would check the car.

He took the stairs, through the hotel lobby and, returning the smile of the receptionist, he pushed through the electric doors. The chilling wind nipped at his cheeks, as he scurried to the yellow VW, and by the time he reached the car, ice was already forming in his nostrils. He fumbled to unlock the door and gratefully climbed in behind the steering wheel.

The car was still warm from its delivery run and, as Craig turned the key, the engine started instantly. He adjusted the temperature control to maximum. The efficient heater was soon blowing warm air to his feet. He studied the instrument layout for a few minutes, and then slipping the automatic lever into D for Drive gear, he drove steadily around three blocks.

He returned to the car park and stopped next to Brandt's grey Cadillac. His watch said it was nearly eleven, time to make his first contact with the helicopter factory.

Craig switched off the engine, locked the car doors and, thrusting both hands deep into his pockets, jogged as fast as he dared on the snow to the warmth of the hotel lobby. Hell's Bell's, it was bloody cold.

From his hotel room, Craig picked up the telephone, and dialled the number on the briefing notes... The Enstrom Helicopter Factory. He waited with apprehension as the line purred its single note.

Alistair Craig was about to take the next step into the web of Ryan O'Rourke's carefully woven plan.

# 7

"Good morning, Enstrom Helicopters, how can I help you?"

"Mike Carrington please." There was a pause. Craig pulled out his notes as Carrington came on the line.

"Ah, Mr Carrington. My name is Alistair Craig. I'm the pilot employed by Sheikh Mohammed Makhtoum, who's purchased one of your Enstrom Hawk models."

"Sure thing," Carrington said. "We've been told you were coming. The ship's ready for you now."

"That's fine Mr Carrington. I'm here to do the test flight and check the extra equipment we ordered. The Sheikh will be taking the helicopter to Florida. I expect you know he has a business near Okeechobee. I'll be doing the flying. When he's completed his business, I'm to have the helicopter shipped to Mr Makhtoum's home in Europe."

"That all sounds fine Mr Craig," Carrington replied. "Sheikh Makhtoum did let us know what was required some time ago. The machine has been ready for a week, awaiting your arrival, I believe. Have you flown the type Mr Craig?"

"Yes.... I've been flying for some time, Mr Carrington.... Several thousand hours. I'm an ex Royal Air Force pilot, but I need to do a couple of flights on her first. I have a current American licence."

"Sure thing," Carrington said again. "You must have plenty of turbine experience, and our Enstrom Hawk's a doddle to fly. Where are you calling from?"

"I got in yesterday, and I'm staying at the Holiday Inn in Marinette. I'm planning to visit you today, if that's okay."

"Why don't you ride out to the factory this morning," Carrington replied. "We're located at the Twin County Airfield on US route 55. It's about five miles out of town."

"Thanks Mr Carrington, that sounds fine," Craig said. "Can we meet before lunch, say twelve-thirty?"

"Sure thing," Carrington said yet again. "I'll be waiting."

At twelve o'clock, Craig left the hotel, and drove to the helicopter factory, with the tyres crunching noisily on the hard packed snow. He followed Carrington's directions along Riverside Avenue, crossing the New Hattie Street Bridge, where it spanned the frozen Menominee River. Very few cars were braving the sub zero temperatures.

He found the helicopter factory as directed, and parked the VW by the small modern entrance. The receptionist greeted Craig with a courteous smile, and introduced him to Carrington who was waiting.

Carrington showed him the factory sales area where several helicopters were parked in a regimental line.

Craig was impressed.

The factory shop floor bustled, as engineers worked on the assembly line, and from time to time, the staccato screech of an air drill added to the general atmosphere of business. Carrington stopped at a dark blue helicopter.

"This is Sheikh Makhtoum's machine, Mr Craig."

Very nice too Craig noted. He knew the type, but was impressed by the spacious cabin. Two seats in the front section, with space for a further three in the rear. He looked inside and produced his notes.

He turned to Carrington.

"What's the range of these Hawks Mr Carrington?"

"Our standard model is the 480L. The Sheikh ordered an additional long-range fuel tank. Now she'll give you about five and a half hours flying time, say five hundred miles with a safe reserve." Carrington consulted a Flight Manual. "But the extra weight would reduce the performance you know."

56

"Yes, I understand that," Craig said, "but it is fairly cold this time of the year, so the weight won't be a problem. Once we are down south there'll be plenty of airfields for refuelling."

Carrington nodded his agreement. "Yes that's true, but in any case, this Hawk model is massively de-rated.... Cruises at three hundred shaft horse power, down from over four hundred, you know."

"I need to do the flying tomorrow, Mr Carrington. Can you fix that?"

"Yes, Mr Craig, that'll be no problem, but why the rush?"

"Oh, I'm the sort of chap who likes to get on with things, and the Sheikh is a man who likes his pilots to be punctual," Craig said jovially. "And your weather doesn't exactly invite long stay visitors," Craig added with a short laugh. He wanted to sound casual to take the edge off the importance of his flight.

"I understand the financial arrangements have been made, and all that's needed is the delivery handover to complete the deal. We'll just need the documents and a bill of sale."

"That's all in hand, Mr Craig, you can take them when you leave today."

Carrington thought of his $10,000 sales commission, and brightened visibly. This would mean he could change his five-year old Chevrolet for something newer, which would keep dear Mabel happy!

"I'll have Engineering do the daily check, and made ready for the flying. Want me to fly with you?" Craig resisted saying 'Sure thing.'

He just nodded.

Carrington motioned to Craig. "Thanks very much for the business Mr Craig. Lets pop back to the office and wrap it up."

As Craig left, Carrington picked up the phone to the Milwaukee Federal Aviation Administration office. A security report to the local FAA office was mandatory for all helicopter sales and movements. Carrington ran through the items listed on the form. The security agent sounded bored and accepted them without showing much interest.

My story would have ended right here if that security officer had been more vigilant.

# 8

Craig returned to the hotel feeling pleased. Things couldn't have gone better. If the remainder of this job went as smoothly, the money was already in the bag! He sat on the edge of the bed, checking the specification of the helicopter, and ticking off the essential requirements for the long flight ahead.

Examining the weight schedule, he calculated that with the extra fuel and two passengers, he'd be one hundred pounds overloaded. But helicopters give better performance at low temperatures as the engine sucked in denser air, and he was confident the Enstrom Hawk would cope with the extra weight. So that was it, nothing more he could do until his next trip to the factory, except report progress to the Sheikh and Brandt. He would then have dinner in the hotel, and hopefully see Christine.

He glanced around the room and picked up a Bible left open and placed by the kind Gideons. He began to read the Ten Commandments. Thou shall not covet...! Hmm.... and he was about to....? He put the book down and dragged his thoughts back to the evening. After dinner he would visit the cabaret in the Lumberjack room. A quiet relaxing drink in the bar first perhaps.

He threw his coat on the bed, and spent an hour going over his flying instructions, making more notes. He sketched out the long route to give him a better perspective of the major landfalls and turning points, and with each note he became more confident. He put the papers down.

He was feeling hungry again, and looking forward to the evening meal, but first he had to face another session with the charming Leroy Brandt.

Craig took ten minutes to give Brandt the results of his meeting, and with a few grunts and goddams, he was told to report again after he'd flown the helicopter. He returned to his room and lay on the bed for an hour, reading an old Steinbeck thriller. At seven o'clock, he went down for dinner.

The waitress came to his table immediately, and handed him the evening menu. She smiled warmly, and leaned over the table to lay a napkin, treating Craig to a fine view of her ample bosom.

"What'll you have?" She said mischievously.

He looked up, holding her eyes.

"I'll have the South African Lobster Tail, melted butter and a baked potato. Oh, and I'd like some wine please."

"Certainly sir," she said politely. "I'll have the wine waiter bring the list."

Craig's eyes followed her as she moved, his imagination working overtime. She was a fine looking girl.

He spent a few minutes ploughing through the indifferent wine list, noticing the absence of any good French wines. He was hardly a connoisseur, but he had taken the trouble to learn the major wine growing regions of France, and the best vintages. The hotel list had a map of France on the inside cover. That would be a fat help, with no French wines to choose. With so much uncertainty ahead, a good strong wine might help him relax. He chose a half-bottle of Spanish Rioja, and ordered by its bin number.

"Thank you sir, a good choice." the waiter said predictably, and returning immediately, he uncorked the bottle, and went about the unnecessary tasting rigmarole this cheap wine didn't warrant.

The lobster tail was served with fresh asparagus and decorated with various titbits of garnish, and a light Bearnaise sauce. On a side plate, a single baked potato was wrapped in silver foil. It was accompanied by a dish of melted butter, and warmed by a candle flame beneath the bowl. Craig sipped the slightly cold wine and cut himself large chunks of white meat, which he liberally doused in the butter. Superb. The

59

Americans could certainly serve lobster, but as tasty as the dish was, he doubted whether this particular lobster tail had ever been nearer to South Africa than it was right now!

Craig followed with green figs and cream, downed the last of the wine, and feeling a bit light headed, he sauntered off in the direction of the music. He'd rather hoped Christine could have joined him.

The Holiday Inn Lumberjack room is the Saturday night meeting place for half the teenage population in Marinette. The room was filled with the chatter of young voices, raised to make themselves heard above the general hubbub. The bar houses an impressive array of fashionable drinks served with the casual indifference of American bar tenders. The solid, dark wooden tables, hewn in the logging tradition, and the sombre tones of the decor, combined to give the bar a heavy but not unpleasant atmosphere. The subdued lighting was so inadequate it was barely possible to recognise faces ten yards away, and the only light came from the tables, each offering a small flickering candle flame, buried deep in a heavy amber glass.

The customers were young, with the expected rapt, with-it expressions….The boys wearing their hair clipped short, with cut-lines and sporting the regulation Tee shirt and Levi Jeans. The girls were pretty, mostly without make-up, except for the black, often smudged mascara.

A combo of piano, double bass and drums was rattling away at some tune Craig vaguely recognised, and as his eyes adjusted to the dark, he walked through the bar to an empty table close to the dance floor.

Almost before he had sat down, the same pleasant dark-haired cocktail waitress with smiling brown eyes, was at his table. She was carrying a silver tray, which she held with fingers spread high above her head. Obviously a professional.

"Hi handsome," she announced loudly, giving Craig a bold eyed appraisal. "What'll it be?"

"Do you have a Tom Collins?" Craig was not sure his favourite drink was served in America.

"Just the one?" the waitress smiled brazenly, glancing pointedly at the empty seat next to Craig.

"Yes please," Craig replied…. trying not to sound too English. The waitress flounced off swinging her hips provocatively.

Craig picked up a menu, and by holding it close to the candle flame, he could just about read the evening programme and the list of drinks, few of which he recognised. The cabaret was to start at 10 o'clock, and there was a picture of a black singer and her backing group.

The waitress returned with Craig's drink, which was served in a tall glass with a white frosty substance on its rim. The glass contained plenty of ice, some cocktail titbits and a sugar-coated cherry. He took a tentative sip and picked up the bar tab the waitress had deftly torn off with the fingers of one hand. Five dollars.... Almost three English Pounds! Thank heaven he wouldn't be staying too long. At these prices, he could see his money disappearing like snow in summer.

Some of the couples were moving moodily on the dance floor, appearing to ignore the music, but as the Lumberjack room filled, the group seemed to find new life and launched into a Rap Rhythm. A few couples were on the floor moving their bodies in time with the faster music, and Craig spent some time watching a particularly willowy girl. She could certainly dance, and seemed oblivious to her audience as she sexily jerked her breasts and hips in a sequence of erotic dance movements in time with the beat.

Craig recalled the good times he'd shared with Tracey. She loved disco dancing too, and for a moment he pictured her on the dance floor, the bright lights showing off her young figure, and the glittering sequins of her favourite dance dress. He dragged his thoughts back, ordered another Tom Collins, and poured it down. A second drink on top of the red wine, and he was feeling decidedly mellow.

Good, that would help him enjoy the evening, and with the added confidence of the alcohol, he opened a conversation with the older of two girls at the next table, and was soon on the dance floor moving in time to a modern version of an old Beatles hit.

At ten o'clock, a black pianist replaced the group, and several extra lights brightened the stage. Disco lights flashed, and as the introduction rose to a crescendo, a black singer swept on to the cabaret floor. She was wearing a stunning white satin dress that emphasised her smooth black skin. She looked a million dollars, and immediately launched into the 'Hey Big Spender' song, immortalised by the Tiger Bay girl, Shirley Bassey.

Craig clapped enthusiastically, and was still applauding when Christine leaned over his shoulder.

"Mind if I join you, Alistair?" She whispered, intimately.

Craig stood up and touched her arm. "How lovely to see you again, Christine. I was really hoping you might come this evening."

She gave him a warm smile. "I did say I would see you here, remember?"

"Yes, but I thought perhaps you were being polite. Anyway, I'm glad you could make it. What shall I get you to drink?

"I drink Gin Slings," she said with a laugh. "Supposed to be slimming."

She was wearing a black velvet dress, edged with white lace, and deeply veed to reveal a glimpse of her full breasts. Her hair was swept up in a formal style, making her look older. Around her neck, a matching velvet choker supported a silver heart shaped locket. Whose photograph did she keep there? Craig wondered. The only other jewellery was a silver bangle on her left wrist. She looked wonderful. Flirtation sparkled in her blue eyes. Craig looked into them, holding them, feeling a glow of excitement. How interesting. So physical attraction could still make his skin tingle?

The cocktail waitress returned to take their order. Craig ordered the Gin Sling, and sipped at his third Tom Collins while they watched the show. The singer ran competently through her repertoire and received an appreciative handclap after each song. Then, with an encore, she threw a flurry of farewell kisses to her audience, and swept off the stage.

After the cabaret, the music became quieter. Craig broke the silence. "Can we dance, Christine?"

He took her hand, and slipped his arm about her waist as he escorted her to the small dance floor. They moved to the music with a respectful one-inch of air space between their bodies.

"I take it you are working here in Menominee, Christine? Why are you so far from home?"

There was a pause before she replied.

"Oh, I suppose I'm recovering from a bad relationship really, but I shouldn't be telling you. It's just that I got this opportunity to work in

America. It seemed too good to miss." Craig pulled her closer as she talked.

"I'm a secretary to an Irish businessman. He travels a lot. I'm his PA. I look after his airline bookings and appointments. I'm here at the hotel for a company meeting. Tomorrow, I fly to New York. What about you? You're a long way from home too."

Craig needed a few moments to think. What should he tell her? Best a watered-down version of the truth.

"I'm taking a long holiday, but I have to do some business for my firm at the local helicopter factory first. I'm in the aviation business. I only plan to be here a couple of days, then off to Florida where it'll be a whole lot warmer. I suppose I'm really a beach boy at heart. I just love the sun...."

Craig continued the small talk, but was disappointed that Christine seemed so uninterested in responding. Unnatural really.... two English people so far from home. Why was she withdrawn? The thought crossed his mind, still carrying a torch for a lost boyfriend? Not his problem, he thought uncharitably as they continued dancing.

The conversation remained firmly in the realm of small talk. Craig was faintly annoyed. He wanted her to show some interest in him. He pushed his cheek against her hair and pulled her closer again, feeling the firmness of her body.... his thoughts were running haywire. She was wearing a perfume he remembered from somewhere.... one of the Chanels?

The combo took a short break, and was replaced by the Chicago pop group's classic record, 'If you leave me now'. The tune had special memories for Craig, and he longed for some close company. He whispered to Christine.

"Why don't we go to my room for a quiet coffee, Christine?"

He felt her body stiffen, and immediately regretted the foolish euphemism.

She pulled her head back and said discouragingly. "Don't rush things, Alistair. Let's have another drink and get to know each other. You seem a nice enough guy, and I'm enjoying being with you, but I think you've had a little too much to drink. I'll let you off for being suggestive."

They continued to dance, and Craig was regretting his earlier assumption. She was a sensible girl, and wasn't going to jump into

63

bed with him, just because they both came from England! Just like him to get it wrong. Too much bloody booze! She was right, of course, and he would do better to concentrate on the job he was being paid to do.

Craig's depression lifted a little as they danced. They talked quietly, against the background of mood music, while the disc jockey played another of Craig's favourites from the Seventies. The guitar group then returned to strum out the last few numbers, and close the show.

Christine tugged at Craig's hand.

"Let's have the last dance, Alistair…. I've really enjoyed being with you tonight. Perhaps we can see each other again tomorrow, but I'm not sure what time I have to leave. I'm just waiting for the call from my boss. He did say we would be leaving fairly early. Why don't you ring my room first thing? We could meet for lunch if there's time."

"Yes, of course. I'll be back from the helicopter factory about twelve." Craig said, squeezing her hand. "It's a date, then."

Craig thought she gave him a strange look, but the moment was forgotten as they danced. The group said their goodbyes as they moved off stage, and the dancers left the dance floor. Craig walked slowly with Christine to her room.

"Thanks for a lovely evening," she said almost formally. "Hope to see you for lunch then. Goodnight Alistair."

She briefly kissed him on the cheek, and turned away.

Craig waited until she reached the end of the corridor, and waved. Then with some gloom in his heart, he took himself off to his room.

He looked into the dressing table mirror and grimaced at the oafish face that stared back. His eyes were fuzzed and his hair a mess.

Too much bloody booze!

"Stupid sod," he said to the empty room.

So much for his romantic ideas of bed with Christine.

"Stupid sod," he said to himself again.

Christine picked up the telephone and dialled.

"Mr Makhtoum. It's Christine here. Alistair Craig has gone back to his room. He's been drinking a little, but seems able to hold it, enough anyway to date me for lunch. He didn't talk much, or give anything away."

She listened carefully.

"Yes I will, Mr Makhtoum. Goodnight." She put the phone down.

Meanwhile, Alistair Craig moodily threw off his clothes and flopped across the double bed. With the fuzz of alcohol, and a troubled mind, he soon fell into a deep sleep, and as the night passed, he found himself fleeing from Leroy Brandt and O'Rourke.

Christine was at his side.

Sheikh Makhtoum was shouting.

He needed him urgently.

The ground was sticky with soft mud. He was stumbling. The villainous Brandt was almost on them.

Threatening.

If only they could reach the helicopter!

# 9

The jangling tone of the bedside phone woke Craig. He fumbled for his watch. Six-thirty. He picked up the receiver.

"Hallo, dear boy." It was O'Rourke. "I'm calling from Chicago Airport. Just catching the early flight for New York. I'll be going straight to the ship from there. How are things going? Are the instructions okay?"

Craig gathered his wits. "Oh, er fine, Mr O'Rourke, the helicopter is laid on and things are going just as you planned." Craig outlined to O'Rourke the meetings with the Sheikh and Brandt. I've arranged the test flying with Carrington. "All we need now is some fine weather."

"Good, then it seems we'll be meeting again on the *Champagne Princess*. Have you actually flown the helicopter?"

"No, that's scheduled for today. The Enstrom Hawk is what we need. She's a good solid helicopter with the special equipment I need for the flight. We've no problems."

"That's fine Alistair. How are your nerves?"

"Bit apprehensive," Craig answered truthfully, "But for a quarter of a million dollars, the nerves will be alright."

Craig thought he should reassure his paymaster. He also wanted some information. "Can you tell me who I'll be flying, Mr O'Rourke? Sounds like someone important. It would be a help to know." Craig put the question casually.

"A very important man, but I can't tell you more, only that it is vital the flight goes precisely as planned. The flying will be difficult, but it's the reason I chose you. Don't let me down, dear boy." O'Rourke added, "It'll be worth it once the job's done and you reach the *Champagne Princess.*"

O'Rourke chuckled fatly. "Keep thinking of the money. We'll crack a celebration bottle of bubbly together."

"I'll keep you to that," Craig said with good humour.

"Good, then we'll be meeting again soon. Bye Alistair. Good luck with the flying."

Craig ran a shower. He was thinking of O'Rourke's comments…. Someone important. Yes but whom? Best to forget it for a while. The flight was almost here and the rest of the money would soon be in the bank. He thought back to Christine. Why couldn't he stop thinking about her, and how bloody stupid to suggest getting her into bed. Had he destroyed his chances of a better relationship? At least she hadn't ditched him on the spot…. but what was the point in getting to know her? She was leaving for New York. In forty-eight hours he'd be a thousand miles away.

When this job was over, he would have to start thinking about regular work. His old job might not be open to him. Still with plenty of money in the bank, he could pick and choose his jobs a bit. Perhaps he could fly for Bristow Helicopters on the new Sikorsky S-92. A fine helicopter and a good secure company, a combination that would fit in well with his life style.

Craig dressed, had breakfast and telephoned the helicopter factory. The welcoming voice of Carrington came on the line.

"Good to hear from you again, Mr Craig. Everything's ready for you out here. Still the same time for our meeting?

"Yes, eleven o'clock. Weather Okay?"

"Sure thing. Clear as a bell, but a mite cold. The Hawk has a good heater, but this spell is proving a bit too much. Bring something warm to wear for the flying."

"Thanks, I've bought a fur Anorak. What about the extra fuel Mr Carrington? Any problems?"

"Engineering seemed surprised you wanted that much fuel. But you're the customer. Your machine has a Chadwick range extender fitted. You'll have an extra fifty gallons and still keep within the

67

weight limit," Carrington pointed out. "With full fuel and luggage, the 480 Hawk can only lift two passengers you know."

"That's all I need," Craig assured Carrington. "Mostly be flying alone, and when I get back to Europe, I'll have the fuel extender removed. I'll be with you at eleven, and don't forget I'm leaving in two days, so please make sure she's ready."

"Yup, that's all organised. The helicopter will be finished by lunchtime so you have a day in hand. See you later this morning Mr Craig. Bye for now."

Craig replaced the receiver. He'd got the right man and so far no snags. Things were working according to the plan, and he was glad the Hawk was in top condition for the long flight. He'd be even happier when he'd actually flown her. It was important he felt relaxed at the controls. Some helicopters had undesirable characteristics, and with the prospect of a thousand miles of night flying, all his attention would be needed for the difficult navigation.

If only O'Rourke had been more specific about his passenger. 'Someone important' was all he would say. No point in worrying. In less than forty-eight hours he would know.

Shortly before eleven o'clock, Craig was again driving on the icy roads to the Airfield. He parked the VW outside the helicopter hangar. Carrington was well wrapped up, and already walking out to greet him. He shook his hand warmly.

"Good to see you this morning, Mr Craig. Let's go inside. The helicopter is one hundred per cent ready."

Carrington left the office to get some coffee. Craig looked around the room. A 'one million scale' Aeronautical Topographical chart of the Great Lakes was pinned to the wall. Craig examined the geography of the area, and mentally traced the long route he would take. First the ice landing on Lake Michigan, then north to Beaver Island.... through the Mackinaw straits to Lake Huron.... next, the dash across the Canadian border to the landing site on Lake Ontario, and finally, the long sector following the Saint Lawrence River to the coast. It looked one hell of a long way.

Flying a small helicopter through the Adirondack Mountain range at night would be especially difficult. He'd need to keep his wits about him. Still for a quarter of a million dollars, that's what he was being paid to do! A high price to pay to get one man out of the country. No doubt he would pay a high price himself, if he got it wrong.

Carrington came in with the coffee, interrupting his thoughts. "The Hawk's being pushed out now, Mr Craig. We'll get airborne in fifteen minutes or so."

"Can we go through the Flight Manual first?" Craig asked.

"Sure thing," came Carrington's standard reply as he turned to the shelf behind him.

Alistair Craig knew precisely what to look for. The technical logs, and Flight Manual give the performance of an aircraft more accurately than any owner could. Craig thumbed carefully through each page, and it was comforting to have a good machine for the difficult flight ahead. The two men left the office for the helicopter-landing pad.

"I need to spend the first few minutes checking the aircraft's night flying systems, particularly the fuel flows. Then do some autorotation to get my hand back in." Craig was referring to the technique of landing the helicopter without the engine, in case of emergency. A few practices would soon bring his confidence back.

The sun shone brightly in the clear cold air, as the two men strapped themselves in the cabin. Craig followed Carrington's cockpit check, using the Flight Manual. The Enstrom Hawk was an uncomplicated helicopter, and in minutes, Craig had the jet engine started and was climbing away from the airfield. He flew around the Menominee area for a while to take in the local landmarks, and check the navigation aids and airframe systems. All the Hawk's systems were serviceable, and she was handling well. Craig completed a few gentle turning manoeuvres, and once he had the individual feel of the controls, he practiced several simulated engine failures to the main runway. After the third gentle touch down, Carrington commented, "You handle her well Mr Craig, you've obviously been flying for some time."

"Royal Air Force training," Craig replied, "Supposed to be the best in the world, but she's nice to fly anyway."

Craig air taxied to the landing pad, closed down the engine and braked the rotors. Two blue-overalled engineers lifted the Hawk onto its wheels, and pushed it through the hangar doors.

"Well, that's fine, Mr Carrington. Now if I can have the documents, that will complete the formalities. You will make sure I can collect the helicopter tomorrow, without fail." Craig looked sharply across the table.

"Sure thing," came the inevitable reply. "I'll meet you here. What time will that be?"

"I'll arrive in the morning, in plenty of time to refuel. I'm planning a 4.15 pm take off, once I've checked the weather.... so let's say one o' clock."

Craig was soon on his way back to the Holiday Inn, while Carrington was discussing the quick deal with his shrewd plant boss, known locally as FLB. He'd been a military pilot, and successful trial lawyer, specialising in defence cases, before he bought the Enstrom factory.

"One of the few guys we get who knew exactly what he wanted. Something slightly strange about the guy. He was rather tense and in one hell of a hurry, but he could certainly fly that helicopter. Rather odd though, taking all that fuel and leaving late. Still.... the money has been paid, and the customer's always right."

Carrington's shrewd boss was curious.

"Where's he taking that chopper?" He asked uneasily.

"Business and vacation apparently. Florida he tells me, and then intends to ship it back to Europe. Ex British Air Force flier, who's the Sheikh's personal pilot, and the EFT dollar transfer hit our bank two weeks ago. The money's as right as rain. Swiss bank.... Seven hundred and fifty thousand dollars, sir."

The boss seemed satisfied. "That's Good. Check everything's okay before he goes. Customers like that don't grow on trees."

"Sure thing boss," Carrington assured. "I'll do that. He's collecting the ship tomorrow. There'll be no snags."

Craig reached the Holiday Inn car park, and left the VW against a sheltering wall to give the engine some protection from the biting wind. He was glad to get back to the warmth of the hotel. The second visit had also gone without a hitch. Now all that remained was the final refuelling check and engine runs, and he'd be ready. Twenty-four hours to go, and as the day of the big flight approached, he was becoming more apprehensive. He would go over the flight plan again tonight. The reward for a successful run was a hundred and fifty k's, but the penalty for failure would be disastrous on the frozen expanses of the lakes. Freezing to death would be a slow process, not a pleasant way to go. It was purely a matter of careful planning and attention to detail. Success would not come any other way. Time to report the results of today's meeting to Brandt. He picked up the house phone.

The gravelly voice of Brandt answered.

"Yeah?"

"Alistair Craig here, I've just got back from the helicopter factory. Shall I come up now?"

"Give it ten minutes," The phone went dead.

Craig wandered over to the window and sat down. The receptionist looked over at him, and smiled. "Enjoying your stay, Mr Craig?" She enquired politely. "How are you finding our weather?"

"Colder than I would have liked," Craig said, cheerfully.

"Scheduled for a heat wave shortly." The receptionist replied, with an impish smile. "The weatherman says the temperature is due to go up to zero!"

Good, thought Craig. He didn't relish the idea of being on the ice refuelling the helicopter in the sub zero temperatures they'd had recently. The cold might cause all sorts of problems.

"Staying long sir?"

"Probably not.".… Craig began to explain, but the conversation was interrupted as the desk phone rang.

Nice girl to have behind reception, Craig thought. Almost time to visit Brandt.

Brandt was alone. He jerked his head at Craig. "Hokay man, how're yo makin' out?" He barked. "Han' I doan mean wit de blonde lady."

Craig was getting used to Brandt's gruffness. "All arranged exactly as the instructions," he answered blandly.

Craig handed over the aircraft documents.

"Here's the invoice and Bill of Sale." He said stiffly. "The Helicopter's got the equipment we need, and the factory has fitted the special fuel tank. The radio is okay, and there is a Bonzer radar altimeter, which I need for the night flying. The ship has a GPS satellite system and an ADF for the navigation. Couldn't ask for more. Nothing to do until tomorrow morning, when I do the final refuelling and take off checks. The Airport people think I'm leaving for Florida on holiday. No problems at all."

Craig smiled. He tried some sarcasm.

"Oh, and the blonde's fine."

Brandt ignored Craig's humour. "Let's hope der won't be none, jest so long as yo gits everythin' right man. Have yo checked out de route?"

"Yes," Craig understated, "there'll be no difficulty with that, providing the good weather holds. Are the pick up times still the same?"

"Ah'll let yo know if anythin's different. Yo jest stick ta dem instructions. De whole plan is timed to da minute han' we doan need no goddam screw-ups." Brandt mellowed slightly. "S'far she's so good. Let's 'ave a drink." He said, reaching for the drinks tray. "What'll yours be, Cap'n?"

"Not during the day, Brandt. I like to keep a clear head if you don't mind."

"Mebbe dat's a good idea, if yo're goin' flyin'," Brandt said with a snort. "Anyway, here's ta success han' all dat dough."

Brandt took a deep draught from the glass. "We won't be meetin' again until de first pick-up on de lake. Dat's five thirty tomorrow, an' ah'll see yo der, out hon de ice. Now jest git along to yo room fer some rest Cap'n, der's gonna be plenty fer us to goddam do."

Craig returned to his room and slumped on the bed. The tension was building up. The big day was almost with him. Not just another flight. This was something special. Over a thousand miles at night. But with a hundred and fifty grand as the prize, it was becoming like the mythical pot of gold at the end of the rainbow. As long as it wasn't as elusive!

The remainder of the morning was spent going over the flight plan. Craig had committed to memory the visual navigational aids he could expect to see at night. The weather was the big factor. Historically, this part of the United States expected long clear periods at this time of the year. That would be due to the Anti-Cyclonic high pressure and intense cold. The weather forecasts confirmed it.

Craig looked at the telephone, and wondered if Christine would be in her room. He picked up the handset.

"Hi, Christine, how about that lunch you promised? You haven't forgotten I hope."

"Hallo, Alistair, thanks for calling me. I have been trying your room, although I knew you might not get back for a while."

Her voice dropped.

"Alistair, I'm sorry, I have to leave in a few minutes. The New York flight goes at one. I've only got time for a quick chat if you want. I can meet you in the hotel lounge in a few minutes?"

"Yes, of course, I'll go down now."

Craig grimaced. Just his bloody luck. That sounded like the end of a promising relationship. Perhaps if he took Christine's address he might see her again when he got back to England.

She seemed preoccupied. The warmth they'd shared on the dance floor had gone. He said he hoped her new job turned out to be what she wanted. She gave him her English phone number, and Craig promised to contact her when he got back home.

As the Holiday Inn courtesy bus left the forecourt, Craig waved goodbye a little sadly and returned to the reception.

To snap him out of his doldrums, he booked a massage session, and went to the hotel pool. He swam twenty lengths in leisurely style, and then visited the Health Studio, where he submitted himself to the resident masseur, who went about his body pummelling and muscle kneading with unusual gusto. He was then directed to the solarium, where he relaxed under the powerful sun lamp. Tomorrow he was in for twelve hours of continuous concentration, as he navigated the long flight to the waiting ship. A few hours of utter relaxation would settle him nicely for the big effort.

Craig followed his swimming and massage sessions with an alcohol free dinner and took himself off for an early night.

To help him sleep, he read an Ian Fleming, non-James Bond, short story, but with his thoughts on the flight, sleep would not come easily, and it was an hour before drowsiness overtook him and the book slipped from his hand.

# 10

Alistair Craig awoke at 7.30. He was travelling light, so he packed his few belongings and stowed the flight planning charts in the side pocket of his travelling case. With a final look around his room, he went downstairs for breakfast.... but his appetite had gone. He nibbled at a piece of toast and forced down some coffee. He sat in the resident's lounge for half an hour reading a local periodical.... then checked out, and once again made his way to the airfield.

Only a few hours to go, and as he drove on the frozen road, he could feel the tension mounting in the pit of his stomach. He made a conscious effort to relax, clenching and unclenching his fingers on the steering wheel. As soon as he could get down to the routine of the helicopter, he'd be okay, he reasoned. Anyway, perhaps a little tension would keep him alert, and he mustn't forget what this flight was all about.... getting back the cottage he loved.

From the airfield Flight Control Office, he telephoned for the Texaco bowser, topped up the fuel tanks, and made a final check of the oil and hydraulic fluid levels. The Hawk started easily, and Craig spent several minutes checking the fuel flow from the new range extender. The extra heavy-duty battery was neatly stowed, and Craig was satisfied the helicopter was ready to go. So long as the weather didn't turn nasty. The TV weather forecast and his phoned enquiry to the Michigan Meteorological office confirmed that the day and night were expected to remain clear, with just a slight southerly wind, which would keep his speed up. The forecaster did mention there had been a report of isolated thunderstorms.

That would have to be watched.

Craig ran the rotors until the operating temperatures and pressures showed normal. Engine oil pressure a steady 90 PSI, and well into the safe green sector of the tiny dial. The turbine outlet and main rotor gearbox temperatures, were also normal. The ammeter indicated a healthy charge, and Craig was relieved to receive a blast of hot air when he pushed the 'Flippo' heater switch to 'On'. He made a careful check of the instruments, and operated the landing lamps and navigation equipment.

Satisfied, he closed down the engine, stopped the rotors, and walked round the Hawk, refitting the engine intake muffs and tying down the rotor blades. He locked the cockpit doors and baggage compartment and, after a final look round, walked across the tarmac to the Air Traffic Control tower to lodge his flight details. His stated destination was Green Bay, a local site. He then made a further check on the weather.

From the warmth of the flight planning office, Craig spent the rest of the morning making final amendments to the en-route checkpoints, using the latest wind information. With the flight documents packed, he returned to Marinette for lunch.

At 3pm, he parked the VW at the Standard Garage, and returned by taxi to the airfield in good time for the scheduled departure. Craig prepared the Hawk for flight, stowed his bag and ticked off the pre-flight checklist, and with the engine running smoothly, he pulled tight on his seat harness, checked his watch for the scheduled 16.15 hrs take-off time, and called on the helicopter's radio.

"Menominee tower, this is Enstrom Hawk 'November 480' requesting lift off and departure clearance for Green Bay. We're landing at a private site six miles south of the city."

The controller was casual.

"Okay Enstrom, we've no conflicting traffic. You are cleared to go. Set altimeter at twenty-nine-point-niner. Air Traffic will be closing shortly, and going off watch."

Good thought Craig. They'd soon lost interest in him.

With the sun low on the horizon, Craig lifted the Hawk into the cold air, beginning what for him, would be the longest, and most difficult flight of his flying career. But because of his meticulous planning, and detailed preparation, he felt confident as he set the Hawk in a steady cruise climb, and set course to the south of Menominee Airfield, and headed for the first scheduled waypoint. With no radar coverage, Air Traffic relied entirely on his filed 'flight plan' and verbal position reports.

Twenty miles south of Menominee Airfield, he left the Air Traffic Service frequency, and switched on the Green Bay VOR. Tracking on this radio beam would make the first leg easy.... just keep the left-right tracking needle in the centre of the dial. He cross-referred to the GPS moving map, which confirmed a 100-knot groundspeed. The small town of Peshtigo passed below.

At 16.45 hours, the helicopter was tracking parallel to the frozen shore of Lake Michigan. Craig looked out over the lake, to see a continuous sheet of black ice stretching out to the distant horizon.

This would be the ten-mile crossing to the Door Peninsula, and as the land mass slipped away, Craig felt the stark, icy grip, and cold hostility of one of the largest frozen lakes in the world. He thought for a moment, of the next thousand miles that had to be flown over the same desolate wasteland, and shuddered.

Craig checked the power to maintain the Hawk in a level cruise at the scheduled three thousand feet. He levelled on the cyclic to give 100 knots indicated air speed, the speed that would make good the planned arrival time, and for the fiftieth time, Craig pondered the identity of his passenger. Must be pretty important to O'Rourke. A veritable fortune just to get a man out of America. Who could he be, and what had he done?

Craig didn't want to know too much, and closed his mind to the problem. Just regard the flight as a routine Air Taxi trip.

He reached the Rockwood turning point on time, and with the reddish glow of the sunset on the instrument panel, he swung the Hawk away from the Air Traffic notified track, to head for Green Bay, and the first rendezvous, and landing site, fifty miles out on Lake Michigan.

Crossing the peninsular, Craig was now flying over the main expanse of the lake, which stretched another ninety miles to Illinois.

He checked the GPS map, pinpointing his position, one mile south of the town of Kewaunee, and entered the ATA on the flight log. He then tuned the homer receiver to the transmitter beacon at point Romeo, and listening carefully, he could just hear the distant Morse signal. It was barely audible. He would be out of range for an accurate bearing, but the ADF needle was drifting around the dial in the right direction, and as darkness closed about him, Craig turned up the volume to confirm the identification code of the homing beacon, which would take him to his first landing on the frozen surface of the lake.

And now the signal was coming in strong, *dit-dah-dit, dit-dah-dit*, R for Romeo as the needle locked on to the helipad transmitter. It showed five degrees to port. Craig again checked the GPS. Just twenty miles to run. Craig gently turned the Hawk to the new heading, making a small allowance for the crosswind.

Time to begin losing height.

He lowered the collective lever smoothly, noting the correct drop in engine torque, and reset the rotor speed with a blip on the turbine governor.

Passing two thousand feet, and the GPS now said only ten miles to go.... say, six minutes flying and about a minute late. He would make that up as he increased speed in the descent. He glanced at the outside air temperature gauge above his head. Minus ten degrees Fahrenheit. Forty below! It wouldn't do to hang about, once he was on the ice.

Craig checked the homing compass again. Still bang on track.

'Piece of cake,' he thought momentarily.

He re-checked the identification signal, which was now very loud.... beckoning, *dit-dah-dit, dit-dah-dit*, Romeo, Romeo, and as he scanned the area ahead, there it was, a small cluster of lights, but unmistakably in the shape of a letter H.

Craig checked the altimeter as the needle passed one thousand feet, and made small corrections to the throttle governor, to keep the rotor speed in the all important green sector of the dial. At four hundred feet, he flicked on the two powerful landing lights, and the icy area below lit up.

Manoeuvering the helicopter towards the lights, Craig saw the grey Cadillac. He poised the Hawk in the high hovering position, inspecting the landing area, and as he flattened the clawing rotor blades, the Hawk gently dropped the last few feet, and with a shudder, the aluminium skids gripped into the surface of the frozen lake.

Alistair Craig was about to keep his appointment on Lake Michigan.

He ran through the shutting down procedure, minimum pitch on the rotor blades, throttle to flight idle, centralise the main rotor disc attitude and allow the engine temperatures to stabilise. Landing and internal lights off, and with a final lurch from the skids, the rotor blades stopped.

Craig had landed the Hawk just fifty feet from the car.

He climbed down, and pointing his torch, stepped carefully on the uneven ice. The driver opened the passenger door.

"Hop in, man," commanded the gravelly voice of Leroy Brandt. "Any problems?"

"Straight forward run as planned," Craig replied as he pulled on the door and sat next to Brandt. He looked over to the back seat, where there was a third man.

His passenger!

The man was unconscious, and slumped drunkenly against the car door with his head buried in his arms. He was either very ill.... very drunk, or he'd been drugged.

Brandt spoke softly to Craig, "Listen fellah."

What was the sudden change in Brandt's tone? Now a velvet purr. The voice used when a favour is being asked. Craig stiffened. Something had gone wrong!

Brandt placed a friendly hand on Craig's shoulder.

"Hit ain't quite de deal yo thought, Craig," Brandt began quietly. "Yo see, hit's a hundred times more important, han' we're gonna pay yo a load more dough."

"You have ta git him to de ship," he said pointing to the third man. "han' its now worth one million dollars ta yo fer a home run.... an' in case yo have any doubt Craig, ah said one million!"

*A million dollars.* Craig's thoughts raced, well over half a million pounds! What the hell was going on?

He felt a sudden chill as he turned again to face the back seat. The semi-conscious man lifted his head, and began moving his lips in an effort to speak. The eyes were glazed over. He sounded a low moan

78

as saliva trickled from the corner of his mouth, dribbling down to his chin.

Craig could see the lined face more clearly in the dashboard light. A face the world knew, and which appeared constantly on their TV screens.

He could not believe it, no it just could not be! He looked again so there could be no doubt.

The man slumped in the back seat was the President of the United States of America!

# 11

My God, thought Craig. What the bloody hell have I done? What have I got myself into?

For a moment he felt stunned, as surely as if he had been struck a hammer blow on the back of his head, and in spite of the cold, he could feel the sweat of anxiety running down his spine. He was mentally trying to cope with the enormity of a situation in which he was an active part. Even the leading player.... what have I done? He thought again.

How far away his cosy Sussex home....? How insignificant his tiny ambitions? That sunny day in England on the Downs at Chanctonbury Ring, how many years ago? The decision made that he would look for some short cut to the money he needed.

He recalled O'Rourke's seemingly off-hand proposal by the winner's circle at Goodwood racecourse. 'How would you like to earn some real money?" And Craig had been offered a quarter of a million dollars. Five years wages for one week's work! But the rules had changed, and the stakes increased four-fold. One million dollars no less, to engage in what must be the biggest conspiracy in history. The kidnap of the President of America. Could he get out of it? Was there anything he could do? And as if reading Craig's thoughts, Brandt spoke.

"Now jest keep yo cool man. He hain't no different as far as yo're concerned. Jest means de ransom's higher an' yo cut gits more, han' if yo wanna git de feel of dat million bucks, jest take hit easy man, han' git him ta de goddam ship."

Craig's mind was reeling. He couldn't think of anything to say. His only concern was the President. He found himself staring at the twitching eye. Brandt continued threateningly.

"Han' doan git no funny ideas neither, mah instructions are ta shoot anyone who tries ta screw up de plan from now on." The eye jerked viciously, as Brandt produced a snub-nosed Colt .45 automatic.

"Hokay den," he snapped. "Now lets git goin, we've got jest five minutes ta git airborne. Ah need ta give de President de next shot of de dope ta keep 'im quiet, an' you git de chopper cranked up fast." He waved the gun at Craig. "Be wit yo hin a coupla minutes."

Brandt lifted the President's sleeve to the elbow, and sank the point of a hypodermic needle into the exposed vein. The President's eyes flickered and closed. The head rolled forward.

Craig was scared, but forced himself to recover from the shock, trying to put some calm into his voice as he faced Brandt.

"Okay, okay, let's keep things friendly, Brandt. For one million dollars, you get the de luxe service." He could barely control his quaking throat. "Just leave the flying to me."

Craig was trying to work out some escape from the desperate situation, but it wouldn't help to alert Brandt. He'd known the flight would be difficult, had known it might be illegal, but the kidnap of the American President, the most powerful influence in the world! He could not be a party to it.

Craig's thoughts were in turmoil as he climbed into the pilot's seat, and automatically ran through the starting procedure. Even in the few minutes the engine had not been running, the oils had thickened in the intense cold, and the starter ground more slowly against the engine. Thank God for the heavy-duty battery. As the engine compressor struggled to reach light off RPM, Craig opened the throttle, the turbine fired, and after a few hesitant seconds, accelerated to its normal idling speed.

Brandt carried the President to the rear door of the Hawk, bundled him aboard in a sitting position, and strapped him to the seat. Brandt pulled the cabin door closed.

"Let's start de flyin' man," Brandt ordered, jerking the gun towards Craig, "An' remember, we doan want no heroics or nuthin'."

Craig went through the cockpit drill, with his mind still in a daze. All ready to go. He lifted the collective lever, and the three whirling blades cut into the dense cold air, but now with the extra weight of its two passengers, the Hawk lifted more slowly into the black night sky, then ducking its nose, gradually picked up forward flying speed to climb away. There was nothing he could do to help the President while in the air, except concentrate on getting clear of the dangerous no man's area of the freezing lake. Almost a thousand miles to navigate with the most important cargo he had ever carried in his life....

*Not such a piece of cake,* he reminded himself.

Craig tried to forget his predicament as he settled into the long climb to three thousand feet, but with its extra load and the massive amount of fuel, the Hawk was struggling to make the height. On the second leg, Craig would navigate visually by maintaining a constant range from the twinkling lights on the land to the east. The wind was behind now, which was a blessing, and he prayed for the clear skies to continue.

At three thousand feet, the air temperature dropped to minus fifty degrees, and Craig had a moment's panic checking the transmission oil temperatures. The needle was only just giving a positive indication on the dial, and the engine temperature was well below normal. Craig thought through the consequences, and reasoned that all would be well. She was just within limits and running OK now, and the temperatures could only improve as the flight progressed.

Craig had time to consider his dilemma again. If only he could get the Hawk down somewhere near the police or the military, and without arousing Brandt's suspicion. But where was that? Potluck wouldn't be good enough. In any case, a change of course towards the lights on the land would be noticed instantly, and he must not risk any shooting. But if it came to it, would Brandt really shoot? That, Craig decided, was a poker hand he was not prepared to play. Best, perhaps, to try to get under the man's guard by faking co-operation.

Craig broke the silence. "You getting a fair slice of the action when the job's done? With this sort of money you can buy a whole load of luxury, fast cars, yachts and all the girls you can handle." Craig thought it a good idea to get on some common ground. "And by the way, can I use your first name Leroy? When do you think we'll get paid?"

Craig studied the gunman from the corner of his eye, but could make little from his expression. Brandt's good eye flickered at Craig.

"Jest call me Brandt man, like everyone else, han' doan keep talkin' so goddam much, yo makin' me nervous." And then he volunteered, "Yo'll be paid after we git de ransom money. When we git ta da ship, we make fer Florida.... de dough's ta be collected der." He looked intently at Craig. "We may need yo services in da chopper ta track de dinghy, ah'll let yo know Craig."

"How much is being demanded?" Craig was pleased he had got the conversation going.

"A hundred million in cash, or we send 'em back de goddam President piece by piece." Brandt grinned savagely at his own humour.

"What makes you think they'll pay that much?"

"Can't say man." Brandt shrugged his massive shoulders. "But de boss seems pretty shoh."

"How did you manage to kidnap him?"

"Beautiful plan. Gas. Put dem all out.... H'only needed a coupla men on de inside to fix things.... den de ambulance from Government House in Milwaukee to de Caddy, han' across de ice to da chopper. Dem goddam gumshoes must 'av put roadblocks everywhere, but dey never thought about de lake. Boss shoh figured dat one out." Brandt sniggered with satisfaction.

"O'Rourke seems a very clever man."

"Yo'll find out soon enough," Brandt snorted. "But if ah were yo, ah wouldn't be too goddam nosey, man."

Craig didn't like Brandt's tone, and suddenly realised the seriousness of his own position. Once he had served his purpose, why should they pay him anything? A simple shove over the side of the ship would save the money and keep him quiet permanently. But if O'Rourke planned to use the helicopter again, he would be needed for some time yet, but what then? Would there be a chance to escape with the helicopter, perhaps at the next landing point or when the ransom was being collected? He would need much more information about O'Rourke's plans.

Craig decided that come what may, he could not continue as a willing accomplice. If any chance to escape presented itself, he must try to get himself and the President free, give himself up, and hopefully face a light sentence, perhaps even get the sympathy of the Court. But would the chance ever come? O'Rourke was a clever, careful man. He would not underestimate him.

The helicopter sped on through the night sky as Craig returned to the chart on his kneeboard, and scanning the dark horizon for a visual reference point, he identified the twinkle of lights that would be Traverse City. He estimated the angle and plotted the relative bearing as a position line, to calculate his groundspeed. Sixty miles in thirty minutes. Good. He was covering the ground at two miles a minute. Craig worked out his arrival time at the next landing position, point Sierra. He would be early, but better to have some time in hand, which he could kill later if necessary. The wonderful moving map GPS was a Godsend, but couldn't always be relied on. The Yanks occasionally switched the satellites off! So he would stick to good old-fashioned map reading.

To keep the conversation going with Brandt, Craig discussed some routine flight details. He would ask some more important questions that might help him to escape later.

"How's the refuelling to be done Brandt?" Craig asked casually. Brandt looked up.

"We're ta refuel when we land hon de next lake…. dats h'Ontario, somewhere near da middle, so tha'll be no goddam snoopers. Yo've got da position an' de homer code."

He looked at Craig suspiciously and continued in his standard gruff tone.

"Jest yo git de chopper dere, okay man? When we land, a pick-up truck'll meet us. Him'll 'ave a two 'undred gallon tank of de gas ta top us hup, an' let's make it goddam quick so we don't git busted."

Craig knew the position of the landing point at Sierra, and all the refuelling details, but the idea was to get the man talking.

"You sure are organised," Craig complimented. "You seem to have thought of everything. I wouldn't mind joining an outfit like yours, once this job is paid off," Craig lied. He didn't want to give Brandt any hint of the escape he was going to plan.

"'Fraid not Craig, dis'll be de one han' only job," Brandt volunteered. "Den we all go our separate ways wit de dough an live de life of goddam luxury."

"If they pay up, how's the money to be collected?" Craig decided to risk some big questions.

"Big rubber dinghy, moored in de sea miles hoff Miami Beach. Used hundred dollar bills, han' wit all dat dough aboard." Brandt smirked. "She should be de most valuable goddam ship in de whole of Florida. Dey'll be anudder homin' transmitter on de dinghy ta guide us der, han' like ah said, der was some talk of usin' de chopper as a back-up ta locate de dinghy. Technical failure or sumpin', but wit me han' mah gun on board, jest in case yo gets hany fancy ideas man." Brandt concluded, pointing the Colt dangerously at Craig.

"That would be easy," Craig said. "No problem for me to pinpoint the dinghy with the GPS. Then you transfer the cash." Craig was hoping he could make himself sound useful, if only to save his own neck. "What if the money is marked or the dinghy is being watched?"

"Hit won't be," Brandt harked confidently. "But hit'll be okay if de whole goddam Navy han' Air Force is watchin'. Makes no goddam difference. Dey don't git der precious President back 'til we git de ransom han' free passage. Hany attempt ta mark de dough or some kinda double cross, han' it'll be curtains fer our famous Texan boy here." Brandt spat the words out contemptuously.

There was a long silence, as Craig admired the brilliance yet simplicity of the plan. He was worried. It could easily work. An amber light flashed in the cockpit accompanied by an urgent 'bleep, bleep'. Craig's attention was drawn to the rotor rpm needle. Too low.... his mind had been elsewhere and the rotor speed had gradually decayed. Craig adjusted the throttle governor a fraction. The light and the horn stopped signalling as the Enstrom Hawk resumed its steady beat.

Craig scanned the instrument panel.... the rows of dials glowed eerily in the red panel light. Speed, altitude and course okay. Engine temperatures and pressures.... showing safely in the green. The Hawk was performing well, and in spite of his predicament, Craig felt, as always, the immense satisfaction of flying well. He played with the controls for a moment, to adjust for changes of trim as the fuel was burnt up.... a few blips of the electric trimmer and the sleek helicopter settled into its new attitude, cutting through the bitterly cold night air.

Craig needed all sorts of information before he could formulate an escape plan. Was there any one higher up in the gang? Or was it all Ryan O'Rourke's show? How many of the gang would be on the ship? Where did the Sheikh come in?

"Does the *Champagne Princess* belong to O'Rourke?" Craig asked innocently, "Or is someone else involved?"

"Hokay... 'okay man, no need fer de smart stuff." Brandt snorted at the loaded question. "O'Rourke is one of de top men, but him's workin' wit de Arabs on dis one. De Sheikh Makhtoum is sharin' de dough. De Princess was specially chartered some weeks back, han' she cost plenty, so we're sending de tab ta de goddam feds." Brandt's pock marked face twisted into a wry smile. "But she's a real beauty. Two decks han' five cabins on each, han' a stateroom. Used ta belong ta some Greek tycoon. H'onassis or sompin'. Once we're aboard, we kin relax in comfort man, han' let de goddam Government do de worryin'. Dey'll be chargin' around like scalded cats lookin' fer de President, but hit makes no difference. Hit'll be de money or America be runnin' anudder h'election."

Craig was amused at Brandt's attempted eloquence, but the man was softening.

"How big is the heli-deck on the ship?" Craig asked. "Wouldn't like to make it all the way there and mess up the landing."

"Princess his a two hundred footer, han' could take two choppers dis size. Crew of three han' de girl."

"A girl?" Craig echoed in surprise. "What on earth is a girl doing involved in all this?"

"All part of de plan Craig, han' someone yo already know. Yo see, hits de English lady yo met back in de hotel. She's a nurse if yo didn't already know, brought hin by de boss special, ta look after de President. But ah shouldn't git hany more romantic ideas, man. Like you, she has a job ta do han' is bein' paid plenty ta keep de President quiet, han' in good shape."

So that was the score. It explained so much. No wonder Christine's behavior at the hotel seemed strange. Of course she had known why

Craig was brought into the plan, but had been told to say nothing. But still something very wrong there. She would have to be a pretty hard type to work with a man like O'Rourke, and from their brief conversations, he knew that she wasn't. And she was a nurse into the bargain! He'd never met one who was not totally dedicated to her profession.... helping her fellow man. Hardly the sort of work that was coming up next! Would she change her attitude to him on the ship? Perhaps he would even have a friend in the enemy camp.

Craig was still thinking about Christine two hours later, and he wondered how deeply she was personally involved with O'Rourke. What the hell was an innocent like her doing in a massive kidnap like this? Perhaps she was sexually involved? The paid mistress doing O'Rourke's bidding. But a nasty crook like him? Surely not. She was twenty-five and O'Rourke must be over fifty. No, none of it made any kind of sense, but his spirits lifted with the realisation that he would be seeing her again, but right now his main priority was to get the President safely to the ship.

The second leg was proving uneventful, except for a brief period when the stars took on a wispy hue, and fearing cloud, Craig swung the Hawk into a sharp turn towards the lights of the distant shore. Small helicopters are not equipped for blind flying, and it would be dangerous to fly into cloud. But at night it was difficult to see the clouds coming up. He would just have to stay constantly on the alert.

Craig plotted a second position line, taken from a distant VOR beacon. They were abeam Beaver Island, not far from the Canadian border; it was time to make the turn east to Lake Huron, and head for the Tobermorey turning point. Nearly three hundred miles covered and less than two hundred for the next landing. Craig checked the timing, and consulted the computer. Good, the groundspeed was steady. He made a routine check of the instrument panel, and was pleased to note the fuel state was in accordance with his flight plan calculations.

The long flight was beginning to give him leg cramp and his buttocks ached. He shifted his flying position to get the circulation going, and looked over to his passenger. Brandt was staring out the side window, the eye calm and the gun nowhere to be seen. Perhaps that meant Brandt wasn't expecting any trouble. The President's position remained unchanged, which was worrying. He was breathing badly, and Craig hoped he'd not been given too much of the drug.

In the faint light of the instrument panel, Craig examined the President's even features. The son of a previous President, whose election campaign should have been sunk by the revelations of his war career, or lack of it, and a whiff of electoral fiddling in Florida, but who'd still gained office once again, and was now the most important man in the world. How fickle of the voting public. How the wily politicians ran rings round them all. But hadn't the Brits done exactly the same! A Prime Minister with a dodgy record in Parliament, a truck load of lies, but still the masses voted traditionally. Craig didn't have much time for any of the Westminster men.... left or right!

But back to the present. Would the mighty American nation allow its coffers to be sacked to the tune of one hundred million dollars? It was surely the highest ransom demand in history, but Craig knew O'Rourke was right. The American people would pay, reluctantly maybe, but it was only money—and they would certainly pay.

Each time a Columbia space shuttle left the launching pad at Cape Canaveral, the American nation kissed goodbye to a similar sum, and it followed that to obtain the safe return of their President, they would pay this demand without flinching.

But then the real fireworks would come. Once the nation's first politician was safely home, then not one million.... not one billion dollars would hide the kidnappers from the fury of America, and no corner of the earth would remain unchecked, until the villains were brought to book.

For my money, Craig considered, Mr. Ryan O'Rourke, his henchmen, and sadly Christine were in bad trouble, and would probably enjoy a very short life of luxury.

The President stirred, and for a moment his eyes opened and looked up to the cabin light. The pupils were badly dilated. Craig looked into them, willing the President to believe he was an ally, but nothing was said, and the movement attracted Brandt's attention.

He looked at Craig sullenly. "How're we doin' Craig?"

"About two hours to go and everything's fine. Is the President Okay?"

"Don't worry yo self about 'im," Brandt said coarsely.

"He'll be enjoyin' de rest from politics. When we git to de next landin' ground, ah hav'ta give 'im anudder shot wit de hypodermic." Brandt patted his breast pocket. "A good dose of sompin' called Hioscine, keeps 'em dozy fer hours yo know"

Craig thought for a moment. He hoped O'Rourke had got the dosage right. His dentist had once told him that Hioscine was being withdrawn as an anaesthetic, as being too dangerous for weak hearts. One or two patients had actually died in the dentist's chair! The President looked decidedly ill, and so far Craig was only an accomplice to a kidnapping. He didn't want to be a party to murder.

"I'm worried," Craig said with concern. "He hasn't moved since we took off."

"He's okay Craig. Knocked out by de drug jest as he should be, but hits goddam cold up here man." Brandt was rubbing his body for warmth.

Craig checked the heater position, but it was at maximum. Just pray that it wouldn't freeze up or fail. A light rime ice had formed on the inside of the windscreens. Craig could hardly feel his toes.

For the moment, the plan must simply be to get the President to the ship as fast as possible. Hope that Christine knew what she was doing, but somehow he must stop Brandt injecting more drugs. He leaned back to check the President's pulse. It seemed sound.

He needed another position check, and consulted the moving map. Now abeam Providence. Better start tuning the second homer.

Craig programmed the orange LED digits on the ADF receiver to 797 Khz, and switched the set to 'Identification' mode. He turned up the volume control and listened. *Dit-dit-dit, dit-dit-dit....* three short dots… S*ierra*—S*ierra*. The homing needle moved sluggishly, but was trying to point ahead. At least Craig knew the transmitter beacon was working. He felt relieved. The refuelling checkpoint was vital, and providing the beacon continued its beckoning signal, Craig could relax, and just follow the needle home. Less than one hundred miles to Lake Ontario, but apart from the scattering of lights from the town of Providence on his right, he could see nothing but an inky blackness ahead.

Craig should have been more alert! The darkness was a warning of an ugly Cumulo-Nimbus cloud, blocking his flight path, and in a second Craig lost all visual reference as the Hawk plunged into the turbulent killer. A vivid flash of lightning struck out at the Hawk. Craig could smell the electricity in the cabin. He looked out desperately for some external reference.... nothing.... He'd flown smack into the middle of a dangerous thunderstorm.

The Cumulo Nimbus cloud is dreaded by everyone who flies. It can form by day or night, and rapidly build up from the ground, sometimes to forty thousand feet. Inside these clouds, flying conditions become chaotic, as powerful air currents tear at the airframe structure, and have been known to snap a Boeing Jetliner in half. Passengers call them 'air pockets', but they are really giant stacks of rapidly moving air that hold massive amounts of freezing rain, and occasionally golf ball-sized chunks of hailstones. The airlines know the dangers of these killer cloud formations, and equip their aircraft with sophisticated weather radar, that pinpoint the worst of the storm cells, and enable their pilots to steer clear. But Craig had no such help.

With the first violent jolt, Brandt yelled. "What's happened Craig? Turn her back fo Chrissake man." But Craig's hands were full, as the small helicopter was buffeted and flung about by the fierce turbulence—the attitude changing alarmingly. He quickly flicked out the Autopilot, as the Hawk rolled on its side. As Craig fought to keep control—the only instrument that could help was the tiny Artificial Horizon indicating the helicopter's attitude. Craig desperately focused on the single reference, as he shouted to Brandt.

"Tighten your safety belt Brandt," Craig yelled—Hold on to something—make sure the President is strapped tight."

The next violent buffet yanked the cyclic control from Craig's grasp—the navigation bag slammed up to the cabin roof, and smacked back against the side of Craig's head as a bubble of air hammered through the spinning rotor blades. Hailstones peppered the windscreen, with the sound of a hundred machine guns—the cabin now a constant roar from the hail and the thunderous bangs. Brandt screamed in terror as Craig wrestled with the vibrating controls, calling on every ounce of experience to keep the Hawk level in an effort to ride out the storm.

A second blinding flash of lightning exploded inches from the windscreen as a bolt of turbulent air sucked at the helicopter from below. Craig yanked back on the cyclic, as the helicopter entered a dive and rolled inverted—its three passengers hanging in their straps. Then with another flash, the Hawk dropped its nose and plunged vertically towards the ground, with the altimeter reeling off the height. Craig was losing control, and knew they could crash and in a desperate bid for survival, he set the controls for autorotation as the Hawk plummeted towards the surface of the frozen lake below.

As the altimeter passed one thousand feet, the instrument readings fluctuated wildly. The Artificial Horizon had toppled outside its limits and could no longer help Craig hold a level attitude. With a final tearing crash of thunder, the helicopter spun completely out of Craig's control. Brandt howled in blind panic cowering—waiting for the inevitable crash. The radar altimeter wound crazily past five hundred feet, its low altitude warning light flashing out the emergency, and imminent collision with the ground.

So this is how you die, thought Craig. No special feelings—no past life before you. The last few seconds just tick away, like any other occasion, perhaps only twenty more to go and then blackness. First perhaps a fierce pain, and then quiet. Quiet for evermore. Alistair Craig was going to die the way he had lived—in a helicopter. He opened his mouth to scream.

Suddenly, the cabin brightened as the stricken machine dropped clear of the storm cloud. Heavens be praised, Craig could see. He renewed his grip on the three flying controls, and with the frozen surface of the lake coming up fast, he pressed with his left foot to stop the spin, and hauled on the collective and cyclic controls together, in an effort to slow the downward plunge. Thank God, the helicopter stopped spinning as he got the rotor disc level.... please, let there be enough height to pull out of the steep dive.

Craig yanked even harder and held his breath as the Hawk responded slowly—they weren't going to make it. Less than two hundred feet to go! The altimeter was showing almost zero. This would be it, Craig mouthed to himself.

In desperation, Craig put both hands on the cyclic and pulled with all his strength against his feet, causing the rotor blades stops to rattle against the mast. And then, miraculously, the Hawk's dive slowed, the vibration gone as they levelled, barely twenty feet above the ice sheet, screaming across the surface of the lake at almost two hundred miles an hour. Craig's heart thumped, as the ice whizzed by. But they were alive.

He gratefully pulled the Hawk into a steady climb, back to one thousand feet.... his stomach still churning. He levelled the Hawk once again and took a deep breath to clear his head....to gather his wits about him. He gulped in another lungful of air, and swallowed hard. That was just too close. He checked the instruments and trimmed the Hawk to straight and level flight.

The cabin was a mess. Craig recalled his flight bag being slammed around the cabin. He felt for the bruise that must be on his head. The navigation charts were scattered everywhere. He checked on the President. He was slumped forward, but the seat straps had held firm. He must have remained unconscious throughout the emergency.

Brandt was hunched with his head in hands, shaking in fear, and with the realisation that the helicopter was flying normally and he was alive, he opened his eyes, and looked hesitantly at Craig.

"Yo must be de greatest pilot in de world man. Ah'd already said ma goddam prayers."

Craig doubted whether Leroy Brandt had ever said a prayer in his life.

# 12

Craig was silent as he re-trimmed the flying controls for the Hawk to settle in level flight at one thousand feet. Then, thinking about Brandt's comment, he looked across the cabin. He knew he'd made a bad flying mistake.

"I suppose I'd like to accept the compliment Brandt, but to be honest, we were just lucky. If the base of that storm had been any lower, we'd have bought the farm."

Funny, thought Craig, how that typically RAF slang phrase came to mind, after the danger had passed. He checked the instruments again, and was relieved to see the readings were normal, although during the turmoil, he recalled seeing the rotor RPM needle well outside its normal limit. So long as nothing in the rotor hub and drive system had over-stressed. He would need to inspect the rotor stops and control linkages, when they landed.

He checked the radio. The homer needle that had guided him was now drifting aimlessly around the dial. Of course. Why hadn't he realised? Those monstrous Cumulo-Nimbus clouds were so active with static electricity, they acted like a radio transmitter all by themselves, sending off spurious signals that had confused his ADF receiver, and beckoned him into the trap. He'd have to wait until the helicopter was out of range of the cloud's misleading signals, before the homer could work normally again.

"Is de helicopter Okay?" Brandt's voice was still shaking.

"As far as I can tell," Craig replied. "Those storm cells can finish off a fixed wing aircraft this size in seconds, and with its delicate rotor system, a helicopter is ten times more vulnerable."

"An' yo do it fer a livin' man?"

"We don't normally fly single-engined helicopters at night, and in daytime you can spot those storm clouds miles away. Pilots avoid them like the plague."

"Well, as far as ah'm concerned, yo kin keep it, but ah still think yo handled de chopper goddam well. Ah really owe ya."

"Thanks, Brandt, but we've got to find the next landing site quickly. We've only thirty minutes fuel left at the most."

But even as Craig spoke, the homing needle moved slowly around the dial to point ten degrees left, and stay there. The cross check on the GPS indication, confirmed the Radio Compass signal. He then checked the compass was accurate by pushing the test button, and was relieved to see the needle obstinately return to its original position.

"Good, we're back in business," Craig murmured, as he altered course, and busied himself setting up the helicopter for the next approach. He would soon be on the ground again, and he wondered if there might be an opportunity to escape then, or raise the alarm. But he was at least twenty miles from the nearest town, with not much hope of getting away without some transport. The refuelling truck was a possibility, but it was unlikely he would be allowed anywhere near it alone.

Could he get Brandt out of the helicopter on some pretext or other, and just fly off? That wouldn't work. It needed at least two minutes to get the Hawk airborne…. more than enough time for Brandt to spot what was going on, and it wouldn't do any good to get himself shot. No, for the time being his position was hopeless, and no doubt O'Rourke had considered all the possibilities, and knew it too. He'd just have to wait until a better opportunity came along.

With the storm well past, Craig concentrated on the homing signal, making several drift corrections, to allow for the wind. Soon the small group of lights indicating the landing ground at 'Sierra' showed ahead. Craig reduced power, settling the Hawk into a steady descending approach, and for the second time this night, picked up the lamps displaying the landing 'H'. At five hundred feet, he switched on the lights, and could make out the refuelling truck standing alone on the broad expanse of ice. He hovered close to the truck, and in a swirl of powdered snow picked up in the rotor wash.... he touched down, with a light crunch from the skids.

They were safely on the ground, this time in Canada, somewhere on Lake Ontario. Craig checked his watch, and was surprised to see he was still on schedule. The previous danger seemed to have lasted an age, but had not, in fact, delayed them for more than a minute.

As the drooping rotors slowed, the truck driver was already manoeuvering his vehicle alongside the helicopter. He jumped out, and ducking under the blades, opened Craig's door. He was heavily muffled, with an Eskimo hood protecting his face from the cold. On his feet were large fur boots.

"How're you doing?" The driver greeted Craig as though he was directing him to a parking lot. "Everything okay?"

"Had some trouble getting through a storm," Craig said in a matter of fact tone, "but we're in good shape."

"How's the passenger?" The truck driver jerked his head to the President. "I have to phone through and report."

"Can't tell, but it will be best if we don't waste time. He hasn't moved for a couple of hours, and in this temperature, it's important we get him to the ship soon. He's going to die from the cold if we don't hurry," Craig added.

Brandt had climbed into the back seat with the President, and was preparing the hypodermic syringe.

Pulling the anorak over his head, Craig jumped out to help with the transfer of fuel. He shuddered as the freezing air clamped its arms around him like a grizzly bear, and shivering in the cold, he accompanied the driver to the rear of the truck. Two yellow drums were strapped to the tailgate, with a neat hand-operated pump screwed into the lid of the first drum.

Craig inspected the clean plastic pipes, and noticed the clear filters. The drums were stamped, SHELL AVIATION JP4, and under the stamp was the famous sea-shell logo recognised all over the world. The hand pump was fitted with an anti-static lead that would prevent any sparking during the refuelling operation. He was impressed.... the system had been well prepared, and dispelled his earlier doubts.

Dirty fuel can stop engines, and a stopped engine over the sea would kill. He didn't fancy dropping out of the sky like a stone into the freezing waters of the Atlantic Ocean.

Craig connected the earth lead to the helicopter's skid, unhitched the fuel nozzle from the truck, and as he busied himself with the task of feeding the hose into the main fuel tank, he found it difficult to appreciate, apart from the intense cold and the darkness, that he was doing anything other than a routine on site refuelling operation that he had done dozens of times in England.

But this was different.

The refuelling site was not some convenient rural helipad, by the Oak trees in the heart of the English countryside, or a quiet parochial airport on the sunny Sussex coast, but the frozen surface of one of the largest lakes in the world. His unwilling passenger was the President of the United States of America, and his pay for the job would be equivalent to his normal salary for the next five years!

'Some have greatness thrust upon them,' he said to himself, but couldn't decide what had made him recall Malvolio's famous words. One million dollars would certainly have given him some kind of greatness, even if he didn't intend to take the money. The cottage dream would have to go now.

With the biting cold numbing his fingers, Craig filled the fuel tanks, while the truck driver pumped steadily on the handle. He carefully secured the filler cap, disconnected the earth lead, and returned the hose to the truck. The driver stowed the equipment, coiling the hoses around the drums, and turned to Craig.

"She's taken one hundred and fifty gallons. Want anything else?"

"I need to inspect the helicopter. Perhaps you could hold the torch for me," Craig asked. He climbed up to the main rotor hub, and checked the pitch links and rotor blade stops. There was no sign of damage. Climbing down he turned his attention to the tail rotor, and was grateful to find the assembly had not suffered from the terrible hammering.

As a diversion, he rotated the tail rotor blades while pretending to study the gearbox. The driver was fiddling with the hose stowing equipment and fuel cock at the rear of the truck. Brandt was occupied with the President. Was there anything he could do now?

Could he disable the driver in some way and get away in the truck? What could he use as a weapon?

Brandt called to Craig. "C'mon man, lets git goin'."

Craig abandoned his plan, and signalled to the driver to move clear.

The refuelling had been completed quickly and without fuss, and the only conversation had been directed to essential matters. Ryan O'Rourke's team had been well chosen. Still, if they were all to be paid anything like a million dollars, he could afford the best. The uncouth Brandt might be out of place, but he obviously knew what was needed, and was presumably being well rewarded. Assuming the ransom was paid, O'Rourke would no doubt take the lion's share, and even after paying off the rest of his gang, he was shortly going to become very rich indeed. But why on earth would one man need so much money? It didn't make any kind of sense. One tenth of the ransom would be more than could be spent in a lifespan. No, there had to be more to it. Craig was perplexed.

He climbed back into the comparative warmth of the helicopter, and looked at Brandt. "Stage two accomplished. We'll get airborne, and this time I'll be flying lower, around one thousand feet. I'm not risking another of those storms."

Craig glanced up to the stars, where the familiar Cassiopeia constellation sat opposite the 'Polaris' Pole Star and twinkled happily in a clear sky. There was no sign of cloud, but he would stick to his decision to fly low.

He switched on the cabin lights, and looked behind him to check on the President. Brandt had rolled back the President's sleeve. The President's face was chalky white.

"Brandt," Craig's voice was iron. "The President's in trouble. He could be dying for all we know." He leaned over the seat and pressed his ear to the man's chest. There was just a flutter of movement. He tried the pulse but felt nothing. Things looked bad. The breathing was shallow and the pupils badly dilated.

"He won't last much longer, Brandt. We have to get going fast." Craig settled into the pilot's seat. "And no more drugs." Craig's sudden tone of authority confused Brandt.

"Hell no man, de boss told me ta give 'im anudder shot of de dope when we land here, han' dats what ah'm gonna do."

"Now look Brandt," Craig's voice was furiously controlled. "As far as I can tell, the President is barely breathing, any more drugs and he'll be gone, and my orders are to get him to the ship alive. Don't you see? A dead President won't be worth ten cents." Craig had to continue to play the part, but he was deadly serious about the President's condition.

"Okay den man, p'raps hits best if we do it yoh way," Brandt conceded. "Yo've gotta point der, han' I kin see de bad shape he's in." Brandt rolled down the sleeve and slipped the hypodermic back into his pocket. Craig was relieved he'd gone along with his suggestion so easily. He fastened the door lock and tightened his seat harness as Brandt took up his position.

"Yo do de flyin' han' ah'll take care of de President," Brandt said. "He'll be hokay." He seemed to have recovered from his confusion.

Now to tackle the last and probably most difficult leg of the flight, terminating, he hoped, on the deck of O'Rourke's yacht.... the beautifully named *Champagne Princess*.

# 13

The final leg to the *Champagne Princess* would require more attention, and Craig would follow the course of the Saint Lawrence River as it flowed down to the sea. Two hundred miles to the Adirondacks, then a short climb over the White Mountains, and another two hundred miles to the New Hampshire coast. He unfolded the next section of the chart.

With the engine started, Craig quickly had the rotors running in flat pitch ready for lift off, and the last leg of the flight.

"Ready to go?" Craig checked with Brandt and tried to take the apprehension out of his voice. "*Champagne Princess*, here we come." And for the third time, Craig lifted the helicopter into a low hover, and as Brandt waved off the truck driver below, the Hawk gathered speed, and transitioned into a steady climb for its final rendezvous.

Craig levelled the Hawk, and began the track to Kingston at one thousand feet.

Lake Ontario is drained by the mighty Saint Lawrence, and with the moonlight, Craig could follow the broad sweeps of the frozen river. In other circumstances, with the spectacular vistas and natural beauty of a great river, cutting its way majestically through some of the most rugged scenery and largest tracts of Pine forest in the world, this would have been a memorable flight. But in the darkness, the beauty of the landscape below remained unseen, and with his important passenger and the sub zero temperatures, Craig would remember this flight for the rest of his life, but for very different reasons.

The Hawk swept low over the river and at forty degrees below freezing, not even the odd night trapper braved the cold to witness the helicopter's swift passage.

Craig was desperately tired after nine hours at the controls, but knowing that he had broken the back of the flight, his spirits lifted.

He shifted his position, flexing his legs and arms to keep the circulation going. God, it was cold.

Would his numbed body ever recover? Would it help to visualise himself lounging on some holiday beach, under a hot sun? How about Mallorca, where he once spent a wonderful holiday with Tracey... the temperatures in the nineties every day. Or the beautiful La Manga in Spain, by the warm Menor Sea. If he wanted to see those places again, he had better keep his head down now and complete this flight safely, he told himself.

The President still hadn't moved, and Craig prayed he could hold out for just another couple of hours. If only he could get the cabin temperature up.

Should he try to make a break for it? Just head for the nearest lights. But a landing at night, without surface lighting. That just wasn't on. More likely find himself colliding with the high ground, not to mention what Brandt might do.

Craig looked across the cabin. Brandt's head was resting against the side window with his eyes closed.

What sort of background could he have? Do you opt to become a criminal, or do circumstances put you there? What would it be like to grow up as an uneducated black in the rough and tumble of the West Indies, where you'd have to get what you wanted with your fists? Craig had seen the run-down tenement areas of Georgetown. How could places like that produce anything other than Brandt's type?

An open university for crime, and the Europeans and their union did nothing about it!

And how about the inhabitants of the houses below? Who really wanted to live and work in freezing temperatures for six months of every year? Surely, nobody chooses that lifestyle. No, they were locked into their lives as surely as Brandt had been born into crime. Was there anyone in the world who really chose his own destiny?

A flickering VOR needle drew Craig's attention. The back bearing from Ottawa. He swung the Hawk on to an easterly track, the final heading for the coast, and as the snow-covered summit of the Adirondacks came into view, he pulled in more power to gain height. Tracking over the more populated region, beyond the hills, he knew the radar saucers would be controlling the Air Traffic, and Craig wondered what height he would need to fly to show up on the radar screens. There must be a local transponder code for emergency. Try the seven's, the same as England, but in this terrain, it was unlikely a small helicopter would be identified under three thousand feet. He checked the tell-tale interrogator lamp on the set, hoping it might bleep. But nothing. Perhaps when he was nearer the coast. But would the radar controllers be interested in a slow moving radar return, ambling along miles below the speed of the jets? Anyway, while the Hawk was over land, he would keep the Transponder Squawk going.

The Ottawa beacon faded out of range, and with some apprehension, Craig selected the final homing signal, T-for-Tango, radiating he hoped, from the good ship *Champagne Princess.*

"What are you going to do with your share of the money, Brandt?" Craig broke the long silence. Brandt looked up.

"No definite plans, not 'til ah see de colour of hit. Hav'ta git out of America, han' thought ah'd take m'self ta Europe. Always fancied Switzerland from de movies yo know. Nice property by one of dem lakes, with a fancy yacht moored 'longside. Mebbe a cool Italian car. Meet some nice gal, han' stay respectable."

For all his upbringing and uncouthness, Craig couldn't help thinking how Brandt's ambitions ran along similar lines to his own, probably everybody's. He wanted to be a family man. A nice home, a good companion, a few luxuries. What else did one do with the allotted three score years and ten?

"How did Christine get on board the yacht so soon? I was only talking to her in the hotel this morning."

"She flew hup from Menominee ta New York. De Princess was docked in de New York harbour, han' will 'av sailed a few hours ago. Him has de timing worked out ta de minute, and de goddam feds won't be lookin' for de President so far from Wisconsin. Once we're hon de ship, we kin make fer Florida in comfort, han' ah'll be glad ta git away from dis goddam cold."

101

"That will suit me too Brandt, but I was more concerned with the President's health. As long as Christine knows her job. You realise the consequences for us all if he dies."

"He won't die man. De boss knows what he's doin,' han' its all goin' ta work out okay, yo'll see"

The lights of Montpelier City passed beneath the Hawk, and Craig could just make out the white peaks of Washington Mountains, the highest point in the range. Good, that would leave just one hundred miles to go, but it was vital to pick up the ship's homing signal before leaving the coast. Craig checked the frequency on the ADF receiver.

"Don't you think the Government will catch up with us eventually? Craig ventured. "Can't stay on the run for ever you know."

"Don't worry man. De boss went over all dat before we started. Sho, de feds is gonna be real mad at handin' over all dat goddam money, but yo see, dis is a tight hoperation, only seven in de team han' from different countries. Soon as de dough's paid, we all skip. De boss is goin' back ta Ireland. Ah guess de Sheikh Makhtoum fellah goes home ta Arabia. De ship's crew ta somewhere hin de Middle East, an 'ahm jest goin' ta disappear. Europe or Australia, or mebbe as mah fancy takes me. Yo and de girl kin return ta England. Right. Don't even know de name of de truck driver, but ah guess, like us, he's getting a good share of de dough."

"Guess dem two guys in Milwaukee will get da grilling from de Feds, but da boss sho paid 'em plenty."

Nicely done, thought Craig, and for the first time he could see O'Rourke getting away with his outrageous plan. Soon the President would be a prisoner on the *Champagne Princess*, one of a thousand ships that would be cruising in the coastal waters off Florida, and the money would be handed over as demanded. What else could the US Government do as long as the President was a prisoner? Yes, it might very well work, but somehow it was up to Alistair Craig to see that it did not. There'd be time to think about his own plans later. The immediate priority was to get them all safely to the ship.

The slopes of the tree-covered mountains passed below, and as Craig reduced height there was nothing but darkness ahead. Was it another storm? Craig strained his eyes.

The general area of grey seemed to stop abruptly in a long white line either side of his flight path. Of course, it was the surf breaking on the Atlantic Coast. Only an hour's flying to the ship. Craig's tension eased a little.

And now the homing signal was sounding in Craig's earphones loud and clear. *Dah-dah-dah,* Tango, Tango. The continuous note was music to Craig's ears. He had virtually made it. A twelve hundred mile flight at night in unfamiliar territory was no mean feat, and his tired body again felt the satisfying sensation of a well-planned, well-flown trip.

The Hawk was now down to five hundred feet, with the radar altimeter flashing furiously. Craig experienced a moment's panic as he left the safety of dry land and scampered over the forbidding waves of the Atlantic Ocean. The homing needle was solidly pointing the way ahead as Craig maintained a steady course and the early morning sky became brighter.

Craig asked Brandt to check the President's condition. The face was still pale and drawn, the eyes closed, and the mouth half open with saliva still trickling across his chin. The blanket covering the chest moved spasmodically, but at least he was still alive. Thank God he'd not been drugged a third time.

Thirty minutes later it was Brandt who spotted the ship.

"Der she is Craig," he shouted excitedly, pointing ahead. "Der she is…. We've goddam well made it."

Craig quickly confirmed the indication of the homer. It checked, perhaps only five minutes to go, and as they flew closer, a flood of relief flowed through Craig's tired body. Hallelujah. *They had made it.*

She was a long low luxury yacht, the sort you saw advertised in the posh yachting magazines with a price tag in millions, and as the first arc of the morning sun nibbled at the sky, the gleaming white hull of the ship was framed in the golden glow of a beautiful sunrise. *Champagne Princess* indeed. She certainly lived up to her name.

The Hawk passed low over the ship's bows on the run in to give Craig a closer look at the landing deck. Hell, it was small. He pulled into a steep turn with the rotor blades flapping their protest, then back on the cyclic and down with the collective. The *Champagne Princess* was lined up dead ahead for the final landing run.

For the last time, Craig settled the Hawk into a standard slow approach to the heli-deck, where several figures were standing. He concentrated on the restricted landing area ahead, positioning the helicopter just clear of the ship's stern rail.

Establishing a high hover, Craig carefully edged nearer the Champagne Princess, with the tips of the rotors whizzing inches from the handrail of the upper deck. In the confined space he gently lowered the Hawk vertically and, as the skids made contact, he squeezed the collective lever to the floor, transferring the full weight of the helicopter to the deck. For a second, the Hawk jerked awkwardly on its skids, and then gripped. Craig breathed out slowly with satisfaction.

They were down.

He wouldn't have wanted to try that particular landing in the dark.

# 14

The twelve-hour flight was the longest Craig had ever flown. But the job was done, and for the last time, the three rotor blades of the Hawk slid to a halt. Craig was thinking.... considering his words.

Ryan O'Rourke, the man who started the whole thing from Goodwood months ago, was walking towards him. Christine was standing close as Craig opened the cabin door to climb out. Two other men were standing close on the heli-deck.

O'Rourke greeted Craig boisterously.

"Well done dear boy, well done," he said, "I knew you were the man for the job." He held out his hand. "Welcome to our little ship, Alistair."

Craig was tired, but angry at the way he'd been tricked into making the flight. He scrambled down from the cabin, and ignoring the man's bonhomie, rounded on him furiously.

"Why the hell didn't you tell me the truth about this job?" He bellowed. "For all you know, we may have just murdered an American President with those drugs of yours. We're never going to get away with any of this, you know. And why didn't you tell me that girl was going to be here?" He pointed accusingly at Christine. "I suppose she was keeping me watched at the hotel, and I don't like being treated that way." Craig was genuinely angry, but he hoped he wasn't overplaying the part.

O'Rourke waited for Craig's outburst to subside, fixing him with the penetrating laser gaze. After a deliberate pause, he smiled at Craig disarmingly.

"Now listen dear boy," he said evenly. "Just calm down and stop the tantrums. Remember how much we are paying you. The fact is we are all in this together now. We can't afford any Prima Donnas on the team. The President is in no danger.... indeed our plan will not succeed if that were allowed to happen. What I told you, dear boy, was absolutely necessary. We needed a good pilot, and you were our choice. You've done a good job."

He moved closer, and placed his hands on Craig's shoulder in a fatherly manner. "Do you think I could have asked you to help us kidnap the President of the United States, and if you refused say, 'Well, don't tell anyone we're intending to.'"

O'Rourke looked fiercely at Craig, waiting for the reply.

The logic was inescapable.

Craig was still fuming at the man who had dragged him into this dangerous conspiracy.

He jabbed his finger.

"But what if he dies from an overdose of those drugs?" Craig challenged. "We're all guilty of murder."

"It appears I have to repeat myself Alistair. As I have already told you. The President will not die, dear boy. Christine here will see to that. You see I know about these things, and for one hundred million dollars, I have made it my business to be right."

O'Rourke's bland forehead wrinkled with impatience.

"Now have I made myself clear, dear boy?" He said pointedly.

Craig decided he wouldn't annoy the man further.

"Yes, I suppose you're right," he conceded, "but it would be an understatement to say I'm not happy about what you've done."

"One million dollars will buy all the happiness you can handle, dear boy, now let's stop arguing like children, and get the President to his quarters." O'Rourke turned to look in the rear cabin.

"He's not moved much during the flight," Craig said with genuine concern, "I'm worried."

"The President is in good hands now Alistair." He beckoned to Christine who was holding a large blanket.

She was wearing a thick duffle coat, and as O'Rourke opened the President's door, she moved closer to Craig and said a little stiffly, "Alistair, I'm sorry for the way this has happened, you must believe me. It is good to see you again, but I can't say much now." She looked nervously at O'Rourke, who had moved out of earshot. She lowered her voice to a whisper. "Try not to upset Mr O'Rourke, Alistair. He can be very difficult. I'll tell you everything later." She squeezed Craig's arm briefly. Her voice picked up for O'Rourke. "Anyway, I'm really glad you're both safe, but we'll need to get the President to his cabin quickly."

A ship's crewman came up to the helicopter. He was dark skinned, with a lined face, and weather beaten features, probably from working too long at sea. Another Arab, Craig decided. How many of the gang did O'Rourke have on board?

Christine looked up sharply and addressed the man directly. "We'll need the wheelchair Ahmed." The 'get it' did not need to be said.

The crewman Ahmed, helped O'Rourke carry the President from the helicopter, and lifted him into the wheelchair. He was still unconscious. Christine placed the blanket over his lap.

"Right Christine," O'Rourke said. "This is where you take charge of our famous guest. He's to be confined to the locker room under the bridge. Then, I want you to give me a report on his condition. But you are to keep his door locked all the time. You'll get the key from me when required. Brandt will help you get him on the bunk."

"Yes, I understand, Mr O'Rourke. He looks weak, but I can take care of him." She placed a hand on the President's cheek and dropped her head to his chest. She looked up. "He needs to be moved into the warm immediately."

Craig was relieved to see Christine take charge and wheel the President away. O'Rourke returned to the helicopter as Craig was parking the blades.

"We'll need to cover the helicopter," O'Rourke instructed. "Make it look like cargo, in case we get looked at from the air. When they get the ransom letter, the whole damned Air Force will start searching for us, but there's been no radio or TV announcement yet. The Government will probably keep the news of the kidnap quiet for a day or two, but my plan covers that possibility."

O'Rourke stared at Craig intently. The eyes narrowed.

"The people of America, and the rest of the world, will want the President back safe and sound. The ransom plan is based on just that."

Craig said nothing.

They were joined by another crewman, presumably the second man Brandt had mentioned earlier. That meant at least two Arabs on the ship, Craig decided.

O'Rourke touched the man's shoulder.

"Alistair, this is Ramzi Yousef. He's in charge of the technicals, engines and so forth. In ship's terms, he's our first mate. Ahmed is his number two. He keeps the galley ship shape for us."

O'Rourke jerked his head towards Ramzi and Ahmed.

"Help us with the covers."

The men dragged a wide tarpaulin over the helicopter's rotors, and tied the corners to the ship's handrails.

Craig ducked under the cover to check the switches in the cabin were off, and shut the cabin doors.

"I expect you have had enough for one night's work dear boy. You'll need some sleep?" O'Rourke motioned in the direction of the bow. "You're in cabin three on the starboard side. Have a good rest. We'll have much to discuss later. We may need your services again, so please keep alert. The *Champagne Princess* will be sailing for Florida. We'll be there in forty-eight hours. I can't wait to get out of this cold weather. Now off you go, dear boy." O'Rourke concluded on a note of dismissal.

Craig picked up his case and climbed the steps to the upper deck. He found his cabin at the far end of the gang-walk.

He pulled the cabin door closed, and without undressing, threw himself on a bunk bed. As he unwound, his thoughts went over the night's events.

He'd just completed the most difficult flying task of his career, and had safely brought the President to the ship, even though his motives were not as O'Rourke had intended. His part in the kidnap was done, and it was time to think of how he could sabotage the ransom plan, save the President, and get himself out of this mess.

But what about the man who'd planned and carried out the kidnap? How well he'd put his gang together to burgle the American nation out of one hundred million dollars. An astronomical ransom demand. Surely, too much money for one man.

Down the ages men have always sought wealth and the power money could bring. But one hundred million. What kind of man needed such a colossal sum? The desire for wealth could not be O'Rourke's motive. If he needed money, he didn't have to take on the whole American nation. With his criminal talent, why not a simple bank raid? A security van, or bullion train robbery? Even a computer swindle seemed to run into millions these days.

No, there had to be another compelling reason for what O'Rourke had done. Was he a paranoid with delusions of grandeur? A lunatic with a deep-rooted grudge against America? The US Administration had declared war on worldwide terror. But surely terror is an intangible. You can take on a country, assassinate its leaders, kill it's population, even defeat its government and topple its President, but Craig failed to see how you targeted an intangible like terror, any more than you could attack murder.

Craig turned the problem over and over in his tired mind, but could not come up with anything that fitted the facts. Lunatic or not, this amazing man had a desperate need for millions of dollars, and was prepared to go to extraordinary lengths to get them. Whatever his motive, Ryan O'Rourke was firmly in the saddle. It would be up to Craig to see if he could be unhorsed.

Craig's thoughts returned to Christine.

She was definitely out of place in the role of kidnapper's moll. Could it be that she too was a reluctant member of the gang? That made sense. The attraction he felt for her was still very much alive. With three days on the ship, he hoped there'd be time for him to discover more about her.

Craig put his head down and slept fitfully, as the *Champagne Princess* began reeling off the thousand miles to Florida at twenty knots.

During the morning Christine opened his cabin door. She stood looking at his mop of untidy hair. When he didn't stir, she closed the cabin door quietly, and left to report to O'Rourke.

He was quite good looking, she thought, and didn't seem like a criminal. Perhaps he'd been tricked into the kidnap, too. She'd had enough of gangsters, and was already regretting the attraction she felt for him. Should she tell him she had no intention of taking any of the ransom money Mr O'Rourke had promised? That she had vowed, come what may, she would take care of the President, and keep her plans to herself.

She knocked on O'Rourke's cabin.

"Ah, Christine. You look well." he said, light heartedly.

She paused for a moment before forcing a smile and said a simple, 'Thank you.'

"And how is the President?"

"He's still unconscious Mr O'Rourke, and it's difficult to tell. His pulse is weak and he won't be able to cope with another dose of Hioscene. It will take at least a day for him to recover."

"And our pilot?"

"He's been sleeping for most of the morning. Hasn't left his cabin."

"Good," O'Rourke said with satisfaction, "but remember I want the President kept under sedation for the next two days."

"I've told you, Mr O'Rourke. That's dangerous. He has a weak heart, and has been drugged too much already. You must give him at least a day to recover or I can't be responsible for what happens."

"Very well, Christine, I will take your professional advice. We mustn't do anything to damage the President's health. No doubt a rest from his warmongering will work wonders." O'Rourke smirked at his own humour.

She didn't like O'Rourke's tone.

"Keep an eye on them both, and when Alistair Craig wakes up, ask him to come to my cabin. Make it about six o'clock."

Christine left O'Rourke, and looked in on the President. Then she returned to her cabin. If only she could share her worries. Where was it all going to end? Was there any possibility of help from Alistair Craig? Would she ever see England again?

She pulled out her handkerchief, buried her head in the pillow, and sobbed quietly.

110

# 15

The envelope that dropped through the letterbox looked like any other, except for the unusual mode of address. The Vice President of the United States of America. It said. Care of: The White House, Washington DC.

The President's Senior Intern was churning through the day's early morning mail. She picked up the white A4-sized envelope to check for the security inspection stamp. No items were processed as far as the Presidential administration office without having passed the intricate security inspections. She looked up and glanced out along the wide Jefferson Boulevard and pretty avenue of grass that led to the wonderful Smithsonian Museums. The Lincoln Memorial sat solidly on the skyline. Her morning walk from the quaintly named 'Foggy Bottom' to the office, over the Potomac River and Arlington Park, was always a delight, and she loved the living in America's finest City.

She looked more carefully at the envelope and gestured to her boss. He glanced at the address.

"Shall I open it, sir?"

"Why not? Don't think the Vice President has taken to having his private mail delivered to the White House. Bound to be from some environmental nut, protesting at the cost of the Iraq occupation, or the next space shuttle, or something."

The Intern slit the envelope and began to read. After the first few lines she frowned, and passed over the letter. "I think you should see this one, Sir."

The letter was typed in capitals on a plain sheet of paper, with no date or address. It had been produced on a word processor, and couched in cosy, but business like terms. It lacked conventional punctuation.

\* \* \* \* \* \*

DEAR MR VICE PRESIDENT ... *The letter began* ...

YOU MUST NOW BE AWARE THAT AT 15.15 HRS ON THE 5TH DECEMBER THE PRESIDENT OF THE UNITED STATES OF AMERICA WAS ABDUCTED FROM GOVERNMENT HOUSE IN MILWAUKEE CITY AFTER THE BUILDING WAS GASSED

TWO CYLINDERS WERE LEFT TO AUTHENTICATE THIS LETTER ... THEY WERE MANUFACTURED BY BENSON CHEMICALS IN TORONTO AND NUMBERED 357S AND 358P ... YOUR PRESIDENT IS NOW HELD PRISONER BY THIS ORGANISATION AND IS UNHARMED ... HE WILL BE RETURNED TO THE PEOPLE OF AMERICA UPON RECEIPT OF THE PAYMENT INDICATED BELOW

MR VICE-PRESIDENT YOU HAVE FORTY-EIGHT HOURS TO ACT ... IF YOUR GOVERNMENT DECIDES TO IGNORE THIS DEMAND THE PRESIDENT WILL BE KILLED HUMANELY AND THERE WILL BE NO FURTHER COMMUNICATION FROM THIS ORGANISATION ... HOWEVER IN THIS INSTANCE AND TWELVE HOURS BEFORE THE PRESIDENTS DEATH WE PROPOSE TO NOTIFY THE SECRETARY GENERAL OF THE UNITED NATIONS AND THE WORLD'S PRESS ... THIS ACTION IS OF COURSE INTENDED TO HASTEN YOUR HAND

TO SIGNIFY YOUR ACCEPTANCE OF THE TERMS OF THIS DEMAND YOU SHOULD INSTRUCT NBC TO CANCEL THE JAY LENO SHOW DUE TO BE TRANSMITED AT 11 00 HRS ON 7TH DECEMBER … THEN TO TRANSMIT THE NBC NATIONAL NEWS FIVE MINUTES LATER THAN THE NORMAL 12.00 HOURS

WE HAVE TO EMPHASISE THAT IF AT ANY TIME WE LEARN OF ANY ACTION THAT IS INTENDED TO DISCOVER THE LOCATION OF THIS ORGANISATION OR DURING THE COLLECTION OF THE RANSOM … SUCH ACTION WILL BE REGARDED AS A BREACH OF THIS AGREEMENT AND THE PRESIDENTS LIFE WILL BE FORFEITED

THIS MR VICE PRESIDENT IS A SINGLE AND FINAL COMMUNICATION WE AWAIT YOUR ACCEPTANCE OF THE TERMS OF THIS DEMAND AS AFORESAID

There was no name or signature. Just four startling words. 'THE AL QAEDA IRA '
The Administration Officer smiled grimly at the Intern, and turned to the second page.
"What the hell's coming next?" He said with apprehension.

APPENDIX.

THE SUM OF $100,000,000, (ONE HUNDRED MILLION US DOLLARS) IN USED UNMARKED BANK NOTES OF ONE HUNDRED DENOMINATION IS TO BE PARCELLED IN FIFTY PACKAGES OF TWO MILLION DOLLARS EACH … THEY SHOULD BE CONTAINED IN POLYTHENE WRAPPING AND SECURED TO A RUBBER DINGHY… THE DINGHY IS TO BE MOORED WITH A SEA DROGUE EIGHTEEN NAUTICAL MILES FROM MIAMI BEACH AT A GPS POSITION LONGITUDE 13.55.60 DEGREES WEST … LATITUDE 38.22.45 NORTH

A HOMING TRANSMITTER RADIATING ON 200 KHZ IS TO BE FITTED TO THE DINGHY AND IS TO BE IN POSITION BY 18.00 HRS BUT NOT EARLIER THAN 17.00 HRS ON THE 8TH DECEMBER

PROVIDING THE TERMS OF THIS DEMAND ARE MET THE PRESIDENT WILL BE SET FREE AT A LOCATION WHICH WILL BE ADVISED

ALL TIMES ARE EASTERN STANDARD TIME

APPENDIX ENDS

The Administration Officer breathed out apprehensively with a low whistle, and carefully placed the ransom demand on the desk, as if it were a delicate porcelain vase.

He looked uncertainly at the puzzled features of the President's Intern.

"Have this taken down to the lab for a forensic report. Priority to this office." He squeezed his eyes closed and wondered what the hell he should do now.

He felt a growing knot in his gut.

"Al Qaeda and the IRA…. Working together! Get me the Vice President's office, and put a call through to security. This would explain the comings and goings of the top brass yesterday."

He smiled grimly as the thought crossed his mind that he might always remember this day.

"This could be a true bill."

# 16

Meetings had been taking place in the Secretary of Defence's office continuously, following the news from Milwaukee the previous day. Within an hour of the Al Qaeda demand, a summit meeting was called.

The Vice President was a staunch Republican, who had served as running mate to the elected President. He was a younger man with a fine war record, and well versed in TV manipulation and public relations. He would enjoy the meeting for very personal reasons.

He had serious Presidential ambitions. One day a new Kennedy!

In the White House, important meetings are held on the second floor of the west wing, in the Oval Room, normally reserved for foreign heads of state business. It is a pale yellow and blue room* in the Adams style, and overlooks the lawns and rose gardens that lead to the entrance steps of the West Portico. The high, white painted ceiling is elaborately decorated with scrolls and acanthus leaves in yellow and gold. Five gilt framed paintings of past Presidents hang on the curve of the east wall, with Peale's painting of George Washington centred above a white marble fireplace. The marble is Italian.

* August 2005

On the adjacent wall, a long glass fronted bookcase houses a thousand books on American history, and the Constitution. The tall doors are solid English Oak, and lead directly to the private study of the President.

Those summoned were the three heads of the Military Services with their aides, the Central Intelligence Agency, the Federal Bureau of Investigation and the lesser known National Security Agency. A male secretary holding a top-secret clearance sat to one side of the long mahogany table, where the ten men arranged themselves five-a-side. A sparkling crystal flower bowl sat on a lace mat alongside a voice actuated Panasonic recorder, which was humming quietly.

The bright rays of the morning sun reflected from the polished parquet floor, to spotlight a fine Thomas Tompion Bracket clock, which ticked audibly on the mantel-shelf. Below the gilt framed clock door, a silver plaque was signed *Elizabeth R.* A gift from the Queen of England. Around the long table, the ten men sat deep in thought, and from time to time looked up at each other apprehensively. The expressions were grave and these men might have been playing poker or a high card game at the gambling tables of Monte Carlo

But the objects before each man were not playing cards or dice, but a yellow file marked with a Red Star, and stamped.... TOP SECRET. Clipped to each file's cover was a list of persons present, with a vacant space for each man's signature. To one side, sat a pad of yellow notepaper, a new pencil, and a carafe of Evian sparkling water.

No ashtrays were allowed.

The report read:

*At 15.15 Hours EST on 5th December, the President of the United States of America was abducted from the second floor office of the Governor's Building in Milwaukee. The President was alone reading official papers. Personal body guards were stationed in the corridor with six FBI armed security agents on the same floor. There were four outside guards with infra red detection devices, covering all entrances to the building. Other staff were resident in the building, including the President's personal security team.*

*Standard Closed Circuit TV (CCTV) cameras were in position on all corridors, and covered the four acres of surrounding grounds, which were also*

patrolled by dog teams. The inner security walls were laser protected, with operation triggered by infrared detection and direct contact.

The Presidential Sikorsky helicopter was parked overnight on the helipad lawn. The usual 24-hour guards remained on board.

The outside guards were killed using long-range 'stun guns' and we believe that a least three different weapons were used. The telephone, telex and dedicated telefax and computer lines were disabled at the PBX position. The disconnection was made internally. The electricity supply to the house alarms was broken at 15.10 hours. An NSA security cleared contractor's service vehicle was known to be working on the electricity sub station during the day. It was signwritten 'Milwaukee Electrical Services Corp,' and checks are being made on the company now. It had been security cleared for two years.

Entry to the house was made through the main door, using codes known only to Federal Personnel. The codes are changed every four hours when the President is in residence. Two 'door-entry' security agents were asphyxiated and unable to challenge the intruders. They were found dead. Names of those lost have been withheld.

The building's alarm devices failed to function, due to interruption of the power supply. The automatic emergency generator did not come on line, and was found disconnected from the main circuit by a magnetic device attached to the relay. Internal federal personnel must also have been involved to accomplish this.

The occupants of the house were asphyxiated using Pentathol 30, a gas that was released into the building through the air conditioning system. Pentathol 30 is one of the Trilone group of nerve gases. It is invisible and odourless and renders persons breathing the gas unconscious in less than a minute. The effect usually lasts for an hour, but long exposure to the gas is frequently fatal. A six inch pressurised canister of Pentathol contains enough chemical to incapacitate every occupant of this building. The electrically controlled door lock of the President's room was broken by use of an unknown device, but there is evidence of considerable heat being employed. Probably a high-powered portable laser.

Two men carried the President on a stretcher from the building to a stolen ambulance. The ambulance was observed and timed leaving Government house at 15.21 hours. No traces of a struggle were evident, but broken phials of Hioscene and Valium were found in the President's room. It is assumed he was either anaesthetised or drugged to facilitate his removal.

At 15.30 Hours, a wounded agent recovered from the gas attack, and called house security, NSA HQ and the State Police. That call was timed at 15.32 Hrs. The stolen ambulance, which carried markings of the Milwaukee General

*Hospital, was found abandoned on Highway 385, two miles south of Milwaukee City. We are checking for any witnesses. At 15.40 hours, roadblocks were erected on every road leaving the City. They were positioned at five, fifteen and twenty five miles radius. All traffic was stopped and searched. At the time of this report no information on the President's location has been received.*

*The evidence points to considerable involvement of Federal, security cleared internal staff. At present the surviving personnel are under arrest awaiting FBI interrogation.*

*At 09.30 hours today, a ransom demand was received in the Vice President's office in the White House. It advises the United States Government that the President is a prisoner of Al Qaeda. The ransom sum demanded is one hundred million dollars.*

*See full text at the Appendix.*

*Senior Officers of the armed forces, the CIA, FBI and the NSA have been informed. No information has been released to other governments or news media. The committee is to assess the situation and recommend a course of action that will ensure:*

*1. The safe release of the President.*

*2. The arrest of the persons responsible.*

*3. Recommend actions to tighten existing security and changes in procedures.*

REPORT ENDS

The men rose to their feet as the young, good looking Vice President strode into the room to take his place at the head of the table, carefully positioning himself between two flags of the 'Stars and Stripes.' He was a relative newcomer to the White House, but a long term Republican. A rich Republican of course, having been brought into the campaign because of his youthful good looks, in an attempt to recapture the charisma of the 1960's John F Kennedy ticket.

He was an ambitious politician who knew how to progress. Even at Harvard, he'd vowed to make it to the top. Politics was simply a question of avoiding the snakes and climbing the right ladders. He'd seen too many top statesmen felled by a murky past. God had blessed him with the looks of Brad Pitt, the American voters wanted, and now he was a short step from achieving the highest office in the world. If it took one act of sabotage, one small act of disloyalty to

118

make that step, he thought darkly, he would do it. *The American dream. An all American college boy makes it to the Presidency.*

Raising a hand, the Vice President began to speak. The room fell silent.

Here was an opportunity to make his mark. With the President absent, it fell to him to take his place until the democratic process elected a successor. If he played the cards well it could easily be him! He coughed once for attention and spread his arms to embrace the meeting; just as the PR guys have taught him. He set his jaw and adopted a grim smile that in difficult times, looked good on camera.

"Gentlemen. Please be seated." He waited for the chairs to stop rattling and coughed again to clear his throat.

"You know each other," he opened pleasantly…. "And there is no need for formal introductions." He placed both hands on his lapels in accordance with the coaching, and swept his eyes around the room confidently. "Can I then open the meeting, and trust you have all studied the agenda?" He patted the table with his knuckles. The men looked up in unison.

"I can hardly express enough the gravity of the difficulties we face," he continued darkly. "Our task this morning is to agree a course of action that will secure the release of the President, and let me say immediately gentlemen, there is no price limitation on what has to be done. We have just forty-eight hours to make a decision" He pulled his lips together. "Gentlemen, it would appear that Al Qaeda are beating us in the security war."

The Vice President looked at the only three men who really mattered…. the CIA's Director, Vic Cramer, the NSA boss, Captain Ron Grant, and the Head of the FBI. This was Government business, and the lesser military men were present to implement decisions.

The Central Intelligence Agency's Director, Vic Cramer, was a good man, a good man with a reputation. But the Vice President didn't like him. Cramer made no bones about his view of Presidents being transitory figureheads, who passed fleetingly through Government. He'd seen five since his time in the Agency. He was too perceptive, and too clever by half. He would immediately see the possibilities for the Vice President. But politics was a desperate business. He'd know that too!

119

Cramer was an ex-policeman with twenty years tough service. He started his career in the Hoover days, but when the CIA Director proved to be a Russian double, he had been transferred to take his place in the nation's top intelligence position. At fifty, he must have seen it all, and would know the hopelessness of the situation they faced. He'd have to be 100% loyal to the President and no doubt promote a policy based on the intelligence, which meant appeasement. He would recommend the only course of action that might succeed. The soft option. The soft option of paying up to secure the President's release. But getting him back would not promote the Vice President's personal ambitions. All so much simpler if he never returned...! This was power politics. Top echelon stuff! Cramer would have to be handled carefully, if he was to persuade the others to adopt the riskier tactics that would allow him to make that last step up the ladder to the Presidency.

Across the table, Captain Ron Grant, head of the NSA, drummed his fingers. He was altogether a different kettle of fish! A political animal that could be bribed for political gain, and might back the risky strategy. The word was that he might be considered to run for State Governor when the Republicans got fed up with their bad run of losers in the Primaries. He would go along with the Vice President if he thought it would mean a step up and the votes that would follow.

The FBI man sitting next to Ron Grant was a simple street detective. When it came to sending out hundreds of investigating agents to pound the streets for information, he'd do well. His bureau would back any plan that was politically uncomplicated. No.... he would not present the Vice President with a problem and would go along with the majority.

Next came the Service Officers, led by that army buffoon, General Orville Mann. Purple Heart and all. The Marine and Air Force men would back any line of direct action that kept them in favour with the politicians. Mann was typically one of them. A crash, bang, wallop operator. It would be interesting to see how the personalities clashed. No doubt the other service guys would huff and puff, but offer nothing, then follow their leader.

The Vice President continued. He gestured to Cramer with an outstretched palm.

"First, I am calling on the CIA Director for his report. Mr Vic Cramer please." He shot Cramer an uneasy glance. This was going to be difficult. Political hardball!

Vic Cramer climbed to his feet. He was tall, with the craggy looks and resigned eyes of too many years in the intelligence business. He seldom smiled, and the tightly closed mouth and firm set of the jaw said he was a man of authority, a man used to being obeyed, a formidable agent with all the tough qualities needed for the CIA's top job. He knew the hopelessness of the position, and looking round the table, he could see that the other men knew it too. How many times had he chaired similar meetings, to discuss the President's safety? He always knew an assassination or a kidnap might one day happen, hopefully after he had retired.

But here he was with this public outrage on his doorstep. The President himself had lectured Americans almost daily on the necessity of beating these Arab terrorists through force. To hell with the toothless United Nations. There must never be another 9/11. Never another assault on the American way of life. The bombing of Iraq, and the toppling of Saddam Hussein were for starters. Those next in line were already being warned. Morocco, Syria, and Iran, would soon come to heel just as the daft, self-styled Colonel Gadaffi had U-turned his politics in Libya. Then there was North Korea, waiting for their turn, unless they got to their nuclear bomb first!

But now the Al Qaeda mob had reversed the position. The man they hated most was their prisoner. Cramer knew the worst would happen: A stubble-cheeked President repeatedly paraded on *Al Jazeera* TV, with a gun held to his head by three hooded terrorists, in the customary Arab fashion, and the public outrage at the failure of American security, the CIA, and their subordinate agencies. His own job was at risk. Retirement with a massive pay-off was only a few months away, leisurely tours of the speaker's circuit, another fat fee for just being there, and repeating the same crap. Probably now all gone!

He pulled at the knot of his tie, and looked along the expectant faces. His voice was grave.

"Gentlemen," he began. The words came softly through a thick brown moustache. The opening words that had to be said for the tapes! "I endorse our Vice Presidents remarks," he said drily.

121

"We do indeed have a grave situation. As you can see from the report, this kidnap is the result of considerable planning and attention to detail. We've known for months that these Al Qaeda operatives have access to the most sophisticated modern materials and systems. But this time, the President's abduction was carried out with significant assistance from within our own agencies. A worrying trend. But may I say, not the first time we have had double agents in our ranks," he said testily. "But to continue."

"May I first give you a little background of the terrorist organisation we face and the methods they employ." Cramer turned his notes, exhaling slowly as he smoothed his jaw. "Osama Bin Laden from Al Qaeda. As we speak, the world's most wanted man."

"Since 9/11, we have seen Al Qaeda bring many smaller terrorist organisations such as the regional Qaeda cells under their wing. A shrewd move by Bin Laden, to extend his influence to more countries of the world. It allows him to use his vast reserves of capital to continue Al Qaeda's bombing operations on a regional basis. His declared aim is, as we all know, to rid the Middle East of American interests, and support for Israel. We know Bin Laden has recruited the Egyptian Islamic Jihad, with its anti-American interests. Then the Algerian armed Islamic group GIA, who attended terror-training camps in Afghanistan, and who align themselves with Salafia Jehadir. Salafist Groups and GSPC support the Taliban with fundraising and propaganda, and are allowed to live in their mosques by the daft British. Their 'Social Services' even pay them to stay there and live off the state."

He decided he needed a dig at the Government, and looked squarely down the table to the Vice President. "I think we should all remember it was our own Government who originally gave life to the Taliban, with financial support against the Russians!" Cramer mellowed his tone like a college lecturer and went on. "I say this only to highlight how complex these issues have become, and how political priorities change." Cramer was beginning to enjoy his discourse. "But to move on."

"These terrorist groups are most active in Europe and the Middle East. One of Bin Laden's senior operatives is from the Baluchistan area of Iran, and an active supporter of the Mujahadeen. Since the Iraq war, he has been hiding out on the Pakistan border. Our

122

intelligence tells us that Bin Laden himself may be there. We also know of a Tunisian Fighting Group, whose founder lived in the UK. As ridiculous as it might appear, Great Britain is now the safest haven for terrorists in the world."

He looked up from his papers to embrace the room, and lowered his tone.

"This meeting will have taken note of how the British Government have bowed to European legal pressure, and the English Courts, and released the four terrorists from Guantanamo, even following our advice that they represent, 'a significant threat' to their own people's safety. They have even released their own terrorist detainees from Belmarsh prison in London, and within weeks, are surprised to find their Underground train stations and buses bombed."

Again Cramer paused, to give effect to his words. Good intelligence ensured good decisions. He laid his papers on the table. Cramer would put the blame where it was deserved. He looked up to the head of the table. Another dose for the two-timing Vice-President. He knew plenty about the IRA, and didn't need notes. How well he recalled the Catholic Kennedys' support for Noraid. Funds shipped to Ireland that probably killed hundreds. He continued his theme ominously.

"And now we have evidence of the most serious alliance. The Irish Republican Army, who have decades of bombing operations and terrorist experience in Northern Ireland and mainland Britain, have joined Al Qaeda. They are taking on America."

The men look troubled as Cramer continued his theme.

"Their intelligence operatives are among the best in the world. Al Qaeda has had sleeper agents in America for many years, thanks to the liberal immigration policies of our own administration. These two monsters are now working together."

"We can expect few, if any, clues to help us locate those responsible. I believe the abduction at the Government Offices in Milwaukee would have required many terrorists' specialists, and it seems highly likely, that some of these came from within our own agency. As you have read, all surviving staff are currently under interrogation, but that is 'stable door' stuff. They may provide us with relevant intelligence. We are also presently assessing American Agents we know have the knowledge and access to equipment to make this kidnap. Our overseas divisions are reporting back from Europe, the Arab countries and South Africa."

He paused again. The bright sun coming through the bullet-proofed window, flickered on his forehead. He gestured for the sunblind to be pulled. The room darkened as he continued.

"We are considering the involvement of the Irish Republican Army, and are in discussions with the British MI6. A senior British Agent is flying here as we speak. We are agreed, it would seem that the co-operation of these two could only be, first.... finance. Finance for the IRA whose supporting funds has become severely limited since the 9/11 attacks and the British *Good Friday* agreement. And secondly.... publicity. Publicity and revenge for Al Qaeda. They will be the driving force in this operation, and fund provider for the abduction. We consider it unlikely that other countries would be involved, but I have dispatched agents to all areas for information."

"The action taken here prior to this meeting is the setting up by the police of the road blocks referred to in the report. They were in position within ten minutes of the discovery of the kidnap. Instructions have been issued to Highway Patrols, the state Police and Government Agents to make checks at Road, Rail, Sea and Airports. Further roadblocks have been spaced at fifty-mile intervals in all states throughout the country with search teams being held in readiness. I find it difficult to believe the President's captors could have avoided the extensive roadblocks, and are probably still located inside the dragnet we have laid down. If they are in the cordoned area, our search teams will find them. Non commercial and private flights have been prohibited, and we are checking all air movements in the last thirty-six hours."

He brought his hands together, and pointed his index finger down the room for emphasis. He needed the meeting's full attention for what was to be said next. All eyes were on him as the fidgeting stopped and the room fell quiet.

"But Gentlemen, there is an alternative view. I do not believe the kidnappers will be found using routine intelligence and search methods. The indications are that their escape route had specialist knowledge and our President may already be held prisoner outside the country." He sipped a glass of iced water as the bracket clock on the mantelpiece struck the hour.

124

"Rumours of the President's absence are already circulating in the nation's press, but at present I have their editors on hold, awaiting a Press Conference. The news of the nationwide roadblocks and searches will break today. The story could hit the new stands this morning. As an interim, the cover plan I am using is that a national security exercise is taking place."

He paused meaningfully. This is the part the Vice President would not want to hear.

"Gentlemen, as much as I would like to take on the people responsible for the kidnap of our President, we cannot do so and I must spell it out to you all, loud and clear. We cannot take any action that will risk our President's safety."

Cramer looked up to gauge the meeting's reactions.

"I am of course aware of the many counter measures available to us, and it will be for this committee to decide on their use and I must repeat, yet again, the controversional view. We cannot take any action that will risk our President's safety."

Cramer paused, clasping a finger in his right hand, as he made each point in turn.

"For example, it would be a simple matter to leave traceable substances on the currency and the dinghy. There are radioactive materials available to us with delayed action, which can be identified and traced by a micro radio receiver. An AWAC aircraft flying at thirty thousand feet, or a surface vessel at five miles could receive them. Both would allow us to tail the kidnappers and we know of no other country that has equipment capable of detecting such substances. Certainly neither Al Qaeda nor the IRA would have them. We are able to impregnate dollar bills with poisons that will cause death or incapacitate ten minutes after being touched by a bare hand. We could install laser and sonic devices that paralyse any body within sound range. We have other, as yet untested, techniques available to us," he concluded, as he grasped his smallest finger. "So, gentlemen we could utilise any, or all of these methods to locate, and if necessary, kill the kidnappers."

Yet again he went quiet, as he allowed his words to be considered.... then resumed, as he changed the nature of his argument.

"However, Gentlemen…." He picked up the meeting agenda and waved it in his right hand. "I have to emphasise, the most important aspect of our terms of reference. This being the *safe release* of the President, which is our principal objective, which none of the measures I have outlined, could guarantee."

Cramer raised his voice. "I must repeat…. The safe release of the President. Al Qaeda is employing a simple, but highly effective tactic. A single ransom demand that requires nothing but a single ransom payment. Unless the persons holding the President choose to make further contact, it is not even a matter we can negotiate."

He dropped his voice to ensure the meeting's attention.

"Gentlemen, as much as I dislike using these words," he looked hard at the glum expressions around him, "We are impotent here." He allowed the significance of the word to register. "If we want our President returned safely…. I see no possible course of action that does not jeopardise his safety. I believe therefore, we must accept that, as an interim, this Government is being forced to pay the Al Qaeda ransom. I do not consider the amount to be of any consequence. I am therefore asking this committee to accept the CIA's view that we pay this ransom demand. We have access to some of the most experienced ransom negotiators in the world. If contact can be made, such a man may well reduce the amount we pay, but I have to emphasise, we must pay the full amount, or any lower level that can be negotiated."

Vic Cramer picked up his papers and swept his eyes around the room. Perhaps an olive branch? He continued evenly.

"With the President safe, we will then use our intelligence and service forces to locate the kidnappers. I'm sure our military here will plan a suitable operation to recover our dollars, and annihilate those responsible."

Cramer looked squarely down the table. "The CIA trusts it will have the meeting's support in securing the safe release of our President in accordance with our mandate." He looked past the NSA boss, and rested his gaze at the far end of the table, where an overweight man in uniform was shaking his head. This was General Orville Mann.

"As a precautionary measure," he looked steadily at the Army General, "I have issued instructions for the necessary quantity of dollars to be held in readiness at Fort Knox. An executive Jet is at

Dulles Airport on twenty-four hour standby, awaiting orders to fly the ransom to Fort Lauderdale Executive Airport. An unmarked US Customs launch is available at Miami harbour, and I have arranged for a suitably-sized dinghy capable of holding that quantity of dollars, plus the radio transmitter, to be prepared. However they will be recorded in a way that we know is undetectable, which will assist us with our later plans, once the President is safe."

The Army General could contain himself no longer, and waved for the attention of the meeting.

The Vice President spoke first. He looked uneasy.

"You have something to say, General Mann?"

Orville Mann rose heavily to his feet. Over two hundred pounds of him.

A national disaster was the stuff of life for the General. Probably expect to ride roughshod over the Governments team, using a badly thought out sledgehammer plan, Vic Cramer decided. The other men knew what to expect, and looked at each other with understanding. Generals were impulsive operators with no political finesse or diplomatic training. This one was an arrogant Texan, dressed in full uniform with a row of medals and three star epaulettes. A pompous oaf with a double chin, and short sandy hair clipped close to the skull in traditional military style. The eyes bulged from too much drink, but did not flicker as he glowered down the table.

Vic Cramer met the General's gaze and winced. The others lifted their eyes to the ceiling.

Orville Mann launched straight into the meeting, with a parade ground bellow.

"Fellahs," he began in a loud Texan accent. "This situation is jest too simple. Forget all this namby-pamby talk about negotiation and handin' over millions of the taxpayer's dollars. We jest want our President back and need to give this Al Qaeda gang a lesson they'll never forget. Now's our chance to get our own back for 9/11." He raised a clenched fist. "Sure we wrap up the dollars for bait, and when they come a sniffin'....." He banged down on the table. "Wham, we go for 'em all guns blazin'. I kin give you a crack commando team that'll nail these kidnappers in five minutes. Why doan you jest hand over the whole operation to the army and my boys. That's the only treatment these Arab hoodlums will understand." He released a burp. "Jest give me and mah boys the authority."

The General slumped back in his seat with a snort, and glared at the others.

Vic Cramer was not surprised at the man's outburst. Where did they get their Generals from these days? Give this man an atom bomb and he'd solve the world's problems. If the lessons of Iraq and Vietnam had taught him nothing, the man was never going to learn. Should he squash him now? No, this was serious politics, and he could see his reputation vanishing in an instant if he allowed himself to become involved in a 'personality' dispute with the Army.

"Thank you, General Mann," Cramer said softly. "The CIA appreciates the army's view, and we may of course be forced to adopt such tactics at the end of the day, but I have to reiterate our strict terms of reference. That is the safe release of the President, and the Army's plan will not achieve that with any certainty. At this stage the capture of those responsible is a secondary consideration and to repeat myself, my agency's view is that this aspect of the task will be passed to the military for action later."

There were nods of agreement from the moderates around the table. "Yes Sir. We want the President back. We can't take chances with his life." Good. He was making progress and carrying the meeting with him. He hoped the General's contribution had been recognised for what it was. *Crass rubbish.*

The Bracket clock struck the next quarter hour.

"So there you have it gentlemen, to summarise my recommendation, we agree to pay this ransom without counter activity. I will ask for the availability of an experienced negotiator. My department is already in touch with such a person, who is a member of the British secret service. He has experience of many successful operations at international level. Once the President is safely exchanged, then, and only then, will we commence our counter operation. We will have the co-operation of many countries to set up a worldwide dragnet. The routine implementation of these decisions can be left with my Agency."

He closed his presentation formally. "I therefore recommend this course of action to committee."

Vic Cramer folded his notes and sat down.

# 17

The Vice President rose to his feet. The veneer of calm was slipping. Oh, for his speechwriter, and the conveniently placed autocue.

Which way to jump?

"Thank you, Mr Cramer. You have given a comprehensive assessment of the situation, and the difficulties we face. I'm sure the meeting now understands the CIA's position and formal recommendation."

He needed to marshal his thoughts. Cramer had made an impressive argument, which made too much sense. He suspected there could be support for the CIA's plan, but they would be of no use to him and his ambitions. So how to pull these guys round to his way of thinking? Think back to his PR men and their training. Of course, Politics....The American people.... And their expectations!

"It seems therefore, that thanks to Mr Cramer and his CIA's clear assessment, we have a simple decision to make." He extended his right palm to the meeting, turning it left and right. "To meekly pay up or to fight!" he said, raising his voice.

"On a personal basis Mr Cramer, I have to say I cannot accept the passive position suggested by your CIA. I believe that your proposed surrender to the demands of Al Qaeda ....The murderers of three thousand New Yorkers, remember.... will not find favour with the voters. Our great American people will expect us to take more decisive action than your office now proposes. Before we proceed, may we examine the rescue options you outlined, and the special techniques you have reviewed?"

The Vice President had already lobbied Ronald Grant, the wily boss of the NSA. He wanted to progress in the world of politics. He already knew which way Grant would vote.

"We will hear the views of our National Security Agency?" He smiled down the table. "Captain Grant, Sir?"

Captain Grant.... known as 'Big Gee' to his associates, was the head of the National Security Agency, an Agency the average American may never have heard of. Grant` was a craggy, cunning operator. He also had political ambitions and planned to leave the Agency and run for office as a Republican. He could see weeks of Government turmoil ahead, and if he could be seen by the media to emerge as a powerful ally of the Vice President, the votes would follow.

The word on the block was, that internationally, their warmongering President and his fawning British Prime Minister had worn out their newly found popularity. With each Al Qaeda attack, the European countries were getting nervous and changing sides. Osama Bin Laden had warned that he would take revenge on the countries that backed the American invasion of Iraq. Bombs had exploded in Casablanca, the British Embassy in Turkey, Madrid, and Italy, and the Al Qaeda Jihad had bombed London. The Taliban were already returning to Iraq.... blowing up hotels in Baghdad.... taking hostages. Sunni suicide bombers had wrecked the first-ever democratic elections in Iraq.

Britain was getting tetchy at the loss of the so-called *special relationship,* which never really existed. The world was thinking it was time for policy changes. A time that could not be more ripe for him to make his move. The Vice President had hinted at a possible Governorship of California, or even the Vice President's position. He just needed to make sure it became vacant!

As Grant climbed to his feet, he caught the eye of the Vice President. They both knew and agreed on what should be said!

"Mr Vice President, my Agency has taken detailed advice from our senior officers and anti-terrorists specialists at Fort Bragg in North Carolina. We find we must take an opposing view to Vic Cramer and

130

his Central Intelligence Agency." He paused deliberately as he offered a half smile. All eyes swivelled towards him.

"I have the utmost respect for his wide experience and knowledge of such matters. But I have to remind this meeting...." He raised his hands for emphasis and flicked two index fingers in the air.... "The President's kidnap is not only political, but a national security matter."

"It is my National Security Agency that has the ultimate responsibility for our President's safety, and I have to tell you that the kidnap situation such as we now face has been under review for many years. It has been discussed in absolute detail with successive Presidents. All incumbents understand the risk they may face, and I know our President has the courage and the will to accept that risk. I agree with the view, that the American nation will expect us to take the initiative, with more decisive action than has so far been proposed."

The Army General was showing interest again. Grant waited for several seconds to give his next words added weight. Now the crunch!

"My agency has discussed this abduction with the Government's special section Middle East advisors in Fort Bragg. We believe that Al Qaeda is unlikely to release the President, even after collecting the ransom. They will use him to extract maximum worldwide publicity. We can expect a series of 'press releases' demanding more concessions from the west, and the release of various prisoners. Guantanamo, Germany, the United Kingdom. Then, when the time is right.... the President will be killed. A message to the world of the strength of Islam."

He chose his next words carefully. Words intended for the press.

"Gentlemen, time is not on our side. We must take action now. Action.... immediate and direct. To get our President back. Action that will be demanded by the people of America."

The faces around the table lit up. Only Orville Mann seemed unmoved, as he doodled a jumble of triangles and circles on his notepaper. Thirty years in the Army, and he'd seen it all. The eyes said so. Damn the Fort Bragg guys. He'd get the job done with his own men.

Captain Grant continued severely.

"I have discussed the implications and options with my senior NSA and service colleagues, and offer the following course of action, which we recommend to the Government."

He allowed a long pause again, to give effect to the words.

"We must mount a rescue operation."

Grant noted the men's reactions, and produced a large-scale map of the Florida Keys. He opened it out on the table. The dinghy's central position was marked in red. Grant continued easily.

"The Government will agree to pay the ransom. The NBC television code will be used. The dinghy will be placed at the stipulated pick-up point, and fitted with the homing device as demanded." Vic Cramer's gaze was rooted on him as he spoke. Grant avoided direct eye contact as he continued.

"The packages, containing a quantity of dollars, will be fitted with an explosive device. For this, we will use the specialist services of Fort Bragg's Delta Force, and Rangers.... our more senior members will know of their expertise, and long record of success in similar operations. The explosive device will temporarily stun any person within a range of fifty feet. The explosion will be accompanied by a simultaneous and continuous release of an anaesthetic gas, which will smother the area. The detonation is to be remotely controlled by a radio beam, and triggered from an airborne observation post, and in case of bad weather, a standby surface position, using the English Plessey *Heli-Tele* system. You may know Gentlemen, that this camera equipment has a telephoto lens capable of magnifications which will enable the dinghy to be accurately observed from twenty five thousand feet, or at a range of five miles."

Grant pulled at his neck tie, wiped his brow, and went on

"It seems certain that the President is being held near the ransom pick-up point. Our contact with the kidnapper at the dinghy will therefore be the first link in a chain that must lead us to his location. The person or persons collecting the ransom, will be taken to our interrogation unit in Miami, where that location will be obtained." He raised his eyes to the meeting, and produced a grim smile. "By extreme torture, and such mind-altering drugs as may be necessary. They always work. However, it may be possible to induce co-operation with a money offer. With the President's position known, a rescue team will attack and secure his release. The plan will use a

132

team of free-fall parachutists from the Rangers and Delta Force's anti terrorist operatives. They will use underwater boarding techniques from submarines and two supporting Chinook helicopters. The kidnappers will be killed in the shoot-out."

The Army General was rubbing his hands and smiling broadly. The plan would keep him happy, but it would not deceive Vic Cramer, who would see through the power play in seconds. He would know that such an attack was far from a perfect solution, and unlikely to succeed.

Grant continued his briefing confidently.

"If the meeting accepts this NSA plan, the detailed implementation may be left with my Agency. We will liaise with the CIA and specialist sections of Fort Bragg's men. They will provide the Rangers and Delta Force personnel."

Grant glanced around the table, and settled purposefully on the Vice President. He was smiling again. Grant finished his address with a contrived air of urgency.

"Gentlemen, time is pressing.... I would formally request, Mr Vice President, on behalf of my Agency, to have your specific approval to implement this operation."

Grant gathered his papers.

"And may God bless this nation.... and our endeavours."

Captain Grant sat down thoughtfully, making a mental assessment of those in the room who might support him. Vic Cramer was not going to be one of them! His hand was already raised as the meeting broke into half-a-dozen side conversations. The CIA Chief tapped on the table for attention. The lobbying was already under way.

"Gentlemen," Cramer said coldly. "I cannot believe our National Security Agency has a serious programme. A programme so obviously full of holes. I must ask you all, yet again, to consider the danger to the President, and our strict terms of reference. If we opt for such a risky strategy, the President's life will be lost."

He hesitated before slinging the next barb. He was in dangerous territory.

" I have to remind you of our Fort Bragg's previous failures. Its famous Delta Force's record is not unblemished, and as much as I admire their undoubted skills and courage, they are not a perfect solution, something we must have. You will recall that in a similar mission in Somalia, they failed in their attempt to capture the Warlord, Aidid Farrah in Mogadishu, and lost seventeen American soldiers and at least one thousand Somalis were killed. We dare not risk a repeat of that embarrassing operation, which President Clinton himself was forced to stop."

"I do not accept, nor do the CIA's advisers believe, Al Qaeda or the IRA would take the life of the President in the short term. He has greater publicity value as a hostage, as has been shown in the past. The risk to the President's life using the NSA's proposed plan is unacceptable. I understand the desire to appease the American voter, but you politicians live in a rose tinted world of diplomacy. You have little first hand experience of the Libyans who will blow a Pan Am 747 out of the sky, destroy a World Trade Centre with Islamic suicide pilots, or even the New York drug dealing gangs, or the real world of the Mafia, the murderers and their kind."

"I'm afraid we must appease this gang. Gentlemen, the money involved is nominal in Government terms. It can be allocated within the annual security budget, and must be paid. And providing we can establish a relationship with the terrorists, it is the only plan that could ensure the release of the President. We have no safe alternative, gentlemen."

"Once the dollars are handed over, and we have the President safe, we should then move on to direct action against Al Qaeda, and I would then have no hesitation in supporting the NSA plan at that point. I therefore ask you once again, Gentlemen, to consider carefully the most obvious and the simplest option that will secure the safe release of our President."

Gritting his teeth, Cramer sat down.

The Vice President looked down the table. Vic Cramer was a powerful man and his judgement was well respected. The expressions were confused. Only the Army General seemed unmoved. The big guns of the CIA and the NSA were at loggerheads as usual, and perhaps he could use the split to his advantage.

He tapped the table once. The room fell quiet again as he rustled his papers.

Cramer had put his case convincingly, but he was the Vice President and they all damn well knew that at the end of the day, he called the shots.

Cramer looked intently at the Vice President as he prepared to speak. They had locked horns too many times in the past. He didn't trust the man, any further than he could throw him!

The boyish looks and handsome features may have secured the women's vote, Cramer thought, but there was a scheming head on those broad shoulders, and there was no doubting the man's talent for politics. He also understood the Vice President's darker motives, and could feel the mood of the meeting slipping away from his appeasement plan.

The Vice President's eyes rested on the long uncurtained windows, through which he could see the extensive Rose Gardens planted in 1962 by Jackie Kennedy. Only in summer could the beauty of the hundred or so colourful varieties, chosen by the Kennedys, be appreciated. Now in winter, the tightly pruned stumps lay dormant under the pale wintry sun.

The Vice President routinely coughed and tapped the table.

"Gentlemen, it appears we are divided. I see merits in both the CIA and the NSA's positions, but before I come to my decision, does anyone have anything to add?"

The FBI Chief spoke for the first time. At fifty-one, he was a pragmatic, and a realist. He was also a sharp dresser.... The Brooks Brothers well-tailored suit was cut to perfection.

He knew the CIA's softly, softly plan would be ditched by the Vice President, but the kidnap gang had to be caught somehow. Personally, he couldn't see either plan saving the President's neck, but it wouldn't do to antagonise his successor. Best to simply go along with the majority, but the proper words had to be said for the tapes.

"Mr Vice President, I agree.... There is considerable merit in both Vic Cramer's and Captain Grant's proposals, but on the evidence and the advice my Bureau has, I believe paying over the ransom money is still no guarantee these terrorists will release the President. They will want to make fools of the American people. They would be in possession of our money and our President. We cannot trust these kinds of people. So in the final analysis, I have to add my support to Fort Bragg and the NSA. These modern day terrorists, particularly Al Qaeda and the IRA, are ruthless, and will not hesitate to imprison their hostages for years. They hold a pathological hatred of America and the successful capitalism of the West. If anyone needs convincing, take note of the Brit's Terry Waite problem, and the Hezbollah record in Beirut. These Islamics have only one goal, and I share Captain Grant's view, that all Al Qaeda, and for that matter their Irish hoodlums, must be exterminated like rats, or not one future American President will be safe. If we allow these kidnappers to collect millions, and get away with it, every crackpot radical group in the world will be on our doorstep."

Cramer was shaking his head, as the FBI man carried on in full flow as if addressing an election rally.

"Let's trap this Al Qaeda mob.... make an example of them. Let the world know that the USA is not a soft touch. We understand the risks to the President, but it is a situation that has been foreseen, and as we have heard, he would accept that risk. In such circumstances, I must support Captain Grant and the NSA rescue option, most whole heartedly."

The Vice President was pleased. Good. Two-votes-to-one. He now had the FBI and the NSA's support for a rescue plan, and for what it was worth, General Orville Mann and his Army. The CIA was democratically outvoted. The Presidential door was opening! He was ready to step into the President's shoes.

He gestured to the room in general.

"It seems, Gentlemen, that we are decided by majority. I have to propose then, that this meeting adopts the rescue plans of the NSA, which have the support of both the FBI and the Fort Bragg military." He glanced purposefully to the secretary as he scribbled rapidly. "But the differing views of the CIA will be noted," he said testily. "The majority is clear and will be minuted for the record. I know the people of America, and the nation's press will respect positive action and I propose to advise the Senate, that I am endorsing a rescue plan. It must be put into effect at the earliest possible moment." He turned to the defeated CIA boss.

"Mr Cramer, I have to thank you for your concise assessment, but the decision of this committee is against your plan of appeasement, a decision I know you will accept in good grace." He shifted his stance uncomfortably. "However, your Agency's co-operation with all aspects of the planned rescue is required, and you will receive a written memorandum in confirmation at the end of this meeting." The Vice President exhaled audibly.

"Will you now liaise with the other agencies, and detail the plans for the operation. Have these before me by 18.00 hrs. Arrange a further meeting of all those present today for 10.00 hrs tomorrow. Formally advise the services, CIA and FBI, and my office personally, of the location. See my secretary. It is important that all communications on this operation are subject to Grade One concealment, and security clearance."

The Vice President raised a well-manicured hand to confirm his decision, and placed an arched palm on the table. Now for some more rousing words for the press office.

"You understand, Gentlemen, that Osama Bin Laden, and his murderous IRA accomplices, who are responsible for this violent assault on our country's law and order, must be captured and punished, together with all those associated with this monstrous kidnap. Anything else is unthinkable. Meanwhile, I personally want details of every development connected with the kidnap. Gentlemen, the task is immense."

He pulled his lips together with satisfaction as the Tompion Clock struck a second hour.

"Be vigilant."

137

# 18

Alistair Craig lay on his bunk listening to the steady whine of the twin turbines as the *Champagne Princess* carved through the Atlantic swell at twenty knots. He looked around the cabin as he reviewed the happenings of the last twenty-four hours.

The cabin was furnished as comfortably as a luxury five star hotel room, and, apart from the constant rumble from the engines below, it was difficult to appreciate he was at sea. An oval window boasted Venetian blinds and a low central table stood between two leather armchairs. The carpet was dark blue. There was even a walnut desk and a telephone. The cabin walls were pale grey, with several nautical prints positioned on a precise diagonal, and the impression of a town house living room was heightened by a bowl of blue and white hyacinths on the central table. Only the bunk bed, with its short ladder and raised sides, made any concession to the sea.

Climbing down from the bunk, Craig pulled a maroon sweater from his bag. As he dressed, his thoughts ran over the long flight. He winced as he recalled the Hawk's headlong plunge into the turbulent storm. He'd been more than lucky to come out of that in one piece. But he'd succeeded. The President had been brought safely to the ship, so his part was over. If O'Rourke left him to his own devices, he could think through his predicament. He wondered what the President's state of health would be after the heavy dose of drugs.

He'd been sedated continuously for twelve hours, and he hoped that Christine would know what to do. If she had been trained as a nurse, the President was in good hands. As his thoughts returned to her, there was a short tap-tap at the cabin door. It was her.

"Hallo Alistair, please can I come in?" she asked sheepishly.

She was wearing a chunky woollen fisherman's Jersey that was too large for her trim figure. Her fair hair was tied back under a tea cosy hat. She stood looking at him framed in the cabin doorway. Craig could see she had been crying and, before he could say anything, she came closer. She had a sad, hunted look, which spoiled her beauty.

For a moment she stood before him, seemingly wanting to make up her mind about what to say. Craig offered his hand. She clasped it quickly. "Oh Alistair," she burst out. "Alistair, please help."

He faced her, holding her hands for comfort. Within a second she was clinging to him, crying.

Now what? Craig wondered.

"Oh Alistair, what am I going to do?" she sobbed softly. "I never had any idea this was going to happen. I feel absolutely terrible for what I've done. Please tell me it's all a bad dream. I could never hurt anyone, and Mr O'Rourke is expecting me to keep drugging the President. He thinks I already have, but I can't Alistair, I simply can't."

Craig stared at her in surprise, trying to take in the dramatic change. She continued to sob between words.

"It's become a nightmare.... when I first saw you at the hotel, I knew you were the helicopter pilot they'd hired to do the flying. Brandt told me I must not say anything about working for them and coming to the ship. When you got friendly, Brandt asked me...." She hesitated and avoided Craig's eyes, "Brandt asked me to tell him everything you said. To spy on you for him. I was getting dragged further and further into it all. When I took the job, Mr O'Rourke said an important man wanted to leave America quickly, and that you would be flying him. He was ill, and they needed me to nurse him until he was well enough to travel. That was what I was told."

She buried her head into Craig's shoulder as the words poured from her, now a jumbled torrent. "But when I got to the ship, they told me the truth. At first I didn't believe them. No one could kidnap the

American President, it just couldn't happen, but when I actually saw you land in the helicopter, I realised how wrong I was."

There was bitterness in her voice.

"Alistair, I don't want their filthy money. I just know we are all in terrible trouble. Please tell me what to do. You won't tell Mr O'Rourke about me?" she pleaded.

She wrung her fingers together and looked tearfully into Craig's eyes.

"I can't go on with this anymore Alistair, I just can't. Please believe me."

He pulled her closer. He was certain of one thing. His earlier doubts about her were right. She was a reluctant member of O'Rourke's team, which at least meant there were now two of them against him. Something he could use to his advantage. Christine was shaking as she continued to cry. What was he to do about her?

He weighed the situation as he squeezed her reassuringly, and came to a quick decision. He would have to throw in his lot with her here and now. He looked down at her more like a brother.

"Now listen to me Christine," he said slowly. "I don't want any part of this terrible business any more than you do. O'Rourke tricked me too. But now there are two of us, we're in a better position to help the President. Can you let him know he has two friends on board and I am trying to help?" He continued holding her until the crying spell stopped.

She managed a thin smile for him.

"Oh thank heaven," she said with relief. "I just *knew* you'd be able to help. I knew you couldn't be one of them. I'll tell the President as soon as I can, but he hasn't fully regained consciousness yet. His pulse rate is low, but quite steady. He'll be OK after some rest and the drug has worn off, but I'll have to get back to his cabin in a minute."

The tension in her voice eased as she composed herself. "Alistair, you can't believe how relieved I feel. Just talking to you has made me feel better."

Craig wiped her cheek dry with the back of his finger. "Just be careful, Christine. We must not let O'Rourke see us talking together for too long."

"I understand, Alistair." Her mood lightened and became chatty. "I gather you got caught in a bad storm. Leroy Brandt is still talking about you saving them, and your handling of the helicopter. Says you were marvellous." She looked admiringly at Craig. "Have you been a pilot for a long time?"

"Well yes, I used to fly in the Royal Air Force, but only got this job recently. Thought I would make some easy money, but like you, I had no idea what I was letting myself in for."

He decided not to tell her about his earlier marriage and his plan for getting enough money to buy back his cottage.

"Christine, somehow we have got to help the President."

Craig moved over to the window. The ship was moving quickly. He lowered his voice. It wouldn't do to be overheard.

He turned back to her. "So how did you become involved with the O'Rourke man, Christine?"

She fiddled with a stray lock of hair and looked at Craig intently. He wiped her damp cheek again. The warm gesture seemed to reassure her. She began talking intimately.

"When I was in England, I worked as a receptionist at the Seven Hills Hotel near Weybridge, in Surrey. Do you know it, Alistair?"

"Yes I do, actually. There's a helicopter landing-pad in the hotel grounds. I flew some businessmen there for a meeting." The mention of a familiar name made Craig homesick to be back in England. Would he ever see those places again?

"I was getting over a bad relationship, and the job came at a time when I needed a change. It sounded glamorous at the time. A trip to America. A new country. Cruising on Mr O'Rourke's yacht. Meeting new people. I had to go for it," she added with a tense expression. "So here I am."

Craig listened attentively. "Please go on, Christine."

"Well, of course, now I know what's going on, I just want to get away. I never dreamed for a second that Mr O'Rourke was planning something like this. How could anyone get away with kidnapping an American President? But it all seems to have been too easy. O'Rourke is certain the ransom will be paid, and now that he has him prisoner on the ship, he's probably right."

She paused, blinking rapidly, as if unable to believe what she was about to say.

"Then I found out that Al Qaeda is behind it all and O'Rourke is an IRA man."

"*What* did you say, Christine?" Craig interrupted incredulously. He felt a chill as she said the dreaded words. He shuddered at the startling news. *"Al Qaeda and the IRA?* Are you sure? My God it can't be possible! How do you know this?"

"It's true all right," she said emphatically. "I've been listening to Mr O'Rourke talking to Brandt and his business colleagues. The Al Qaeda people planned the kidnap. They're using the IRA to do the work. O'Rourke is one of them. It's all a scheme to get money and revenge for what America has done to the Arabs."

She looked earnestly at Craig as she continued quickly.

"And Sheikh Makhtoum is not a Sheikh. His proper name is Khalid Mohammed. He's an Al Qaeda assassin from something called the Islamic Observation Centre. He was some sort of project engineer, who held a Ministry post in Qatar as a cover for his terrorist activities. Now he's been specially brought in to oversee everything, and is the one who will collect the money. He's very high up in the Al Qaeda gang, Alistair, and I'm sure both Ahmed and Ramzi are Al Qaeda men too. They talk to each other in Arabic all the time."

For the second time in twenty-four hours, Craig was stunned. From this lovely girl's mouth had come those dreadful words. The murderous Al Qaeda no less, the first international terrorists of the 21st century.... now linked up with the equally murderous Irish Republican Army.

Well, ... well! Craig reasoned. He'd read about the Khalid Mohammed man, who was an absolute Al Qaeda fanatic, and not a man to be crossed, he felt sure. But, he knew nothing of the other two. So that's what it's all about! Suddenly things were falling into place. He was right, there could be no simple reason why one man needed such a vast sum of money. It had to be some kind of international organisation. But the monstrous Al Qaeda, headed by Osama Bin Laden, a Saudi with a university education and access to family money. The new player, who ignominiously entered the world stage in September 2001, when his little known terrorist organisation attacked America by slamming two passenger packed Boeings into the twin towers of the World Trade Centre, taking three thousand New Yorkers to their death.

Another hi-jacked airliner was used as a Kamikaze bomber, and deliberately crashed into the Pentagon, and then a fourth was lost over the innocent fields of Shanksville, killing a further forty-three souls.

Overnight Osama Bin Laden became the world's most wanted terrorist, and as he continued to bomb soft targets, which associated themselves with Western interests, a $25 million bounty was posted for his capture. Dead-or-alive. Middle Eastern British and American Embassies were a favourite target for his suicide fanatics. Then, a hundred holiday makers were slaughtered in a Bali nightclub, followed by the terror of a 1000 lb bomb at a Madrid railway station, where another two hundred Spaniards perished. The bombings would just go on and on. Suicide bombers, driven on in the belief that their act of martyrdom for the Faith would lead them to a heaven, where seventy-two virgins awaited their pleasure. Bin Laden was forced into hiding to a 'safe house' in Karachi, but continued to release videos spitting out hatred for America and their obedient poodles in Britain. He needed world-wide publicity, and so welcomed joining up with the IRA man who shared his hatred for the enemy, and could progress his aims. What a shrewd move to recruit the IRA for their dirty work.

But what of the hated IRA? The same men of terrorism and death, who operated underground in the Republic of Ireland. The madmen who once tried to wipe out the entire British Government by hurling a 100 lb mortar bomb at 10 Downing Street. The murderers, who killed a dozen defenceless young musicians at a sleepy seaside town, because they were a 'soft' target, and played in a military brass band.

But hadn't the British Prime Minister assured the country that the IRA was giving up their claims to Northern Ireland? The much-trumpeted Peace Treaty? The leading political figures appeared nightly on TV to support the process, while, all the time, the original hard-core IRA Lieutenants waited for the Good Friday agreement to come tumbling down. They had been let down by the old guard. The new men, the Real IRA, was born. The new merchants of death. The British weren't going to use a few fine words to destroy a political agenda to re-unite Ireland that had been founded in the Irish Republic, more than a hundred years ago.

And now the Real IRA was summoned to join Osama Bin Laden and his terrorists. What a combination! Two organisations whose interests were so uncomfortably close. Bin Laden wanted America bashed again, and forced to withdraw the occupying troops from the Middle East as surely as the remaining IRA hardliners wanted the British kicked out of Northern Ireland. What if they both succeeded? What a coup! The imperialist Yanks, given another lesson for meddling in the domestics of Middle East policy, the loss of their precious Iraqi oil and their war-mongering President. And the Brits would finally give up their claim to Ireland at the toe of O'Rourke's boot!

Craig marvelled at the project. It fitted in with his earlier thoughts, but he could never have envisaged his own personal involvement. The whole nightmare was outside his small world. He turned to Christine.

"Look Christine, I've got to think this thing through. Get back to the President's cabin now, and say absolutely nothing to O'Rourke. I'll meet you later when we can." he said comfortingly.

Christine smiled at Craig, and with an affectionate squeeze of his hand, she left his cabin.

Craig closed the door, his thoughts in turmoil.

He returned to the window to consider Christine's dramatic revelation. The constantly changing patterns of the sea caught his attention as the ship cut through the waves, now thrusting him along to a new danger. The murderous Real IRA, he thought again. The new force born of the Good Friday agreement, and O'Rourke was one of them! Now working alongside Osama Bin Laden. Truly a pair of king sized snakes in the grass. O'Rourke, a man Craig had regarded as just another well-heeled Air Taxi passenger. A wealthy Irishman, who could afford racehorses and helicopters.

And what of the infamous Osama Bin Laden, the head of the world's most hated terrorist organisation. A typically bearded Arab, who was portrayed by the media as a madman, and whose Christ-like features were routinely shown on TV and in the papers.

And Craig had been plunged well and truly in the middle. What chance now of his own survival! What sort of men were these guys, who were hell bent on taking on the world? What the hell drove them? How well Bin Laden had chosen the henchman for his latest attack on the West. Ryan O'Rourke, the fervent officer of an illegal army.

From what appeared in the papers, Craig knew all about Bin Laden, the Khalid Mohammed man and his Al Qaeda terrorists, but O'Rourke was very much a new kid on the block. He must be an absolute fanatic to take up with the Arab terrorists. Still fighting an underground war against the British. Most of his IRA officers had left and offered to give up their weapons. A peaceful settlement of the Irish problem was temptingly in sight.

But Craig could not have known of O'Rourke's complicated background and the deeply rooted hatred he possessed for the British. A hate instilled in him since childhood, by a father crippled in the Irish Civil War by the infamous Black and Tans. The brutal men of violence taken from British prisons, and hastily formed into an army whose purpose was to occupy Ireland and quell the civil riots using the cosh.

Each day, as he grew older, the young man's hatred for the occupying British soldiers intensified, while his crippled father struggled with life from a wheelchair. Then, as the post-war economic depression of the 1960's began to bite, there was no food. The young Ryan O'Rourke toiled for sixteen hours a day in the fields of Augnasheelin, to earn enough to pay the rent, while his sick mother was obliged to wash floors to keep starvation from the door. Just when the depression was lifting, his father died.

O'Rourke was then sixteen, and with his father's death, he made a vow of revenge. The Britishers were established in the North of Ireland.... they thought it was part of England! They disposed of the Stormont Government, and replaced it with rule from Westminster. They had divided his country and put up a border. But one day, he vowed, he would boot them out, the British bastards, who had callously killed his father, would be booted out of his homeland. Forever.

He studied hard and won a place at Dublin University, where he read political and social history. He became the loudest in debate. His studies of the Irish problem served only to strengthen his passionate nationalistic feelings, and as he traced back the long history of the Civil Wars, and the trouble brought to Ireland by the cursed British Protestants, he became more outspoken.

He quickly made his unwelcome mark in university life, and it was not long before his radical views came to the ears of senior officers of Sinn Fein, the political wing of the Irish Republican Army. Twice he was called before the Dean and asked to account for his anti-British outbursts, and his tutors soon marked him down as a potentially dangerous young man who should be avoided.

After one particularly fanatical speech, Sinn Fein approached him, and being wholly in sympathy with the IRA's aims, he was recruited as a junior officer, and following a series of successful reprisal operations in Belfast, he quickly progressed to become the commander of the South Armagh Brigade.

He was made responsible for 'Special Projects' and the planning of many harassment raids across the border, and at the request of Colonel Gadaffi, he personally carried out the murder of an American diplomat in London as a 'reprisal' for the American air raids on Tripoli. This was followed by a series of bombings, culminating in the horrific murder of Lord Mountbatten, as the quiet world statesman innocently left Mullaghmore for a day's fishing.

With each successful operation, O'Rourke's stature within the IRA grew. He was appointed to the Army Council, and with the assistance of a Government Minister, was able to import M-60 firearms, Semtex-H, and the micro bomb switches needed to promote the Irish cause.

As each year passed, the hatred within him festered, while, to the outside world he appeared to be an educated, and rather shrewd businessman who made money from horse racing.

The struggle between Catholic and Protestant dragged on into the nineties, and it became apparent that the British Government was totally committed to a policy of troop occupation in Northern Ireland. The political differences between North and South were fought on the streets of Belfast, and at selected civilian targets in the United Kingdom. Each week brought accounts of shootings, bombings and murder. Protestants in the North were being gunned down in their homes, or blown to pieces in their motorcars.... or captured and even tortured. The shooting at the kneecaps and ankles was a particularly barbaric trademark practiced by the IRA killers. The Catholics would first kill or maim a Protestant who associated himself in some way with the British presence, and immediately the

UFF, an opposing faction from the Protestants, would retaliate with the murder of a Catholic. Tit for Tat, the murders continued with no hope of a settlement.

The politicians huffed and puffed ineffectively, while the Dublin High Courts routinely mocked the British, by refusing the extradition from the Irish Republic of known terrorist suspects. The warrant for Brendan Burns was defective, Owen Carron's offences were judged political, Patrick McVeigh was an identification mix up, and Father Patrick Ryan simply would not receive a fair trial in England.

Known IRA members, former MPs, Catholic Priests and run-of-the-mill villains were regularly freed by the Irish Supreme Court, while the politicians wrung their hands, spouted fine words around the conference table and dreamed up short lived 'peace agendas.' The Anglo-Irish wrangling rumbled on. Back in Ireland, a new effort was made to draw a peace line. First Gerry Adams announced the ceasefire, which from day one he steadfastly refused to confirm as 'permanent'. The politicians whooped and the Nobel Peace prizes were bandied around. The American President shook hands with the terrorists, while all along the grassroots IRA lieutenants kept their low profile and waited for the peace agreement to break down.

When a 1000 lb bomb intended for the English Grand National was intercepted, the media talked of a split in Sinn Fein policy. It became apparent to O'Rourke that the previous long-term wrangling and occasional guerrilla tactics would never succeed. Nothing short of an outright terrorist war against the British would solve the problem. A dirty war that concentrated on Britain's 'soft' targets. The working people in the streets who'd elected the politicians. A concentrated effort of daily shootings, bombings and whenever possible, the killing of any of their leaders or their celebrities, even their cursed protestant churchmen. Such a campaign of terror would eventually become unacceptable to the people. They would have to give in and force Westminster to withdraw the troops he loathed so much.

There had to be a final effort and so, when he was approached by Sheikh Makhtoum, and asked to work with the Al Qaeda network, he had the perfect answer. A true 'double whammy.' The Brits given a bloody nose, and yet another American President bumped off! What a spectacular world coup!

So O'Rourke was given the task of hatching an anti-American operation, and now that the Americans had stopped funding Noraid, they were as bad as the British. As a man with long experience of terrorist operations, he knew about security systems and explosives. Bin Laden promised him the money, and millions of it. Money to buy explosives for the Semtex bomb factories, and the necessary guns. Perhaps the SAM missiles to take out the odd airliner as it departed from Heathrow.... or a few rocket grenades lobbed into their government buildings. The powerful Czech RPG-7 could be bought for five thousand pounds from disinterested Libyan arms salesmen, who asked no questions. But hundreds were needed.

So he would do Bin Laden's bidding to get the money.... take on the Americans and, by joining forces with Al Qaeda, he would have access to the sort of men he needed for his own plans. Men who would give their lives for the cause. Al Qaeda's first quarrel was with America. Little old Britain was for them a minor prize. But O'Rourke wanted the minor prize. The alliance was a natural one for two evil men.

The contacts were made. Ryan O'Rourke, the tall well-dressed gentleman who respectfully raced thoroughbred horses, the perfect cover provided, for the regular comings and goings from England to Ireland, where only the best racehorses are bred and trained, now in cahoots with the infamous Osama Bin Laden.

And Al Qaeda's plan? The taking of an American President, and a ransom demand for one hundred million dollars.

Not some lunatic brainwave, but the culmination of mutual hatred and a desire for revenge. And if the President was dead? Then so be it. O'Rourke's father had died in the cause and nobody cared. Only the money was important, and the American people would surely pay.... one hundred million dollars. Nothing, really.... they could afford it. Less than fifty cents from the pocket of every American.

O'Rourke even considered how the heightened security throughout America could be used to his advantage. The incumbent was having a bad time, as American voters started to appreciate how they had been misled into a war with Iraq. He'd scraped through the election, with the help of some dodgy voting from Florida. He'd be out in the country states, visiting the Government Offices, setting out the administration's new policies, albeit with an army of security. That would be the time to act.

O'Rourke also knew of the disenchanted Government Agents whose loyalties could be changed with the right amount of Al Qaeda dollars. Men on the inside, who were necessary to perfect his plans.

O'Rourke had studied. He had lived with this vision of a united Ireland for half his life. He understood security. Understood the infinite lines of protection that surrounded a President. Agents who had the government authority to kill at will. Government Agents from the National Security Agency, the FBI, the CIA and the lesser known 'special' service who were never more than yards from their charge on a twenty-four basis. Men who pledged to forfeit their lives if necessary. But sometimes, fallible men, greedy men, who could be persuaded, by the right amount of money, to change sides.

Craig pressed his fingers to his temple to help him think.

Who was going to stop O'Rourke and his Al Qaeda backers? Who, in the whole world had any kind of chance of upsetting this careful plan?

The thought frightened him.

Only himself.... Alistair Craig, the only person who was in a position to do anything. He had been well and truly pitch-forked into the hot seat, and for a thousand reasons he had to stop these villains.

Craig thought back to Christine. A faint flicker of hope. The sudden way she had poured out her feelings. Now he had an ally on board, an ally in the enemy's camp.

The thought stayed with him, but how to take advantage of that was another matter!

# 19

A salty spray peppered Craig's cheeks as the *Champagne Princess* reeled off the miles to Florida. He looked down over the ship's side, where a plume of white foam gracefully arced out from the bows as the sleek hull cut through the water. Craig made his way purposefully along the upper gang-walk to O'Rourke's cabin.

With the breeze in his hair, Craig paused to take a deep breath, and for a few seconds, with the fresh tang of the sea in his nostrils, he tried to forget his troubles.

He reached O'Rourke's cabin and found the door already open. He knocked once, and stepped inside. O'Rourke was poring over a GPS plotting table. He had a long straight edge in his left hand, and was stepping out distances with dividers on a chart. He appeared to be doing some navigational calculations.

Craig shuffled his feet. O'Rourke looked up.

"Ah, Alistair, my dear boy," O'Rourke said with a cordial smile.

Craig reflected how well the friendly Irish brogue concealed the man's true nature. He studied him more closely, and found it difficult to believe the violent character that must lay concealed beneath the smooth exterior. He thought back to his first meeting at Battersea Heliport. If he thought this man was dangerous before, what now? He must be a hundred times more careful! O'Rourke left the plotting table, and sat on a comfortable lounge chair under a long window. He motioned to Craig.

"Make yourself at home, dear boy. I take it you are rested after your long flight? Can you handle a drink?"

"Something soft will suit me fine at this time of the day," Craig answered. "My standard orange juice if you've got it."

He tried to keep his voice casual, but winced at the proximity to a terrorist such as O'Rourke, and the enormity of what he was doing. O'Rourke began fussing at the drinks cabinet.

Craig sat on a low stool taking in the startling colour scheme. Maroon and gold. Very regal, but how inappropriate! He pictured the wealthy buyer pompously passing instructions to the shipbuilder:

*"And I want the State Room to have a Regency theme, you know, lots of maroon and gold with vertical stripes. Anything you can do to give it a Presidential air."*

And the shipbuilder had scornfully obliged his tasteless paymaster in full!

One wall was a vulgar combination of broad maroon and grey bands each capped with a gold ribbon, while the adjacent wall was heavily mirrored, exaggerating the overpowering effect of the stripes. A tall chest boasted gold handles, and even the deep pile carpet was maroon with more gold motifs. A very much out-of-place crystal chandelier hung apologetically from the ceiling, casting a spectrum of rainbow colours across the floor. The air was chilled by the fierce air conditioning and smelt of Jasmine.

Craig shrugged his thoughts aside. A crude and distasteful cabin, he concluded, and one in which it would be difficult to relax. Typical of a rich owner. Too much money and too little taste.

He turned to face his unwelcome paymaster. O'Rourke handed him a glass.

"You did well dear boy, but I knew it could be done. Brandt told me about you running into a storm, but says you coped with that little problem rather well, which of course reflects on me. I know a good pilot when I see one."

Craig was cautious.

"I'm sure you also know that weather is always the unpredictable factor in flying. Luck was with us last night. Things could have turned out differently. But I got one hell of a shock when I realised who you had got in the Cadillac. I was concerned in case Brandt had given the President an overdose of the drug, but I spoke to Christine this morning, and I gather he is recovering."

Craig thought he should continue to reassure O'Rourke.

"Still, as you say, I like money the same as anyone, and one million dollars is going to keep me in the lap of luxury for a very long time. I was upset last night after I landed, and I apologise for the things I said, but you can count on me Mr O'Rourke." Craig forced a smile.

"Well that's fine, dear boy, I'm glad you see it my way," O'Rourke answered levelly, "You see, once our plan is completed, we'll all be a lot richer, no-one gets hurt, except perhaps the pride of the American people, and we go our separate ways to live a life of great comfort. Do you think you were spotted at any time?" He concluded amiably.

"Most unlikely," Craig replied. "The route over the lakes kept the helicopter clear of the populated areas, except on the final stage, when we followed the river to the coast. But it was dark, and small aircraft would not be that uncommon in the Vermont region. I kept the helicopter low under their radar. There'd be no reason for anyone to take particular notice of the helicopter, and we did have the navigation lights off."

"Good, that's the way I planned the flight, dear boy. Any difficulty with the refuelling?"

"No, just like clockwork… Apart from the cold. You seem to have thought of everything."

O'Rourke moved back to the cabinet and poured a drink for himself. He said over his shoulder.

"Brandt will have told you about the letter demanding the money. Think of it, dear boy, sacking the coffers of America to the tune of a hundred million dollars. I'll go down as the most successful criminal in history."

He turned around to face Craig.

Craig saw the faintly glazed expression come into O'Rourke's eyes. Were his thoughts back in Ireland and his misguided aims? And even if his madcap scheme worked, would the Bin Laden men let him stay alive? Al Qaeda had arranged for him to do their dirty work and when all was done, he wouldn't be needed. Perhaps that's why the Arab Makhtoum would be joining the ship. To bump off O'Rourke!

That would be more Al Qaeda's style. Craig suspected a real double cross coming up.

"We collect the money on the tenth." O'Rourke went on. "That leaves three days to enjoy the sea and some sunshine. The satellite weather forecast is good, so you can relax for a while, dear boy. You needn't have too much to do with the crew. Just Ramzi Yousef, the engineer and our galley man Ahmed Massoud. He helps Ramzi run the ship. Both good men."

"How many on board, then?" Craig asked casually, but needing to know the answer.

"*Champagne Princess* is a fully automated ship, dear boy, latest computer-controlled turbines and autopilot, runs herself, so a crew of four is more than enough. Now you and Brandt have joined us, not to mention our famous guest, we're a party of seven. Lucky seven, I'd say. Quite cosy, don't you think, dear boy?" O'Rourke chuckled fatly.

Craig assumed the tone of O'Rourke's bonhomie.

"I have always fancied a luxury cruise," he said trying to keep nonchalance in his voice, "and picking up a fortune in dollars gives it an added relish."

"You may still have some flying to do, Alistair. I'm keeping the helicopter on standby in case it's needed. The Sheikh is now in Florida, and will be picking up the money in my launch, but the helicopter could be needed. I'll let you know about that later. Another drink, dear boy? Nothing too exotic just yet, we'll leave the champagne until we have the money safely in the bank, don't you think?"

Craig put his glass down. "No thanks Mr O'Rourke, I fancy a walk around the ship if I may," he said, summoning up a smile. "Stretch the legs…. Ciao …"

Craig raised a hand in farewell as O'Rourke motioned him to the cabin door.

Later, Christine came to O'Rourke's cabin to tell him that she had given the President the next dose of Valium. She gave O'Rourke a complicated explanation of the danger of keeping the President under sedation for a long period. O'Rourke questioned her patiently and then picked up the intercom to talk to Brandt in the engine room.

153

As the sun lowered in the afternoon sky, Craig leaned against the bow rails taking in the stiff breeze. The conversation with O'Rourke had been an effort, but he was satisfied that he'd given him no cause for suspicion. He wondered if he could dream up some pretext to visit the President?

Brandt introduced him briefly to the two crewmen.

Ramzi and Ahmed were both from Saudi Arabia, it seemed. Their English was limited, and they preferred to keep themselves below decks. Craig did not underestimate either man. There was a sly understanding between them. Ahmed was alert and sharp eyed, and Craig could easily imagine either of the two men dressed more formally in the role of suited businessmen or bankers. However, the two seemed content to take orders from Brandt, without question.

Craig then spent half an hour casually inspecting the ship. He stopped at the radio room to try the door, but it was solidly locked. Peering through the porthole, he could see the VHF transmitters, and a radio compass direction finder. There was also a Global Positioning System, a Loran receiver and Decca radar. No doubt the scanner tube was on the bridge. The shelves contained the usual safety equipment, lifejackets, lights and rescue gear.

He wandered forward to the Bridge, where Brandt had returned to the helm. The large diameter steering wheel twitched periodically as the ship's autopilot fed in heading corrections. The instrument panel contained two rows of switches controlling the various lights, cabin heating, bilge pumps and the radio services. The ship's compass and radar screen were housed in a hooded pedestal bowl, to the right of the wheel. The dial of the speed indicator registered a steady twenty knots and Craig noted that the heading was 175 degrees.

Brandt was wearing a roll neck sweater and a sailor's cap, which hid his greasy hair. He turned his good eye towards Craig.

"How yo doin' Craig." he said amiably. "Glad ta hav'yo wit us. Still owe yo a thanks fer last night. Guess yo glad de flyin's done, mah frend.'

"Yes, I wouldn't want to tackle that flight again, Brandt, and it's good to be aboard a luxury ship like this. If you care to show me the controls, I can take turns with the steering."

Brandt shrugged.

154

"Thanks Craig, but today me han' Yousef are sharin' de watches fer a while, han' de steerin's completely automated. May ask yo ta give us a hand tomorrow, if yo like."

"I'll be happy to help whenever," Craig said looking out at the sky. "Thank heavens its getting warmer too. Never experienced anything like that cold last night."

"Don't suit me neither." Brandt said in a chatty tone, without his usual quota of goddam this and goddam that, Craig noticed.

"Ah just love de sun yo know, lots of surf han' sand fer me. Ship's makin' good time han' we'll reach de Carolina coast by tomorrow. Florida de day after."

As Brandt talked, Craig casually noted the layout of the various controls…. the engine start-up…. power settings. It would help to know as much about the ship as possible.

"What's her range?" Craig enquired, with professional interest. He was considering the possibility that the *Champagne Princess* might need to call at some port to re-fuel.

"Gas tank's are full, enough ta make hit ta Florida han' stooge around fer a day or so." Brandt made a fingering gesture. "Hit's all laid on, han' dat dough's shoh beginnin' ta feel good."

"I'll drink to that," Craig said. "Mind if I go back to the aft deck and take in some air? See you later, and let me know when you need help at the wheel."

The sun was sinking into the sea behind the ship as Craig slid the wheelhouse door shut and made for the aft deck.

The helicopter sat forlornly with the corners of the covering tarpaulin flapping gently in the breeze. Craig picked up an aluminium-framed chair and propped it against the handrail. The evening was just warm enough to sit on deck. The twilight night-sky was clear, and the first of the evening stars twinkled as Craig moodily studied the changing patterns of the sea. A steady twenty-knot breeze whipped over the deck, and Craig moved his chair closer to the sheltering wall. He looked intently at the helicopter. The Hawk had served him well, and if O'Rourke was thinking of using the helicopter for the ransom pick up, it must be ready to fly again. Could he use it again to help them escape?

Something like two or three minutes was the minimum needed to climb into the cockpit, get the engine started and the rotors running

155

at flying speed. That was probably two and a half minutes too long to prevent O'Rourke or Brandt stopping him. In any case, the crew had tied the rotors with the tarpaulin, and with the blades secured, the engine couldn't even be started! No doubt O'Rourke had worked that one out already.

Craig looked gloomily over the stern rail, and down to where the waves bubbled and boiled under the attack of the powerful twin screws. The ship's frothy wake stretched out to the darkening horizon, as the *Champagne Princess* hurried smoothly through the Atlantic swell.

Craig frowned as he wrestled with the problem. If he couldn't find a way out of this predicament soon, he might as well throw himself down there right now!

# 20

Craig directed his thoughts to the probable events of the next few days, going through the various possibilities and what he could do to upset O'Rourke's plan. But as he examined and rejected each idea in turn, he came more surely to the conclusion that O'Rourke had perfected his operation. He seemed to have thought of everything. A chess Grand Master, who had devised a sequence of moves, which led inexorably to the winning checkmate position. The tactics were simple, but foolproof. The *Champagne Princess* was a prison, a luxury moving prison, without bars.

Craig was free, yet free to do nothing. His conclusions depressed him. He heard footsteps, and looked up to the boat deck to see Christine. She paused at the top step.

"Hi there." Craig offered his hand to help her down. "Make yourself at home, but its a bit draughty here."

He reached for a second deck chair, which he arranged alongside his.

"I'm well wrapped up and quite warm enough," she chirruped, flapping the long sleeves. "Does it suit me?"

"You look just fine," Craig said sincerely. He stood up and looked along both gang walks. None of the others were on deck.

Craig lowered his voice. "How is the President?"

"He's regained consciousness, but is feeling sick," she replied. "We managed to talk, and I told him about you. That you are not one of the gang. I also told him about Sheikh Makhtoum and the IRA, and who the Sheikh really is. It seemed to unsettle him. He wants to talk to you, but I've said it will probably be impossible. He asked me about the ship and where we are." She looked gloomily at Craig. "Somewhere off the east coast of America, was all I could say."

"The big thing is to keep O'Rourke fooled," Craig said. "If he thinks the President is under sedation and locked in his cabin, he may not be so careful. May give us a chance."

"So far Mr O'Rourke has left the President entirely to me. I've said he needs to be visited regularly to take his temperature, pulse and so on. Brandt has looked into the cabin a few times. One thing though, the President needs some food. Leave that to me."

"He wants to know if we can get a message to anyone, the Police or any of the Government Agencies. He gave me a codeword we could use."

Craig frowned with impatience.

"I've been thinking about that particular problem all day. Perhaps he can tell us how we go about it."

Christine fell silent for a moment looking puzzled, as though she'd lost her place in a book.

Craig found himself staring at her. She had a cover-girl beauty that reminded him of Julia Roberts from the 'Pretty Woman' film. She was pretty all right, enough to have been a model. The unflattering duffle coat couldn't hide her fine figure and the intriguing swell of her breasts.

The ash blonde hair fell heavily to her shoulders, unfashionably long. She wore very little make-up around the eyes, which were the deepest blue Craig had ever seen, and in happier times would probably sparkle mischievously. Her complexion was clear, with the hint of a dimple at the corner of a lovely wide mouth. She was wearing a light red lipstick, which discreetly matched the red of her long nails. Yes, a fine looking girl Craig thought, and one he wasn't going to forget easily.

"How old are you, Christine?" Craig asked suddenly.

She blushed with surprise.

"You're not supposed to ask a lady that question," she scolded mockingly. "How old do I look?"

"Twenty four or twenty five?" Craig volunteered.

"Actually, I'm twenty six."

"Tell me about yourself," Craig asked candidly.

"Well, I was brought up in Somerset, a charming old village called Crowcumbe, just outside Taunton, the County town."

Craig knew a little about the area from one of his old RAF flying postings at the nearby Westonzoyland Airfield. He had converted to Meteor Jets there in the early days of his aircrew training. He recalled the quaint village names…. Middlezoy, Stogursey and Stogumber.

"Please tell me about it, Christine. I've always thought that the West Country was the nicest part of England."

She shook her head as she held Craig's eyes. "There's not much to tell, Alistair. I was the only child. Mum and Dad ran the local pub, the Carew Arms in Crowcumbe. It was a country pub with ship's beams, stone flagging and a skittle alley that still uses wooden bowls and nine-pins. My parents worked hard and wanted a good life for me, but I found village life very restricting. I remember it was quite an occasion when we got dressed up to visit relatives in Bristol, not thirty miles away. For me life consisted of getting up, breakfast, village school, then evenings with friends and church on Sundays. Not very exciting, I'm afraid."

Craig studied her with new interest as she settled into her story.

"My only passion was horses, and when I was fifteen, Dad bought me a beautiful Irish Cob Hunter…. big feet and a huge head, but I loved her. I called her 'Folly.' She was an honest ride, and I spent hours and hours hacking over the Quantock Hills. Even followed the local staghounds a few times. We used to meet at Crowcumbe Court with the Bassett hounds. All the excitement of the chase…. really terrific."

"Then, at eighteen, I fell in love." She looked away shyly as she said the words. "At least I thought so at the time. He was a local boy, stationed at the Army camp at Norton Fitzwarren and much older than me. I gave up horses and just lived for him, and in no time we were lovers. For me, my first experience. You know, long summer walks in the country, finding some disused barn. Then a friend's flat,

159

or the back of his old car. I didn't see it at the time, but for him it was just a local affair, but I was in love and didn't care."

She looked thoughtful.

"Then one day, he told me he was being posted to a new camp up North, and he would write. He did. Just once. To say goodbye. That tore my heart out, and it took me a year to get over him. I decided to forget men for a while, and concentrate on improving myself at work. I trained as a nurse and worked hard, long hard night shifts, with plenty of studying. Eventually I passed my exams, and after five years, became an SRN. That's a State Registered Nurse, you know. A good qualification, which got me several jobs in some of the big hospitals." She stopped in mid- flow, putting her hands to her cheeks, thinking back.

"Please don't stop Christine," Craig said warmly, "I want to know much more about you."

She looked up and found Craig's eyes on her. She made a helpless gesture.

"Well, when I was twenty-four, it happened again…. This time I was miles from home in the Freedom Fields Hospital in Plymouth. I was working well, and was respected by the staff and happy. He was a newly qualified doctor, just arrived from London, obviously intelligent and a real gentleman. Lots of fun, and from the first day he treated me like a queen. In no time at all he was saying he loved me and we talked of marriage. I couldn't believe it, but I wanted it to happen."

She paused and smiled at Craig sweetly, apologetically. She looked out of the cabin window, then back at him.

"Don't be embarrassed Christine, please go on," Craig encouraged.

She glanced down to her lap, the memories flooding back.

"Well, the sex started immediately, and I would go round to his flat. Tidy up and buy flowers to give it a homely touch. That flat was our home and for me, a promise of what was to come. I would cook in the evenings, make myself look nice, and wait for him to come off duty."

"One evening as I waited, playing some records, I noticed a handwritten envelope addressed to him…. A lady's writing. It was post-marked London and was from his wife."

160

"That was enough. I cried and cried and just wanted to get back to my quiet village in Somerset. I left the hospital and managed to get selected for a training course in hotel reception work with the Trust House Forte Company. I did well, the managers liked me, and I was given a job near home at the Castle Hotel in Taunton, where I buried myself in the reception cubicle and could watch people, but not be touched by them."

"After a few months, I became restless again, and having been bashed twice, I wanted in some masochistic way, to be bashed again. So I got a transfer to a hotel near Weybridge. It was there at the Hilton Seven Hills that I met Mr O'Rourke. He used to fly in quite often by helicopter. When he outlined his proposal, I couldn't have been more ready. Just the change and excitement I needed, but I never had any inkling of the real plan. You know the rest, Alistair. But I'm really not proud of any of it."

She sat primly, looking at Craig with a schoolgirl expression, fiddling with a stray wisp of hair to hide the embarrassment of telling her story.

Craig looked directly into her blue eyes. She smiled back docilely

"Thank you, Christine, for telling me about yourself, but you really do need some looking after you know. You can't go on running away for ever."

He still had an odd feeling that he knew was entirely due to this lovely girl. He wanted to touch her…. reassure her in some way. Instead he said, "Well, just for the record Christine, I'm not married, so you are safe with me."

For the first time she gave Craig a full, lovely smile.

"Thank you for telling me that Alistair, but I can't see us getting very romantic in our present situation. Now as I have told you so much about myself," she insisted. "What about you? Flying helicopters must be fascinating work. When did you start?"

Alistair Craig moved his chair fractionally closer and, as the *Champagne Princess* sped through the dark Atlantic waters, her two reluctant passengers sat talking intimately, discovering their common interests as Craig related his story, and listened attentively as Christine exchanged hers.

161

An hour passed as the luxury yacht swept them on, and the ship became quiet. Craig stood up and held her more intimately at the waist, holding her to him and then broke away.

"Christine, it's getting late, time for us to go." He squeezed her hand and kissed her gently on the cheek. "Thanks for talking with me this evening. We had both get off to our cabins. I'll see you again in the morning."

"Goodnight, Alistair. I really do feel much better."

Craig walked back to his cabin thinking more and more about this super girl who had so suddenly burst into his life. But he was being daft, he told himself. Just two frightened people clinging to each other, to hide from the danger surrounding them. Best to put her out of his mind for the time being, and think more positively of the escape plan he had to come up with. But as he sat in his cabin, his thoughts obstinately returned to her.

He arranged the pillows on his bed, and finding an old Ian Fleming paperback on the bookshelf, he propped himself against the headboard, and was soon lost in a highly unlikely story of a one-man financed rocket being diverted to explode in the heart of London. Another madman, but infatuated with gold instead of Irish nationalism.

* * * * * *

Forward in the Stateroom, O'Rourke was also taking things quietly. Considering events to come. He looked at his watch. Almost midnight. Shortly time to relieve Brandt, and take the next watch on the bridge.

He crossed to the drinks cabinet, selected a White Horse whisky and poured a generous measure. He took a long first swig of the pale gold liquid, and paused as the alcohol warmed the back of his throat.

He settled back in the comfortable armchair. Things were going well, he considered. His months of planning and attention to detail were paying off. Of course, he would have preferred to take the ransom in gold, but one hundred million would weigh seven or eight tons! So it had to be dollar bills, the international currency of greedy moneymen. Neatly stuffed into packages of two million each... Fifty

162

of them! Nicely transportable.... For the crusade! O'Rourke swigged again, smiling to himself with satisfaction.

Yes.... the combination of the helicopter and the ship was the key to success. No doubt the American Government had already searched high and low in every state for their beloved President, and would be keeping watch at all the exit ports.

But the beauty of his plan was the quick getaway from Milwaukee using the ice crossing to the Lake Michigan rendezvous. The Great Lakes routing to the ship was remote enough to avoid detection. That, and the flight being made at night was the secret.

The pilot Craig had done a good job, and he was pleased with his judgment. The girl, too, was co-operative, and could be left in charge of the President. Now it was just a matter of waiting for the cancelled Jay Leno show and NBC news that the US Government would pay. Soon Makhtoum would appear in the launch with the heist. Just forty-eight hours to go and his plans would produce the millions that would be used over and over against the damned British.

The exit plan to Cuba was in place, and from there he would return to Ireland with the money and the clamour of his fellow IRA countrymen. The guns and bombs could be bought and the right men recruited for the terror campaign. But there was still much to be done.

He poured himself a final stiff drink, and a second for Brandt, and slipping on his coat, he walked forward to the Bridge. He greeted Brandt and handed him the whisky. "Thought you might like a little something, Brandt. Here, pour this back."

Brandt stood up from the steering wheel. "Well dat's kinda thoughtful of yo Boss," Brandt said. "Could do wit a drink."

"I'll take the next watch. You stretch your legs, but I'd like you to check the President before you turn in. If the girl is about, she'll give you the latest report. She seems to have settled down, but keep your eye on her just the same."

"Ah see she's already gettin' acquainted wit de pilot guy," Brandt replied. "De two of 'em av' been chattin' on de rear deck fer most of de evening."

"I don't see any problem, Brandt. Probably help by giving them something to think about while we make for Florida. Now there's nothing more for you to do for a while. Tomorrow we listen to the

163

radio for the Government's answer. Mr Jay Leno won't appreciate being cancelled but that's the signal for a 'go' as far as we are concerned."

Brandt handed over control as O'Rourke settled behind the wheel. "So long, boss. Speak later."

He stepped through the wheelhouse door, and stood on the boat deck looking out to the horizon. The inky blackness of the night sky merged with the dark sea. Only the comforting swishing from the bows, and the constant drone of the turbines, disturbed the silence. Brandt stepped down to the lower deck, and walked back quietly to the President's door, listening. He looked back to the stern. No sign of Craig or the girl. Satisfied, he crossed to the port side and retired to his own cabin.

On the bridge, O'Rourke consulted his chart and set the autopilot to a new heading. He adjusted the auto throttles to 70% power and switched the radar auto-alarm to sound at five miles. He then checked the ship's position on the Satellite navigator, made some notes, and sat back.

He relaxed and allowed his thoughts to roam over his future as the *Champagne Princess* carved off the miles. It had been a good move to join the Al Qaeda men, even though the cultural differences left them little in common. But none of that mattered. What did matter was the coming together of two dividends from one operation. Money for him, and a dead President for the Arabs. A final insult for the Yanks.

The recent so-called Irish peace initiatives were doomed to failure. He'd seen to that with his control of the right men in Sinn Fein, and the damned British would soon realise it. With the money in his hands, plans could be made for the terror campaign in Britain. They would be made to pay for the years of oppression inflicted on his countrymen and, with their soldiers booted out, his Republican Army would be greeted on the streets of Dublin as heroes. He might even be called on to become a political figure, perhaps ultimately the President of the Republic of Ireland! It was all going to be worthwhile. A united Ireland could once again hold her head up in the free world.

His father's death would not have been in vain.

# 21

Christine awoke early and quickly jumped off the bed to get dressed. Despite their circumstances, there was something about each new day on board that she liked. A refreshing feeling as the sea swept yesterday's troubles behind. Perhaps it was something to do with the steady breeze as the *Champagne Princess* scythed into the wind, or was it the endless expanse of the sea reaching out to a clear horizon?

Like Craig, she had laid on her bed thinking about the attraction she felt for the man who had literally flown into her life. He had blue eyes and the fair wavy hair she preferred. He was tall with a firm physique, and she liked him being a pilot, but not so good looking as to have a string of girls chasing after him. She would look nice for him today. Not much to choose from, she thought as she opened the wardrobe.

The sky was clear so it would be warmer. How about the white cotton blouse with blue trimming at the cuffs and neck? That would match the light blue of her jeans. She was proud of her figure, and the tight jeans emphasised her femininity.

She spent more time than usual arranging her hair, and decided on some make-up. She pulled on the jeans, gave herself a sideways glance in the long mirror, and pinned on the Wedgwood Cameo brooch Dad had given her for her twenty-first birthday.

She sat on the bed thinking how extraordinary it was, that she was dressing up for a virtual stranger, especially when there was so much danger ahead. Though she felt safe enough tucked away in her little cabin. Somehow this powerful ship and the promise of a lovely day made the danger seem unreal. As though she was watching it at the local cinema. There was nothing that she could do, except look after the President, unless she could come up with an idea. She just hoped they could think of an escape from their predicament.

O'Rourke had told her to report to him first thing each morning. She climbed the steps to the upper deck, and paused to breathe in the sea air. The temperature was noticeably higher, and the sea shimmered in the early morning sun as she stepped hesitantly into the wheelhouse. O'Rourke and Brandt were on the bridge.

"Good morning, Mister O'Rourke. Can I get you both some coffee?"

O'Rourke handed the wheel to Brandt, walked over to Christine, and kissed her on the cheek. She pulled away. O'Rourke seemed not to notice.

"That would be welcome, Christine. Perhaps bring some breakfast too will you?"

O'Rourke glanced up at the mackerel sky, tinted red and gold by the morning sun.

"S'going to be a nice day," he commented mechanically. "Perhaps warm enough for you to get some sun later."

O'Rourke returned to the instrument panel, and busied himself with the autopilot controls, making adjustments to the heading and engine power settings.

"I'll take my food in the cabin, Christine. Brandt will stay on the bridge."

"Yes, of course, Mister O'Rourke, and I'd better have a look at the President, too. He'll need another injection," she lied.

"Yes, give him a careful examination, I want you to keep him sedated and keep me informed of his temperature and pulse rate."

Christine left O'Rourke and went below deck to the galley where the crewman Ahmed was preparing food. She relayed O'Rourke's breakfast order and helped shell the eggs. She needed to take something for the President, and when Ahmed left with the breakfast plates, she grabbed two slices of buttered bread and some cooked

166

meat, which she hurriedly took to her cabin. Then she returned to the galley and assembled a breakfast tray for Alistair. She knocked on his door.

"Hallo, Christine," Craig said warmly. "Oh, some breakfast. You really are an angel."

She placed the tray on the table. "Mr O'Rourke is on the bridge, Alistair. Brandt has taken his watch. I managed to get the food for the President. I'm taking it to him now. Is there anything you want me to say?"

"Nothing important," Craig replied morosely. "Just that I'm working on a way of getting out a message, but the more I think about it the more hopeless it seems. The ship's not even due to call into port for fuel."

"Well, I'll just tell him you are making plans to contact the Government."

"Be careful though, Christine. Don't get caught talking to him."

"I understand, Alistair, I have to speak to Mr O'Rourke first so I can check where everyone is on the ship."

After breakfast, Craig dressed and put on a loose T-shirt, slacks and his soft trainers. He wanted to have a more detailed look over the ship today, and check on the radio room.... if only he could get in, but O'Rourke kept the room locked, and wasn't likely to let him borrow the key!

He also wanted to inspect the engine room. What if he could sabotage the turbines in some way? Force the ship to stop, or pull into a port for repairs. A naval patrol ship or some other vessel might come to investigate. Yes, that was a possibility he must consider further. Then there was the steering gear.... Could that be tampered with? How did the sea-cocks work? That was a dangerous area.... he might finish up scuttling the ship and drowning everyone on board, and heaven knows how O'Rourke would react if he was discovered tampering with anything.

He walked the length of the ship to the foredeck, checking the ship's equipment. The sun was high, and shining warmly from the clear blue sky. Craig leaned over the handrail and looked down as the surf rushed by. He was intrigued to watch the sea, as it obediently parted ahead of the thrusting bows, and race down the hull in a frenzy of whirlpools and mottled spray.

167

He stopped at the speedboat secured by the davits.... now if he could get that launched? But what chance was there of lowering the boat and getting the engine started without being seen? Absolutely none.... and he mustn't forget that Leroy Brandt, and presumably O'Rourke had a gun which he suspected they wouldn't hesitate to use.

Craig became aware that O'Rourke was watching him from the bridge. He gave a cheery wave. Now what?

"Come up on the bridge, dear boy," O'Rourke beckoned with good humour.

So the Al Qaeda cohort wanted to talk! Craig made his way to the foot of the steps leading to the upper deck, and climbed up.

"Good morning, Mr O'Rourke," he said a little stiffly. "What a change in the weather."

O'Rourke beamed. "Most welcome, dear boy, and in this sea we are making a good twenty knots. We've sailed five hundred miles since yesterday. We reach Freeport around ten o'clock tomorrow. Are you fully recovered from your epic flight?" O'Rourke enquired, changing the subject. "Your big pay day is almost here."

"I'm looking forward to it," Craig nodded, trying to put enthusiasm into his voice.

O'Rourke gave Craig a conspiratorial smile. "I understand you're going to give us a hand at the wheel today."

Craig stared back at O'Rourke's bland forehead, where the black comma of hair was stiffened with hair gel.... close to the left eye. So the IRA man still had his vanity. He answered, "Yes, I'll be glad to help on the bridge. Give me something to do."

"Thank you, Alistair, that will share the load." O'Rourke rubbed his hands. "Why don't you take the midday watch?"

"Yes, that'll be fine, but if you don't need me now, I'll stretch my legs and maybe get some sun."

"Good, make yourself at home, dear boy." The lips parted into a slow smile. "Enjoy yourself while you can."

Yet again, that glazed expression. Craig didn't like his tone. What did he mean by that? Best to stay out of the way.

O'Rourke's eyes followed Craig, as he made his way to the bow.

The pilot appeared to have settled down. That was good. He was glad neither Craig nor Christine were giving him cause for concern.

He'd be a lot happier when NBC confirmed the ransom money was to be paid.

He considered for a moment. He knew the Government had no option but to accept his demands. It was more a question of whether they would take a risk when handing over the money. As long as he kept the President alive, he knew they would not, but they would want proof of the President's well being. No, the real hunt would come later, but by then he expected to be thousands of miles away.

A pity about Craig and Christine. They were a nice couple and were getting on well together. He liked that. It stopped them having too much time to think about their own demise. Not for a couple of days yet, as he needed Christine to keep the President doped, and he might have to use Craig again, but when the time came, he would get them together and do what had to be done. Once their bodies were overboard, all traces would be gone.... the sharks would see to that! With the money in the bag, the President would have to follow them. He didn't like that part of the plan, but that was the agreement he'd made with the Sheikh.

Then a bullet for the disposable Brandt, and the *Champagne Princess* would be abandoned in the Cuban harbour at Port Cardenas. He would simply disappear with Sheikh Makhtoum and his two men. The political situation between Cuba and America would not allow too much rousting about. All the Government would have to investigate would be an empty ship, a few bodies and a dead President. Al Qaeda would have got what they wanted, and he would have the money.

What a terrific combination of motives, Al Qaeda politics and his IRA thirst for money! The international media would be alight. The news would run in every page of the world's press for weeks. Al Qaeda had breached the innermost security of the President, and his Real IRA was back in business.

He was on the verge of collecting the millions his men needed to bash the British, kindly donated by the people of America. Almost too simple, he thought, but simplicity was the keynote of the ransom plan.

Brandt arrived on the bridge. "Everythin' okay Boss?" he said in his usual gruff tone. "Guess it's mah turn ta do some steerin." The eye twitched at O'Rourke. "De girl's been up fer an hour han' Craig's been snoopin' aroun'. Dey spent time together in Craig's cabin jest now, thought yo should know boss."

"Thank you Brandt, I have spoken to both of them this morning. I'll leave the ship to you for a few hours.... Keep the heading on one-seven-five, and the engines at seventy percent. I'm going to listen for the morning NBC news," O'Rourke chuckled.

"I don't expect there'll be any general announcement of the President's absence. They'll want to keep it a secret for a while. A hundred million dollar secret," he concluded jovially. Pleased with his own joke, O'Rourke loped off to his cabin, chuckling curiously.

* * * * * *

Craig spent the morning considering other escape possibilities. Could he force the ship to stop or get off in some way? Make it to shore.... not unless he could swim fifty miles, and was immune to sharks! So how could he make contact with the outside world? He wandered over the ship's three decks on the pretext of getting some exercise.

The engine room was no help. The two Arabs, Ahmed and Ramzi, constantly attended it. They seemed content to eat and sleep in the hot noisy atmosphere. Craig studied the two massive turbine engines. There was no way of sabotaging them without some special tools.

Neither crewman said anything that would help. The oppression of the small engine room made Craig want to get back on deck for some fresh air. He would find Christine and have another chat. She looked quite stunning this morning, and he particularly noticed the open neckline. Was that for his benefit?

She was sitting by the helicopter looking out to sea as he approached.

"Hi, Christine."

She looked up shading her eyes from the sun. Craig moved close to her as she spoke.

"I've managed to talk to the President this morning, Alistair. He's recovering quite well. He wanted to know about the ship," she said in a troubled tone, "and about O'Rourke and the Al Qaeda man back in Menominee, Brandt and the others." She looked straight at Craig. "Even you and me. He knows the IRA people are a bad lot and

170

seemed surprised there was a connection between them and the Al Qaeda gang." Christine spoke through troubled lips, as if not wanting to say the words. "When I mentioned the ransom collection, he said his Government will pretend to pay, but the agents will capture the person collecting the money and negotiate some deal. Apparently something like this has been considered. Its all been discussed and planned for many years."

"Yes, I suppose that's quite likely," Craig said, shrugging his shoulders. "But they still need to know where we're being held prisoner.... That is what we are you know.... Prisoners."

"What are you saying, Alistair? Don't you think Mr O'Rourke will let us go when it's all over?" She stepped toward him, trembling.

"It's a possibility.... let's hope we get out of this mess first," he said to comfort her. "If we do, I'm going to take you to a quiet place in England, where we can talk together all night if we want. One way or another, this nasty business will be over in two or three days, so just keep your fingers crossed, Christine." Craig smiled in an effort to give her some consolation.

They sat talking until it was time for Craig to help on the bridge.

Brandt showed him the main controls, which were straightforward, and with a parting "maintain the one-seven-five heading," he ducked out of the wheelhouse.

Craig noticed the ship had wandered a few degrees off the heading. He made a correction to the autopilot. The *Champagne Princess* responded instantly taking up the new course. He pulled up a high chair so that he could monitor the instrument cluster and look out over the bows toward the horizon, just thinking about his problem. Should he stop the ship now? That wouldn't accomplish much, except to alert Brandt and O'Rourke, and getting himself clapped in irons alongside the President wouldn't help at all.

No, it came down to getting a message out in some way.

He looked at the problem logically.... Messages.... now how can they be passed...? Telephone. His own small phone was gone and he'd already seen that the ship's radiotelephone was securely locked in the radio room. In any case, the VHF electronic display radios would need an entry code, which he didn't have. How about a bottle message? That would be the hell of a long shot. He'd have to do a lot better than that!

171

Craig gazed gloomily over the smooth surface of the sea and looked up. They must be getting near land. A flock of seagulls had joined the ship, and were keeping pace, flying lazy circles in the updraft above the ship's bow. As they wheeled closer, Craig shaded his eyes from the sun.

Above him, a long white scar scratched the clear blue of the sky. A high-flying Jet, probably at about thirty thousand feet with its four engines pulling a condensation trail composed of millions of ice crystals that fanned out behind the aircraft. Probably one of Boeing's Jumbo airliners on the airway from Europe.

Craig visualised the three hundred or so passengers trying to relax.... munching their way through the packaged cheeses and roasted nuts. To relieve their boredom, the pilot would be drawing their attention to the American landfall urging them to 'Keep your seat belts fastened,' with a drawled.... 'Like we do here up front.'

As Craig followed the fast moving jet, he wondered if the crew were similarly inspecting the small dot on the ocean below that would be the *Champagne Princess.*

But what was it nagging away at Craig's brain? Telephone.... Radiotelephone. Messages?

Of course! Why hadn't he thought of it before? The two-way radio in the helicopter! 'Stupid fool,' he mouthed to himself. Talk about overlooking the bloody obvious!

From the cockpit of the Hawk, he could speak to the Jumbo or any other aircraft that was within radio range. All he needed was the frequency. Glory be! But why the hell hadn't O'Rourke thought of it? Surely he couldn't have overlooked something so obvious. Perhaps he had removed the VHF set while Craig slept, or simply snapped off the aerial.

If he could get to the helicopter, his problem might be solved! It would have to be at night. Where would the ship be then? He did some mental calculations and checked down the ship's GPS moving map display. The small white cross indicated the ship's position.... Just fifty miles off the coast, and accurate within a few feet! The long magenta line indicated the magnetic track being made good, and the ship's speed was shown below the display. Nineteen knots. He'd need to make a note of the co-ordinates so he could radio out their exact position. The big jets would be approaching Florida, probably for landing at one of the major airports, Miami, Orlando or Tampa. He could look up their airways control frequency on the Jeppesen IFR Charts.

That was the plan. Wonderful. But risky. If he was ultra careful, it would work.

Later, he told Christine.

"If you get caught, Mr O'Rourke will kill you. It's too dangerous, I know it is," she implored. "You'll never be able to get to the helicopter without being seen, Alistair. There's always one of them on the bridge. I don't want to lose you. Please," she tailed off.

Craig had to make her understand. There was precious little time.

"It's a chance we have to take, Christine, and the only one we are likely to get. I'll do it after midnight. If I can get inside the helicopter, it only needs a single radio call to make contact with an aircraft.... that will be enough. The pilot will do the rest. It will be simple, but time is running out. I'm going to make the call tonight." Craig held Christine's hand.

"I need to work out the details. You just act as normally as you can Christine. Do some sunbathing. Give O'Rourke the impression you are enjoying being on board. We'll speak later."

In the privacy of his cabin, Craig drafted the text of the message. He would pass the *Champagne Princess's* exact position with details of the ship. His pilot's licence number and the codeword the President had given Christine would authenticate the call. He would also pass the ship's speed and course.

Having completed the text, Craig carefully folded the paper and slipped it into the Ian Fleming paperback for safety. So far.... so good. He would wait until midnight, when the crew should be asleep. The only problem would be to stay unseen by the man on the bridge. Once inside the cockpit, the covering tarpaulin should keep him hidden.

Satisfied with his work, he returned to the rear deck. Christine was on a sun bed, one leg lifted in the classical pose of a model. Craig felt vaguely embarrassed as he found his attention riveted to her full breasts and the provocative curve of her thigh. The blonde hair was fluttering about her shoulders in the warm breeze. Craig pulled up a light aluminium framed chair and sat close to her.

173

"The message is ready Christine," he whispered. "I'm making the call about midnight. Tell the President. We don't want him to try anything desperate now. If I can get the message through, we could all be free in forty-eight hours. Just so long as O'Rourke doesn't suspect anything, we can get away with it."

"The President is not really well enough to leave the ship, but I will tell him what you are doing. Should cheer him up no end."

She suddenly went quiet as O'Rourke appeared. She changed the subject and began talking about the weather in a louder voice.

"And how are my two guests?" O'Rourke beamed at them. The Adolf Hitler lock had slipped. "Enjoying the sun, I see."

Craig thought he was glancing furtively at Christine's curvy figure.

"Make the most of it, you two. We all have a great deal to do shortly when the ransom money arrives. Sheikh Makhtoum will soon arrive in the launch, then we set a leisurely course for Cuba Island."

So, thought Craig, the Al Qaeda man will be back in the business. Collecting the ransom and, once he had the President and the money, O'Rourke and Brandt would have served their purpose. Both could be disposed of! If that were Makhtoum's plan, he would surely be on the death list along with Christine. The possibilities were frightening. He'd need to keep a close watch on the crewmen, Ahmed and Ramzi.

He looked at O'Rourke, trying to sound casual, but with a $64,000 dollar question.

"Once the Sheikh arrives, how do we hand over the President?" Craig asked. He thought perhaps O'Rourke might want him to return the President to Florida.

O'Rourke's expression changed instantly.... his eyes were hard, and the voice without feeling. The laser look was back.

"I'm sorry, dear boy, but that will not be possible. You see the beauty of my plan is that no one knows our identities, except of course, our famous guest. It has all been agreed with our Arab friends." The voice was full of greed as he rolled his lips. The brown eyes glittered. "Once we have the ransom....the millions of dollars....The President will have to find his way overboard. He'll be unconscious of course, and will feel no pain, if that is your concern, dear boy."

Again Craig felt his anger rising. On a warm sunny afternoon, under a clear blue sky, O'Rourke had calmly announced he planned to kill an American President. He felt a loathing horror for the man. What a monstrous bastard. How he longed to get his hands around the man's nasty throat and squeeze the last breath out of his windpipe.

"Surely you must have appreciated that from the beginning, dear boy." O'Rourke concluded indifferently.

Craig's face flooded with anxiety. He could see the alarm in Christine's eyes too.

"But that's murder." Craig's heart went to his mouth as he burst out angrily. "You can't just take a man's life in cold blood. We'll all be equally guilty you know. I thought we were just after the money."

"There really is little alternative, my dear boy," O'Rourke continued without emotion, "Unless you want to see us all caught. I should think we'd get at least thirty years in a state penitentiary, or more likely the electric chair, and that dear boy, is not part of my plan."

Craig's pulse surged. He felt sick in the pit of his stomach. Christine was holding back her tears, her hand to her mouth. So it was to be murder after all. Could he have expected anything else from the bloody Al Qaeda? Or the IRA, both with a history of mass murder? And what now, his own chance of survival, or Christine's? By God, he just had to get the message through tonight. It was now their only chance of staying alive.

He glared at O'Rourke as the hate for the man boiled in his groin. Should he go for him now? Strangle the bastard! But with Brandt and the crewman in the background, he knew he couldn't hope to accomplish anything by starting a fight. Getting shot or injured would only destroy his big chance tonight.

"I suppose you're right," Craig forced himself to say. "It's a terrible thing to do, but as you say, we are all in this too deep now, I suppose, and I don't want to end up in jail any more than you."

"That's a realistic assessment, dear boy, I'm glad you see it that way." The voice was flat again. "I don't see how the murder of a President should make any difference, a President who is responsible for the death of a thousand innocent civilians in Iraq, remember." O'Rourke was staring at Craig with his curious glazed eyes. "And where would you like to leave us? We'll need to get your share of the ransom ready."

175

Was the bastard still playing with words?

"Cuba will suit me fine," Craig replied evenly. "From Havana I can catch a jet anywhere, probably make for South Africa," Craig said, throwing in any name for the sake of saying something. "But shouldn't we wait until we've got the money?" Craig's voice was furiously controlled.

"Of course," O'Rourke said, levelly. "How sensible of you, dear boy. I think I'll go forward to catch the breeze."

Craig watched the man's retreating back. By God, he would get that man…. and when he did it would be something damned unpleasant. He looked back to Christine. She was deathly pale.

"Surely he won't do it," Christine blurted out. "Not kill the President?" She began sobbing.

Craig tried to comfort her. "That's just not going to happen, Christine. Now we know the truth about that maniac, it's ten times more important I make that call tonight."

He considered their position. If the President were to be killed, then he, and presumably Christine, would suffer the same fate.

Fate? What he really meant was death, and he mustn't forget it. Like most people, he had thought about death many times, and because of his occupation, had sometimes been close to it.

But he had no intention of dying. Not now he could sabotage Al Qaeda's plans and save their own necks.

It was a question of succeeding tonight. That single act of communication would enlist the help of Government's forces, who even now would be frantically searching for clues. Craig would give them that clue tonight.

He looked at Christine's frightened features, and cursed their circumstances. In two days, he knew he'd fallen for her and, in spite of the danger, he was sure Christine was the girl he wanted. She had allowed him to kiss her. Was that because, like him, she was scared, or was it because she felt the same way towards him? Was this the beginning of a good relationship, the beginning of the thing he wanted…. a secure future?

Did they have a future? Did Christine recognise the danger? Would she realise that O'Rourke intended to kill them both along with the President?

He decided not to tell her.

# 22

Craig checked the time.... Twelve thirty. Time to get going. Apart from the constant throb from the engines, and the steady slap of water against the hull, the *Champagne Princess* had been quiet for an hour.

Making up his mind, Craig crossed to the window and peered through the slats of the Venetian blind. A full moon! Bars of moonlight filtered into the cabin, and settled in silver strips on the cabin floor. No one on deck. Silent as a graveyard.

Slipping back the lock on the door, Craig stepped into the night to be greeted by a cool soft breeze. He stood motionless for five minutes.... listening, as the moon's shadows slid silently across the ship's silver superstructure. A persistent tinkling from a slack rigging wire echoed round the ship as it slapped rhythmically against the aluminium mast.

Otherwise, all quiet.... okay to move.

Craig looked up to the velvet black of the night sky. The full moon squatted like a large cheese on the smooth surface of the sea. It reminded him of the Wiltshire Moonraker. Another quirk of the English!

Craig hated the silence and would have preferred a choppy sea. Rough weather. Anything except this eerie calm. Any unusual sound would be heard in every part of the ship.

He must get to the helicopter without being heard. Their very lives depended on it! He moved a few trial steps and paused again. Still the comforting sound of the sea, as it kissed and gurgled along the hull, and the tinkling of the rigging.

Walking on tiptoe and keeping in the shadows, Craig felt for the handrail leading to the Heli-Deck, and carefully lowered himself step by step down the ladder. It was vital to stay out of sight of the helmsman on the bridge. He looked back.... just the dull red glow from the port navigation lamp, and an amber light from the masthead.

He was surprised to see the Perspex nose of the helicopter reflecting the moonlight. The steady breeze had tugged the tarpaulin clear of the Hawk's cabin. Half the windscreen was now uncovered. Once inside, could he be seen from the bridge, he wondered?

Craig gave it another five minutes. If he was challenged, he was taking a late night stroll! "Couldn't get to sleep Mr O'Rourke.... thinking too much about tomorrow, I suppose. I'll be getting back to my cabin now.... Goodnight."

With a last look back to the bridge, he made up his mind. 'Go' he whispered to himself, as he chanced a dozen quick steps to the helicopter and dived under the covers. Tensing his muscles, he felt his way to the passenger door with his heart thumping. As he pulled on the door handle, a seagull skimmed by, letting out a loud screech. The door catch released with a metallic click that echoed round the ship. Craig winced... listening. No reaction. Thank you for the cover, my friend. Thankfully, still quiet.

He held the door open and slid into the familiar cockpit, breathing slowly and deliberately to release the knot of tension. Now where were the navigation charts? Should be between the seats. He flicked on the pinhead light from the torch and picked up the bulky Jeppesen manual. He risked a second flash and thumbed through the alphabetic section for the airway frequency. He traced his finger down the list. God, there were dozens! K... L... for Lauderdale. M for Miami Control. Approach. Tower. Weather and ATIS information. Ah.... There it was. 118.4 Mhz for arriving aircraft from the east. Now to get the radio going.

The Master switch had to be 'On', but first he must check that none of the other aircraft systems were selected. He didn't want the high intensity strobes to flash out his presence, or the whine of the fuel pumps to give him away. He carefully checked every instrument on the panel in turn.... then, holding his breath, he placed his finger firmly on the Master Switch and pushed. Phew.... Silence.

He selected the Collins VHF radio and tuned the LED digits to the Miami Airways frequency, then slipping on the noise-cancelling Clark headset, he listened, fearful that any second he might feel the cabin door flung open and the sharp dig of a gun in his ribs.

The silence was comforting as he waited for the COM set to warm.

Craig listened for an aircraft.... any aircraft. But nothing. Craig waited five minutes. Listening. Surely there must be some routine two-way transmissions from Air Traffic Control to aircraft using the Airways.

Had the radio suffered from the sub zero temperatures? Could the circuit boards be distorted or the battery discharged? Had the radio simply failed at the worst possible time? Please not. That would be the cruellest luck, but as he considered the possibilities and adjusted the squelch and volume controls, a faint crackle of static told him the transmission key of a distant radio station was being triggered. Craig's heart lifted as the 'oh so welcome' drawl of an American accent came over the air.

Craig lowered the volume to a whisper.

*'Miami control. This is Continental Flight 'Seven-Seven-One'.... Boeing 747 Heavy.... out of London. Checking Nassau VOR at Flight Level Tree Zero. Estimating point Rumba at Fower-Fife. We have weather and airfield information 'Juliet'. Seven-Seven-One over."*

Craig consulted the airways chart. Great. An incoming Continental Airline 747 from London, with about ten minutes to go to Miami Airport. He'd be less than a hundred miles from the *Champagne Princess*, and well within radio range. Now where was the note he'd prepared for the message? Ah, it had slipped between the passenger seats.

Craig withheld his transmission until he was sure the two-way exchange was completed. Due to his sea level position, he couldn't hear the Miami Controller's reply, but the interference from the carrier wave told him landing instructions were being passed.

The 747s pilot acknowledged the Air Traffic instructions. *"Roger Continental 'Seven-Seven-One is cleared high speed to Rumba and leaving Tree-*

*Zero for One-Fife-Zero. Changing frequency to approach with call sign only."*
The airliner was descending from thirty thousand feet to fifteen thousand, heading for Miami, and about to change frequency.

Craig took a breath. He had to be quick. It was now or never! Clutching his prepared notes with fingers crossed, Craig flicked on the torch and pressed the 'Transmit' button. The T for Transmit light came on. Good. He was live on air! Craig spoke slowly and deliberately in a carefully measured tone.

*"Continental Seven-Seven-One. This is an emergency call of international importance from Champagne Princess. Mayday ... Mayday ... Mayday. Do you read me over?"* Craig was using the internationally recognised 'Mayday' signal for distress, which takes priority over all other radio traffic.

Nothing happened. No response!

Surely the jet had heard his call.

Craig waited a few more seconds, and was about to repeat his transmission when the 747 pilot's voice came in hesitantly.

*"Ah... Erm... Roger.... This is Continental Seven-Seven-One. Champagne Princess, we read you loud and clear. Pass your Mayday message."*

He'd made contact. Craig silently whooped for joy.

*"Continental Seven-Seven-One. This is a Mayday call. Codeword 'Kingpin' I say again. The codeword is 'Kingpin'*

Craig was using the identity codeword the President had given to Christine that would authenticate his call.

"The President of America is held prisoner on this ship.... The *Champagne Princess....* Registered in New York. I say again. The United States President is a prisoner on this ship."

Craig paused, and then continued slowly, with a further pause between each phrase to allow time for the message to be accurately copied.

"Position at 23.45 hours UTC, 27 degrees, 40 minutes North... 75 degrees... 31 minutes West. Ship moving on heading One-Seven-fife degrees magnetic at twenty knots. Three Al Qaeda terrorists on board. They are Ahmed Mohammed, Ramzi Yousef and Leroy Brandt, a Cayman Islander. Also an English nurse. An IRA man is in command. His name is Ryan O'Rourke. Advise your Government, the terrorists intend to kill the President when a ransom is paid. The money is to be collected by a Khalid Mohammed who calls himself

Sheikh Mohammed Makhtoum. This is English pilot, Alistair Craig. Licence number 47981.... Mayday. Please acknowledge over."

There was another long pause. Then a somewhat incredulous voice replied. "Roger *Champagne Princess*. Your Mayday received and copied. Codeword Kingpin you say? Will relay to Miami Security."

"Thank you Seven-Seven-One. Regret I cannot continue. Mayday signing off."

Craig switched off the radio and let out a long sigh of released tension. He felt a surge of excitement rush through his body.

It was done.... it was bloody well done! The all important fuse had been lit. Craig could sit back and await the result of tonight's work, and a massive weight was lifted from his shoulders. With one well-placed call, he'd sabotaged Al Qaeda's monstrous kidnap, and because of one small oversight in O'Rourke's otherwise perfect planning, his months, maybe his years of scheming, had been destroyed in thirty seconds. Craig switched off the electrics and crept out of the cabin.

There was one more job he could do.

If things went wrong with a rescue, or O'Rourke showed any sign of acting before the ransom, he'd already decided he would take a chance with the helicopter. He set about loosening the knots holding the tarpaulin. Enough to allow the rotor blades to at least start turning. It was not much of a plan, but if all else failed it would have to do.

Now to get back to the cabin.

Craig peered into the dark along the gang-walk. Nothing. Apart from the solitary light atop the mast, and the red and green navigation lights. But as he came to the locker room, his heart stopped. A face at the window. Craig momentarily choked, but quickly recovered as he realised it was the President. The porthole slid back an inch.

"Did you make contact?" The President whispered hoarsely.

"Yes Sir. A Continental Jumbo Jet approaching Miami. I gave the ship's position and the codeword. The pilot acknowledged my call."

"Thank God and well done. Now get back to your cabin safely. I'm Okay in here. Don't worry about me. Christine will keep in contact."

"Yes Sir, I will. And just hold on. We'll be saved now."

Craig slipped into his cabin and leaned against the door as the tension slowly unwound about him, but he felt better than at any time in the last three days. He had quietly struck back at Al Qaeda and O'Rourke. Just a tiny blow.... but a blow that would slay the dragon. Even now the massive wheel that Craig had set in motion would be turning. The jet Captain would be relaying Craig's Mayday message to Miami Air Traffic Control, who in turn would alert Government Security. Already a meeting would be taking place.... examining the detail of Craig's message. Planning a rescue.

But how would it come? By air? An approaching helicopter would be heard miles away. A submarine then? Possibly. But a boarding party would have to storm the ship in seconds to have any chance of success. No doubt stun grenades would be used like the Iranian Embassy siege in London years ago. A good team could do it. But it would have to be a good one!

There was nothing more he could do. Just keep the helicopter possibility in mind, and let the President know of the escape plan he held in reserve.

For the moment his motives were not suspect, and slowly, very slowly he was turning the tables on O'Rourke and his Al Qaeda accomplices.

Craig lay back on his bunk bed. So now he must wait, probably only until tomorrow, but he could not help thinking that in twenty-four hours, much will have happened on the *Champagne Princess*, and the world would know you could not expect to take on the United States of America and get away with it.

His whole future, the President's and Christine's now hung by a thread.

But the thread was very thin!

# 23

Continental Airways Flight number 771 was Captain Hopkins' last trip before a welcome three-day stand-down. With a couple of days to spare before he returned to his Columbia home in South Carolina, he was planning on driving to Marco Island on the Mexican Gulf and take in some sun, some sand and a little golf, but he badly needed some sex!

On the ten-hour flight from London he shared a few light-hearted moments with the stewards, but he knew his senior Captain's position required the girls to remain aloof. He was particularly interested in the willowy blonde who was new to the airline. With luck she might not yet know the form, and she seemed pleased to respond to his small talk. During the movie, while the passengers were glued to the small screen, he invited her to join him, 'for a day on the beach' at Marco Island. Perhaps stay overnight? He threw in innocently.

"Can I think about that?" she had said with a knowing smile.

At least she hadn't said no.... which, probably meant yes!

On the let-down to Miami Airport, Hopkins made the initial call to Approach Control and was telling his co-pilot to fly the remainder of the procedure, when the unexpected voice of Alistair Craig came through, interrupting the landing routine.

At the sound of the key word 'Mayday,' the two pilots paid instant attention, listening carefully and making notes.... Hopkins acknowledged the call.

"Well I'll be damned." He looked across the flight deck to his co-pilot, who was grinning.

"What next!" Hopkins said dryly. "I've had some cookie messages in my time, but that one beats the lot. *Champagne Princess*, eh? What else...! And the President himself, no less. Nicely done.... even had the funny sounding Arab names! These amateur radio hams are sure screwy as hell. They don't miss a trick. Fancy yachts and our old friends, Al Qaeda. That one was even a crazy limey."

Hopkins had received similar calls from hoaxers before, and if the Federal Aviation authorities allowed these idiots to buy multi-channel VHF sets in a Miami store for a few hundred dollars, what could they expect? Something should be done, but he would have to report the unauthorised transmission to the security office, which meant a special form and probably lots of questions. A bloody nuisance too. He had other things he wanted to do!

He set the throttle and flap controls for the 300-knot descent and handed over to the co-pilot. He would just have time to go back and chat with the new stewardess. He brushed his hair with a palm, straightened his uniform, and left the flight deck for the passenger cabin. Judy had changed into 'arrival dress' and was snatching a brief rest in the crew seat. She smiled up at him.

"What do you think then, Judy?" he said invitingly. "A couple of days in the sun together? We'll stay at a five star hotel with a room overlooking the Mexican Gulf, and the tastiest food in town. The relaxation will do us good. What do you say?"

Her eyes were alight. "Oh, it sounds wonderful," she said excitedly. "I'd love to come." The eyes dropped a fraction. "But I'm not promising anything you know.... let's just get to know each other first."

Which meant, Hopkins decided, 'Yes' but not immediately, maybe after an hour or two!

"Sure that's understood Judy, we'll just have a swell time together." Hopkins cheerfully lied. "We can meet up in the aircrew restaurant after de-briefing. See you there."

"I'm looking forward to it." Judy said wistfully.

She gave Hopkins an intimate smile as he turned for the flight deck. How exciting. Lots of the girls married company pilots, that's why she joined Continental, although she'd been warned by the others what to expect on a night stop. She felt flattered that the Captain had chosen her, and he was rather good-looking, even if a little old. Still, if he could handle such a big aeroplane!

Back on the flight deck, Hopkins took the Captain's left hand seat, resuming the approach to Miami, and was soon vectored by radar to intercept the ILS beam for runway Two-Eight. He'd fly a manual approach and, with the localiser and glide path needles crossed squarely in the centre of the Flight Director, he positioned the big jet along the centre of the Localiser and Glide Path beams and, at fifteen hundred feet, called to his co-pilot for the landing gear to be dropped and the final landing checks made.

As the green centre lights of the runway raced underneath, the three hundred-ton jet closed on the striped threshold markings at two hundred miles an hour for the touch-down. At fifty feet, Hopkins pulled back on the control column to check the landing attitude, holding the wheels of the complex undercarriage system inches from the runway. Sixteen puffs of burnt rubber squirted from the tyres as they kissed the tarmac. The engine thrust reversers engaged and howled their protest, as they slowed the aircraft to fast walking speed. Hopkins turned off the landing runway and steered his Jumbo on the yellow centre line that led to the Airport Terminal.

He handed over to his co pilot and selected the VHF ground control frequency to receive taxying instructions, and with the four jets whining at idling power, followed the green parking lights and manoeuvred the big aircraft smoothly against the passenger disembarking gate. The two pilots ran through the closing down procedure and completed the on-board post flight documentation. Then, with the passengers unloaded, they handed over to the ground crew supervisor and made their way to the Operations de-briefing room.

Hopkins had forgotten the hoax *'Mayday'* call, and with his thoughts firmly on the lovely body of Judy, he hurriedly ran through the formalities of customs and completion of the Voyage Report for Continental Flight Seven-Seven-One.

Under the section of 'any other items' Hopkins stopped to think.... should he include details of the radio ham's hoax? He thought over the problem for a moment and glanced at his watch. To hell with it, he decided. He didn't want to hang around being questioned by some stupid FAA security investigator, especially with the lovely Judy all teed up and waiting for a night of sex. With a mild mental reservation, he signed off the form with a 'nothing to report' and picking up his flight bag, hurried to the aircrew restaurant.

Captain Christopher Hopkins.... 'Hoppy' to his friends, was a young-looking fifty. He was an experienced airline pilot, having been with Continental for twenty-five years, and Captain for the last eighteen. His senior Captain's position, and social status, had captured the affections of the pretty twenty-five year old girl who was now his wife, but fifteen years of marriage and two children had removed the sexual excitement, and his marriage had gone stale. Still, his flying job brought him a steady flow of adventurous, and attractive, females, and from time to time, offered him a particularly desirable stewardess.

Such was Judy. She would not have been with the airline for more than a month, probably not yet seduced by the flight deck.... But she had a sexy body and sure as hell, she must do it, he reasoned. He recalled his chauvinist party joke. There were just two types.... those who did, and those who haven't been asked!

Hopkins decided not to change, since he didn't have much time, and Judy probably liked the uniform with the four gold rings and the wings. He would stop at some romantic restaurant on the drive to Marco Island, get a few drinks inside her, and hopefully before the night was out he'd be tucked up in bed with the young girl at his side.

Hopkin's co-pilot, Roger Woodley, also cleared crew customs with his Captain and completed his section of the Voyage Report for the Ops section. He wasn't too happy at the Captain's instruction to ignore the hoax call, but it didn't do to upset the senior Captains.... Not if you wanted to get on in Continental!

He changed out of uniform, smoked a quiet cigarette, and then walked through the main terminal to meet his wife. Recently married, they had just bought an apartment with a panoramic view of the Atlantic in a neat condominium facing Miami Beach. They lived in the Penthouse suite with a balcony overlooking the mighty, five hundred dollars a day, Hilton-Fontainbleu Hotel. Twenty floors of unashamed luxury, complete with ice rink, Olympic sized swimming pool, and eight tennis courts, where the resident coach is an ex-Wimbledon Champion.

As Woodley arrived in the long, curved passenger terminal of Concourse B, he was disappointed to see Caroline was not waiting to meet him. Probably still at the apartment, checking her newest dress, or more likely, arranging her hair. But they had a good marriage and he loved her very much. So what the hell if she was late again? A woman's privilege!

With time on his hands, he moved idly to the Continental ticket sales counter where he knew the desk clerk.

"Seen Caroline yet?" Woodley asked.

"Not this evening.... but she'll make it sooner or later, Roger."

"Yeah, usually later."

There seemed to be no particular topic for conversation, so the desk clerk asked the standard aircrew question: "Have a good trip?"

"You know how it is," Woodley replied mechanically. "The usual ten hour bore from London, apart from some Limey radio ham calling a '*Mayday*' over the Atlantic to say he'd just kidnapped the President."

Woodley might just as well have let off a gun. Two CIA agents watching the ticket sales counter moved in and grasped the co-pilot by each arm.

"May we have your identity?" one said sharply.

Startled, Woodley produced his Airport identification tag, and was asked to accompany the two agents to a private office. The door was locked from the inside. These two guys were the size of Arnold Schwarzenegger. Woodley was frightened. Surely nothing could happen to him at an airport.

"You can sit down."

The two agents stood uncomfortably close. Intimidating.

"What do you want to know?" Woodley said nervously.

"Tell us about that radio call for starters," the senior agent demanded. "And don't take too long.... we're in one hell of a hurry."

Woodley related details of the hoax transmission.

One agent listened attentively as the other made notes and spoke into a radiotelephone. As Woodley finished, the agent grabbed his

arm roughly.... "We need the position of that ship," he barked....
"*Champagne Princess* you said?"

"Yes, but we were convinced the call was frivolous... we took very
little notice.... but the Captain wrote down the text. He may still have
it. But what's so special about this hoaxer? We get them all the time."

"Can't say," the agent responded, "but we have orders to check.
We'll need to speak with your Captain."

That would be damned difficult, thought Woodley, who knew
about Hopkin's date with the stewardess.

"Er.... He'll be gone by now.... on stand down I think.... Er, two or
three days," he said awkwardly.

"Where?"

Woodley knew about Marco Island, and didn't want to make
trouble for his Captain.... but telling lies to these two big guys might
get him into even more trouble.

"I'm not sure. I think he's driving with a friend to Marco Island."

The agent could see the co-pilot was covering for his Captain. He
would have to tell him. He put tension into his voice.

"Now listen Captain Woodley, I'm afraid you will have to stay with
us for a while, and what I am about to tell you comes under the State
Department's Official Secrets laws. We can't allow you to discuss this
matter with anyone, and I mean anyone, not even your wife. So we're
keeping you with us." He paused to let his words sink in, and said in
a quieter voice. "The President has been kidnapped and we need the
position of that ship. *Now where is Captain Hopkins?*"

Woodley was speechless. "The President kidnapped? I don't believe
it! Someone is pulling your leg. You can't keep me here, I'm meeting
my wife."

The agent pulled a wallet from his pocket and flipped open a CIA
Agent badge at Woodley. "I'm afraid it is true, and with this I can
keep you here or any other place I want." He snapped the wallet
shut. "Now just co-operate and things will be fine, Mr Woodley.
We'll take care of your wife. Just tell us where your Captain has
gone."

The agent's eyes glittered impatiently as he faced Woodley who was
trying to think things through.

"Well.... don't keep me waiting, you're not going anywhere, and I'm
not in the mood to play waiting games."

"Er.... Marco Island," Woodley faltered. "He's staying at the Marco Island Hotel, I think. He's driving with a girl, one of the stewardesses," he stuttered. "But please, his wife mustn't know."

"What's the make and colour of his car, and who's the girl?"

Woodley was scared and just wanted to get back to his wife.

"A two-thousand-one Mustang.... light blue," he blurted out. "I don't know the licence number but you can get it from Airport security. The girl's name is Judy. She's blonde. Just joined Continental. I really don't know any more. Now can I go? I won't say a word to anyone."

The senior agent fired orders at his colleague. "Get that licence plate number and have all cars on the lookout. Circulate an APB for Hopkins and the girl's description, and have his car stopped. I want that pilot brought to this office in one hour."

He turned to Woodley. "Sorry, no.... we'll let you know when you can leave."

The Agent picked up the phone. As the line purred he looked up to his colleague. "Call me on the radio as soon as you've got the pilot."

# 24

Hopkins drove slowly through the Everglades, one hand on the wheel and the other arm around Judy's slim waist. A sleepy, late night music programme was playing a Johnny Mathis romantic.... one he'd specially tuned to get her in the mood. In around two hours he planned to be at Marco Island. The setting of the hotel must have been designed for weekend love, Hopkins thought. Each room having a private balcony overlooking the beautiful Mexican Gulf with its glorious sunsets, swaying palms and white sandy beaches. The luxuriously appointed bedrooms, the tennis courts, swimming pools, and international class restaurants, offered its holiday guests the utmost in luxury, seclusion and comfort, and if you couldn't make a seduction there, Hopkins decided, you had better give up trying!

They would arrive in the early hours, have a late nightcap in the bar and then after their long trip, it would be so natural to fall into the king-sized bed. Hopkins was a good lover, and once in bed, it would be logical to extend his area of command from the flight deck to the hotel bedroom. Judy snuggled closer as his free hand cupped her breast and he felt the first stirring of an erection.

"How far to go?" she purred.

"About a couple of hours Judy, but I thought we'd have a break on the way, to stop off for some dinner. There's a nice Italian restaurant I know in the next town. Why don't you just relax for a while?"

Hopkins slipped his hand under her blouse and began to smooth an already erect nipple. She moaned softly and parted her legs, her hand reaching for his thigh. He was hard. Things were going well, Hopkins thought. She was already as good as his. Perhaps he should stop the car now....?

The flashing blue light of a Highway Patrol car suddenly appeared ahead blocking the road. Three more Patrol cars were parked menacingly either side. The area was bright with red and blue lights. Hopkins quickly withdrew his hand and returned it to the steering wheel. Damn.... some kind of roadside check. Rather odd at this hour, Hopkins thought as he brought the car to a stop and his passenger hastily adjusted the buttons of her blouse.

A Police Officer walked purposefully to the driver's door. Hopkins noted the Smith & Wesson model 28 revolver attached to his waistband that said 'Don't mess with me.' He wouldn't argue.

Hopkins lowered the window.

"Good evening officer. Anything wrong?" He looked up sternly. Thank God he was still in uniform, which usually gained some respect from officialdom.

"Captain Hopkins, Captain Christopher Hopkins?"

"Yes." Hopkins face was granite.

"I'm afraid I need to ask you some questions sir. Why don't you step into the patrol car?"

What the hell now, thought Hopkins? Was she married? A jealous boyfriend? Had his wife started some kind of police enquiry?

"Well, ah yes, but what's going on, officer?" Hopkins made a point of flashing the four gold rings on his sleeve. "I'm a Continental Airways Captain, and I've just finished a long transatlantic flight.... it's getting late." Hopkins jerked his head imperceptibly to the girl. "Don't give me a hard time, officer."

"I'm not giving you a hard time Sir," the officer said flatly. "You either come with me or I'm arresting you now." He didn't like cocky civilians in uniform, especially not randy sods like this one, he thought, noticing Hopkin's partly unzipped pants.

In the patrol car, the Police Officer's tone became mellower. "I'm sorry I have to stop you at this hour, but I have instructions to take you back to Miami Airport. My Police Chief wants the details of the radio call you received from the ship off Miami."

191

"Oh, for Christ's sake," Hopkins raised his voice. "You haven't stopped me at this time of night to ask about that! Who the hell told you?"

"Your co-pilot."

"Well, it was just some damned hoaxer."

The officer's expression was bland. "My Chief doesn't think so, and we need the position of that ship."

Hopkins was still boiling. "I'm telling you officer, it was just a hoax call. We get them all the time," he almost yelled. "If you want the information, I wrote the details on a spare log sheet, but as soon as I realised the call was a phoney, I tore it up."

"We'll need to find the pieces then," the officer said quietly, as if explaining something to a rather dense child.

"Well it may still be on the aircraft, but more probably it's been thrown away by the aircraft cleaners by now."

"Okay, I'll radio through to Miami and stop the cleaning team. Let's get back to Miami fast. You travel with me in the patrol car. One of my officers will take your lady back to the airport." He glanced to the girl with a knowing smile. "I'm sorry, but those are my orders."

Hopkins swore under his breath. Of all the bloody luck.... so much for bed with Judy.

At the Airport, Hopkins was taken to the security office where Woodley was held.

"Roger, these guys need our help."

"Yes, Sir. I've already given them the details of the phoney 'Mayday' call.... but it all sounds horribly serious. These men are from the CIA. They know about the ship's position report. They want the map co-ordinates."

\* \* \* \* \* \*

Back at Miami Airport, a team had already been dispatched to the aircraft to locate the discarded log sheet that contained the all-important position report, but it was possible the vital clue had been destroyed.

"If necessary I want that Jumbo torn apart rivet by rivet," the agent barked, "and if its not there, you'll get hold of the trash containers and go through them piece by piece with a fine toothcomb. Don't even think about coming back until that paper is found."

During the agonising wait, the room filled with cigarette smoke. A fresh-faced young Operations Officer opened the door. He was wearing two thin gold rings. He put his head round the door, and addressed the CIA security agent.

"Look here," he demanded indignantly. "I've got a flight to get off to London in an hour, and I can't have the whole damned airline held up while you security chaps play hide and seek."

The agent looked up slowly, devoid of humour and pointed his identification badge at the newcomer. The young officer could see he had said the wrong thing.

"Listen turkey, that aircraft or any aircraft anywhere on this whole fucking airport sits right where it is until I say different, understand? Now stop proving you're a clown, and piss off."

"All right, all right. But you guys seem to think you own half of Miami." And having relieved his feelings slightly, the young officer left the room.

Just then the phone rang once.

"Okay boss. We've got it."

# 25

Four eyes scrutinised the torn scraps of paper as they slotted into place like a jigsaw. In less than a minute, the vital clue was sellotaped to a single sheet of paper.

"Okay" the CIA Agent said with satisfaction, "This is what we need." He consulted the maritime chart. "Confirms the ship's position off the Florida coast.... not too far from here. *Champagne Princess*, eh? Great name for a ship." The Agent's orders were specific. He turned to his number two. "Fax a copy to the Chief in Washington along with my report. No e-mails.... I'll warn him it's coming, but get it coded. We don't need to sell tickets for this show!"

In Washington, Vic Cramer studied the transcribed telefax and breathed a sigh of relief. He hadn't dared to believe the first news coming from Miami, but if Al Qaeda had the President on a ship, and he knew its location, he could start planning. He'd been unhappy having to meekly pay over the ransom and hoping for the best. He always knew that there was more to this than a simple ransom demand. Now with the news of an Al Qaeda involvement, it seemed more likely this was the next round in their ongoing boxing match with the country.

What a coup for the Bin Laden man, and in his view a probable 'goodbye' for the President, but this break changed everything. No more pussyfooting with handing over the millions. It would be good old-fashioned time for action. So long as the report was genuine. His follow up enquiries were encouraging.

Cramer looked through the papers again and turned to his secretary. "Have this re-coded and passed for fax distribution. FBI, NSA and all Grade 1 destinations."

He picked up the red phone.... a direct line to the Vice President's Washington office. The line buzzed.

"Good evening, Sir.... Cramer here.... We've located the pilot's note from the log. All just as he says, Sir. Confirms the President is alive. I'm faxing a scrambled brief to you. Yes, Sir. He's held prisoner on a ship a few miles off the coast. Cape Canaveral.... the *Champagne Princess*.... Yes Sir, we think it's genuine. I've put a trace on her now. The message gives the latitude and longitude and a guy called Alistair Craig is on board. English pilot apparently, but it doesn't say why he's involved. I've checked with the British Civil Aviation Authority and got an answerphone, but our Gatwick agent confirms the guy is a registered professional helicopter pilot, and known locally in Sussex.

The message says there's a gang of four on the ship. All armed.... Yes Sir, as we suspected, our friends Al Qaeda are responsible and that Khalid Mohammed fellah is one of them. They seemed to have joined up with the Irish Republican Army, would you believe.... I'm getting on to the British M16 right now. There's a helicopter on board too. A thing called a Hawk. Small single engine jet. Guess it was used to get him to the ship from Milwaukee, but we had no reports of any chopper movements at the time." He paused for breath.

"No, I can't believe we missed it either. I'm on to the helicopter factory. Up in Menominee. Yes Sir, that part checks out. The helicopter left there shortly before the abduction.... but here's the real bad news Sir. The pilot guy says once the gang have the money, they will kill the President!"

He paused to let the significance sink in.

Cramer continued grimly. "No, there's no doubt about that part of the message."

"I have to say Sir, that in view of the threat to the President's life, we have no alternative but to use the Fort Bragg rescue plan.... Yes Sir, I am discussing an operation with Grant and the Military. We've decided a simultaneous boarding, using an airborne and underwater team is the best tactic. I'm setting up a meeting in Miami for nine am tomorrow. I'll be leaving in thirty minutes."

The Vice President was thinking rapidly. Things had changed. If the rescue succeeded, he could kiss goodbye to the Presidency! But what if it didn't? He smiled to himself.

"Yes, I understand what you are saying General Cramer," he said cautiously. "You have my agreement. I'll fly to Miami with you for the meeting."

"Thank you, Sir, I'll meet you at the Airport."

Cramer replaced the phone on its cradle, and absently looked out of the window. He turned over the news in his mind, going through the options.... trying to decide how the rescue could be planned. He dug his fingers in both cheeks, exchanging a grim glance with his deputy.

But by God, this was the lead he had prayed for. He would make damn good use of it. An hour ago the position was hopeless.... the kidnap gang held the aces. Now with this one piece of vital information, the odds had shifted. But how on earth did these Qaeda terrorists get established over here? How the hell did Bin Laden manage to control them from his Afghanistan dug out? Weren't the godammed IRA confined to the British backyard?

No doubt they had been encouraged by the weasel-mouthed US Congressmen, who were forever going on about Human Rights, peace in the world, and our Catholic brothers fighting for the Irish cause.

The whole of America wanted to give Osama Bin Laden and his Arab brothers a dammed good shagging, but it had always been good for the two million Irish votes to express sympathy for the IRA, and what they cosily liked to think were their Irish ancestors. They'd even allowed a senior Sinn Fein officer to meet the President and shake his hand. Come to think of it, one of the Kennedy's Catholic clan had married one of them!

But the world knew of the constant threat from the Al Qaeda gangs in most major countries, Bin Laden's men could come from anywhere. But at least their ongoing recruitment and training programmes in Afghanistan had been stopped. The IRA was a more complicated outfit. They were allowed to move freely from state to state. But he knew from British Intelligence, that they would kill the

President if it suited them. Somehow he just had to prevent the lunatics pulling the trigger.

Cramer picked up the Hotline to his opposite number in England.... the steely lady who bossed the Brit's MI6 from her cosy office overlooking the River Thames. Could a woman really hold down that job? He was about to find out.

It would be mid-day in England and he noticed the clicks and bleeps as she came on the line. So, in spite of the scramble, GCHQ at Cheltenham was listening in! Should he use her Christian name? He had when they met last year in London.

"Elizabeth, this is Vic Cramer, Central Intelligence Agency. We have a lead.... an English pilot.... he radioed a message to a Continental Airliner. The President is a prisoner on a ship near Miami. It stacks up Okay. But if the message is for real, it's an Al Qaeda operation with one of their top men on board. And the bloody IRA is involved too. Yes... we need you."

"I agree.... yes, anything you can do at your end. The file is being coded for you right now. Should be on your desk in ten minutes."

"Fine, I'll have our HSCT sent over for you.... Yes, Ma'am.... around an hour. The HSCT? It's Boeing's X-33 version of your HOTOL. Misted fuel engines that push her along at 5000 MPH. Atlantic and back in three hours. Yes.... 'Special Category' at present, but we've been flying the ship for two years. Northolt. London? Okay, Ma'am. I'll advise our flying operations."

Cramer dropped the phone.

Why the hell did the Brits scrap Concorde?

Vic Cramer pushed his chair back from the desk. He didn't have too much time for the Brit's so-called Secret Service. Secret? He'd even seen it announced in the press when the new MI6 boss took over. Too many pansies who'd graduated from Sherborne College. Blake, Philby. But he'd also seen their tough spy school in Beirut and they were certainly no Yo-Yos over there.

But it would be MI6, the Brit's overseas intelligence gathering organisation, who understood IRA tactics. They'd had enough practice, and perhaps the guys from England would have some ideas! A negotiator might be needed. Who was the guy the Brits used to get that religious fella, Terry Waite out of hock?

Whoever he was, he'd damned well succeeded, paying less than a quarter of what had been set aside. If he could get the responsibility for this operation off-loaded to MI6, it might help save his own arse when the shit hit the fan. He knew it was going to! Meantime, he was the Chief of United States external intelligence, and would be expected to come up with the goods. He made up his mind and turned to his deputy.

"Now, deputy, get this written down. Here's what I want you to do. Get on to it right away."

"First, call the NASA senior controller at Canaveral. Obtain a high-resolution photo of the area around the *Champagne Princess*. Get the largest photo enlargement they can achieve of the ship. Have the results sent to me at the Miami office by internal courier immediately.... and I'm talking hours, 15.00 hrs this afternoon.... latest."

"Book a Boeing 747 AWAC reconnaissance aircraft. We'll need an airborne operations command platform. Have the Learjet standing by at Washington Airport to fly to Miami... Make that Washington-Dulles. I'm sending the HSCT to England for the MI6 lady. Call Captain Grant and ask him to meet us at the airport. I'd like him to join me with the planning and briefing at Miami. The Vice President will be travelling with us. Have our Agents available to meet the English lady at Miami. Check with her UK office for timing."

The deputy scribbled rapidly as Cramer continued firing the orders.

"Next set up an operational meeting for all service chiefs and heads of departments for 09.00 hours. Get on to the Air Force and the Navy. I need a Lockheed U2 spy plane and two Chinook C47 helicopters at my disposal for observation duty. Have them positioned immediately to Fort Lauderdale Executive Airport.

All flying units to keep a listening watch on UHF channel Bravo. Radio transmissions to be scrambled on security frequency Quebec."

He paused for a moment scratching the stubble on his chin between thumb and forefinger. He made a note on a pad.

"The codeword for this exercise will be the Presidential 'Kingpin.' I say again. 'Kingpin.'

"Advise Admiral Forbes I want three submarines to surround the ship at three miles range. They will remain submerged until cleared by me personally. If the *Champagne Princess* moves they will follow discreetly. They must not, repeat not, be observed."

"Contact the Operations section at Fort Bragg and draft in a team of Delta Force divers. I need twenty underwater specialists. Also, a team of Rangers parachute free-fall agents available to commence training exercises. They are to report to Fort Lauderdale tomorrow. We'll need to get hold of a ship similar to the *Champagne Princess* to run a practice operation. Position it to Fort Lauderdale harbour to await further instructions."

Vic Cramer snapped his briefcase shut.

"Have you got that?"

The deputy read back his shorthand notes.

"Okay," Cramer continued, reaching for a table lighter. He badly needed his smoke.

"Draw up these instructions into official Agency orders. Bring them to me for signature in ten minutes. I'm leaving for the Airport in twenty.... I'll need all calls passed to me on the R/T closed line. I'll be in touch.... oh, and by the way, I'll need you in Miami by eight am.... Be there."

Cramer drove fast through the late night traffic using the howler and lights. By keeping his speed to eighty, he covered the twenty miles to Washington Airport in fifteen minutes. Flashing his ID badge, he cleared security at the VIP gate and raced to the aircraft apron. The car screeched to a halt by the waiting Lear Jet 55.

Captain Grant and the Vice President were already aboard with the engines running as Cramer hurried from the car to climb the aircraft's steps. The pilot released the aircraft's brakes, lurched forward and began taxiing at high speed to its assigned holding point 'Kilo' ready for a priority cleared take-off.

The Vice President greeted Cramer with a handshake as the aircraft accelerated down the runway.

One hour after receiving the call from Miami, Cramer had set in motion his Government's reply. The Lear Jet was climbing to forty thousand feet, heading south at six hundred miles an hour, while its passengers formulated the rescue. A NASA satellite confirmed the ship's position, and enquiries had confirmed Alistair Craig's identity.

Craig's vital information had turned the tables, and if he succeeded in getting the President back alive, he'd make sure the English pilot was rich for life!

His initial assessment of the risks had been wrong. The kidnappers did intend to kill the President as Grant had predicted, but the fact relieved him of one hell of a difficult decision. Now the only option was to go in fighting. It was just a question of how soon!

With the *Champagne Princess* located, the submarines would be vectored in to shadow her. Then he had to get a boarding party on the ship. That would be done using either the Delta Force divers or the Rangers parachute team. Which tactic was best? Then why not use both?

The divers would be more risky, as there would always be that vulnerable moment as they surfaced. The highly experienced Delta Force might board the ship in thirty seconds, but would that be fast enough to prevent the President's death? He could use twenty, fifty or even a hundred men in a rescue attempt and still not succeed. No, it was not a question of numbers, only accuracy and speed, and if the gang was intent on killing the President anyway, they would probably do it at the first sign of a rescue.

The critical time would be when the first diver surfaced, or the parachutists were spotted from the ship. How long would it take to locate the President's cabin? They would need the plans from the builders, and might even have an educated guess in which cabin the President was held. But he wasn't being paid to guess! Then why not go for all the cabins? Lob a stun grenade into each. Yes, that must be the way. Study the ship's layout and have a total boarding party of twenty men. But would twenty be too many? One wrong move might wreck the plan. Perhaps it would be better to have a select team of, say, six real specialists, and reduce the chances of being seen.

As a reserve, they would have more men standing by on the Chinook helicopter. The instant the first team was on board, the second wave could move in, but such a rescue plan would have to be worked out in fine detail and timed to the very second. If it failed, he felt sure the first bullet would end up in the President.

As the Lear Jet raced south, thrusting aside the fibrous wisps of high Cirrus cloud, Cramer outlined some other possibilities to Grant and the VP.

What about using gas?

The special section had some pretty effective substances. Could the ship be smothered with the stuff? That possibility would need to be explored more closely. He made a mental note to speak to Fort Meade as soon as he landed. If there were airtight compartments throughout the ship, the gas plan wouldn't work, but that was something he could check when they'd seen the ship's plans. No doubt Admiral Forbes, with his naval background, could help on that one.

For the next hour, the three men emptied their immediate thoughts and sat back with a comforting Scotch Whisky. Forty thousand feet below, the thin necklaces of orange light, tracing out the roads criss-crossing the Carolinas, rushed lazily beneath the Lear Jet at ten miles a minute. Vic Cramer looked down at the darkened landscape, and for the first time since the disastrous news of the President's kidnap had reached him two days ago, he felt his confidence returning.

He was in with a chance.

The *Champagne Princess* was a small, unarmed ship with only four men to protect her, while he had the entire resources of the United States to call on. A true David and Goliath act, but this time Goliath must win! But why the bloody hell hadn't the daft British squashed these IRA hoodlums years ago, instead of landing him with the problem? Too much pussy-footing by the wet politicians, no doubt!

At seven am, three hours after take off from Washington, the Lear Jet screamed low over the swampy Everglades, and descended smoothly down the narrow beam of the Instrument Landing System to Miami Airport. With a screech of tyres, it touched down behind the HSCT arriving from London.

The two aircraft were met on the runway by the illuminated, 'Follow Me' sign of a marshaller's VIP vehicle, and threaded their way through the maze of taxiway lighting to the reserved parking bay, where, in two hours, a meeting was to be held that would decide the fate of the most powerful politician on Earth.

# 26

Alistair Craig was woken from a shallow sleep by the rays of the morning sun streaming into his cabin. He parted the Venetian blinds and peered out to see an early morning mist that promised a warm day. Everything was unusually quiet. No noise from the turbines. The ship had stopped and must be at anchor. He checked the time. Seven am. Only three days on the ship…. but it seemed an eternity. He felt the tension coiling in his stomach.

With the realisation that O'Rourke intended to kill the President, Christine became withdrawn. Craig tried to console her…. Suggested O'Rourke wouldn't carry out his threat. "Try to behave as naturally as you can," he urged her. "Let O'Rourke go on thinking you are resigned to the situation. He'll have enough to think about himself just now." She would do her best, she assured him. Craig discreetly changed the subject.

For the twentieth time, Craig cursed for getting himself and Christine into this horrendous mess. Still, he had his plans…. It was just over twenty-four hours since he'd got the message through to the Continental pilot. He considered how a rescue would come.

The deadline for the ransom payment was only hours away.

He felt encouraged as he recalled the small signs he'd detected yesterday…. almost certainly indicating that the American Government was setting up an operation.

There was the high wing training Cessna, which had completed two distant orbits, but within observation range, using powerful binoculars. The perfect cover for a trained AOP spotter, who knew exactly what he was looking for. Then the ultra-high aspect ratio Lockheed Jet that had completed several straight-line observation runs at high altitude. The type was equipped with sophisticated photographic equipment that produced pictures with so much detail, you could see the colour of a man's tie fifty thousand feet below.

No, the two aircraft added up to more than coincidence, and he was sure a team of specialists would be studying the detail revealed on the photographs. They would be relaying information to the Government Officers planning the President's rescue.

The clincher was the two dolphins circling the ship. Craig knew the US navy used them for covert observation duties. These dolphins were fitted with tiny transmitters that would be relaying information to their training base. The clever mammals could even be trained to make underwater kills with a friendly nudge from a poisoned hypodermic. Yes, the wheels of the machine were in motion. It was just a question of when the operation would start.

The best time for a rescue operation, Craig knew, would have to be at half-light. Early morning or dusk. Tomorrow the ransom was to be paid, so the rescue had to be made tonight at dusk. That would mean around six o'clock.

Craig caught his reflection in the circular shaving mirror, and was relieved to note the firm set of his jaw. He was determined that somehow he must make use of his presence on the ship. Why, any crack Commando team would give an arm to have a spy in the enemy camp. It would be up to him to take advantage of the position.... if the time came?

He slipped on a T-shirt and grey slacks, and decided to walk round the ship to get another look at the Hawk. He still held in reserve the possibility of using the helicopter if the rescue failed to come, or showed signs of going wrong.

A rhythmic slapping greeted him as he walked quietly aft along the gang-walk to the Heli-deck. A tarpaulin tie-down had been loosened by the fresh breeze and was flapping gently against the fuselage. How helpful! If he had to use the helicopter, a lot of time would be lost getting the ropes untied, but now half the work was already done.

How long would it take to untie the remaining ropes? Could they be untied fast enough to start the engine and get airborne? Had O'Rourke overlooked the possibility of using the helicopter? The kidnap plan had been carefully conceived, and Craig felt sure O'Rourke must have considered every aspect. Yet here was the helicopter, and providing it had not been tampered with, it offered a possible means of escape.

Craig looked up at the three rotor blades that sagged under the weight of the heavy tarpaulin. Once the engine was started, could the blades cut through the cover and throw it clear? He studied it.... trying to imagine what would happen. Probably no.... the blades wouldn't accelerate fast enough.... could not build up enough inertia. Using the helicopter was too chancy. No doubt O'Rourke had reached the same conclusion, even assuming he hadn't already sabotaged the machinery in some way.

For the time being, Craig decided, the helicopter was out.

Craig looked moodily up at the sky beyond the helicopter, where a group of seagulls was circling noisily above the stern. One bird broke off and coming in low, settled with a noisy clatter on the high tail boom. Craig allowed his thoughts to drift a million miles away to England, and his Sunday walks on the Downs at Chanctonbury, where no doubt other gulls were also wheeling and soaring above the gnarled old Beech trees, but in a happier rural setting.

Somehow when all this was over, he would take Christine home to Sussex, settle down and start a new life. Forget the money and his cottage.... what on earth had made him think it was important? But wasn't he forgetting the key part he had played in O'Rourke's plan? Would the help he had given in thwarting the ransom demand be recognised? Perhaps the American Government would insist on a long prison sentence. What might he get? Five years.... ten? He squeezed his eyes closed and clenched his fists. No, that must not happen, it wouldn't be fair, after he alone had sabotaged the Al Qaeda kidnap and the IRA's ransom attempt, and saved the President's life.

"Enjoying some early morning air, dear boy?" O'Rourke's smile was tinged with suspicion.

Craig stepped back from the helicopter, not knowing why he had done so. He turned to face O'Rourke's bland forehead.

204

"Not much longer to wait now, and we will all be a lot richer," O'Rourke said breezily, "The Americans are going to pay up all right," he continued smugly. "NBC announced it after the newscast today. I arranged for the Jay Leno show to be cancelled.... nice touch, don't you think, dear boy?"

Again O'Rourke chuckled strangely to himself, and stroked the comma of dark hair towards his right eye.

The gesture irritated Craig. "So they really do value their Texan President at one hundred million," he mused. "Sheikh Makhtoum will be leaving Miami in the launch tomorrow afternoon, collect the cash, and be with us within the hour. We then enjoy a leisurely cruise down to Cuba, where a certain member of the Government has arranged an escorted entry to Port Cardenas, in exchange for a million dollars in US hard currency. Shall I bore you with another of my little aphorisms, dear boy.... money will buy anything or anybody."

Craig couldn't help reflecting that when it came to governments and big business, he was probably right.

"Once we are safely in Cuba, you will be at liberty to do as you please. Our little team will disperse and never meet again. Where do you intend to go then, dear boy?" O'Rourke's words were laced with innuendo. He seemed curiously interested in the reply. Craig found it difficult to look squarely into the man's eyes, while keeping up a pretence of his greed for the money.

Craig adopted a concerned expression.

"Cuba will be my best bet for a while, then I'll go to South Africa.... perhaps spend a few weeks in Cape Town lying in the sun, while the fuss dies down.... then home to England eventually."

"And how do you propose to cope with one million dollars in cash?" O'Rourke continued his interrogation. "You'll need a couple of large cases, and somewhere to bank the money."

"I suppose the usual Swiss Bank, you know, anonymous numbered account. I'll make the deposit from Cuba. America doesn't have anything to do with Castro." Craig was thinking quickly, but the idea seemed reasonable enough to avoid O'Rourke's suspicion.

"Excellent, excellent, dear boy," O'Rourke said with enthusiasm. "I'll give you details of a suitable Cuban bank when you receive your share of the ransom. But what about Christine? You two appear to be getting on very well together, I see."

"Oh, I'm not at all sure about that," Craig said carefully. He found it difficult to keep up the conversational tone.

"Well I'd understand if you wanted to take her back to England with you, dear boy." The expression was wooden. "Perhaps you may care to look after her."

"You'd better ask her that question," Craig's mind was teeming, "But we do get on well together, and I'll certainly help if I can."

"Good, then that's all settled," O'Rourke said amicably, as though arranging pairings for the village tennis club tournament. "That will relieve me of a job. Think I'll get some breakfast."

O'Rourke turned his back on Craig, and sauntered off with a light whistle. He paused at the steps leading to the upper deck, and peered into the darkness of the locker room holding the President. Seeming satisfied, he climbed the steps in the direction of the bridge.

Craig swallowed to relieve the dryness in his throat. That had been difficult going. He pulled a deck chair under him and sat back, looking out at the bright sun as it climbed smoothly into a cloudless sky.

He tried to make something of O'Rourke's small talk. What was he trying to accomplish by throwing him and Christine together? He wouldn't forget what O'Rourke had told them. The President was to be thrown overboard, a cold-blooded act of murder, and he would not allow himself to be misled by O'Rourke's apparent good humour. He still had no idea that the President was conscious. He must be having one hell of a difficult time shut away in the tiny locker room in semi-darkness, faking unconsciousness all day, and eating only at night. God what must it be like in there, three days without hygiene, living on the scraps of food that Christine managed to get to him. But O'Rourke was totally taken in by her reports, and for some reason, he felt disinclined to go into the locker room himself.

Craig's thoughts returned to O'Rourke.

So money would buy anything or anybody, would it? Well, in twenty-four hours he might well be finding out how wrong he was! As his attention was drawn back to the clattering and chattering of the seagulls, Christine appeared, looking down from the upper deck.

She was wearing a pretty 'outdoor-girl' cotton blouse, tightly belted above white jeans, showing off her trim figure.

Her blonde hair hung loosely, and Craig noticed the match of the light blue of the blouse and her eyes. He found it difficult not to be aroused by her beauty, but she looked unhappy.

"Hallo, Christine," Craig called up to her, a little artificially in case O'Rourke was listening. "Come and join me down here." As she sat close, he adjusted his chair so that he could see down the ship and observe anyone listening.

"Have you spoken to the President?" Craig whispered.

"Yes, he's just about recovered from the worst effects of the drugs, and is able to talk. He badly needs exercise, but all I could do was give him enough massage to keep his circulation going. I have to report to Mr O'Rourke next, and he thinks I am injecting enough Hioscene to keep the President sedated. Apart from going to the locker room a couple of times, he seems satisfied. I have to keep the door locked though and O'Rourke holds the key," she said dejectedly.

"The President says that once the Government have traced us, they will attempt to capture the ship, probably after dark. I have not told him what O'Rourke said about his own position, but he seems to know anyway. He's told me to leave his door unlocked tonight, which I will arrange once I have the key again…. might give him a chance to make his own escape."

"I have been thinking about that," Craig said, "and if necessary perhaps we could go over the side, but unless there were some boats about, we'd probably just drown, even assuming we didn't get shot in the water, but we can't make any positive plans now…. everything depends on how a rescue comes. It could be a helicopter attack, or another ship, but I really think they would use a submarine and make a commando type attack. O'Rourke doesn't suspect either of us. He has just told me he's received some codeword that confirms the government are going to pay the ransom. He has no idea what I've done, and thinks he's safe on the ship. We must keep constantly on the lookout for any sign of action, I'm absolutely certain. It will be tonight, but whatever you do Christine, try to behave normally and let O'Rourke continue to think we are just waiting to get our hands on the money. With a load of good luck we could be okay." He squeezed her hand. "You know how I'm beginning to feel about you, Christine."

They stood facing each other as he looked longingly into her blue eyes, his hand resting lightly around her waist in an affectionate embrace.

"Do you like Sussex Christine? I mean, have you thought about living there?"

She dropped her eyes shyly, and did not reply immediately, then, suddenly pulling him to her, she kissed him full on the lips surprising Craig. For a moment, she held him tightly before pulling away.... her eyes alight.

Smiling, she took a tissue from her pocket to wipe the lipstick from his mouth, but then took his face between her hands and brought her lips to his again, pushing her body to him as she kissed him on the mouth passionately.

"You're a wonderful girl." Craig panted as she released him. "I think I already know the answer."

"Alistair," she said eventually. "I can't believe this is happening. I've always hoped I might meet a nice guy like you, but here we are, in an impossible situation. I like you a lot, Alistair, but these last few days have been a nightmare. I'm just hoping we can get out of this mess. I'm so worried that horrible man will do something terrible. Let's pray we can get off this ship before we make our plans together."

She looked again at Craig, and hugging the memory of their kiss, she relaxed into a warm smile as he held her eyes. Her hair fluttered intriguingly against her cheeks in the evening breeze.

With a lovely girl like this, what the hell was money in comparison, thought Craig? If only he could get them both away from O'Rourke, and back to the safety of Sussex. Get his old job back and start out afresh with Christine, who now meant so much to him. He studied her again as she looked out to the horizon, shading her eyes. The sun highlighting her long blonde hair. Her skin shone with health.... Yes. She was the girl all right.... but so long as she felt the same way about him once the danger was past. Somehow, some way, he would get them out of this trouble, as surely as he had got himself into it. It was just a question of planning ahead for any eventuality, and being ready to act the moment any opportunity presented itself.

But he knew things would get difficult once a rescue started. There would have to be a lot of shooting, probably from both sides. But anything O'Rourke could put up would be totally swamped by the rescue team.

But suppose a rescue was not coming. Perhaps the high flying Lockheed Jet was just part of some ordinary Air Force navigational mission, and the small Cessna aircraft was on a routine training flight, or on its way to one of the Bahamian Islands for the weekend. Perhaps the Captain of the Jumbo Jet hadn't taken his Mayday call seriously, or for some reason he'd not been able to report the call.

Please God… Not that.

But no…. the co-pilot would also have heard Craig's emergency message, providing he had been on the flight deck at the time. So much could go wrong.

If nothing happened tonight, Craig decided, he'd have to get another call out.

He looked at some of the other escape possibilities. What about the speedboat that sat on the foredeck? Was there any way he could get it launched quickly?

"Let's take a look around the ship again, Christine."

They walked forward along the starboard gang walk. The speedboat was a well-known Fletcher…. a fast runabout with two massive Penta outboards, but it was solidly securely by the stout davits, and had probably never been used since the *Champagne Princess* was commissioned. Another dead end, Craig decided. It might be possible to release the boat, but never enough time to get it launched and the engine started. The noise alone would be as good as sounding an escape alarm.

Once again, he had to face the inevitable. They were in a prison, and if he gave O'Rourke the slightest warning that he was planning to get away, a shout to Brandt and a couple of bullets would quickly be the end of them both.

In any case, as the ransom deadline got near, O'Rourke probably had a constant watch set up, and even as the thought came to him, the radar dish high up on the bridge started to rotate slowly. So the watch had already started! Perhaps O'Rourke was expecting something after all.

Craig examined the scanner.... not the type of radar he was used to. What would be its range? Ten miles or so.... but he guessed its main function would be collision avoidance, and he doubted if it was capable of detecting an aircraft.... that would be a help.

But what if submarines were used for a rescue? The radar would be useless, unless of course the *Champagne Princess* had underwater radar.

He could only hope the person in charge of the rescue had taken all these factors into account.

He said a fond farewell to Christine with a goodbye kiss and returned to his cabin for the afternoon.

He sat at the desk, his mind churning through the next few hours, as ever looking at the escape possibilities, and how he should prepare for any one of them.

One thing was certain. He had the edge over O'Rourke, who would be in for one mighty surprise when the government forces descended on the *Champagne Princess*, and the boot of the first commando landed on her deck at his feet.

# 27

The briefing room serving as the centre of operations had been hastily prepared using an American Airlines final departure lounge. To a casual visitor, the two capital A's of the Airline's bright red logo, blazoned on one wall of the room, gave no clue to the importance of the meeting that was about to be held, and the momentous decisions that would be taken.

A one-twentieth-scale model of the *Champagne Princess* was positioned on the make-shift stage in front of a central lectern. On the wall behind the stage, two bright spotlights illuminated a map of the Florida Keys. Under the lectern, the words, 'Operation Kingpin' was sign-written in red plastic letters. Two armed policemen guarded the entrance, checking identity papers of all visitors as the room filled with Fort Bragg's most important military and security men in America.

At 09.00 hours precisely, Vic Cramer walked on to the stage.

He sat with Captain Grant at the head of a horseshoe table, with three senior officers of the Armed Forces, together with the head of the FBI, two members of the Senate, and the team leaders of the Delta Force's underwater and Ranger's free-fall diving teams.

The Vice President sat quietly to one side of the stage. He was studying his fingernails.

Cramer's eyes flickered around the table, nodding briefly. He introduced himself with a curt, "Vic Cramer."

He picked up a long ruler and tapped the wall-chart behind him.

"Gentlemen, I am here to open this briefing, and provide all agent operatives with the background for this rescue operation." Cramer gestured to his left.

"Captain Grant is in charge of the rescue manoeuvres. He will provide the main briefing shortly."

Grant stood up briefly and nodded to the room.

Cramer went on.

"I am sure you have all had a chance to reassess the position since our last meeting and in the light of the information received yesterday. A transcript of the message, received by Captain Hopkins of Continental Airlines, is in front of you. It gives the position of the *Champagne Princess....* the target ship, where our President is held prisoner."

"Our high level reconnaissance has confirmed the ship's position remains the same, and this is being continually monitored on a minute-by-minute basis."

"The purpose of this meeting is therefore, to brief your operatives on the rescue plan, which is to secure the release of the President. Captain Grant of the National Security Agency will organise the rescue operation. I am the Operations Director. The rescue operation will commence at 19.00 hours precisely."

"That is tomorrow, Gentlemen. We have therefore...." He glanced at his watch, and looked up at the circle of men meaningfully, "Just thirty-four hours to prepare for this operation. It is code-named 'Operation Kingpin.' You will note the revised plan results from information we now have, that Al Qaeda do not intend to release the President, even when the ransom money is paid."

There was anger in Cramer's voice, as he continued.

"These kidnappers are a well known, leading Al Qaeda cell. The English pilot's message advises that they also have an IRA Senior Officer on board. He is in charge of the ship. His name is a very Irish Ryan O'Rourke."

Cramer allowed himself a smile as he continued.

"British intelligence is checking out the name. First reports say, he is a known Officer of the recently formed Real IRA. We are awaiting more detailed information on this man."

Cramer, looked down to his notes. The difficult Arab names were coming up.

"The Al Qaeda names we have, we know of only too well. Ahmed Massoud and Ramzi Yousef.... remember them, Gentlemen. But it appears the overall leader of this kidnap operation is our old friend, Khalid Mohammed, and less anyone is tempted to dismiss any of these Arabs, let me tell you that Khalid Mohammed is an experienced terrorist who specialises in political assassinations, car bombing, aircraft hijacking and reservoir poisoning.

Ultimately, he was the man who masterminded the 9/11 World Trade Centre bombing. When he is in transit, he uses the alias of Sheikh Makhtoum, a racehorse owner. Intelligence says he has been threatening a further major attack on us for months. This is it. Let me tell you more about the man and the organisation we face."

"Khalid Mohammed is an Islamic religious fanatic... a lover of violent Jihad at his early youth camps. He left his native Kuwait at sixteen, and came here to enrol in a Baptist college in North Carolina. Once again, we seem to have been playing nursemaid to these terrorists. He has a nephew, one Ramzi Yousef, who was responsible for the 1993 bombing of the World Trade Centre. He actually made the bomb. This will be the same Yousef, who the message says is now on the target ship."

Cramer allowed himself a moment of revenge. He'd lost a very good friend in that 1993 attack. "Once the President is safe, I want you to get him!"

Knowing smiles answered back. If these men from Delta Force and the Rangers could succeed and grab this Al Qaeda lot in one fell swoop, what a cauldron of villains he would have nabbed. A real dent in their terrorist network.

"Men, let me now turn to the IRA outfit. This is an illegal Para-Military group, who operate from bases in the Republic of Ireland. They enjoy considerable sympathy from both sides of the Irish border, mainly the Catholic support, and even from some members of the British Parliament and the USA. They profess to be a political organisation, but have been responsible for the murder of two

213

thousand civilians and servicemen in Northern Ireland. I give you this information, gentlemen, so that you do not underestimate these Irish terrorists. They are intelligent, highly experienced, and ruthless killers."

Vic Cramer leaned forward to grasp the lectern with both hands. His expression remained grim.

"There is, I am sad to say, the possibility that the President has already been murdered, although Al Qaeda should understand that Government Agencies will require proof of his well being before any ransom monies are released. But these can be irrational men, with irrational thinking. They are capable of anything if they believe their Allah is with them."

"However, Gentlemen, Operation Kingpin remains the same. We must board the target ship swiftly, and in total surprise. The persons on board are to be overpowered and taken into custody, but it is officially recorded that all Agents have the United States Government's authority to kill as may become necessary, to secure the safety of the President. There will be no recriminations, men, I assure you."

Cramer picked up his notes and wiped a handkerchief over his brow.

"So, Gentlemen, before I pass you to Captain Grant, let me close my brief by repeating our principal objective. The release of the President of America. I want you to keep that objective constantly in your mind."

He embraced the room with a confident smile.

"Only then may we succeed." Cramer gestured to his side.

"Now to the operation itself, and for this I will pass you over to Captain Grant of the NSA. He will brief you in detail on the rescue plan you are to execute. Over to you, Captain Grant."

Grant stood up. He was holding a small laser pointer. He circled the *Champagne Princess* with its pin-point of red light, and let it come to rest on the ship's main deck. He gave it a flick.

"This is where the attack starts, Gentlemen. We will be using our most experienced operators from Delta Force and Rangers. The two rescue teams will make simultaneous boardings. These are an underwater team and an airborne team, each consisting of twelve men. The airborne team will comprise the Rangers, who will make the parachute drop from a Hercules C130 aircraft. The underwater boarding will be made by Delta Force. They will approach initially by submarine, to a range of three hundred yards. They will then leave the airlocks, remaining underwater, until they can surface alongside the target ship. Each man will be equipped with CS gas canisters, stun grenades and semi-automatic AK47's."

"Arrangements have been made for two, full-scale practice rescues, using a vessel similar to the Target Ship at 14.00 hours this afternoon, and again at 19.00 hours tonight. You will find reporting details of this in the notes. I have to emphasise to all Agents and team leaders that the number one priority throughout Operation Kingpin is the safe recovery of the President. As our CIA Chief has briefed, other lives and property are a secondary consideration."

"The airborne Rangers boarding team will wear matt black suits, with a single red armband for identification. The Delta Force diving team will use matt black and yellow suits, and employ underwater breathing apparatus of the recirculating type, to minimise the surface escape of air. Underwater teams will be equipped with cartridge-propelled grappling hooks. Team leaders are to practice their men, until they can be out of the water, and up ten feet of rope to the ship's gang-walks, in ten seconds. When the first man is spotted by the kidnap gang, there will be just seconds to save the President."

"Next the airborne attack. A Hercules C130 with twelve Ranger parachutists will make a precisely timed exit from fifteen thousand feet. Your men are 'free-fall' spot landing experts, and we anticipate at least half should achieve a landing on the target ship's deck. The first drop will be a high altitude chute opening using 'Paracloud' canopies."

"The second drop will free-fall to seven hundred and fifty feet, and time their descent for a deck landing thirty seconds later. In the semi-darkness the parachute approach should remain largely undetected until the last few seconds. Out of a total of twenty-four men, we expect at least eight Rangers will land on the target ship, and combined with the twelve men of Delta Force's underwater team, that should give us a total of eighteen men aboard within seconds. Let's hope the gang won't know what hit them."

"Two further Army teams from the Chinook helicopter and the launch *Cutlass* will close in at eighteen-ten hours. Their function is to lift the President off the ship and transfer him to the Chinook. From there, he will be flown to the military hospital at Opa Locka. Finally, the medical team in the second Chinook will move in at eighteen-fifteen hours to remove casualties and transport the injured to the General Hospital in Miami."

"We understand there is a British pilot on board, and if possible he is to be safeguarded, but I must emphasise that the primary purpose of this entire operation is to secure the safe release of the President."

Captain Grant paused as a giant photograph of the *Champagne Princess* was wheeled into the briefing room on a long stand and set up behind the model ship. The picture was a massive enlargement fifteen feet long. Alongside the photograph was a smaller blueprint line-drawing, showing the layout of the ship's structure, indicating the numbered cabins, the bridge position and engine room.

"Now, Gentlemen, if the Rangers and Delta Force leaders will move forward, we may examine the target ship in detail."

"We have just received this photograph from NASA, taken obliquely from forty thousand feet by our Lockheed U2 reconnaissance jet. Enlarged twenty times, we can identify a paint mark on the deck, and I will now ask Naval Commander, Captain Forbes, to continue with the briefing, giving more detail of the ship and the planned boardings."

Forbes was a middle aged, wiry looking man, wearing naval uniform. He had the lined, weather beaten features that suggested too many years at sea. He stood close to the shoulder-high photograph, and spoke quietly with a rasp in his voice, the 1940's voice of Humphrey Bogart in the classic, Casablanca.

"Men, the target ship here, the *Champagne Princess*, is a twin turbine vessel, two-hundred and fifty feet long and forty feet beam. She draws twenty-five. The ship has seven cabins and the London Lloyds register lists her as one hundred-fifty tons. Make no mistake men, a vessel like this is in the same performance class as our latest naval destroyers, but the ship-makers build these hulls with all the fancy fittings for the millionaire trade. She has anti-collision and weather radar, and probably Sonar for underwater work. A specialist agent has the task of disabling the underwater Sonar antenna at 18.55 hours."

He turned to the photograph.

"This picture clearly shows the outline of a helicopter on the aft deck. It has been partially hidden under covers, but we have determined the helicopter is made by the Enstrom factory in Menominee, Michigan. The type is known as the 480 Hawk. The smaller, thermal-image picture reveals that the engine has not been run in the last three days. We are sure the helicopter was used to put the President on board, and the FAA team are checking its most likely route."

"As Captain Grant has told us, there are to be two main rescue attacks by the Airborne and Underwater teams. The twelve-man teams will be split into six, two-man sub teams. The Rangers airborne team with red armbands will be, 'Red A (Alpha)' numbered one to six, and 'Red Alpha B.' The Delta Force underwater team 'Yellow B (Bravo)' will also be similarly numbered. Both teams will make the timed boarding as your individual briefs, and each two man sub team will be allocated a cabin number. For the underwater team, the easiest boarding points are at the centre and aft…. Here, and here."

Forbes picked up the long wooden pointer and indicated each area on the ship as he continued.

"There are seven main cabins, and a Stateroom, which I have numbered. Cabins one to four are located on the starboard side, adjacent to the radio room. The remaining three cabins, numbered five, six and seven, are on the port side. The Stateroom is forward here, under the bridge."

"Each cabin corresponds to the team number. Team number one will attack cabin number one. Team number, two attack cabin number two, and so on."

"We think it likely that the President is imprisoned in one of the smaller cabins, possibly a locker next to the radio room, but each team will assume their allocated cabin is holding the President. We understand that the cabins can be locked from either side of the door, and you will be issued with miniature coiled spring hammers which, when released, have a breaking force of eight hundred pounds, sufficient to shatter all conventional locks."

"You must expect the President to be incapacitated, and require moving by stretcher. This will be the responsibility of Red team Alpha Two, who have the medics operatives."

"This is the sequence of events as they appear in your briefing notes, and individual teams will receive further briefings with your team-commanders, before this afternoon's first practice at Fort Lauderdale."

"Men, I have no need to impress on you the importance of Operation Kingpin. I have to repeat, success will only come if all agents are totally familiar with the ship, and accomplish their tasks on schedule. So in summary men, please now refer to your written briefs. Here is how the timing looks."

The room fell quiet as the men rustled their papers.

OPERATION KINGPIN.

RANGERS AND DELTA FORCE OPERATIVES.

18.50 Hours. ALL TEAMS TO POSITION TO THE TARGET AREA AND THEIR INDIVIDUALLY ASSIGNED POSITIONS.

19.00 Hours. FIRST EXIT BY RANGERS PARACHUTE TEAM RED ALPHA ONE FOR THE TIMED ARRIVAL ON THE TARGET'S DECK AT 19.05 HRS.

19.03 Hours. SECOND EXIT BY RANGERS FREE-FALL PARACHUTE TEAM RED ALPHA TWO FOR A DECK ARRIVAL AT 19.05 HRS PLUS 30 SECONDS

19.05 Hours. DELTA FORCE UNDERWATER TEAM YELLOW ALPHA AND BRAVO TO SURFACE FOR BOARDING TARGET AT 19.06 HOURS.

19.15 Hours. CHINOOK HELICOPTER AND HSL 'CUTLASS' TO CLOSE IN ALONGSIDE TARGET SHIP.

\* \* \* \* \* \*

"As soon as any team have the President safely in their custody, two green Verey lights will be fired, with a five second interval between them. Once this signal is observed, the planned timings are to be ignored, and all units will close in immediately to capture the remaining persons on board."

Forbes walked around the scale model of the *Champagne Princess*, and continued.

"I want all members of the attack team to study the layout of this ship until you can board and move about her blindfold. Each team must be able to locate their assigned cabin in seconds, and if necessary, in total darkness. You will carry infrared glasses on your headgear. We know the gang are armed, and you can expect resistance with firearms. There will be casualties, but I repeat, surprise is the strength of this plan. It may be possible to secure the President's release, without a single shot being fired."

"Gentlemen do you have any questions?"

A hand went up at the back of the room.

"What happens if the first rescue wave is spotted, and the target ship starts moving before we board."

"A specialist Delta Force underwater team have the task of disabling the ship's driving gear at H hour minus five minutes, and I promise you, the target ship will be immobile. Nuclear subs U2 and U3 are a separate operation, and can surface against the target if it became necessary. They have instructions to ram the *Champagne Princess* if necessary, to prevent her moving."

"A Chinook helicopter is also holding a reserve team that would be called in. The *Cutlass's* Captain has instructions to move in ahead of the planned schedule with a further rescue team. But teams Red Alpha and Yellow Bravo are the first wave key-men, and once you are on the ship, we anticipate odds of at least five to one in your favour. The rescue operation will be completed in less than five minutes. Providing the first boarding teams do not get seen, Operation Kingpin will be successful."

"Any further questions men?" The room remained quiet.

"Right gentlemen, will you now proceed to your individual briefing areas as shown on the notes. Transport will be available for the first boarding practice at 14.00 hours."

Vic Cramer thanked Captain Forbes, and walked across the room. The Vice President was talking to the service officers. He seemed pleased. Just like a politician. The voters would be satisfied, and he was happy to see his agents, the G-men, go in with all guns blazing!

"Thank you," The Vice President said, addressing no one in particular. "A good briefing, and you seemed to have taken into account all possibilities. Is the operation going to work out the way you have planned?"

Something of a loaded question Cramer decided.

219

"We are dealing with men Sir, human fallible men. All I can tell you is that we've planned 'Kingpin' using the best advice of the specialist sections of our Fort Bragg men, my CIA, the NSA, and the military. Delta Force and the Rangers are the most highly trained government agents this country possesses. If they cannot pull off the rescue, I'll know we've given it our best shot, and it probably wasn't possible anyway."

Vic Cramer stood for several minutes studying the model that was about to become the stage for the most difficult rescue operation he had ever attempted. If this hand-picked team followed their orders, the whole operation might prove too simple. But just one tiny mistake, and he would have an international disaster on his hands.

Tomorrow, around seven o'clock, he would know the outcome. Come hell or high water, Operation Kingpin just had to succeed.

# 28

The *Champagne Princess* was quiet.... as quiet as any time of the day. A large orange sun settled into the gathering mist as the fluffy fair weather Cumulus clouds collapsed into the sea. With dusk closing around the ship, a chubby moon climbed cautiously into the darkening sky and the brightest of the evening stars began their merry twinkle.

It should have been a lovely evening.

Craig's watch showed 18.00 hrs, and he wondered what the night would bring. He knew an attempt to rescue the President must come tonight, under cover of darkness. So that meant little more than an hour to go.... But an hour of uncertainty, an hour of taut nerves, and knotted stomach muscles. O'Rourke and Brandt were on the bridge, Ahmed and Yousef, presumably down below. The only sound came from the sea, and the background hum of the radar dish, as it circled monotonously above the bridge. If O'Rourke felt sure the ransom was going to be made tomorrow, he might well be off his guard tonight.

Craig strained his eyes to the darkening sea, where the moonlight rippled on the waves, and painted its silver shadows across the ship. Craig walked quietly along the starboard gang way. Everything was so damnably quiet. But what was that?

He looked up again to the darkening sky. A distant throb from an aircraft. He felt a flicker of optimism. Yes, and as the sound became louder, he was certain. A muted rumble of an approaching high-flying jet, and listening more anxiously, he could hear the unmistakable sound of a second aircraft, a turbo prop and a heavy transport type, in a holding pattern overhead the *Champagne Princess*. So, if they were the government aircraft, a rescue was coming by air after all. Craig's thoughts raced. An airborne operation, so it had to be an attack with parachutes.

The jet engine note was typical of a Boeing AWAC flying at reduced power. It would be in command of the operation. Fitted with sophisticated ground tracking radar and infrared night vision that produced images as clear as daylight.... just the job for an airborne observation platform.

Christine came up on deck and whispered to Craig. She had heard the aircraft too.

"What sort of aeroplane is that, Alistair?"

"It's a high altitude observation AWAC, I'm absolutely sure, Christine, but there are two of them, circling the ship. It could be the start of a rescue. They'll be using parachutes to board the ship."

Craig was thinking rapidly.

"Have you still got the President's key?"

She nodded.

"Good. Now listen Christine, go to the President and tell him there are aircraft overhead, and to be ready to leave his cabin. If anything goes wrong, I've decided we'll take a chance in the helicopter."

She looked frightened and her blue eyes looked anxiously into his.

"Once O'Rourke knows the ship is under attack, he's quite likely to hold the President as an escape hostage, but who can tell? Or he might decide to shoot us all. If that seems likely, I'll get the helicopter started."

He pointed to the rear of the ship.

"Tell the President to make for the helicopter deck as soon as the blades are going.... that will be the signal. If I can get aboard and spin up the rotors quickly enough, we can get away if we need to. In the confusion, we could make it."

He put his arm around Christine as he spoke, guiding her. She was trembling.

"When you get reach the helicopter, get into the cabin on the left side. I'll have that door open. Tell the President to get in the front alongside me. We are bound to be heard. Just keep your fingers crossed I can get the helicopter started in time."

Craig looked back to the Hawk.

"Be sure the President understands what we are doing Christine. I'm going down to the rear deck to see if I can get to the ropes."

Christine kissed him quickly on the cheek and hurried away.

Craig walked purposefully along the gang walk to the helicopter…. planning.

He sensed footsteps behind…. began to turn to face them…. then a flash of light in his head and the world crashed sideways about him.

A massive blow to his head jarred every bone in his body, as though he'd been hit by a truck. It was followed by a pain in his leg, he would never have believed possible, a fierce pain that screamed up his leg and exploded into his gut.

Craig's legs buckled beneath him.

He'd been struck with surgical accuracy, on the boss of the bone at the back of his knee, a fierce blow on the Medial Condyle of the Femur, a blow that induces the worst pain it is possible to inflict on a human.

Craig felt himself slipping, and tried to take hold of the ship's rail, as the deck rushed up to meet him.

A hundred miles away he heard O'Rourke's angry voice.

"Brandt, drag him back to his cabin. Make sure he's securely tied. I'll be along in a while. We'll soon see what he has to say for himself…."

Craig felt himself lifted roughly….

Then darkness.

# 29

Eight miles above the unconscious Craig, at forty two thousand feet, the Government's rescue plan was building up smoothly.... the countdown to H-Hour had begun.

The two aircraft Craig had heard were a Hercules C130, with its crack team of parachute Rangers, and the controlling AWAC Boeing 747 circling the *Champagne Princess*. The Rangers were the top 'delayed drop' specialists in the country, and each man had made at least one hundred free-fall drops at night, to a precision landing area no larger than a tennis court, and only the previous night had carried out a practice descent to a similar ship. A dress rehearsal for the actual operation. Fifteen had landed on the ship's deck, and tonight Vic Cramer would be satisfied if only half that number succeeded on the *Champagne Princess*. They would arrive in darkness.... unseen and unheard, while silently gliding the last thousand feet to the target. Once on board, they would be expected to overpower the crew in seconds.

The three submarines were positioned in a circle at a range of three hundred yards, and the underwater team of Delta Force divers would leave the air locks in pairs to start the swift underwater swim to the ship. They were using self-contained underwater breathing apparatus, and timed to surface alongside the ship at H Hour, precisely as the first parachutist touched down. The high-speed launch *Cutlass* was lying out of sight, and would race the three miles to the ship in two minutes. She would head the second wave attack. Cramer had reserves of two further submarines, the Chinook helicopters, and the Delta sabotage specialists, who would already be disarming the ship.

It was a good plan.... timed to the second.

Sure, Cramer thought, he was using a sledgehammer to crack a walnut, but the cost factor, for once, was not a consideration. Providing the airborne and underwater rescue teams remained undetected, the President was as good as saved. His Rangers and the Delta boys were well keyed up, in anticipation of the important task ahead, and would swamp the ship in complete surprise. Every cabin would be stormed, with a stun grenade placed in each. All his men would need to do was locate the unconscious President, and the job was done.

The odds had shifted in the Government's favour, and for a moment, Cramer bathed in the accolade of success that was shortly to be his. He had planned this operation well.... Yes that was the secret. Method.... Organisation.... Timing. The only way to beat these twenty first century Arab Guerrillas. The infamous Bin Laden was about to be well and truly socked!

Captain Grant was in control of the massive screen before him. The radar returns beamed down to him from the AWAC, and picking up the R/T microphone, he called the pilot of the Hercules parachute aircraft.

"Airborne Red Alpha One leader, report your status."

The reply was instant.

"Red Alpha One Leader.... In position with Rangers descent team ready to leave the aircraft. Time check now Eighteen-twenty-five hours. Confirm the first exit at nineteen hundred. H-hour, minus thirty-five minutes. And counting."

"Roger, Airborne Leader Red Alpha One.... Check in Red Alpha Two."

"Okay sir, Red Alpha Two also in position holding over the Delta Zulu.... Ready to commence second Para drop at nineteen-zero-tree. H Hour plus three minutes."

"Roger," Grant acknowledged. "Standby Red Alpha Two to await your call in and continue to listen out."

Grant looked up from the radar screen and motioned to one of the three women standing over the operations table. Like the Ops rooms used in the Battle of Britain, several models on the table indicated the positions of the two Hercules, and the surface vessels, with the target ship, the *Champagne Princess* at its centre. One girl moved the model with the tip of a long snooker cue. Grant studied the table plan for a moment, and looked up at the white digital clock counting down the minutes and seconds, to H-Hour.

He picked up the microphone again. "Underwater Yellow Leader, report your position and check positions of numbers two and three underwater units."

There was a short pause, then a crackle of static as a broken transmission came in.

"Underwater Yellow Two checking in Sir and also in position... Range from target three hundred yards.... Bearing zero-five-five degrees.... Periscope depth at twenty feet. Delta Force Underwater diving teams are standing by to enter airlocks for tracking to target. Time check now Eighteen-three-zero.... Thirty-five minutes to H-Hour, over."

"Roger Yellow One. Hold position as briefed. Yellow three to stand by for fast surface if called."

"Number three standing by Sir, your message understood."

From his airborne observation post, the hard lines on the face of Vic Cramer relaxed into a taut smile. He was satisfied with the way Grant was handling the operation.... slotting into place, as their prepared plan swung into action with clockwork precision. The *Champagne Princess* and her crew of Al Qaeda murderers were about to feel the anger of the American nation, and they would just not know what had hit them.

He was a little unhappy at the request from the British Anti-Terrorist Squad, to ensure any IRA operatives among them were killed. Apparently on the direct orders of the new Prime Minister. Something to do with not having a Florida Four! Well that might be the way it was going to work anyway. His job was to get the President out, and to hell with what his men did with the others on the ship.

Grant spoke into the microphone again.

"Come in *Cutlass*, report your position."

"As briefed sir. Came the reply. *Cutlass* holding clear of target at Two thousand yards range.... Bearing Two seven zero."

The operations clerk moved the model *Cutlass* to its reported position on the operations board.

"Roger *Cutlass*," Grant instructed. "You commence your run in to the target to arrive with the Chinook helicopter at Nineteen-ten hours."

"That's copied and understood Sir and standing by.... *Cutlass* Out."

Grant and Vic Cramer both sat back with satisfaction, looking over the operations table, which showed the *Champagne Princess* at its centre, encircled by the submarines and the high-speed launch. The two Hercules aircraft were overhead the target, with the Chinook helicopter waiting at the table edge.

The success of the operation relied totally on precision timing, and at this moment each team leader's attention was similarly riveted to his timepiece, mentally preparing for the massive outbreak of combined action just minutes away.

# 30

Back on the *Champagne Princess*, O'Rourke sat on the bridge looking out over the bows, deep in thought.

He was thinking of the changes he might need to make to his plan in the next few hours. He'd made a bad mistake trusting Craig. The stupid Brit, who still believed in loyalty. That loyalty was to cost him dearly. So what to do with him? He knew he'd been careless in allowing him to find a chink in his armour, his perfect ransom plan.

If Craig had made contact with the authorities, he'd need to move quickly. But did it make any difference? If the American Government did know the ship's location, all he needed to do was repeat his ransom demand. No ransom money, or any attempt at attacking the ship, and the President dies. But that all assumed Craig had transmitted the message that he'd so carelessly left in the helicopter.

He had Craig wrapped up securely, awaiting his attention at leisure. Let him stew for a while before he screwed out the truth.... That would be too easy. He'd done it too many times in the past. Information extraction for the IRA was his speciality, and with a particularly stubborn subject, quite enjoyable. But he doubted if Craig was made of such material.

He strained his ears for what he thought was the distant drone of an aircraft again. He couldn't be sure. Relax, he told himself, there was bound to be some routine flow of airline traffic in the area. But why didn't the aircraft noise go away?

Surely the United States wouldn't take any risks with their beloved President's life, and in any case, he assured himself, unless Craig had made the contact, they had no way of associating the *Champagne Princess* with the President's kidnap, one ship out of a hundred that would be off the Florida Keys. But then again, why couldn't he see any?

Strange to be the only vessel in the area. Best to check on the radar again.

But how could an aircraft approach the ship without being observed a mile away? No, his position was unassailable, and they damn well knew it. Still he would be happier when tomorrow came, and Sheikh Makhtoum appeared in the launch with the money. The biggest heist in American history.... no.... in the world! And success would make him the most acclaimed patriot in Ireland.

But he was not interested in the reputation.... just the power one hundred million would bring to the Irish cause.

With the ransom safely in his hands, it then only remained to dispose of the President, and the two lovebirds. Just a little of the gas for each of them perhaps, and a simple 'heave-ho' over the side. The sharks would do the rest inside minutes, especially if he could arrange a little blood to give them the first scent! Then a bullet for the unsuspecting Brandt, and the two crewman, and he would be away. But would Makhtoum give him any trouble, he pondered?

Brandt had been necessary to help with the rough stuff at Government House, but he was a simple black, and wouldn't be missed. Alongside the Sheikh, he'd seen the kidnap of the President through, exactly as planned. The money was as good as theirs.

What did one hundred million dollars look like?

A stack of fifty packs of neatly printed-paper? No.... it was the smile being wiped off the faces of the stupid politicians in Westminster.

The image flooded his mind.

How they would sit up when the security forces discovered his Real IRA possessed laser and infrared rifles, and for those special occasions, the 'Sam Redeye' and 'Rapier' missiles. Why not put the first one in the Palace of Westminster? Really give them something to think about.

With his warm thoughts as company, O'Rourke decided to stroll forward to the bridge, as he decided what to do with Craig. Perhaps a little judicious roughing up first! Let the little twit know how hard the real world could become!

He adjusted the gain and range controls of the coloured screen, to highlight the echo returns from other ships, but there was nothing. The bright leading edge of the transmitter signal circled lazily. The green tube stared back blankly. He mustn't be so edgy. The kidnap he'd worked on for so long was only a few hours from absolute success. He had planned every move rather like a game of chess, and now he held all the valuable pieces.

As long as the President was under his control, the United States Government would do nothing to risk his life. They would do exactly as they were told. He could probably even ask for a massed brass band accompaniment to fanfare his success, and would get it.

The money would be left precisely as he had instructed, and he would cover up all traces and simply disappear. The friendly Cuban government official was his best insurance. Amazing what people, especially people in high places, would do for the right amount of money. The private jet would be waiting and he'd be safely on his way to Dublin.... to the applause.... to the hero's welcome!

Two men sat quietly, each reflecting on the success that was to be theirs. O'Rourke on the bridge of the *Champagne Princess*, secure in the knowledge that his captive President ensured the success of his plan, and the collection of a one hundred million dollar ransom. While at his command post in Miami, Vic Cramer surveyed the position of his specialist teams encircling the ship, poised to launch the attack.

\* \* \* \* \* \*

But even as each man anticipated victory, other circumstances were deciding that neither side's plan would succeed. Fate had a third person waiting in the wings.... and was about to play her decisive hand.

Less than fifty miles away, at Fort Lauderdale executive airport, Captain Mark Stockley, another pilot, the same age as Alistair Craig, was flight planning a routine air taxi trip to the Bahamas.

Jeppesen IFR route maps, the airways clearance, and the technical log had to be attended to for the ops office, but as he prepared his Beechcraft Duke Executive, he little knew that this was to be his last flight, but that in losing his life, he would save a fellow pilot from O'Rourke's terrible torture, and unwittingly assist in saving the life of the President of the United States of America.

# 31

Craig explored the sensations around his aching body. He moved to get up but found his arms shackled to a chair that was in turn secured to the bunk ladder. He was a prisoner in his own cabin. His feet were strapped to the legs of the chair, holding his thighs apart. The Venetian blinds were down and the fading light from the oval porthole told him dusk was approaching. He had never felt so utterly helpless or vulnerable. The back of his head throbbed, where he'd been struck from behind and his wrists felt numb from the tight towelling strips that bound him.

How long had he been unconscious?

He looked across his cabin to the desk clock…. just six thirty.

If his reasoning was correct, the Government forces would have to take action tonight, and if it was to be at dusk, certainly in the next hour.

But something had gone badly wrong, and now he was an absolute prisoner. What had happened to Christine, and why had O'Rourke turned on him? No doubt he'd soon be finding out.

Craig heard footsteps. O'Rourke came into the cabin. He was pulling Christine with him. Her face was tear-streaked and distraught, her hair a mess. He shoved her roughly to the sofa. She collapsed on to it. Had he been violent to her too? Craig wondered.

The black comma of hair was slicked back. The forehead glistened. For a dreadful minute O'Rourke stood silently over Craig, the laser eyes shining angrily…. Christine lay forlornly on her side. Her hands to her face…. She had her eyes closed cowering in fear.

Craig was very worried. He could sense trouble everywhere. Should he try to take the man head on? Try some brinkmanship?

"Who the hell do you think you are, O'Rourke?" he burst out in desperation. "I thought we had an understanding. I don't know what you think you're doing, keeping me a prisoner, tied up like this, but just let me loose now."

Craig had no idea how O'Rourke would react, but at least he was doing something to gain an initiative, giving him something to think about.

O'Rourke stood with his arms folded, looking down at Craig with mild curiosity, as though a child was asking a silly question. He spoke quietly. It was a neutral voice, remote, without colour. Almost bored, but dangerous.

"Alistair, my dear boy…. You have disappointed me." He began ominously. " I felt sure you would understand the nature of your position, and appreciate your prospects with us. But I have overestimated your capacity for rationalizing a situation."

O'Rourke waved at Craig airily, but the laser stare never wavered…. it remained glued on Craig. He produced a wintry smile and spoke slowly and deliberately as though he was acting in a Shakespeare play.

"The *Champagne Princess*," he began calmly, "could have been the entry to a kingdom for you, dear boy. A kingdom of riches, riches only achievable by the peasant masses through the 'millionaire' programmes offered by greedy TV companies, who promise a dream in exchange for telephone money, but keeping the big profits for themselves."

The stage smile creased and vanished. Suddenly, he changed tempo and yelled angrily at Craig.

"But now I find this, you ungrateful and stupid fool."

O'Rourke removed a folded paper from his breast pocket. Craig recognized it instantly. Oh dear God above, he thought, the message he'd used in the helicopter! What a careless idiot he'd been, leaving the evidence for O'Rourke to find! He must have dropped the message in the darkness, probably in the cabin. That spelled really big trouble.

O'Rourke brandished the paper and glared down at Craig.

"So we have a traitor in our midst. All along you have been deceiving me, dear boy, pretending to be with us, helping us with our mission, so now I need to know what you have done. And you will tell me, I promise you."

Craig looked across the cabin to the walnut desk where the colourful Hyacinths now seemed so pointless. On the desk was a tray containing several items of everyday kitchen equipment, a meat skewer, a serrated steak knife, a small teaspoon, but curiously, a knitting needle. There was also a black rubber cosh. Things looked bad. What was O'Rourke about to do?

O'Rourke selected the rubber cosh from the tray, casually bouncing it against his palm. Craig could see he was about to get a beating at least. Christine was sobbing loudly. She turned away and buried her face on the sofa.

O'Rourke continued the monotone in a milder voice, but menacingly.

"Dear boy, we are playing for high stakes here today. You know the figure. One hundred million clean American dollars. This operation is a life's dream coming true. But a dream that required years of waiting, months of planning, and not inconsiderable investment of capital. Until your untimely intervention, I was on the very verge of success, dear boy. You may have spoiled that success, so you will forgive me for taking desperate measures to restore the situation."

O'Rourke's expression returned to the laser gaze. He moved his head from side to side negatively, as though declining a suspicious sales offer from a street trader. The eyes were far a way... Glazed.... The voice distant.

"You see, I had a dream too.... a dream to take revenge on you damned British for the years of oppression. Your forefathers, the Elizabethans, who rained down on my people four-hundred years ago.... who battled against my countrymen in Munster, Leinster and the free counties. Ruthlessly snuffing out their lives, and continuing to do so over the centuries. Your forefathers," he emphasized, jabbing his finger at Craig, "who sent over the evil prisoners.

Prisoners released from the jails. The accursed Protestants. The Black and Tans, who came to my country to quell the riots, and beat a free Ireland into submission with the cosh, much like the one I am about to use on you. The fiendish Britishers who stole my father's life. They will pay. Do you understand these matters, dear boy...?"

He suddenly screamed again at Craig.

"Have you considered them, you stupid Britisher....? Studied the history?"

Craig looked up at O'Rourke's red face. He had to delay the man, gain some precious minutes. Could he keep O'Rourke talking? Could he reason with him? Anything for more time.

"Mr O'Rourke, you must know that neither myself nor any of the British people had control over the invasion of your country. It was so many years ago anyway. I cannot tell you why Britain has been so determined to keep fighting with Ireland. It's the politics of Government.... the people have no direct control. You must understand that. Look to the politicians and the ballot box if you want redress." Craig could feel the man's dangerous reaction building, as he continued to reason. "Just untie me now Mr O'Rourke, so we can talk this thing through in a civilized manner. You can't take on the whole world, you know."

O'Rourke looked down at Craig with indifference. He pulled up a chair, and sat very close, his face just inches away. Craig could smell the man, could feel the miasma of O'Rourke's breathing.

"Dear boy, you continue to disappoint me. You must know the ballot box failed decades ago. The only vote you Britishers understand is the vote of the bullet. But you lie to me too, Captain Craig."

He flicked the paper across Craig's face.

"I now know of your true intent dear boy. You could have become part of our success, shared in the wealth we are to rightfully receive, yet you have chosen to undermine our project with this."

He rattled the paper at Craig again as his temper flared.

"And for what?" he snarled. "Some misguided thought of 'the right stuff?' O'Rourke smirked as he mimicked Craig's British accent. "The proper thing to do? The saving of a President. A President, who murdered thousands of people in Iraq, a man who should mean

235

nothing to you. But you have chosen and you have acted, so now you see, dear boy, I must know what you have done."

O'Rourke's tone rose an octave. He was becoming more agitated as the words tumbled out.

"You may choose now dear boy, choose between the truth or a great deal of pain. Dear Alistair, there is no one who will come to you rescue here. So I must tell you that unless you tell me what I want to know, I propose to extract it in such a way, that you would have welcomed even a second's delay from the terrible pain I must inflict on your unwilling body. You have upset me, dear boy, and I want revenge. You must understand, that it is you who may be standing between the success of my life's work, and ignominious failure. That position is not acceptable to me, dear boy. All I require is a simple answer. So tell me, and I ask for the last time. Did you make contact with anyone over the airwaves last night? When did you use the helicopter?"

Craig was silent, thinking. Brandt came into the cabin. As he saw Craig's bonds, there was alarm, perhaps sympathy, in his eyes.

O'Rourke picked up the cosh meaningfully. "I assure you dear boy, this minor slap is simply your starter. A little encouragement that may loosen your tongue." he snarled furiously and brought his hand down without further warning.

Christine screamed at the same instant that Craig felt the dull thud against his ear, followed by two more hard blows across the mouth. He felt the warmth of his own blood trickling down his cheek, but was surprised how little the blows had hurt. He knew much worse was to come, but somehow he would not give in. If he did, O'Rourke would get away and that would be unthinkable. It must be approaching dark. If only he could delay O'Rourke for a little longer. Help might not be far away.

Craig spoke through swelling lips, his voice thick.

"Please understand, O'Rourke. Nothing I tell you can change anything now. Once the Americans find us, they'll attack this ship. You will be killed for certain. They'll probably kill us all."

Craig was desperate. He was trying anything.

"Listen O'Rourke. I will do a deal with you. You could still escape before they arrive. Have you any idea of the holocaust they'll unleash against you and this tiny ship? When they attack, none of us will

236

survive. Leave us here and get away in the speedboat while you can. I'll help you. You could make it. There must be hundreds of similar boats in these waters. You won't be spotted easily."

Craig knew his puny offer was pointless. But time was the thing!

O'Rourke looked puzzled for a moment. He inclined his head a fraction as he locked the laser eyes on Craig. There was controlled fury in his voice.

"I can see you are still in the land of dreams, dear boy. No American government will attack this ship. Not while we have their President captive. Our insurance all along, you see. So I am inclined to refuse your childish offer, dear boy. There is to be no release for you now, no last minute arrival of the cavalry, but you can ease your path of pain by confessing all. Just tell me who you made contact with?"

Craig suddenly became angry himself.

"All right, you Irish bastard," Craig yelled back. "But let's get the girl out of this. She had no part in my plan. So just let her go. Whatever she says, it will be too late to threaten your project. She knows nothing."

Christine suddenly jumped up from the sofa. She turned on O'Rourke.

"Yes I do, I know everything," she shouted at O'Rourke, "and I'll curse you all to hell. I'll see you and your horrible men on Death Row. I know all about you. You'll have to kill me to keep me quiet." She crumpled against the cabin wall and collapsed in a flood of tears.

Craig was surprised at her brave outburst. How could he protect her?

"No Christine, this isn't your fight. Please go away from here. Please just go for me, Christine."

"I won't leave you, Alistair.... I won't." She screamed at O'Rourke again, "I hate you with all my heart. I want to kill you."

O'Rourke looked from Craig to Christine and back again. He signalled to Brandt.

"Take her to the locker room Brandt." O'Rourke ordered. "Shut her in with the President." He jerked his head to the door. "I mean now."

Brandt didn't move at first, and for a moment Craig got the impression he might even turn on O'Rourke. The eye flickered as he glowered uncertainly.

"Don't just stand there," O'Rourke shouted.

Brandt took Christine's arm, and gently pulled her away as she whimpered. "Aw… please come on Missy," he said quietly. "Yo'll be ok wit me Missy. Now c'mon. Dis ain't no place fer a pretty lady."

O'Rourke waited until they had left the cabin, then turned to Craig again.

"So, you consider me an Irish bastard dear boy. A predictable reaction."

He looked at Craig with a cruel, hateful stare.

"You prefer the painful path, dear boy, your defiance does you credit, but can I assure you that in a short while you will be wishing you had delayed the hurt that will come your way, delayed by even a few seconds. Anything, rather than the intense pain I intend to inflict. You will plead with me to use the cosh again and again, until you are unconscious. Have you changed your mind?"

"No. Just get on with it, you madman. It can't be more painful than sitting here having to listen to you."

"Damn your eyes then Craig," O'Rourke screamed wildly and lashed out at his bruised face a second time. Several hard blows, left and right. Craig's top lip split open, oozing blood as he tried to ride the cosh, but his shoulders were held tightly to the bunk. God, he was hurting badly. What a sadistic bastard this man was. Craig could taste his own blood as it trickled into the corner of his mouth. He closed his eyes to feign unconsciousness in an effort to gain a few more minutes perhaps.

O'Rourke's anger seemed momentarily dissipated by the violence. He appeared calm. His voice became scholarly, clinical. He sat down close to Craig again.

"Captain Craig." he said dryly. "In your cocooned world of comfort in merry England, I'm sure you have little experience of the ultimate measures that can be taken to extract information. You see, I need to know what you have done so I may plan ahead." He patted Craig's shoulder with the cosh, as he spoke.

"Many sadists over the years have devised so many methods of hurting. The mediaeval rack, the thumbscrews, the body gouging.

238

The attack on the most sensitive portions of the male body, methods refined in the torture chambers of the Spanish Inquisition, the Nazis in the prison camps, and to move on to the more modern use of electricity on the genital organs, methods that provide the most interesting variety of pain and the victim's fear of the loss of his manhood. Then there are the drugs that can be injected to send the body into convulsions of pain. But none of these crude methods interest me, dear boy, there's no finesse, because it is your brain I intend to attack while we discuss the next bodily pain I might inflict.... the organ that houses your very mind. Do I need to talk of these things more dear boy? Even the word pain, from the Latin poena.... That which must be paid, by you.... now."

O'Rourke brought his face even closer, so that their nostrils were on the point of touching. The voice was studious, professional.

"Alistair, my dear boy, you might care to know that at my University College in Dublin I intended to become a surgeon. My studies required me to understand the workings of the human body. The vital organs that produce the breathing cycle, the network of nerves the brain uses to control our muscles, the delicate chemical balance that is necessary to keep us healthy, and in particular, the nerve pain sensors, the pain sensors that warn the brain of danger. I understand these things, dear boy, and intend to use that knowledge to hurt you a great deal."

O'Rourke picked up the knitting needle.

"An interesting piece of equipment. So benign in a woman's gentle hands, but so capable of inflicting the worst pain you might imagine. With this I can puncture or remove your eye with a flick of its tip. Even if I let you survive with a sound mind, you might just have seen young Christine for the last time. A disturbing thought I trust."

He brought the needle's tip up to touch Craig's ear lobe.

"All such a pity don't you think dear boy, you were such a suited couple. First good friends, and then, no doubt, soon to become lovers, perhaps even go on to become a happy couple. But now all that is to be taken from you."

"So tell me Captain Craig.... the helicopter radio. Did you make contact with anyone? I'm not a sadist, dear boy, but a realist who needs information. Just tell me the truth and there will be no more hurt. And do not lie to me."

239

Craig wondered how much pain he might be able to bear, how long could he delay O'Rourke? Could he keep him talking? But every minute improved his chance of survival, and would help Christine. A minute nearer the rescue, which must surely come.

He had to try reasoning again, no matter how futile his words.

"Mr. O'Rourke, can't you see what you are doing is desperately wrong? I understand the things you tell me, and yes, the British may have treated Ireland badly over the years. But it is history. The politicians are making progress towards peace in your country, the economy is booming, where once there was no work. Just take off these ropes so we can talk like sensible people."

Craig's words fell on very deaf ears, as he knew they must.

"Mr Craig, I'm losing my patience. It appears you need the first lesson."

It came without warning as Craig began to reply. A blinding flash closed his eyes as the needle entered his ear, piercing the Tympanic Membrane. Craig could only clench his teeth as hard as his jaws could close, fighting for breath, fighting to kill the stabbing pain.... pain in a fierce thrust that drove into the very center of his head. Perspiration flooded from every pore of his frame. Craig's chin dropped to his labouring chest as the pain ebbed and flowed. He squeezed his eyes closed and gasped for breath, until mercifully, unconsciousness took over his tortured mind.

O'Rourke, grabbed Craig's chin and lifted it roughly. The pupils had shrunk to pinpricks leaving the whites showing. Craig had passed out. O'Rourke rammed his head down roughly.

Brandt returned. He looked scared as he saw Craig's bruised face and the congealing blood dripping from his ear. He flinched visibly, and dragged his eyes away.

O'Rourke noticed the change and turned to Brandt.

"He's okay Brandt, but stubborn." He said wearily. "Leave him for a while, and call me when he comes round. I'm not finished with him by a long way, the foolish boy. He'll talk eventually. They all do."

Brandt spoke with concern. His voice uncertain.

"But boss, all dis hain't necessary. Craig's a decent guy. We doan hav'ta hurt him so bad. Jest leave him to me. I kin get to de truf mah way. He'll talk to me. Ah know he will. He kinda likes me."

"You're going soft, Brandt," O'Rourke said with contempt. "You know full well that this operation is far too important to be put at risk by some inconsequential English minion. We'll do it my way Brandt. You just keep doing what I'm paying you for. Let me know when he's come round again." O'Rourke's eyes glittered impateiently.

Craig sensed O'Rourke leaving the cabin. He must hold on to his state of collapse to gain more time. But could he take another dose of the torture? He knew the answer was no. The pain had receded for a moment…. the ear numb without feeling, but he could still hear, which was a blessing. He remained motionless, counting the minutes.

Brandt spoke softly to Craig. "If yo kin still hear me Craig, why doan yo tell me what de boss wants to know. I doan like any of dis yo know. Seems de boss am goin' crazy. I wanna help you Craig, no more of dis bad treatment. Dat ain't mah way. Ah kin feel wer'e all in sum trouble."

Craig remained quiet. Brandt had changed.

The kinder side of the Caribbean nature. Was he falling out with O'Rourke? Perhaps terminally? Now he could take advantage of that? He said nothing and laid still.

O'Rourke was back.

It meant more pain. Pain that weighed down on him…. pushing him into the depths of his despair. These might be his last moments…. the ferocious throbbing in his head. Death. If it must come…. Please let it come quickly.

O'Rourke stood over Craig and suddenly grabbed him harshly by the hair, wrenching his head back. Craig looked up at O'Rourke through half closed eyes.

He picked up the skewer from the tray.

"Now dear boy, I see you are still with us, so we may continue the treatment. We come to stage two. Possibly two out of several. Let me explain dear boy. I intend to insert this skewer into the most sensitive parts of your head until you give way. There are many cavities we can explore. The next most sensitive will be the Septum, the bone and cartilage that divides the nasal cavity. I told you I have studied the human body. "

O'Rourke was talking as a surgeon, explaining a delicate procedure to his medical students.

241

"This time I propose to pierce the nasal tubes that lead to the brain, dear boy. The Ethmoid bone. It's rather like a sieve. Did you know the Egyptians used to draw the brain down through it when mummifying their Kings? You might even feel your brain moving as your cerebral spinal fluid is released. It will run down your nose dear boy. Think this thing through, dear boy. There will be so much more pain, so much more unnecessary suffering. Possibly permanent damage to your thought processes if I am careless and allow you to live. You will have seen those poor souls whose lives are worthless because of brain damage, by accident or at birth. You are not some paid government spy whose job it is to resist dear boy, and this isn't a James Bond episode."

Craig could feel the cold skewer against his bruised top lip.

"Now once again my dear boy.... Did you make contact on the radio? Did you give anyone the ship's location?" The voice was impatient and filled with hatred.

O'Rourke was becoming more agitated. He was losing his temper. Just what Craig wanted. Anything to distract O'Rourke and avoid the surgical accuracy of the skewer's invasion.

He thought of the way O'Rourke had already hurt him. For a foolish instant, Craig lost his reason and blurted out without thinking: "Well, if you won't listen to sense, damn you to hell, you mad Irish pig. Why don't you just go fuck yourself?"

O'Rourke grunted in anger as he grabbed Craig's head viciously.

"You silly boy.... I am not capable of that."

O'Rourke flicked the skewer close to Craig's left eye, then dropped to the nostrils.

"You've asked for this Craig, you're not going to wreck my moment of glory for the cause with your stubborn stupidity." A slash of pain tore through Craig's body. His head jerked back in agony as the skewer flashed deep into his nostril. A new pain bursting up at him from a different part of his body. Craig cried out, a horrible piercing scream of an animal in the throes of death. O'Rourke twisted the skewer as he forced Craig's head down to it. Craig's body went limp as mercifully, he passed out again.

O'Rourke threw the blood-stained skewer to the floor.

"Fuck you too, dear boy, and if you are able to hear this, I'll be back for some new treatment. This time we'll use the spoon pressure on your eyes. You see, I'm beginning to enjoy our little battle of wills, dear boy. I see you as just another of those nasty Britishers who stamped their feet all over my country." O'Rourke slapped Craig's cheeks and spat in his face. He turned to Brandt.

"Brandt, I need to check the ship's radar again. If Craig has alerted anyone, we might need to move fast. Keep an eye on the remains of our stupid pilot here. I'll be back shortly."

Again Craig came to his senses. Why couldn't he stay unconscious? Why did his obstinate body insist on bringing him back? Back to face more torture from O'Rourke.

But another five minutes had been secured. Craig tried to steer his nerve endings away from the pain in his head. He'd held out as long as was humanly possible. Had gained more time. But was it enough?

Brandt came over to Craig as he opened his eyes. He touched Craig's arms almost affectionately, then dabbed a towel at the blood congealing on his damaged face. Blood was still trickling from the damaged ear.

Craig coughed a mouthful of blood. The voice was hoarse and choked, but hadn't given in. His head hurt like hell as he forced himself to speak.

"Thanks Leroy, you're really a decent guy. But what's happening to Christine?"

"Okay Craig, she's wit de President now, but man, I doan wanna see no more of dis, Craig. Fer Chrissake, jest tell de boss what he wants ta know so dis can all stop. I kin see dis whole caper fallin' apart. De Sheikh is s'posed to bring de launch wit de money to dis location, de boss don't want to move unless he has to. If de money ain't paid tonight, dere's no tellin' what dat man might do t'hus all."

Brandt was changed by O'Rourke's savagery. Yes, perhaps he had another friend on board. Craig was surprised he could still think rationally as he spoke. His voice sounded hollow, echoing inside his head.

"Leroy, you know that O'Rourke is bordering on the insane. Once the Sheikh gets the money, O'Rourke doesn't need any of us. I'm sure you can see that. You don't want to go the same way as the President. O'Rourke needs to be stopped, Leroy. We could do it together. We could get O'Rourke. I'll speak for you later when it matters. But I can't take any more of this and when O'Rourke gets

243

back, I'll tell the madman what he wants to hear. But he won't like it."

Brandt looked at Craig with concern. He was listening…. seemed to be taking it in. Understanding.

"The American Government knows where we are, Leroy." Craig continued rapidly. "I told them on the helicopter radio last night. We can expect some drastic action very soon. I've worked it out. Probably any time now Leroy, I'm sure. They'll attack this ship and once they've got the President, they may kill everyone on board. And they will get him Brandt. Those guys are absolute professionals. Believe me Leroy. I've worked with them. Why don't you throw in your lot with me? Together we could nail O'Rourke. We might all survive then."

There was alarm and uncertainty in Brandt's face. He shook his head with indecision. His voice was confused.

He pulled out a knife from his back pocket and began mumbling to himself. He moved closer to Craig and hesitated.

"Ah think yo mebbe right Craig, ah should have seen all dis sooner. Dat man is crazy, ahm sho'. Ah never really trusted him…. probably was goin' ta kill me too…. soon as dis job was done."

Craig was wondering what Brandt might do next, when the cabin suddenly filled with noise, a high-pitched scream, increasing in volume, getting closer. A fast-revving engine. Brandt looked up and turned to the cabin window.

Craig knew the sound. An aircraft of some kind…. approaching at speed.

It had to be the rescue!

As the noise became louder, Craig heard O'Rourke shouting for Brandt to come up on deck.

Brandt hesitated, looking back…. still uncertain.

Craig was right, and making up his mind, he bent down to Craig's wrists.

"Ahm really sorry 'bout all dis Craig," he said simply. "Ah've jest been too stupid, man."

Brandt rapidly cut through the towelling holding Craig's wrists, threw him the knife, and with a 'Good luck Craig,' he hurried out of the cabin.

244

Craig shook his head and rubbed the numbness from his hands and arms. But he was free! He tore off the strips binding his legs, shakily got to his feet and held on to the bunk bed for support to clear his head. It was humming…. humming and hurting like hell as he gathered his wits about him. But his determination was returning as he forced the pain away.

Craig steadied himself. He knew what he had to do.

# 32

For young Mark Stockley, pilot of the Beechcraft Duke, a small six-seat commuter runabout, tonight's flight was scheduled as another routine Air Taxi business run. Fort Lauderdale Executive Airfield to Freeport in the Bahamas.... a short, two hundred mile hop, that hardly justified the climb to cruising altitude. Operations calculated his flight time as an hour and ten minutes,

Stockley was planning to take off at Eighteen-forty-five hours, a quarter to seven to his four passengers. They were in high spirits, laughing and joking as they loaded their bags and golf clubs in the luggage bay.

"Come on pilot, let's get going, One of the passengers called out good-naturedly. They intended to get in plenty of golf and booze, and maybe even sample the local coloured talent.... Stockley judged from the conversation.

He thought it strange that the Miami FAA Office insisted on checking his intended route. First time he'd known them do that. Some kind of combined Marine and Air Force exercise, was all they would tell him, but his instructions were very positive. All non-military Aircraft were prohibited from the exercise area three miles south of his route. The instructions were precise. Any violators of the exclusion zone could be shot down! Anyway, he had no intention of

246

varying his flight plan tonight. He wanted a quick out and back trip for very personal reasons!

With details of his flight filed with Air Traffic Control, Stockley was cleared to start engines and was soon fast-taxying from the passenger terminal to the assigned holding point for runway Zero-Nine. He hurried through the pre-take off check list. Tonight he was VFR. An all-visual route flying clear of cloud. Only one pilot was on the flight deck for this trip.

Just like his money-pinching firm to save on aircrew costs whenever they could, he thought unkindly, as he mechanically ran through the engine check routine and pushed the engine throttles forward.

He ran up each in turn, increasing power to take-off RPM and exercised the propeller speed governors to ensure the right feathering action. Good.... temperatures and pressures as they should be. Now for the number two engine. He switched to single magneto operation and was irritated to note some fierce rough running. Blast.... a 200 rpm mag-drop was well outside the published Flight Manual limits. Stockley thought through the problem for a moment. She was certainly okay on both magnetos and he had no intention of flying on one!

He looked over his shoulder where the passengers were already well into the six-pack cans of beer.... getting in the mood for their fun weekend. If he turned back to maintenance section now, they'd be mighty annoyed at the delay, and more importantly to him, he would be late getting back. He wasn't at all sure his new girlfriend would wait too long for their nine o'clock date. She seemed to have plenty of boyfriends to choose from, and he had sure worked hard enough fixing the date for tonight. He'd even changed the bed linen!

To hell with it, he decided. Freeport and back was a quick trip. I'll leave the magnetos until I get back. The Beechcraft Duke was a fine twin with turbo-charged 400 horsepower Rolls-Royce Continentals. If the port engine went a little sick, he always had the extra power of the other one to make up the performance.

With the decision made, and dusk gathering around him, he obtained departure clearance from Air Traffic and was soon charging down runway Zero Nine, accelerating to $V_2$ take off speed at 100 knots, but noting with some concern the lower boost and RPM readings of the port engine.

Mark Stockley dragged the Duke off the runway early and settled into a gentle cruise climb. As he gained altitude, he adjusted the propeller and cooling flaps, to allow for the higher engine temperatures. Once he'd turned on course for Freeport and cleared the Miami control area, he could switch on the autopilot and let 'George' do the flying.

The last of the sun's rays had faded behind him, and the sky ahead was getting dark, which meant a night landing at Freeport Airfield. Thank heavens the lighting facilities had at last been updated. The passengers were boisterous, and in good mood, as they settled back with their drinks, watching the smooth sea skate by, three thousand feet below.

As Stockley levelled the Duke at five thousand feet, the starboard engine stopped with a loud bang, accompanied by a frightening vibration. The nose yawed rapidly to the right, and rolled below the horizon alarmingly as the ship entered a dive. Mark Stockley instinctively booted in full left rudder, to check the aerodynamic swing and pulled the nose up.... but with the loss of an engine, the aircraft began losing speed and height rapidly.

The young pilot suddenly found himself with his hands full, as he ran through the engine failure procedure. Hold a level attitude and bring the good engine up to full power. Best to close down the defective engine completely, to reduce the dead propeller drag, but even as he started the feathering drill, things got worse. The port engine wasn't producing enough power to even hold the Duke level.... those damned magnetos.... why the bloody hell had he taken the chance?

Stockley quickly calculated his position. Twenty minutes airborne time, say forty miles out from the coast. Best to turn the aircraft back and make for Fort Lauderdale.... but even as he took up the new heading, the port engine rpm needle started fluctuating wildly under the extra load. He was horrified as the cylinder head temperature rose to the red line limit.... if he didn't reduce power quickly, he was going to finish with two dead engines!

He checked the boost gauge and pulled the throttle lever back an inch to under 30HG, but with the reduced power, the Duke wouldn't hold its height. The engine temperature was now 'in the red'.... probably about to explode. Stockley checked the vertical speed indicator.... five hundred FPM down.... he would be in the sea in less than ten minutes. He was going to have to ditch!

As the Beechcraft continued losing height, Stockley called out to his frightened passengers. "We've got an emergency.... lost our engines. We're going down in the sea. Get your life jackets on, and someone locate the dinghy. Get strapped in tight, I'll yell shortly before we touch down on the water, but get those belts strapped on tight."

With his passengers warned, Stockley switched the VHF to the distress channel to call out the emergency with a 'Mayday.' Thank God they got the call, and would launch the air sea rescue chopper. All he needed to do was ditch the ship well... so they could use the dinghy.

He concentrated on controlling the sick engine as the altimeter unwound. He tried various throttle and fuel mixture settings to at least slow the descent.

The altimeter was now down to one thousand feet.

Hell the sea looked black down there, but he could just make out the direction of the long sea swell. Thank God it looked calm, that would help no end, and as Stockley checked around the cabin preparing the Duke for the ditching, he spotted a ship only a few miles ahead. One of those long luxury cruisers used by the local Miami millionaires, for anything from crossing the Atlantic, to fishing.

That was one hell of a lucky break! If he could put the Duke down near her, the ship's crew would pick them up in no time. He didn't relish the idea of swimming around as shark bait for too long!

Stockley dropped to full flap and fully feathered the failed engine. The altimeter now read five hundred feet.

"Stand-by for the crash landing," he yelled to the passengers as he lined up for a long straight-in approach to the ship, perhaps half a mile to go.

\* \* \* \* \* \*

O'Rourke was on deck.... Yelling for Brandt. The engine noise from the stricken Beechcraft was a howl, rising in pitch as it approached the ship. He pointed in the direction of the aircraft. All he could see were the blazing landing lights.

Brandt shouted, "Dar she is, comin' in real low towards us. Some kinda seaplane. What the hell is he trying to do? Ram us?"

O'Rourke had already made up his mind.

"Leroy, Get the President. Bring him up on deck. Tie him to something. "

He pulled a Magnum 357 revolver from his waistband.

"By my Mother, if they try to come aboard, I'll make them sorry, he screamed."

\* \* \* \* \* \*

Vic Cramer was also surprised as he studied the radar screen and realised the tiny radar trace he had ignored earlier was now turning in the direction of the *Champagne Princess*. What was it, and what was it doing in the area? Some kind of light aircraft?

The damn fool! He'd instructed Miami Air Traffic Control to keep the area clear of all other traffic. If the aircraft kept its present course, it would alert the terrorists and sabotage the whole damned rescue. He watched the tiny trace with fascination as it moved ever nearer to the target ship. He damped a bead of perspiration from his brow. Christ, it was now only three miles away.... surely Air Traffic would head the bloody pilot off.

When the intruding aircraft was within a mile of the ship, he realised that something was going badly wrong. There was no time to check with Grant.

He picked up the VHF microphone and called urgently.

"All Kingpin units, this is KINGPIN COMMANDER. We have an unauthorised aircraft approaching the target .... Abandon scheduled timings. I say again .... Abandon scheduled timings.... Rescue operations to commence immediately. All Kingpin units, commence operations now."

Cramer consulted the operations area map and the target brief.

"AIRBORNE LEADER RED ONE, this is KINGPIN COMMANDER, start your run in and parachute drop now.... I say again, You are to start your parachute drop immediately .... Acknowledge instruction.... Over."

The pilot of the C130 Hercules called back.

250

"Roger Kingpin Commander. Your message received and understood. Commencing run-in to the target now. We have two minutes to release point."

Cramer called again to the Underwater units of the rescue team. "UNDERWATER LEADERS, you are also to commence your operations immediately. I repeat, we have unauthorised traffic approaching the target area. Cancel planned timing and proceed to target ship now. Yellow Leaders acknowledge. Over."

The Submarine Captain replied immediately. "This is Underwater Leader. Your message received and understood, Sir. Proceeding to rescue area with number two now.... Estimate four minutes to surfacing at target."

Cramer glanced anxiously at the radar screen to confirm the position of the unwelcome intruder. Any second now it would be spotted by the terrorists on the ship. If only his crack parachute team could get to the decks first. *Christ, what a shambles!*

As he contemplated the mess on the radar screen, he recalled the Government's stern brief, "*You are to do nothing that endangers the life of the President.*" And now, in the next sixty seconds, all hell was going to break loose on the *Champagne Princess*. There was still the high-speed launch!

"KINGPIN COMMANDER to CUTLASS. Proceed immediately to target ship at maximum speed .... Report when visual contact made.... *Cutlass*, do you read me, Over?"

"*Cutlass* acknowledging your instruction sir. Heading to target at full speed."

And as the helmsman of *Cutlass* rammed the throttles forward, her two outboard Mercury Turbo-charged diesels churned angrily into the sea, and six hundred horsepower from the screws lifted her bows clear of the water. The helmsman's cheeks were flung back into a taut mask as the racing hull planed towards the *Champagne Princess* at ninety knots. In the emergency, Cramer had done all he could to keep the rescue operation from collapsing, and now he could only pray to God that luck was on his side, and hopefully, at least one of his team could get to the ship, before the President was killed.

The race to save the President was on, but a race he had to win or he might as well blow his own brains out.

# 33

The Beechcraft was barely a mile from the *Champagne Princess* as Mark Stockley grappled with the controls to bring the aircraft in for the crash landing. He glanced anxiously at the instruments, remembering his training for this type of emergency. Concentrate on the correct airspeed.... as low as possible to reduce the impact.... hold a nose-up attitude and drag the tail in first. As the plane passed two hundred feet, he yelled to his passengers.

"Hold tight.... take up crash positions.... Heads on your laps.... Soon as we touch down, someone kick out the emergency exit.... Swim for the ship.... We'll be picked up okay. But get those straps tight...."

In the half-light, Stockley lined up on the final approach to ditch alongside the ship. He positioned the Beechcraft as close to the hull as he dared. If he could pull this one off, he'd have something to talk about in the bar for years! He switched on the two powerful landing lights and a treacherous avenue of light beckoned him down to a watery grave.

Stockley gripped the control column with all his strength to hold the crash landing attitude and braced for the impact. As the tail made contact, he closed his eyes and pulled back hard.

\* \* \* \* \* \*

Craig could hardly believe his eyes as he struggled from his cabin out to the deck. He looked down the ship, towards the howling engine.... transfixed, trying to make sense of it all. Christ, how the hell could a light aircraft help? What was going on? What a bloody shambles of a rescue. The wing lights of the Beechcraft came on.

O'Rourke was at the ships bows shouting for Brandt. He was barely twenty feet away.... His back turned. Now was Craig's chance.... he'd be off his guard. Craig fingered the knife, ready to spring. How he'd relish driving the blade home into O'Rourke's guts. But Brandt was standing close... sidling towards O'Rourke as he spotted Craig.... he could see what was in Craig's mind and waved him away.... pointing to the big revolver O'Rourke was holding. Craig considered, measuring feet. Could he get close before O'Rourke turned the gun on him?

Craig made his decision in an instant. Getting shot wouldn't help the President one bit. He'd have to go for the Hawk before O'Rourke went for him!

Driven by anger and with the desperate pain hammering in his head, Craig sprinted down the gangway to the rear of the ship, and barely conscious of his actions, with head hunched down, he cleared the six-foot drop to the heli-deck below.

With a sickening crash, the Beechcraft smacked into the sea.... belly first.... then bounced back into the air and hovered for a second, like a King Cobra, preparing to strike.

Craig stopped to watch, mesmerized, as the stalled aircraft mushed though the air towards him, dragging its tail plane through the water. The nose dropped sharply as the Beechcraft carved through the water at a hundred miles an hour, skimming across the waves behind a twenty-foot curtain of spray.

The doomed aircraft ploughed on through the boiling water, dropping lower.... the port wing slipped into the waves and dipped, slamming the machine against the *Champagne Princess*. Craig couldn't tear his eyes away from the dramatic scene. The live engine continued to rev furiously as the propeller tore into the hull with an ear-splitting shriek.... hot oil splattering across the ship's decks.

For an instant and still under power, the propeller sliced at the ship's superstructure, as though making a last desperate effort to climb back into the night where it belonged, then, with a final boom from the dying engine, the aircraft fell to a shuddering stop and slid back into the sea. Gallons of high-octane fuel spurted from the ruptured tanks as the dying plane rocked in the water. The nose slipped beneath the waves with its young pilot hammering at the cockpit window in a life or death struggle for escape.

Craig mouthed a prayer. "Please God help him."

A flash of orange lit up the sky as the fuel tanks exploded, sending out a fire wall of burning petrol that raced across the water. Craig watched with alarm as the fire licked dangerously close to the *Champagne Princess.*

He looked back to the Beechcraft as the seawater closed in, but had to turn away when he saw the drowning passengers clawing frantically at the windows. Then as the hull sank lower, the passenger cabin flooded, and with a final boom, the once-proud Beechcraft Duke tipped on its nose and sank into the flaming sea.

Fire swirled across the ship's deck as Craig moved again…. Flames and black smoke billowing up from the burning fuel. He threw up his arms to protect his face as he reached the Hawk, and diving under the covers…. He yanked on the pilot's door, and without any preliminaries, threw the master switch, and hit the engine start button.

The starter motor ground hard against the engine for agonising seconds and…. thank heaven, the compressor reached ignition speed, and fired. Craig opened the throttle wide with the engine howling. Now if only the blades would tear through those covers. Craig held the throttle open as the rotors accelerated violently, screaming their protest.

He looked back to the burning ship. Christine was stumbling through the smoke and flames, the President at her side, holding her for support. For Christ's sake hurry, Craig urged. Please run …. Please just run …. Now O'Rourke had seen them, and was on the move.

Craig clenched his teeth and moved the engine speed well past the maximum red sector, as the first blade tore into the covering sheets, and slowed. A strip of ripped tarpaulin sailed out from the rotors, as the following blades sliced, harder and faster. Heaven be praised, the tarpaulin had given way.

The helicopter rocked on its skids as larger pieces were hacked to shreds by the slashing rotor tips, which whirled past Craig at over two hundred miles an hour.... then three hundred.... nothing would stop them now.

Craig checked the rotor speed.... he needed at least five hundred rotor revs for lift off.... still a hundred to go. He held on to the power and glanced at the dials. The engine and gearbox temperatures were wildly outside limits for a take off, but this was no time for caution.

Christine and the President reached the helicopter as Craig saw the first flash from O'Rourke's gun. The windscreen disintegrated as a bullet sang by his head and buried itself in the bulkhead behind him. Christ, that was close.

A second flash, now nearer, and O'Rourke was running along the burning gang-walk towards the helicopter, firing from the hip. Another bullet clanged against the whirling rotors, and whined off into the darkness.

"Keep your head down," Craig yelled, as two more shots splintered the Perspex screen by his feet.

Craig felt a searing shaft of pain from his thigh, as though a high-speed electric drill had been plunged into the flesh. His leg was on fire. Oh God, 'Stop that pain' .... 'Stop that pain' Craig held his breath, biting hard on his lip, anything to divert the excruciating pain from his groin.

He looked up to the night sky. Christ, the stars were flashing.... Was he blacking out? Above the roar of the Hawk's tortured engine, and the wild thumping of his heart, Craig could hear the staccato crack of gunfire, and now each of the stars trailed a white cloud. Clouds. No .... they were parachutists letting off short bursts of automatic fire, which raked the ship's decks and ricocheted off the bulkheads. O'Rourke wasn't going to survive out there for very long.

It was the rescue!

The sky was filled with Commandoes. Five.... now ten.... now perhaps twenty, and already the first wave was landing in the smoke on the upper decks of the *Champagne Princess*. Puffs of explosive burst out in rapid succession as grenades were lobbed into the cabins.

Christine got to the door, wrenched it open and bundled the President into the cockpit alongside Craig. She grabbed the door handle. Craig was already raising the collective lever for lift off as the rotors hit their maximum speed, and the remains of the tarpaulin were flung clear.

"Get in, get in.... hurry," Craig urged Christine.

O'Rourke leapt down the steps into the flames on the lower deck. He crouched ten yards from the helicopter, not daring to come closer to the spinning rotors.

From short range he aimed carefully and squeezed the trigger.

Christine screamed, her hand clasped to her breast. Blood oozed under her fingers and for an agonising moment she clawed at the helicopter door for support as she tried to pull herself in the cabin.

Craig had to get the President away before O'Rourke fired again.

"Hold on, please hold on Christine," Craig implored as he began the lift off, but was horrified to see her grip fail as she fell back to the ship's deck. She was badly hurt and lay motionless against the helicopter skids.... Perhaps already dead.

Craig's brain screamed. The bastard. The bastard had murdered Christine in cold revenge. He must know he's done for.

Commandoes were swarming the decks.... the air filled with gunfire. A long burst was followed by a shrill cry of agony. Craig saw Brandt's bulky frame jerk like a Marionette Puppet as he took the full force of a hail of bullets. He staggered drunkenly to the ship's handrail clutching his stomach, screaming in pain. Blood bubbled and spurted horribly from a ripped artery.

Silhouetted in the flames, O'Rourke moved a yard closer to the helicopter, and holding the gun with both hands, he dropped to one knee, in the classic firing stance of the marksman. The muzzle was aimed at Craig's head. O'Rourke was going to finish him off!

Too late, Craig flung himself sideways as a second bullet crashed into his left shoulder. He slumped forward with the impact, fighting for breath, his face a mask of pain.

Craig shook his head and calling on every ounce of strength, turned purposefully to face O'Rourke with murder in his eyes.

O'Rourke levelled the gun again.

This was the kill.

With an intense stabbing pain lancing from his shoulder, Craig pulled up on the collective lever, praying he would have enough strength to fly. The helicopter lifted clear of the deck and lurched forward on its skids, the flames licking dangerously close. The plastic screen caught alight, burning his feet.

Craig, stinging with pain and fury, gritted his teeth and rammed the cyclic stick forward.

Another bullet flashed.

Craig rammed the cyclic control further forward.... harder. The Hawk's rotors lurched towards O'Rourke, and with a metallic shriek, the first rotor blade scythed into his startled body, slicing the head from his shoulders, even as the arms came up for protection. With blood spurting from the ripped artery, and scattering shreds of O'Rourke's brain tissue, the severed head slithered across the deck, wobbling like a deflated football. With another spurt of blood, the head re-bounded off the bulkhead behind its own corpse, and skidded to a stop below the helicopter.

Craig forced himself to look down. God, O'Rourke's mangled mouth was still moving.... The bulging eyes stared back hideously at Craig, the skin around them blistering in bubbles of human fat.... the black comma of hair crinkling as it smoldered in the flames.

The helicopter began shaking from the massive impact with O'Rourke's body. The flames from the ship were about to set him on fire.

With the pain giving him renewed strength, Craig continued to lift off. He looked up to the rotor blades, which were vibrating violently from the damage to their delicate balance. Would they hold together long enough to get away from the flames? With consciousness slipping away, Craig desperately fought to maintain control. The belly of the Hawk was on burning.... any minute now the machine could explode.

Craig climbed clear of the swirling smoke, and half blinded in a red mist of pain, he was only faintly aware of the turmoil of activity breaking loose about him.

A twin rotor helicopter with searchlights blazing, thumped towards the *Champagne Princess*, as the sky filled with another wave of parachutists, raining down on the ship's blazing decks and splashing into the flaming sea.

Frogmen were breaking the surface and swarming up the ship's hull with grappling hooks and rope ladders. Craig focused on an area to ditch, as he manoeuvered the shaking machine clear of the burning fuel.

The angry sea rushed up to meet them. Craig pulled the emergency jettison lever of the President's door. The door flew off in the rotor downwash, as he settled the helicopter gently on the water, just avoiding the high-speed launch that raced past to the burning *Champagne Princess*.

As the skids touched, Craig held the machine in a steady attitude for a few seconds, to stabilise the airframe, and then deliberately tipped the rotor disc into the water to stop the rotation.

The blades churned and thrashed violently at the waves and skidded to a stop. Craig clung on the controls to allow the broken tail section to settle in the sea, as the red-hot exhaust pipe slipped into the water, hissing and spitting steam. With the sea rising in the cabin, Craig's last action was to release the safety straps, grab the President's arm, and hurl them both clear.

A dozen frogmen surrounded the sinking machine. Two men grabbed the President.

Craig felt himself being pulled to the safety of a launch as the Enstrom Hawk took its final gulp, and disappeared beneath the waves, on its way to the bottom of the Atlantic Ocean.

The sudden rush of cold-water cleared Craig's head, but his body below felt numb. He looked back to the *Champagne Princess*, where two black rubber-suited commandos were dragging the limp body of a girl clear of the flames.

A bright green Verey light climbed into the sky followed by another.

The launch came up alongside the *Champagne Princess*.

Craig called out desperately.

"Christine, Christine. Are you all right?"

She raised an arm to wave.

# Epilogue

Alistair Craig glanced up at the sprinkling of Cumulus cloud that drifted lazily over the gnarled Beech trees at Chanctonbury Ring. Fair weather Cumulus, heralding a fine day. The ring of tall trees was now dotted with the sticky white buds of springtime as they rustled softly in the light morning breeze.

Above Craig, a seagull swooped down…. perhaps the same one Craig had watched nearly a year ago, and with a clatter of wings, settled on one of the topmost branches. Craig listened with amusement as the gulls bickered and quarrelled for the best perches, eventually appearing to agree an acceptable pecking order.

Craig rubbed his thigh, where the vicious pain of the last few months had subsided into a dull ache. After the helicopter crash, he'd lost so much blood that he was on the hospital critical list for a week.

O'Rourke had punched three large-calibre bullets into his body, any one of which should have killed him. The surgeons left the minor damage to his shoulder, while they nursed and patched at the more serious wounds to his stomach and groin. For two weeks, Craig hovered on the edge of death in a coma.

But as the days passed, and the unseen shadows of the window blinds marched daily across his hospital room, Craig regained consciousness, and with his resolve to survive strengthened, he faced

259

each painful visit to the operating theatre, and the long climb back to health with renewed determination.

The obstinate numbness in his aching body, was steadily replaced with feeling, as the damaged tissues and nerve endings got back to work, and he recalled, oh so well, the day a pretty nurse came on duty to tidy his room, and he found himself studying her young body with masculine interest. Hell, now he knew he was going to recover!

Then the ENT specialist operated on the damage O'Rourke had done to his ear and nose. Another two painful operations, but which proved one hundred per cent successful.

"No reason why you won't be fit enough to fly again," Craig was told. "I'll be getting a full report off to your CAA medical examiner today."

But then came the inevitable enquiry, and each day government agents from different departments sat at his bedside. Questions and more questions, as the investigation team pieced his story together.

For days the government seemed convinced he was part of the Al Qaeda gang. So why had he killed O'Rourke? Why had he changed his mind and alerted the 747 pilot?

Slowly, piece-by-piece, the truth emerged as each statement matched the facts.

And then, that unbelievable day, when the President himself visited his bedside with the news.

He had personally intervened, and there would be no prosecution for the part Craig had played in the kidnap, and the President had requested that Craig was awarded a special payment of two hundred and fifty thousand dollars, but less his hospital expenses!

But sure as hell, Craig thought to himself, he'd fixed O'Rourke all right. That man had experienced, if only for a few seconds, ten times the agony he'd inflicted on Craig. The nasty bastard had paid in full for the torture and the bullet aimed at Christine.

Brandt had died horribly too, which saddened Craig. A decent Cayman Islander at heart, who'd turned out to be a friend.

The two Al Qaeda men, Ahmed and Yousef, had also been killed on the burning decks of the sad *Champagne Princess*.

After the investigation came a string of visitors, and of course the American press. For several days the newspapers carried the story, mostly plugging the 'brave English pilot saves our President' line, but one or two pointing accusing fingers.

Craig's picture appeared in the international papers, and on national television, with the President at his bedside shaking hands. On the whole, public sympathy was behind Craig for his part in wrecking the Al Qaeda ransom plan, and saving the President's life.

Craig had even met the Continental Airline Captain of Flight 771 and his co-pilot. They spent a jocular half hour discussing the short, two-way radio conversation, which had so nearly been passed off as a hoax.

Then, accompanied by a battery of whirring cameras and flashing bulbs, they took him to the studio for many TV interviews.

\* \* \* \* \* \*

Home in England, it was back to the glare of more publicity as the pressmen hounded him on his arrival at Heathrow, and followed him to his Sussex home. All he wanted was the peace and quiet he once thought he would never experience again.

But release was on its way, as a new political row was brewing, when yet another Cabinet Minister was revealed with his pants down, and the media instantly lost interest in Craig, to converge on their next hapless victim.

Craig recalled the day he reported to Gatwick for his aircrew medical. His old friend and Civil Aviation Authority doctor, Tony Godwin, passed him fit to regain his aircrew licence, and he was asked to fly for his old firm again. It was good to be back in harness earning his living respectably.

A flock of seagulls suddenly rose at some unseen signal, and resumed their casual circles above the Beech trees.

Craig turned on his pocket radio to hear the midday political programme broadcasting a short extract from the American President's speech to the Senate. Craig listened with more interest, as the familiar voice advised the Arab world of his Government's commitment to a policy of peace in the Middle East.

All good knock-about stuff, Craig thought…. but how far away he was now, how remote. Was there really a time when he'd been so closely involved with the President's very existence? Now, once again

261

the powerful voice of a world statesman…. The voice of a man he would never communicate with again in his lifetime.

But he still had his own life to be getting on with. Tomorrow was Monday, and the start of a new working week. It was that time of the year again. The flat racing season was getting underway and another Glorious Goodwood week was coming up.

Just make sure he didn't bump into another dodgy racehorse owner!

Alistair Craig looked at his watch, a nice replacement, kindly donated by Rolex. Wasn't that how they treated the posh celebrities?

But time to be getting back to his flint cottage, or Christine might get mad for turning up late for Sunday lunch.

# THE END

# Also from Electrocution

www.electrocution.com

Watch out for **Dennis Kenyon's new novel** (as yet unnamed), to do with the diamond trade!

**The Helicopter Pilot's Handbook**, by Phil Croucher. All the stuff nobody ever teaches you!

**JAR Professional Pilot Studies** by Phil Croucher. Written exam material for the JAA ATP, for aeroplanes *and* helicopters!

**JAR Private Pilot Studies** by Phil Croucher. As above, but cut down to suit the PPL exams.

**Canadian Professional Pilot Studies** by Phil Croucher. Written exam material for the Canadian CPL/ATPL, INRAT, etc. for aeroplanes *and* helicopters. Also suitable for despatchers.

**CARs in Plain English** by Phil Croucher. Canadian aviation regulations translated!

**JAR OPS in Plain English** by Phil Croucher. European aviation regulations translated!

**FARs in Plain English** by Phil Croucher. US aviation regulations translated!

**Single Pilot CRM** by Phil Croucher

**The Bell 206 Book** by Phil Croucher

**Finger Trouble** by Lu Zuckerman